BLACK KNIGHT
PERDITION

AGE OF RECKONING: BOOK ONE

CHRISTIAN J. GILLILAND

ISBN: 978-1-7353304-5-7

Black Knight: Perdition
Age of Reckoning: Book One
By Christian J. Gilliland

MARKS MEDIA
Publishing Co.

Table of Contents

For my girls, everything I do I do for you.

Dakota and Danielle, you were the catalyst that led me to find my path.

Nick, Ezben, Elias, Sean and Tara, the work you did to bring this novel to life was simply perfect.

Austin and Dansare, thank you for your support for all these years.

Mom, thank you for making me alive.

Chapter One
Heaven

21ˢᵗ of Cidraa – 346 AG

He fell... The wind blew his hair in all directions and buffeted his ears. It was not painful or necessarily scary... in fact it was exhilarating. For a moment he was in awe of the sensation of flight. He felt free like a bird and considered spreading his arms and flying far away from everything he had ever known. He entertained a dream of building something new for himself. A life rooted in peace and comfort passed through his mind. He imagined trading in his sword for a hoe and fantasized over tilling the ground of his cabbage farm. The thought was peaceful, but it could never happen... for Crinnan Jamiso was dead.

The world beneath him grew smaller and Crinnan realized he wasn't plummeting towards it or flying like he had thought. He had no control over his body, he could fly nowhere. He could do nothing as he rapidly ascended away from the orange, green and blue planet beneath him. His body was climbing into the clouds as if some celestial fisherman had hooked him and was reeling him in.

The darkness of night that had surrounded him was gone. The growling of his attackers and the pain that they had induced was nothing more than a memory. Crinnan's arms flailed as he floated upward, or at least he thought they did. When he searched for his body, he found nothing. Out of all the strange variables of his situation, *that* was what led him to panic.

Crinnan passed through the clouds or what he perceived were the clouds and was engulfed in the brilliant light of The Brothers, the twin suns that hung in the heavens above Duraan. The sudden brightness blinded him for a moment, but his vision soon adjusted. He felt a comforting feeling of warmth spread over him even though he could not find his body. Crinnan was quickly learning that he was no longer a physical being; he was in fact nothing more than his thoughts.

Crinnan tried to clear his mind and figure out what was happening to him. He had trouble getting his thoughts in order, so he started with the basics to ground himself. He was a scout class knight in the elite Century Squad of Black Knight. He favored the sword and pistol in combat. He had two friends, Alec and Elia, and the last thing he had eaten was... beans.

"Beans..." Crinnan whispered as he ascended. "Yes..." The events of his final night on the planet started streaming in. He remembered he had been sent by his sergeant Kavin Preast to scout the area surrounding their camp. Century Squad had stopped in the Izla'Axi caverns West of the Belhaasi Weald to rest. Their mission had been to gather intel on a radio tower that had recently been constructed south of the Great Canruusi Canyon. It was supposedly powerful enough to give the Govian Empire communications abilities throughout the entirety of the country of Izla'Axi. Century Squad's mission was to observe the construction from afar and determine whether they were going to be able to destroy it.

Crinnan had been sent with his squad mates Jeph Scaven and Pancho Lopez to make sure their area of the great Ancient forest city was secure. He remembered walking through the darkness of the Belhaasi Weald, flashlight in hand and a cigarette hanging from his mouth. He recalled it all to near perfection; his memory had become as vivid as if he were watching himself on television. He saw the ambush, something that Crinnan was prone to due to himself constantly getting lost in thought. He watched the monsters leap from the trees and eviscerate him. He watched his guts fall from his stomach as he was gored, and finally witnessed the life drain from his eyes. There was no time for him to fight back before he had been slain and his corpse was dragged away for dinner by the monsters who had killed him.

"No!" he fearfully whispered as his ascent suddenly slowed. A shock of terror coursed through his body like lightning coursing through his veins. He realized he had been killed... he had failed to defend himself and the monsters were probably feasting on his guts at that very moment... yet there he was, somehow conscious and able to think about it... What truly frightened him, however, was the sudden reality that filled his mind.

Crinnan realized exactly what was coming next. He had heard stories about it his entire life, he had been warned by the followers of Dura'ana, the ungrateful citizens whom Crinnan and the rest of Black Knight fought endlessly to liberate from their government. They warned him, they had pleaded with him to turn away from his life of sin and defiance and embrace the ways of Dura'ana, but he turned them all away... They had warned him and Crinnan had ignored them. An eternity of everlasting pain and torture awaited him; Crinnan Jamiso's reward for his defiance... was The Hells.

Twenty-three years was all he'd had. Twenty-three years of living, breathing, eating, drinking, fucking, fighting, and shitting it all back out. As he floated above the clouds of his home and stared into The Brothers' light, he flirted with the idea that it had all been in vain. He pondered over whether his life had been wasted or not. He contemplated whether he had been a failure... Had he been nothing more than a damned tool in a war that had only led him to this death? Had he been used? The realization of how worthless his life had been led him to beg for his tears to fall, yet... Crinnan had no eyes to cry from.

"Fuck!" He shouted as he stared into the light of The Brothers. It was the only word he could manage to spit out. Crinnan had always been a person of few words... more so the type who communicated with glares, sneers, sucker punches and grunts. The single word wasn't, however, an attempt to communicate, it was simply the manifestation of everything he felt inside him.

"Are you real?" He called out as he nervously looked around. "Hello? I know you're there! Come on! Show yourself, let's get this over with!"

A brilliant white light brighter even than The Brothers themselves suddenly and silently exploded from what would have been the center of his body. For a moment everything was swallowed by the light and he was blinded. He couldn't see anything around him, but he could *feel* something.

Everything was silent and it was unnerving for Crinnan. In his short life he had grown accustomed to noise; be it the wind, gunfire, or even the ever-present pulsing of his heart. When his vision finally slowly faded back in, he found that he was no longer a floating nothing. His body had been returned to him, and the sensation of being physical manifested a shocked gasp.

Crinnan immediately looked down at his hands. They were the same hands he had used his entire life; he saw the freckle on the side of his left hand, the pattern his veins made underneath his skin... he saw hair creeping up the sides, the dozens of scars from training and combat... seeing it all again stirred up a strange and foreign barrage of feelings that he wasn't prepared for.

He was completely naked and stood alone on a crystal-clear glass floor surrounded by radiant white light. Far beneath his bare feet, Crinnan saw the planet of Duraan. It was where he had grown up, fought and ultimately died. From where he stood, it looked calm and peaceful. It was all a lie, for Duraan had never known peace.

Crinnan looked up and marveled at the magnificent gleaming skyline of what he perceived was the city of eternal paradise. It was heaven, and he knew that this glimpse was the divine tormenting him. The Goddess Dura'ana was dangling Zion just out of reach of Crinnan's grasp, she was showing him what he could have obtained had he submitted in life. In all her grace and love... the bitch rewarded a being who had suffered immensely in life with one single step upon the outskirts of salvation. Crinnan felt the divine presence again and he knew that he was no longer alone.

"I guess this is it." He whispered with a defeated tone. His fists clenched and his heart thumped rapidly. Sweat lined his hairline and he took a deep sorrowful breath. He was fearful of looking up because he knew exactly who stood before him. "And I guess you are..."

"I am." The voice that cut him off was both a whisper and a chorus, the manifestation of salvation and damnation in one. It was beautiful, and at the same time terrifying. "Dura'ana."

The physical force and immeasurable energy behind her gently spoken words was more than Crinnan could bear. It hit him like a mighty wind, tinged with the most infernal heat he had ever felt and then a biting cold the likes of which he couldn't have fathomed in life. Crinnan felt an immense pressure on his shoulders and his knees buckled. He fell to the glassy floor, prostrated before the goddess. It wasn't out of reverence or duty. It was simply his body's natural reaction to something far beyond himself; a response that he had no control over.

The form of a female adorned in a flowing white dress stood before him. Her glossy black hair reflected the light around her, and the fabric of her spectral clothing seemed to defy the laws of gravity as it floated all around her. Her face, beautiful he imagined, remained hidden behind the same white light that had previously blinded him. Or, Crinnan surmised, perhaps the light *was* her face.

Dura'ana stood in silence before Crinnan. He could feel her hidden gaze piercing him. She dissected and analyzed him. It felt like layers of his mind were being fileted and studied and an immense clamping pressure formed in his skull. Crinnan groaned and tried to move, tried to find any kind of comfort but there was none for him. Heaven was only the beginning of Crinnan's damnation and there was nothing he could do about it.

Clenched tightly in the goddess's right hand was the handle of a long gleaming gold bladed sword. Crinnan recalled its name being Eskaa. It was an ancient Damarsi word that meant *justice* in the modern tongue. In her left hand was a thick book. Sofii Gruud, or *The Book of Mercy* as it was called by her followers. The book swung opened, and Dura'ana looked down at it.

"Crinnan Jamiso." She whispered; her voice was melodic like a chorus of angels. Crinnan only allowed himself a moment to marvel though, for she was not his goddess. "A child with such a powerful lineage. Your ancestors hewed the history of Duraan with their blood... My child, why did you deny me in life?"

"Just do it..." Crinnan painfully whispered. His entire body was tense, and his fists were clenched with fear and fury. "I'm here... so you got what you wanted out of me. I'm not afraid, do what you... do what you do..."

"You *are* afraid, child." Dura'ana corrected him. "You killed those that loved me in life, and you curse me in death. Did my people fail you so? Tell me, Crinnan... give me a reason to spare you."

"I..." Crinnan couldn't think, he couldn't figure out what to say. "I am afraid..."

"Afraid of me?" Dura'ana asked. "Or are you afraid of the fate you have earned for yourself?"

"It doesn't matter." Crinnan whispered as he lowered his head. "I'm damned no matter what I say here."

"You speak truth." Dura'ana replied. "My child... I am sorry, but I gave you an entire life to make the right choice. You simply... didn't."

"Just get it over with then." Crinnan mumbled, his head still lowered. "Send me to the Hells."

"Very well." Dura'ana said. At that, The Brother's light was blotted out and day turned to night. The Book of Mercy in Dura'ana left hand crumbled to dust and blew away with the wind.

"I sentence you to two thousand years in The Hells." She declared, her voice taking on a more authoritative tone. "And then you shall be judged as to whether you may labor in the fields of heaven. May you find peace, child."

The goddess raised Eskaa, the sword in her right hand and pointed the tip at Crinnan. The ground suddenly trembled and tendrils of darkness violently pierced the crystalline floor, embedding transparent shards of whatever Heaven was made of into Crinnan's flesh. The shadow vines began creeping toward Crinnan from all directions, closing in on his body. He watched his fate approach him and his heart pounded yet he did not move. He was consoled only by knowing that he was about to embrace the same destiny that every Black Knight that preceded him had, that he had *earned* his place in the Hells.

The tendrils quickly took hold of Crinnan and wrapped themselves around his wrists and ankles, lifting and stretching his body. Dura'ana reduced in size so that the two of them stood eye to eye and with gentle steps, she approached him.

The light that had enveloped the goddesses face turned to a dark haze and her white dress transmogrified into a glowing black tattered robe. A hood raised over her black hair, and the golden blade ignited in flame. Crinnan squinted his eyes as the goddess approached. He would not turn away; he would face his fate with every ounce of strength he had amassed back in his life.

Without another word on her part, Dura'ana's eyes suddenly burned red, piercing the dark haze that enveloped her face. She threw her head back and released a planet shattering wail. Crinnan's attention was drawn to the skyline of Heaven behind him. The gleaming beautiful spires of eternal bliss exploded and crumbled. A mighty wave of energy was released, soaring past him and buffeting his body with the dust and shards of what could have been his paradise. He watched all hope of comfort and peace vanish before his eyes.

The tendrils tightened on his limbs and Dura'ana leveled her gaze on him. After a few silent moments, the goddess raised the sword and planted it to the hilt into Crinnan's chest. He gasped, and the black tendrils suddenly enveloped his entire body. He couldn't help himself as he struggled and fought as they wrapped around every inch of him. Panic ensued, and as the vines wrapped around his throat, he began to feel claustrophobic. The last image Crinnan saw before his eyes were covered in thick black darkness was that of Dura'ana turning her back to him.

"I never knew you." She whispered with a sad tone.

Then there was nothing.

Heaven vanished and Crinnan once again saw the planet far beneath him. The wind tore at his skin as he plummeted from a height he could never have fathomed on his own. He watched as the world grew bigger and closer, felt the vines tear into his skin like leeches, and tried to scream but he could not. Instead, he gritted his teeth and flared his nostrils as the planet drew nearer.

Crinnan's body finally struck the solid ground, and the world seemed to shatter like glass. The shards of Duraan tore through his skin and left jagged splinters all through him. What wasn't shredded by the glass was ripped apart as Crinnan passed through layer after layer of the rock. His speed did not decrease, friction did not slow him. The glassy jagged underworld took every bit of flesh it could.

Eventually Crinnan broke through the final layer of the world and it opened up, swallowing the once proud Black Knight. Crinnan, who was nothing more than bone and blood at that point, burst into a world sized chasm of darkness.

Had the ground not been engulfed in flame the new world would have been nothing but blackness. Crinnan's bones passed through wave after wave of thick smoke and he began to hear the roaring and crackling of the fire beneath him. He smelled the cooking flesh and heard ear-piercing screaming. The jubilant whooping and maniacal laughter of the demons below was terrifying. A realization quickly struck home, and Crinnan felt more fear overcome the skeleton of a body that was left of him… He had entered the Hells.

The sound of solemn organ music could be heard, faintly at first, accompanied by the voices of a chorus. They sang in an ancient language; one he did not understand. As he drew nearer and nearer to the burning ground the tempo and volume increased, to a point where it sounded like the chorus was screaming as they foretold his doom.

Fear enveloped him. He did not know what was going on but when he was nearly one hundred feet from the ground somehow something flashed before him. It was a sentence spelled out in red glowing words and it seemed to float in the air above him no matter where he looked.

You Have Died

Chapter Two
The Hells

You Have Died

"Well, no shit!" Crinnan furiously spat.

The burning ground was approaching quickly. Crinnan knew he had no more flesh to lose, and he braced his bones for impact. His skeleton slammed into the ground, shattering into more pieces than there were bones. His body spread over the landscape of the Hells, and the strange singing stopped.

For a moment, silence took over. Crinnan lay amongst the flames, unable to move, hardly able to think and even less able perceive what was going on around him. The world was unlike anything he had experienced in life. Back home he had always been able to at least try to defend himself, he had never been completely hopeless.

The fires burned him; the heat was suffocating. Crinnan couldn't writhe or crawl or attempt to find any kind of respite from the pain, he was only shards of bone scattered across the landscape. All he could do was lay and wait for whatever was to happen.

"So, this is forever..." He thought fearfully to himself. His body lay in pieces, sprawled out through the fires of the Hells. Eventually he started to make out the sounds around him. He heard the pleading and screaming of his fellow damned. Watched as laughing, armored demons stomped through the flame in pursuit of desperate fleeing prisoners. He tried to close his eyes but to his dismay there were no eyelids. For all he knew, there weren't even any eyes...

The daily activities of those who accompanied him in the Hells was a sight to behold. He watched as the strong hunted the weak. Some of them planted daggers into their target's backs, some just chopped them in half with giant glowing swords. Everyone screamed, some with bloodlust some with terror.

For what could have been days, Crinnan lay in the same spot on the ground and watched as more bodies fell from the sky and shattered just as he had. As he lay there, he thought of his life. From a young age Crinnan had trained to become a warrior. He had grown to be among the best Black Knight had to offer. He was a spectacle with a sword and pistol and a master of silent execution of his mission. He was a member of Century Squad, a Centurion and like all Centurions, he was famous among the army. He was however, and to his end, very easily distracted.

In life, few people meant much to him. He had two friends, Alec Flinn and Elia Sols. They were all he needed, and all he would allow himself to get close to. Love was easily lost or taken away in his experience. He believed that growing close to people always ended in pain for him. He carefully cared for his friends, however, and they greatly loved him back.

As Crinnan thought about his friends and of love lost, his thoughts landed on the one person he had ever been in love with in his entire life. He had not spoken to her since the war in Kamlot seven years prior. The two had only known each other for a week, and then they never spoke again, but that week had filled Crinnan's heart for an entire lifetime as far as he had been concerned. They were two teenage cadets. She, the daughter of Commander Dorax Emmal, and he, the son of Commander Crinnan Jamiso Sr, both of them depending on each other to survive in the Kamlotian wilderness. Her name was Milinka.

"I will find you…" Those were the last words he had told her before they were scooped away by their parents. Words that had proven to have been a lie. He had never kept his promise, he had never found her… He didn't try once.

Crinnan had heard rumors and news about Milinka, seeing as she was nobility in Black Knight culture but… the opportunity never came for him to meet her again. He had assumed that he had simply become a memory of hers. Or that she had forgotten about him entirely.

Sadly, Crinnan lost his chance to ever find his love again. He remembered hearing the news that she had fallen in battle. He recalled running into the woods and weeping bitterly that night as he had daily told himself the lie that he would see her again. Facing the truth that he would never again see her or love again was heartbreaking at minimum. World shattering at most.

"No!" He heard somebody nearby scream. It tore him from his reverie, and he couldn't help but observe. A dripping, oozing, pale-skinned demon approached. Its steps were awkward, and its large fat belly jiggled from side to side as he walked. The massive creature held a hook the size of Crinnan in its hand and laughed and whooped chaotically as it chased down its prey.

Crinnan watched in terrified curiosity as the creature finally caught up with its target and powerfully swung his hook. The point of the massive weapon impaled the terrified prisoner, and the monster lifted the person's torn and bleeding body up off the ground.

"A worm on a hook!" The demon laughed as he watched the prisoner squirm to break free. "Try being faster next time! It's more fun that way!"

Crinnan watched as the demon reached a massive fat fingered hand out and ripped the prisoner's body from his hook. The strength of the demon and aggression in his action split the prisoner's body in half and Crinnan watched as his guts splashed out onto the ground. The demon hurled the prisoner's top half in one direction, an arc of gore and blood trailing behind, and then his bottom half in another, laughing heartily as he did so.

"Good luck putting your little body back together!" The monster laughed as he taunted. The sound of the poor person wailing in the distance caused the corpulent demon to throw his head back and laugh.

Crinnan lay motionless and silent. Not that he had any choice. He was only a stone's throw from the demon and did not want to be its next victim. Unfortunately, as he had not yet learned, that was not how the Hells worked.

The demon's vision seemed to glaze over for a moment as he reached out and tapped at the empty air in front of his face. Crinnan watched curiously at the strange behavior for a few moments, and then saw the demon gasp in delight.

"Well, well who do we have here?" The creature bellowed as he awkwardly turned toward Crinnan's direction. The rolls in his flesh jiggled as he eagerly stomped his tree trunk shaped feet. His abnormally wide mouth formed into a grin. "A newcomer by the looks of it! A little Black Knight?" He laughed a disturbingly gleeful laugh and licked his lips hungrily. "A newbie! Such a delight, a little virgin! Well, let me say I'm honored to be the one to pop your Hells cherry!" He threw his head back and laughed heartily.

The demon's gaze went out of focus again and he jabbed one of his fingers in the air in front of him. An action that Crinnan found odd. Soon after, a black haze enveloped Crinnan, and the tendrils that had surrounded him in heaven shot out in all directions from where he lay. They returned quickly, carrying pieces of bone with them.

Crinnan groaned fearfully as he felt his body reassemble. His skeleton flew in from all directions and snapped together and he felt his muscles and tissue begin to grow back. For the first time in what felt to him like days he felt his heart begin to beat again. Unfortunately for him, it was pounding.

The demon approached Crinnan's newly formed body and knelt down, grinning menacingly at him. Crinnan was filled with fear and tried to scramble away but the creature threw his hand out and snatched him by the throat with his massive fingers.

"A little warrior in life?" The demon asked, mocking Crinnan with a voice that one would only use with babies. He lifted Crinnan's body into the air and shook him like a doll, grinning wildly and mischievously as he did. Crinnan felt his joints flail and bend in all directions from the force. He grew dizzy and his stomach churned. He couldn't hold back and finally vomited violently.

The demon gasped as the bile from Crinnan's stomach glazed his face. Squeezing Crinnan's throat tighter, the demon reached up and wiped the liquid from his face. "You disgusting little fucker!"

Crinnan gasped desperately for air and pulled as hard as he could at the demon's fingers. They wouldn't move an inch and as Crinnan began to grow dizzy from strangulation, he began to panic. Finally, he narrowed his eyes and swung his fist. He tried to scream and reeled in pain as his hand shattered and bounced off the demon's hide. The demon grinned and squeezed harder.

"Down here," he snarled, "we do the fighting!" He lifted Crinnan higher and then violently slammed him into the flaming ground beneath them. Crinnan felt his newly reconstructed bones shatter and let out a wail as the demon pushed his face against the hot ground.

"Do you feel that you terrorist garbage? Stick your tongue out and taste that burning dirt. That's all you'll be eating for the rest of time, worm!"

Crinnan tried to scream as the scorching hot ground melted the skin of his face. The immense pressure from the demon's palm pushing down on him threatened to pop his skull. He couldn't make a sound or wiggle free; he was at the monster's mercy.

The demon continued laughing and pulled Crinnan's melted face out from the fire. Pieces of his skin stuck to the rocky ground and stretched like taffy until they finally snapped free from his face as he was lifted.

"Let this be your first lesson!" He lifted Crinnan to eye level and licked his lips. The demon's jaw unhinged like a snake and his mouth opened wide, revealing two rows of jagged razor-sharp teeth. Crinnan whimpered out of fear, a noise he had never imagined himself making. He tried to shake himself free with what little strength he had left, but there was no escape to be made.

The demon placed Crinnan's head in his mouth, lining up his neck with his lower set of teeth. Crinnan closed his eyes and braced as the jaw slammed shut, piercing his neck but not fully removing his head. He could smell the demon's putrid breath inside the abnormally large mouth. He felt his own blood gushing out onto the demon's tongue and then cringed as the monster squeezed his fingers harder and then twisted Crinnan's body like one would a piece of jerky. Crinnan's head finally ripped free, and he felt his neck snap. The teeth begin to grind his skull, crunching it into pieces... and then Crinnan heard something strange.

"Hello... Crinnan... Crinnan Jamiso? Can you hear me?"

Crinnan couldn't respond. He didn't have a mouth, no lungs, no vocal cords. He was just... mush.

"I should say I do not know if he can hear me." A slightly modulated voice said as if through a shoddy radio connection. *"I have tried again and again but I have not been able to reach him yet."*

As the creature swallowed and the chewed-up pieces of Crinnan's head began to descend his throat, everything stopped. All went silent, and after a few moments, the world went dark.

You Have Died

Chapter Three
Voices in the Dark

The First Level

"Well thank the fucking Brothers for that." Crinnan groaned as he came to. But how could that have been? He was already dead; how could he die again? Nothing in the Hells was what he expected, nothing made sense. How could he continually die, why couldn't he hurt the demon? Where were the strange voices coming from? Suddenly the text floating in the darkness faded, revealing a much more mysterious message.

Terminal Online

Connection Established, user: Vajinious, user:44232001423932

>Bloodgames v.666.3

>HELLSCAPE by FARSEER

...

...

>System Override Key Accepted

...

...

...

>BetaMode: Enable

```
>Scripts: Enable

...

>godmode.sli loaded

>>ERROR

>>>godmode.sli not compatible with this version. Unable to execute.

>maxlevel.sli loaded

>>ERROR

>>>maxlevel.sli not compatible with this version. Unable to execute.

>sagescript5finalfinalfinalfuckinglast.sli loaded

>>sagescript5finalfinalfinalfuckinglast.sli executed

>Player Entity: 44232001423932 Created

>ERRR: Prisoner Entity: 44232001423932 Already Exists

>ERROR: ERROR MESSAGE IMPROPERLY DELIVERED

>PROCESSING SOLUTION... ... ... ...

>Player Entity: 44232001423932 and Prisoner Entity: 44232001423932
Merged

>ERROR MESSAGE Anomaly REPAIRED

>>Name: <Pending>

>
```

And what was that text? What did any of that mean? Crinnan was overwhelmed with confusion and anxiety as he stood in the darkness.

"It says we are connected, Crinnan can you hear me?" Another voice suddenly called out. It did not sound like a demon or Dura'ana or any of the others he had heard since his death. The voice sounded strangely real, it sounded like someone who was alive. Crinnan opened his mouth and spoke.

"Who are you?" he asked, wondering if the voice could even hear him. Crinnan waited in the silent darkness and felt his heart begin to beat a little softer. "Hello? Can you hear me?"

"He hears me!" The voice cheered. *"I did it!"*

"Yes..." Crinnan replied. "I can hear you. Who are you?"

"Hi!" The strange voice chirped. *"Hey, how is it going?"*

"It's... pretty fucking bad?" Crinnan had no idea how to properly respond to the sudden voice. He didn't know who or what was talking or where they were. He did notice, however, that every time they spoke another strange word flashed in the bottom right corner of his vision. That word was "Vajinious"

"How the fuck do you think it's going?" Crinnan answered with a tone of annoyance. "I am dead and in the Hells. I just had my head ripped off by some fat fucking blob with a damn surprise snake mouth. What is going on, who are you?"

"Yeah, that sucks." The voice sounded young and empathetic. *"So Sage isn't here right now, he had to poop, but he told me to watch his station and wait to see if you responded, and you did!"*

Crinnan didn't know who this mystery pooper or the person talking to him was or what Vajinious meant. That lack of knowledge was grinding on his nerves. He felt like he was alone in this strange dark void and was only able to talk to some idiot kid, and that didn't sit well with him. "What is all this?" He slowly and angrily asked.

"Like you already said. It's the Hells."

"No shit!" Crinnan returned. "I mean who are you, how are you talking to me?"

"Oh!" The voice exclaimed. *"Well, I mean, my name is Lucaas Lynx, but you really won't be talking to me very much."*

"What does the flashing word... Vajinious mean? Why does it appear every time you talk?" Lucaas chuckled in response to the question and Crinnan impatiently waited for an answer.

"Yeah, so that's a funny story. You see Dad... sorry; Sage's real name is Sajinious and he told me to update his username from his NPin allocation. I thought it would be funny to call him Vajinious... you know. Like vagina?"

"Funny joke coming from someone who has probably never seen one." Crinnan quipped. "Though, I mean other than vagina, I have no idea what anything you just said means."

"Well, I mean. That wasn't very cool of you, but I get it. You're upset." Lucaas' seemed mildly offended but soldiered past the insult. *"Sorry, I forgot to mention that to you. We are communicating with you through the NaNe; we are in the physical world you are in the digital. Our name flashes when we're speaking so that you know who is who just in case a bunch of people are talking at once... do you see how my name, LucLynx3 is flashing now?"*

Crinnan saw the name and nodded his head. "Yeah... I see it. But I seriously don't understand what you are talking about. What is... NaNe?" Crinnan asked, perplexed by all the foreign terms. "What is... NPin allocation? What do you mean digital? What the fuck are you talking about?"

"Digital?" Lucaas repeated. *"You know, as in computer-based?"*

"No, I don't damn know!" Crinnan snapped. "I thought I was in the Hells!" Crinnan received no immediate response as Lucaas had gone silent.

"Hello?" Crinnan called out. He suddenly felt alone again, and despite the fact that he preferred to be alone in the real world, in the Hells it just made him anxious. "Wait, don't go. I'm sorry for saying you don't know what a vagina looks like. I'm sure you slay like the best of them... Please don't leave me yet..."

"I should say I am terribly sorry for Lucaas." The original, more mature sounding voice from earlier returned. He had a rather posh sounding accent and Crinnan remembered Lucaas referring to him as dad or Sage. *"My name is Sajinious Lynx, though my friends call me Sage. You are welcome to call me Sage. I should say that if we are not friends by the end of all this, then I will have done a rather unsatisfactory job... and do not call me Vajinious."*

"Oh. Hey. By the end of what?" Crinnan asked. "What is going on?"

"I have taken an interest in breaking you out of the Hells, dear boy." Sage explained. *"It has not been done for, ironically enough, nearly a century. Eon*

the Calamity was the last to do so long ago, but your Black Knight friends sent him back."

"Why?" Crinnan asked.

"Why what?" Sage replied with a hint of confusion in his tone. "I should say they in all probability sent him back to the Hells because he was quite an unsavory fellow."

"No." Crinnan sighed. "I mean why are you saying you'll break me out?"

"Does it really matter?" Sage asked. "I should say information is a luxury at this point my friend. Rejoice in our ambitions, for they will benefit you greatly..." He paused for a moment and the younger voice of Lucaas returned.

"Okay standby for character creation." Lucaas said, confusing Crinnan once again. "Three... two... here we go."

Crinnan gasped as the world around him suddenly grew alive with... power. He felt wind fly past him, felt the breath sucked from his lungs. His head started to throb and it felt like he was being ripped from his own body. His conscience flew backward, and Crinnan stared at a featureless, hairless completely white skinned anthropomorphic body.

"Is that me!" Crinnan gasped, fearful of what he was seeing. "Why do I look like that!"

"Chill out." Lucaas replied. "It's just the placeholder. Standby for system instruction."

Welcome to Hellscape, new user.

A strange, almost robotic sounding voice played in Crinnan's ears. It was neither male nor female and it didn't give Crinnan the sense that it was alive. It didn't stop Crinnan, however from looking around searching for the source of the voice. He saw nobody, which dismayed him.

Congratulations on reaching adulthood, or gaining residency in our great country of Govia. As you are aware, Govia is blessed by the goddess Dura'ana and is seated at the head of the table of Duraan. Through Govia, our world knows peace and prosperity. Order is maintained not only by the efforts of our great and benevolent Emperor Cidro and our valiant heroes of the military on the frontlines, but also by you. You, dear citizen, contribute to Govia's greatness through your devotion to Goddess, Emperor and country. Your work through your designation enables us to maintain and grow the greatness that we have obtained and continually reach for. The Goddess Dura'ana smiles upon you, new citizen, and the Emperor thanks you.

"Say pause." Lucaas instructed.

"What?" Crinnan asked. "Why?"

"Just do it!" Lucaas urged.

"Fine..." Crinnan relented. "Pause!" The voice stopped speaking and Lucaas started.

"Do you understand what is going on?" He asked.

"I don't understand a damn thing." Crinnan replied. "What is this?"

"The voice you hear is the... system." Lucaas replied. *"You are currently no longer a prisoner. Sage has activated his first custom script that is solely focused on you. The "prisoner" Crinnan has been deleted, and "player" Crinnan has been created. Are you following?"*

"So... I'm not a prisoner anymore?" Crinnan asked. "Sage made me a player somehow?"

"Right." Lucaas affirmed. *"It is the first of many custom scripts that Sage and I plan on integrating, but it's the most important. The system sees you as a new player now. New players in the Hells are either people who have just come of age, or someone who has gained citizenship to mainland Govia."*

"Why?" Crinnan asked.

"So, basically... every demon you encounter in the Hells is a citizen of mainland Govia." Lucaas explained. "They all log into the Hells every day and use these avatars that they create to... well to sin."

"Sin is illegal in the Empire." Crinnan said, shaking his head. "That can't be right."

"That's right." Lucaas agreed. "Sin is illegal in the real world. But Govia knows that people just... can't not sin. Govia believes that inside everyone is a small well of evil, that we all can't help but sin and do wrong... they believe we crave it, that we can't help ourselves. Whether they are right or wrong is up for debate, but the simple fact is they know that no matter how many laws they make and how hard they enforce those laws... people will still sin. This is one purpose of the Hells, an outlet for their inherently evil citizens to sin."

"So... people come to the Hells to sin?" Crinnan asked. "Like a brothel or a bar?"

"Exactly!" Lucaas chirped. "It's actually been a very successful way of keeping order in mainland Govia. All sin is illegal in their country, so the Empire created and provided the Hells to its citizens. Govia mandates that all mainland citizens log into the Hells for at least one hour a day to expel their Sins. Some people drink, some gamble, some kill and torture prisoners, some have extramarital or premarital sex... the scope of sin is very wide and the citizens get... creative here."

"That's bullshit." Crinnan snorted. "So the Govians just come here to drink, kill and fuck so that they don't do it in the real world?"

"Correct." Lucaas said. "That way no crimes are committed in the real world, if the people have an avenue to do whatever they please by simply logging into a virtual lawless world where they won't face any repercussions for their actions... then the likelihood of them breaking any laws in the real world has proven to significantly drop. This is how Govia maintains control over their people and is why the punishment for any violation of their laws in the real world is so severe."

"What a bunch of crap." Crinnan snorted. Nothing about what he was hearing was even fathomable to Crinnan. Where he had lived and grown up, far from mainland Govia, if people wanted to fuck... they fucked. If they wanted to kill someone, then the other person had better hope they were a superior fighter… and awake.

"I agree." Lucaas replied. *"Anyway, say resume so the system can continue."*

"Resume." Crinnan said, and the voice picked up where it left off.

Shortly I will guide you through your first steps here in the Hells. Your avatar must be designed, and your character name must be selected. While I speak, I encourage you to think about how you want to look and what you would like to be called. Remember, citizen, your selected name here in the Hells is a permanent choice, but you will be able to update your avatar as you rise in rank and unlock new cosmetic options. But first, allow me to recite a chapter from the Book of Gaardmourn that you may be spiritually filled before you embark on your journey. I will be…

"Say skip." Lucaas urged Crinnan. *"By the Brothers, please say skip unless you want to sit through thirty minutes of scripture."*

"Skip!" Crinnan quickly said, not wanting to sit through any kind of recital of the Govian holy text. The system stopped talking mid-sentence and then started a new one.

I hope that was as spiritually filling for you as it was fulfilling for me to read it to you. With that knowledge and guidance safely nestled in your heart, oh citizen, I will now recite verses two and three of the Song of Cidro's Ascension. I ask that you close your eyes and raise your…

"Skip!" Crinnan nearly yelled.

Now that your spirit is fully and properly filled, we will begin the process of crafting your avatar. Do not be alarmed by the sudden shift in

---

At that, the blackness that surrounded Crinnan seemed to... thicken. It swirled and spun and Crinnan found himself seemingly carried by it as one would a wave in the ocean. It was alarming and unsettling, but it only lasted for a moment before the light and heat of a campfire pierced through.

For the first time since arriving in the Hells, Crinnan found a sliver of comfort. The gentle heat from the small campfire reminded him of home, of making camp with his squad. He looked into the soft crackling flames and felt a fleeting sense of peace.

Would you like to create a new custom avatar or use the data gathered from your real-world image? Please note: while cosmetic upgrades may be installed, your base avatar cannot be changed. Once you finalize your creation, you will not have an opportunity to return to this screen.

"What do I do?" Crinnan asked aloud.

"Whatever you want dude!" Lucaas replied. *"This is your..."*

"No." Sage interrupted sternly. *"While this is a game, I do not encourage you to have fun here, Crinnan. Say real world image, it will be the easiest option for now."*

"Real world image then." Crinnan said.

You have selected "Real World Image". Please confirm your selection by saying yes, or no.

"Yes." Crinnan grunted.

> **Thank you for confirming your choice. Your avatar will retain your real-world image. Remember, this choice is final. Are you ready to proceed to the next step?**

"By the Brothers, yes." Crinnan snapped.

> **Pagan terminology detected. The authorities are being notified of your transgression. Please standby for...**

"Override that." Sage quickly ordered Lucaas. *"Crinnan it is very important here that when you are interacting directly with the system that you... pretend you are Govian. It will make things easier on our side."* He paused for a moment and then continued. *"Lucaas has intercepted the alert and refreshed the system back to the next stage of avatar creation. Do be mindful."*

"Right." Crinnan sighed.

> **Awaiting input. Are you ready to proceed to the next step?**

"Y... yes." Crinnan replied.

> **Please speak the name for your avatar. You may select any name, allow your mind to run wild. Originality is encouraged, though it...**

"Crinnan." Crinnan said. He noticed when he spoke, the system silenced itself until he was done speaking.

Username: "Crinnan" unavailable. Please select a different name. Remember, you may select any name, allow your mind to run wild. Originality is encouraged, though it must be stated that this is a permanent...

"Crinnan Jamiso?" Crinnan all but asked.

Error: Invalid name. Reason: Illegal verbiage, surname of known criminal entity. The authorities have been notified of your transgression. Please standby for processing.

"Oh, by the Brothers. Lucaas!" Sage groaned. *"Crinnan, child, I know I do not have to repeat myself. Govia is very strict when it comes to their censorship of... ideas and people with ideas that go against what they force upon their citizens... Lucaas has intercepted the notification. Try again, but please... do not be foolish."*

Awaiting input... Generating list of available usernames.

...

TurtleCaptain88

HappyRainbow22

MasterBlaster6001

PrettyKitty6969420

TwelveGeeseInATrenchcoat2

aDog99

FlooferNooter

"PrettyKitty6969420?" Crinnan repeated. "What kind of strange name…"

Username: "PrettyKitty6969420" selected. Welcome, PrettyKitty6969420 to Hellscape. Please standby for a breakdown of your Avatar's statistics and abilities.

"Wait what!" Crinnan snapped. "No! I don't want to be PrettyKitty6969420! Go back!" Crinnan waited but received no response from the system. He groaned and he could hear Lucaas and Sage laughing from wherever they were. Crinnan flared his nostrils in embarrassment.

"You guys shut the fuck up." He snapped at them. "This isn't funny."

"I should say you are right, dear boy." Sage replied, quelling his giggling. *"We are being insensitive to your situation and I apologize. We will make a greater effort from here on out to accommodate your fragile situation."*

Avatar Information Sheet

…

Name: PrettyKitty6969420

Rank: 2,114,712,296

Percentile: 100

Player Rating: CURRENTLY NOT RATED

…

HP: 200

Shields: 200

Damage Output: 2x Base

Speed: 1.25x Base

Active Buffs:

...

New Citizen Booster

+100% to HP, Shields, and Damage Output until the next percentile of ranking is achieved.

...

Naked

+25% to Running Speed

...

sagescript5finalfinalfinalfuckinglast.sli

Description Unavailable

Equipped Items:

...

Head: EMPTY

Chest: EMPTY

Arms: EMPTY

Waist: EMPTY

Legs: EMPTY

Feet: EMPTY

Accessory 1: EMPTY

Accessory 2: EMPTY

...

Weapon Slot 1: EMPTY

Weapon Slot 2: EMPTY

> **Abilities Unlocked: NONE**

"What is all this?" Crinnan asked. "Why am I seeing so many numbers... why is it floating in front of my face? It's making me dizzy, what the fuck is going on!" Crinnan lowered himself to the ground at the jarring sight of the strange information being relayed in front of him. What was all this? Was it supposed to mean something to him?

"Those are your current statistics in relation to your personal progress through the Hells." Sage replied calmly and with a soothing tone. *"I understand it is overwhelming to you as you have never experienced anything like this before but remember, as often as I can, I will try to be available to assist you and answer any questions you may have. For now, the system will tell you what you need to know."*

> Your rank is indicative of your overall skill level compared to the rest of the citizens, or players, in Hellscape. By completing quests, slaying monsters, and engaging in friendly battles with your fellows your rank will increase or decrease depending on the outcome. Rewards will be granted upon crossing the threshold of a new percentile. As you are a new citizen, your rank and percentile are at rock bottom. Progress through these lands to achieve a higher rank.
>
> ...
>
> Please note: The lower your rank, the more system assistance you will receive. As you raise in rank and percentile the system aid will gradually decrease. If ever you may rise to the top 1%, you will receive no system aid and your avatar will be no stronger than you are in the real world. Hellscape rewards the strong and those who seek to gain strength; this act of weaning you off system assistance will ensure that you are granted the ultimate reward, tangible personal growth... and cosmetic items.
>
> ...
>
> Your Avatar Information Sheet can be summoned at any time simply by

willing the information in your mind. Hellscape is a place of discovery and growth, and this will be all the help I provide you in terms of system mechanics. The rest is up to you to discover.

...

I leave you now, citizen. Go forth and expel the sin from your heart. Remember, all that is forbidden in our great Emperor's domain is encouraged here. Purge the iniquity from your body, release your sins that you may return to us purer than you when you left.

...

Before I go, I do wish to impart on you the divinely inspired words of the great Highfather Halmaan. "For it was mine eyes that I did lift..."

"Skip." Crinnan said with a sigh and a shake of his head. The campfire faded away and he was once again left suspended in blackness. "So..." He asked after a few moments. "What now?"

"*Now I fear the time has come to return you to the Hells, Crinnan.*" Sage replied. "*I should say I am very much looking forward to you completing the journey ahead of you... But listen; our time with you is... unfortunately limited. The Empire is actively tracking us, and it is quite difficult keeping them at bay. My time with you is nearly expired so I fear I must be brief. Listen close, this is not a riddle. When the darkness fades you will find a sword. I have gained super administrative rights and encrypted your particular entity with a lock that only I have access to. Govia cannot remotely interfere with your actions or your progress. To hinder you, they must log into the game themselves and beat you. Crinnan, I should say that you are no longer the hunted, you have become the hunter. Standby for further clarification.*"

"What does any of that shit even mean?" Crinnan growled. "I don't understand what remotely means, I don't get any of this!"

"*It means that you are turning the game upside down!*" Lucaas chimed in.

"That doesn't bring any clarity..." Crinnan replied.

"I said, stand by for clarity! Crinnan, take the sword and kill the succubus." Sage replied. "We... we must leave now; we have to set up a new proxy before Govia finds us. We will return to you though..." At that Sage and Lucaas went silent. Their names stopped flashing in his vision, and he was left suspended in nothingness. Crinnan was disheartened by the fact that he was suddenly alone again. He wondered just how long he would have to wait for he was quickly growing tired of the darkness, of just sitting and dying and talking to voices that had no bodies...

With a sigh, Crinnan crossed his arms and waited impatiently.

Chapter Four
The First Fight

The First Level

For a moment the silent darkness persisted. As he waited, Crinnan tried to replay the conversations he'd had with Sage and Lucaas in his mind, but it all sounded like gibberish to him. The only words that Crinnan had truly understood after listening to the system and speaking with Sage and Lucaas were sword, kill and vagina. He had no interest in playing any "games" or allowing the numbers of his Avatar Information Sheet to have any bearing on his life. Crinnan did not like numbers or math or logic. He liked being left alone and fighting.

Crinnan thought of the fights he had taken part in in his short life. He'd fought in the Kamlotian Civil war only seven years prior and participated in pushing back a Marauder assault on the village of Empyr near his base. He'd fought and killed pirates, ambushed Govian troops and encampments, and had even once saved a girl from being kidnapped by slave traders. Faces of the dead flashed through Crinnan's mind and a sobering realization overcame him. He was in the Hells... and so were all the non-Govians he had ever killed. The thought of any of them finding him caused him to shudder. They would *really* be pissed.

He took a breath and seemingly out of nowhere became disoriented. An orange flickering light began to penetrate the darkness and Crinnan realized he was heading back to the Hells. It couldn't have come any quicker, he was ready to get out of there. The light faded in and out, throbbing for a moment before Crinnan's vision returned to black. The disorientation grew heavier, and he could hold his eyes open no longer. Within moments, they closed and Crinnan fell unconscious.

***

When Crinnan came to, he found himself naked once again and laying on a stone altar. He immediately sat up straight and was able to see that he lay atop a large hill composed of the same red ground that his bones had settled in earlier. Above him was only blackness and the fires on the ground raged as far as he could see. He reached up and cupped his face in his hands, groaning at the sight of it all. He was grateful that he wasn't suspended in the thick sensationless darkness anymore, but being back in the Hells was little comfort.

The altar Crinnan sat upon was cold and smooth. He absently ran a finger across the surface, noting that it felt like marble. Looking down at it, he saw that it was just a polished grey stone. His eyes scanned the intricate designs on the borders, and he considered what the altar could have possibly been used for. His slight knowledge of altars told him that anyone sitting on top of one was not in a particularly good position, so he threw his bare legs over the side and hopped off.

The red dirt on the ground beneath him was coarse like sand and filled the cracks between his toes. It would have been a decent enough feeling had the dirt been cool, but the dirt was hot and disturbing it sent a putrid brimstone smell wafting up into his nostrils. Crinnan wrinkled up his nose and fanned the air in front of him as he stood.

"The little warrior awakens..." A seductive voice softly whispered from somewhere close by. The sound was jarring and caused Crinnan to hurry away from the altar. He looked around frantically, searching for the sultry voice's owner. After a moment, he spotted something in the shadows ahead; he could vaguely make out the curves of a heavily accentuated female form in the shadows and took a cautious step away from her.

A demonic sounding giggle ensued, and a set of glowing violet eyes suddenly pierced the darkness that surrounded her. Crinnan's breath turned heavy and he backed further away, searching for a way to escape. He took his gaze off his enemy for a moment, and when he looked back, the glowing eyes were no longer there.

"Shit!" He cursed. As he jerked his head around, he felt something slam into his body, pinning him to the altar. Crinnan struggled to break free from her and watched in terror as she overpowered him. Two purple skinned hands reached out and dug their long black nails into Crinnan's wrist as the succubus straddled him and pinned him against the altar.

The demon: a tall, long-legged, purple-skinned and black-haired female smiled as she hovered above him and innocently shrugged her shoulders. Her large naked breasts bounced as she gyrated her hips on top of him and she leaned forward, pushing her tits into Crinnan's face.

"Oh, hey baby." The demoness moaned. She glazed her lips with the black viscous saliva that slowly dripped from her forked tongue. Crinnan gasped and immediately looked away, the abundant chest cleavage pressing hard against his face. He was both petrified and mildly aroused. Her thick thighs squeezed him in place, and she ground against his crotch, leaning down closer and dragging her barbed tongue across the naked flesh of his chest. Pieces of skin tore free and Crinnan gasped in pain.

"Oh no, does it hurt?" The succubus moaned with a tone of false innocence as she pressed her plump lips against his ear. "I can make it feel better baby boy."

"No!" Crinnan snapped. He could feel his exposed self growing hard as the succubus dragged herself over him. He moved his head back and forth frantically, searching for any kind of way out. He was not about to endure whatever the creature demanded from him. This situation was well beyond his comfort zone, and he was prepared to get out of it by any means necessary... and then he spotted it. The hilt of a sword peeking up from the right side of the altar. Crinnan remembered what Sage had told him: "take the sword and kill the succubus."

"Give it to me!" The succubus ordered as she positioned herself to accept Crinnan's cock. "Come on, baby. You've been a bad, bad boy. Give mommy what she came here for!"

"Let go, damnit!" Crinnan shouted as he finally ripped his hand free. The succubus' claws left deep bloody gashes in his skin, and Crinnan reached out and grabbed the handle of the sword. The succubus rolled off him, and a fine black mist engulfed her hands. She smiled wickedly, and Crinnan got to his feet on the opposite side of the altar.

Item Acquired:

...

Iron Short Sword

1h Weapon

Grants lethal combat capabilities to avatar.

Damage Output Modifier: None

Description: A basic weapon with a lethal edge, the short sword can be found on the hip of any of our fine men and women on the front lines. Through the years, the swinging of these blades has provided more and more lands with Dura'ana's favor, and helped the world see the true way that Govia provides.

...

Weapon Equipped to Weapon Slot 1

"You want it." The succubus asked, sensually touching and swaying her body in front of him. "It's either this or eternal torture. Come on, baby. Be my toy, enjoy your time here. Let me have my fun." She moaned as she took a step forward and crawled onto the altar. The black mist on her hands seemed to spread over the stone and begin to rise up above her. "Come on, bring that yummy body over here to mommy."

Crinnan grimaced, curling his upper lip and gripped his sword tighter. Whatever weird fantasy this creature was trying to force upon him, he didn't want any part of it. Or so he told himself. He looked down and saw that he was still erect and felt mildly embarrassed, but he didn't linger. He took a step forward and the succubus smiled.

"You can't hurt me with that, baby." The succubus laughed, nodding at his sword. "You can't hurt me at all. You can only give me... pleasure. That's all you prisoners can do."

Crinnan held his weapon threateningly and snarled at the creature before him. She did not respond how he wanted. Instead, she succubus writhed in heat like a cat, gyrating her hips against the smooth stone of the altar. Crinnan couldn't believe what he was seeing. Sure, it was sexy in a way, but he knew nothing good could come of this. He wasn't going to give in no matter what Little Crinnan demanded...

"Come on!" The succubus snapped, finally flipping onto all fours. She crawled toward him a few steps, and crooked one of her gnarly nailed fingers, beckoning him over. "This is my time, prisoner. You do as I say!"

"Fuck off." Crinnan snapped back. "Come any closer and you're dead!" The succubus stopped crawling and lowered her head to the altar as she suddenly started laughing in response.

"Stupid newbie." The succubus giggled. "Hard to get is so ten years ago." The succubus looked up and then jumped to her feet. The black mist culminated around her hands again and she held them out in a threatening manner. Crinnan kept a sharp eye on her.

"Oh no!" She feigned concern as the mist shot out and knocked Crinnan's feet from under him. He crashed to the ground, landing on his back. Dust flew in all directions around him, and he growled. "Looks like you fell down. Let mommy come and help you!"

"Quit with the weird ass mommy shit!" Crinnan yelled. He rolled backwards and then got to his feet in just enough time for the mist to slam into his chest. He stumbled back again but kept his balance. "It's creepy!" Crinnan groaned.

"That's the idea, honey." The succubus declared as she hopped off the altar. She took a few steps forward and bit her lower lip. "Are you really not going to fuck me?" She asked with a whiny voice.

"No!" Crinnan clapped back. "I don't even fucking know you!"

"Such a waste." The succubus sighed. "I guess I'll just have to eat you then."

"Why do you all eat each other here!" Crinnan yelled. The dark mist surrounded him, and he could feel whatever force was behind it lift his feet off the ground. The succubus extended a clenched fist as she took slow methodical steps toward him.

"Disappointment can be the greatest teaching tool." The demoness purred. She spoke with a teasing, yet mildly impatient tone. "Come, oh mighty warrior. Try your best. Thrust that little sword inside me, make me scream!" She stepped forward, having moved her arms out perpendicular to her body. She raised her chin confidently and slowly walked, moving one bare purple foot in front of the other as if she were walking a straight line.

"Big bad soldier..." The succubus taunted as she neared. "About to be bested by a little dainty lady like me." She flashed a smile, showing off her sharp pointed teeth, and Crinnan watched her forked tongue reach up and lick her lips. "I am so looking forward to watching your face when you realize you can do nothing. You can't protect yourself, boy, you can only..." Crinnan snarled and lunged powerfully. The tip of his sword pierced the demoness's sternum and emerged out her back. Black tar like blood streamed down his hands and onto his forearms and he pushed his weapon deeper, down to the hilt. Without a word, he locked eyes with the demoness.

"W...what?" Her tone was shocked, and a look of fear spread over her face. "H... How can it be?"

"Must be magic." Crinnan sneered. He didn't waste any more time. With a strength he hadn't known in life, he ripped his sword upward, lifting the succubus off the ground and tearing through her flesh and bone. With one final pull, the blade cut through the final bit of her sternum, severed her collarbone and emerged out the right side of her neck. Crinnan let the weapon drop to his side, and the demoness fell to the ground, twitching.

Crinnan's naked body was covered in black blood and he panted as he slowly walked over to the side of the succubus' body. She stared up at him fearfully, a stream of the dark ichor leaking from her mouth. Kneeling, he wrinkled up his face and stared at the creature.

"How'd I do?" He whispered as he held the edge of his blade against her throat. Weakly, the demoness' head trembled, as if she were trying to shake it in objection.

"W... who..." She choked, blood bubbling from the side of her torn neck. "Who..."

"Shut up." Crinnan stood and drove the tip of his weapon through her eye. More of the black blood gushed out, and the succubus released a light gasp. She arched her back one final time, and then went limp on the ground.

Player: Gadrielle.Jaanmor EXECUTED

Player Rank: 1,887,621,113

Congratulations, PrettyKitty6969420! You have advanced in ranking!

Previous Rank: 2,114,712,296

New Rank: 2,001,166,704

Previous Percentile: 100%

New Percentile: 95%

NEW PERCENTILE ACHIEVED - Congratulations, you are showing your true power. Your buffs have been modified.

Cosmetic Items unlocked! See your wardrobe for more details!

"Your turn bitch." Crinnan whispered as he kicked the corpse in the ribs. He snorted at the dead demon and turned away. The fields of fire burned endlessly before him, he watched bodies fall from the sky. He heard the screams of the damned, and the cries of glee of those who pursued them. Crinnan didn't know exactly what to do, but he knew he could now fight. With that knowledge, he took a step forward.

Chapter Five
Disembodied Direction

The First Hell

> **Attention Citizens:**

A strange female voice echoed in the air around Crinnan, and he couldn't help but stop and listen.

> The content pack, DJ's Fury, has been successfully implemented into the Bloodgames program on the Second Level. We invite any and all capable to come and experience the new environment. Rewards will be provided for the first two thousand who participate.
>
> Furthermore, our development team is aware of the unexpected bug that has appeared in the system causing players to respawn as prisoners upon death. We ask any affected by this bug to find a GM on the first level so they may be protected from any misunderstandings with fellow players. Additionally, we ask that all Player Versus Player interactions cease until this bug is fixed. The system will be temporarily locked down as our developers work to fix this issue. During this time, for your safety, logging in and out functions will briefly be suspended. Rest assured; this will not last long. All players currently logged in will be compensated at a rate of

> **two times play time in game during this brief lockdown. We thank you for your cooperation citizens. Praise Dura'ana, Praise Cidro.**

"Whatever that means." Crinnan shrugged as the voice ended. He didn't know anything about the Hells or any of the people within it so most of what he heard was just gibberish. He did find it interesting, however, to hear that Bloodgames matches were going on. He and his friend Alec had watched a number of Bloodgames matches on their television back home in their dormitory, so he was relatively familiar with the whole last person standing idea.

It never occurred to Crinnan, though, that the Bloodgames matches were held in the Hells. Why would it have, Crinnan had thought the Hells were just... a fictional place of eternal punishment after death. He thought it was all a lie created by the Govian Empire to keep people in line... just another story... but then he woke up after his death.

Crinnan had lost track of time. He didn't know if hours or days were passing. He traversed the cracked, ashy, and flaming ground of the Hells, clearing rolling hills, climbing steep grades and crossing wide gorges. No suns in sight, the light was cast only from the fires beneath him...

The things he saw as he walked were... unforgettable. He watched the players rip prisoners limb from limb. He saw people being cooked alive, buried while screaming for mercy, slowly flayed and consumed by their overlords... and the sex was everywhere. He saw demons fucking demons, prisoners fucking prisoners... demons fucking prisoners both consensually and... not... It was obscene, perverted and violent and Crinnan felt incredibly uncomfortable as he marched his naked body toward whatever he was walking toward.

All Crinnan had done since he killed the succubus was walk alone. For a long time, he did not hear the mysterious yet helpful voices of Sage or Lucaas. He wondered if they had abandoned him, or perhaps he was unreachable. Or maybe, they had died themselves. He did not know. Eventually he started to feel like the Hells had a sense of ironic humor and was giving him exactly what he desired when he had been alive, to be completely alone.

In the time that Crinnan walked he had thought of many things. He of course thought of his parents, his most instinctive sort of comfort. In life he had not spoken to them much, for over the years they had grown distant. Crinnan's father was the Commander of the Black Knight Underground Base in Canrom City, the largest city in all of the continent of Redodra. He was a carefree risk taker, had made a career of trusting his heart over his mind and charging head-first into battle... and somehow always winning. His mother was older than his father, by many decades. She was an elf, he a humaan. She balanced his impulsiveness, acted as a voice of reason. She was at times cold, but Crinnan knew she loved him. He of course loved her, but it was not something they spoke of. Very much unlike his father, who rained praises and love down on all his children. That polar experience of parental love was comforting. Crinnan couldn't help but imagine himself as a child once again locked in his mother's silent, yet firm embrace.

He thought of his friends, Alec and Elia and of how terribly he missed their incessant badgering. He wondered if there was any chance of him ever seeing them again. He expected Elia would one day join him in the Hells, but he was quickly realizing that Alec never could. Elia was a faire, one of the native races of Duraan known for their petite bodies and colorful hair. Alec, like Crinnan's father, was humaan, a race that had come to the planet via ships that sailed in the stars long ago. He hadn't seen a single humaan in the Hells which made sense. Govia was not fond of the humaan people, and full-blooded humaans could not join the empire as full citizens.

The Empire considered Crinnan a terrorist. Crinnan had only seen his twin brother Rubaan once since he left the army and became a Govian citizen. He did not look down on his brother for the choices he had made. It was his life to ruin, Crinnan thought. His brother was doing what he felt he had to do to be happy and protect his family and new way of life. Crinnan was glad that Rubaan had the strength to at least try.

After what seemed like an eternity of walking, Crinnan's shoulders were slumped and his gaze was cast downward. Everything was the same for miles, more fire. More ash, more smoke and screaming and blood...

Eventually Crinnan came across, of all things, a well-made of shaped stone. With a dry throat, Crinnan picked up his pace and hurried forward. He placed his hands on the side of the well and looked down inside. For a moment he thought he saw the rippling of water. He leaned in for a better look and a dozen long fingered grey hands suddenly reached up out the well, digging their nails into Crinnan.

"Join us!" The shrill voices within the well echoed. They pulled against his naked skin, trying to drag him within. Crinnan resisted, planting the soles of his feet in the dirt beside the well. He pulled back and batted at the emaciated rubbery skinned arms, cursing and bleeding as he did.

The hands did not let go. They pulled harder and harder, and Crinnan's feet were lifting off the ground. His body was dragged across the rim of the well, and the fingers started to rip into him.

"Join us!" The voices continued. "Join us!""

"Fucking stop!" Crinnan cried out. Finally, with a *well* placed strike, he swung his sword and severed one of the hands. The rest quickly retreated, leaving Crinnan shredded and bleeding profusely.

"By the Brothers!" Crinnan rasped as he pulled himself to safety. "That stings." He groaned. As he fell to the ground, his peripherals were enveloped with a flashing red, as if blood was circling his eyes. He had never encountered a sensation like that when he was alive, and deduced that it was signifying he was hurt?

"Not that the blood doesn't already tell me that." Crinnan quipped as he crashed to the ground. Ash blasted up his butt crack when he landed, but he didn't care by that point. He reached down and touched the muddy blood on him, and then looked at his fingers. His skin was almost completely black from the filth he had accumulated while walking for so long. His hair was matted and disgusting, and the blood on his chest and belly were mixing with it all. He pressed his back up against the stones of the well and rested his head. With a sigh, he closed his eyes.

"Lesson one: never trust a well in hell." The voice of Sage declared. "Are you okay?"

"Never better." Crinnan said, not moving his head or opening his eyes. He took a few breaths and shook his head. "I guess you didn't abandon me then."

"That is correct." Sage replied. "I should say that I am quite sorry it took as long as it did. Avoiding Govia while I manipulate their systems is rather difficult

and is generally met with unpredictable results. Though I finally feel comfortable transmitting again."

"Well I am glad you feel comfortable. Crinnan sarcastically remarked. "The last thing I would want is to inconvenience you."

"I should say there is no need for hostility my boy." Sage commented. *"Though your frustration is understandable."*

"My frustration is understandable?" Crinnan snorted as he finally had a reason to lift his head from the stones of the well. "How could you possibly understand my frustration? I am here, you are there probably in an air-conditioned house with something to drink. What about any of this is understandable? When the fuck was the last time *you* were in the Hells?"

"The last time I escaped was nearly one hundred years ago." Sage casually answered. *"For the first time in our lives, the one known as Eon and I worked together."*

Crinnan couldn't come up with a response. He had not expected that answer.

"Whatever." He grumbled as he rested his head and closed his eyes again.

"I do understand, Crinnan." Sage said softly. *"And I am sorry for the silence, I know the Hells can be a lonely place."*

"It's fine." Crinnan grumbled.

"Dear Crinnan it will be a bit of work and time before we can get you out of there." Sage regretfully informed him. *"We are going to have to rip that dark sky completely open and pluck your data out. The weakest point is going to be the oldest zone and home of the data stream... the Seventh Level of the Hells. Today I hope to get you to the Second Level."*

"The Second Level?" Crinnan repeated. He remembered the disembodied female announcer voice saying that the Bloodgames was in the Second Level. "So, what kind of wonderful journey will that be?"

"You have to kill more demons and eventually a portal will open." Lucaas piped in. *"Killing the succubus helped you, but she wasn't enough. She was a newer player, not very strong. The stronger the player you kill, the higher your*

ranking will go. To get to the next level, you have to cross the 90th percentile marker."

"Terminology, Lucaas." Sage interrupted. *"Remember. He is ignorant."* Lucaas huffed and then continued.

"Just... like. Kill things. Eventually you'll open a portal."

"Crinnan..." Sage sighed and took over. *"There is just so much you do not know."*

"So, tell me." Crinnan insisted. "I've got the fucking time."

"The Hells..." Sage began. *"They are not a real thing I should say. It is... How should I put this..."*?

"They are a sick videogame!" Lucaas chirped and interrupted Sage. *"A twisted version of the utopian Afterscape that Life Links created so long ago."*

"What is a video...game?" Crinnan asked. He had seen videos before on television; he knew what games were but did not spend any time playing them. Drinking or training was more productive in his opinion. The word videogame, however, was foreign to him.

"In Govia, playing a videogame is something that people do to pass the time." Sage replied. *"You see a videogame is a game that the Govians play on their computers."*

"A game for a computer?" Crinnan repeated, a bit dumbfounded by the concept. "People have their own computers in Govia?"

"People have everything in Govia." Sage chuckled. *"Cars, computers, streaming pornography, phones... you name it Govians have access to it."*

"So, the Hells is something people... play?" Through everything he had experienced, Crinnan was starting to vaguely understand the concept of it. But how did anyone *play* any of what he was experiencing? His idea of a game involved cards, dice, paper...sometimes a knife and a rabbit. The world he was experiencing seemed real.

"I will try to explain." Lucaas chimed in. *"People step into a big silver egg thing that's called a Hellpod. It's completely dark inside and they essentially go to sleep. When they wake up, they are where you are, in the Hells. They see it*

the same way you do, except they can just click a button, wake up and go back to their lives. It is not real to them... well, not until now."

"Yes..." Sage agreed. *"You see, long ago in the Ancient times people lived and died just like they do today. However, in those times there was a technology called the Afterscape. Basically, after the humaan aliens arrived, they revealed to the Ancient people that beyond the clouds there was no god, no goddess, only dark. This majorly affected them as they were a heavily superstitious people whose entire infrastructure was built upon the idea of being rewarded or punished after death. As the Ancients learned the ways and technology of the humaan people, they eventually created a virtual afterlife based off the technology of the Humaans. It was one that could be guaranteed to people upon death."*

"So, people died... and went to a computer?" Crinnan asked.

"Exactly." Sage replied. *"You see, everywhere you look – in the air you breathe, in the ground you walk upon – are machines called the NaNe. They are microscopic, you cannot see them with your naked eye. You may know them better by what they do... you may call it magic or sorcery, but I will tell you that it was by far the greatest technology that the Humaan people gave to us. Rather, it could have been. Anyway, one thing that these NaNe do is they record everything about us. They record our memories, our physical features, our learned ways of reasoning and communicating and store it in an ever-updating file called a blueprint. Back in Ancient times when a person died their blueprint would be uploaded to the Afterscape server and they could digitally live forever with their loved ones doing the things they enjoyed. This, of course, was all before the Church won the war and started the Empire. Once the Church or the Govian Empire as they are now called took hold of the world, they redesigned the technology and changed the Afterscape to Heaven and the Hells. When you died, your blueprint was automatically sent to the Hells as punishment for defying the Govian Empire."*

"So, you're saying that not only is there no Goddess, but also right now I am walking around inside a computer?" Crinnan could not believe the words that were coming out of his mouth. It sounded like absolute nonsense.

"Yes. Well, a computer program to be more precise... and a bastardized version of what it once was." Sage's tone had a hint of resentment in it.

"What about... my soul?" Crinnan asked.

"Not my area of expertise." Sage replied dismissively.

"So how will you get me out of here?" Crinnan asked. "I mean, what will happen to me once I get out if all I am is... computer stuff?"

"Data." Sage laughed at the poor ignorant boy. *"Computer stuff is called data... anyway, we will take your NaNe and put it back in your body and then you will regenerate."*

"Bullshit!" Crinnan spat. "That's just so..."

"Unbelievable?" Sage hummed. *"Listen, my boy. All my life I have been in the business of bringing dreams to reality. I want you to think about it for a moment. There you are, in the Hells. I am talking to you whilst you traverse the plane of unending damnation and you are able to talk back. Not only that but I am doing it through a computer. I know it's difficult for someone such as yourself to understand but I should say Crinnan, what is it you believe you have to lose by trusting me?"*

"Whatever." Crinnan replied. "So... how do I... move to deeper levels?"

"Well, like I said you kill people and monsters and raise your ranking... and that's the interesting thing about your situation." Lucaas said. *"The demons you fight are real people. They upload their NaNe into these avatars to fulfill their sick fantasies. They're not... soldiers. Most of them have never harmed another person in their lives. You see, it was never intended for demons or players to be killed in this game. Sage and I, we wrote this script, completely modded the game. We gave you an ability we created called Demon Slayer; basically, what it does is once you reduce a demon's health to zero, their in-game status changes from "demon" to "prisoner". Nobody by default can change what is coded in people's NaNe. Well, nobody but us. What I am trying to say is, if you kill a demon here, they stay here."*

"So, if they die in the game they die in real life?" Crinnan asked.

"In a sense." Sage replied. *"If you kill them in the Hells, their NaNe will respawn as a prisoner in the Hells and will not return to their physical bodies. Their real bodies will stay alive; they will just be devoid of consciousness."*

"What a stupid game." Crinnan said. "Why would anybody play a game like this when they could die?"

"As we have explained... There has been no risk of harm until now." Sage sighed. *"The player versus player feature ensures that hit points never go below one and renders the losing player unconscious instead of dead... we removed that limitation and Govia will not be able to reinstate it."*

"Do the other demons know what they are doing?" Crinnan asked. "I mean, do they realize they are torturing people?"

"It is well known in Govia, yes." Lucaas answered. *"They feel that if a person is in the Hells, then they deserve whatever happens to them. It's kind of part of the appeal. In Govia, sin is illegal in all its forms. The Empire enforces at least one hour of playtime in the Hells daily so that its citizens can sin there instead of causing trouble in the real world. It is very effective, and their social structure basically runs on your player ranking in the Hells."*

"Then killing them sounds good to me." Crinnan said. He was not too keen on Govians in the first place, the idea that even the Empire's citizens were as twisted as its government made him hate it all even more. "It takes a sick fuck to willingly do this to people. I'm fine with ending as many as I can find."

"Then we have to go for now." Sage informed him. *"Remember, raise your rank until you are in the 90th percentile to get to the Second Level. The only thing that truly threatens you down here is yourself. The demons can knock you out and make you respawn but that is all. Do not succumb to the psychological bombardment that awaits you. You can do this, Crinnan. I believe in you."*

"How long will you be gone?" Crinnan asked.

"Until we aren't." Sage replied. *"We have to go now…. we will talk again."*

"Bye man!" Lucaas said.

At that, the word "Vajinious" disappeared entirely from Crinnan's vision and Sage and Lucaas went silent. Crinnan closed his eyes and sighed. He wondered how long he would have to stay in the Hells before he could get out. He wondered how many more people he had to kill before he could get to the Second Level.

Chapter Six
Here There Be Monsters

The First Hell

"Well... here we go then." Crinnan said. He grunted as he stood up, noting that his wounds had closed. The throbbing red in his peripherals had vanished and getting back to his feet was near effortless. "I guess I just... go kill someone then..."

As Crinnan walked, he thought more of his mother to pass the time. He recalled a memory of when he was young, three or four he imagined. His eldest brother Kiersen had pushed him down a flight of stairs and as he tumbled, he knocked down his twin brother Rubaan. His mother was quick to tend to him and slapped Kiersen on the back of the head as she ran past him.

"It is okay loves," he heard her voice soothe as she held Crinnan in one arm and Rubaan in the other, "You will be okay." Crinnan could feel the warmth of her embrace as he trudged through the Hells and wished she could descend the proverbial stairs and scoop him up once again. He sighed as he thought about it all and thought that if Sage and Lucaas truly could help him escape then the first thing he should do would be to call his mother. A slight tremor at his feet pulled him out of his thoughts.

"What was that?" He stepped back and spun his sword in hand. "What's going on?"

The ground shook more violently, and he watched as small mounds of crumbling and burning dirt began to form all around him. He widened his stance and raised his weapon in defense. Whatever was coming, there seemed to be a lot of them.

A black pointed claw pierced one of the mounds and planted itself into the ground. Crinnan watched as more claws emerged and realized that they were legs. The bodies of small shining ebony monsters that resembled vicious looking spiders pushed themselves out of the holes. They had clusters of red blinking eyes at what Crinnan perceived was the front of them and two shining white fangs that dripped with some kind of gummy viscous fluid.

The legs tore through the ground as a spider skittered Crinnan's way. He stepped back, for the monster had a surprising amount of speed, and prepared to defend himself. The beast leaped from the ground and released a high-pitched squeal. When it was within reach, Crinnan swung his blade and bisected the spider. It crashed to the ground and vanished in a plume of thick smoke just as nearly half a dozen other spiders poked through the dirt.

Hell Spider Killed
+100 Rank

New Rank: 2,105,666,285

"Hey, that's lower than it was before!" Crinnan snapped as he heard the information read out to him. "What the fuck!" Crinnan remembered his rank had been two billion last time he'd checked, not two billion one hundred million.

"Oh shit." Crinnan backpedaled as his eyes bounced from spider to spider. One ran up as if it were attacking his heel and he jammed the point of his blade through it and into the ground. When he pulled his weapon up, the remainder charged him.

Hell Spider Killed

+100 Rank

> **New Rank: 2,105,666,185**

"Yeah I know." Crinnan snapped in response to the notification. The first spider leaped through the air and found itself promptly sliced in half. The other four were too fast though and planted their pointed legs into Crinnan's skin before he could react. He howled and staggered backward as he reached up and grabbed one before it could sink its fangs into him. He threw it to the ground and stomped on it as the others rapidly planted their teeth in and out of him.

> **Hell Spider x2 Killed**
>
> **+200 Rank**
>
> **New Rank: 2,105,665,985**

"Shut up!" Crinnan yelled. The spider's teeth were poking holes into his body. Blood was dripping from him and his peripherals were beginning to show the throbbing red again. With a growl, he dropped his sword and grabbed hold of two of the three that remained. He ripped them from his body and flung them as far away as he could and snatched up the last. It flailed wildly in his hands as it tried to stab him with its appendages and he growled and smashed his palms toward each other, squishing the spider into nothing more than a black oily soup that dripped from his fingers. As it turned into smoke and faded into the air above him, the final two charged toward him.

> **Hell Spider Killed**
>
> **+100 Rank**

Crinnan didn't have time to retrieve his sword before the next spider leaped toward him. He caught it midair just as the second latched onto him. With the first spider in his right hand, he reached up with his left and pulled the second off his body. As they both thrashed about, he finally grit his teeth and slammed them together, smashing their bodies against each other. They popped like grapes and their greasy black blood splashed up on his face. As they turned to smoke and vanished, Crinnan lowered his head and groaned in utter disgust.

Hell Spider x2 Killed

+200 Rank

New Rank: 2,105,665,685

"If I say thanks do I get super special politeness points too?" Crinnan snapped angrily at the voice that kept reading to him. He huffed in place for a moment and tried to wipe the greasy spider blood off his body. "That was... weird and gross." He flung his hands about, trying to get the ichor off of him. In his life he'd had his share of blood and monster gore splashed on him, he should have been used to it but Crinnan always felt sick when he was covered in something's innards.

After spending a few moments rubbing his hands in the dirt to get the oil off, he finally decided to sit down and take a small break. He was curious why his rank had changed, why had it dropped one hundred million points? Had he done something wrong? The thought dominated his mind for a moment, and then he realized something.

He wasn't the only person in the Hells. If the ranking system was to be believed, there were over two billion other people involved. Crinnan thought about it a moment and based on his social studies classes in the academy, he recalled the population of mainland Govia being around three billion as of about a decade ago. That fell in line with the ranking system, and with what he had been told by Lucaas about all mainland Govians being required to participate in the Hells to purge sin from their minds. With that in mind, Crinnan realized that the ranking system was more of a tug of war than anything else. Every participant was always gaining and losing rank. That thought led him to realize that crossing the 90th percentile into the 80th might be harder than he thought.

"Of course." He sighed as he stared down at his naked self. "Just like in real life. Everyone's trying to be better than each other... at the expense of those left behind... stupid." He reluctantly stood back up and lifted his sword off the ground. Begrudgingly, he started walking again.

"Walking is stupid." Crinnan grumbled to himself as he kicked a mound of dust with his bare foot. A hand reached out of the dust and grabbed Crinnan's ankle in response. Crinnan looked down, sighed, and then stabbed the hand with his sword. The hand released its grip, flailed wildly for a moment and then withdrew into the ground beneath it.

"Stupid bodyless hands everywhere." Crinnan said under his breath. The Hells was beginning to grate on his nerves. He was tired of walking, tired of being naked... he wanted to just leave. Sage claimed that he was trying to get him out and Crinnan wasn't sure he even trusted him. It wasn't like he had anything to lose though.

The sound of thumping nearby pulled Crinnan out of his whining and general self-pity and he looked up. He didn't see anything in the immediate area and so he started walking toward where he thought the thumping noise was coming from. After crossing a hill, he came to a stop.

Maybe fifty yards from the base of the hill he saw a large bipedal black hairy beast stomping about with a club in his hand that was as thick as a tree trunk. The creature didn't have a neck and its head looked more like a misshapen tumor growing out the top of its torso.

Crinnan looked down at his naked body, over at his sword, and finally to the monster. It did not look like it would be a particularly easy creature to slay, but he felt he could manage. Back in the real world he'd killed plenty of monsters with his friends. This one looked slow and stupid which suited Crinnan's skillset well. He spun his sword and then jogged down the hill toward the beast.

The monster quickly noticed Crinnan. It clenched its fist and arched its back so that its neckless head was facing the black sky and it belted out a mighty roar. The intensity of the beast's voice gave Crinnan pause and for a moment his jog halted. He watched as the hairy monster pounded its chest with its free hand and locked its glowing red eyes onto Crinnan.

"Well, here we go I guess." Crinnan mumbled as the beast took a step toward him. Crinnan ran and so did the monster. As they neared one another, the beast lifted its club to strike. Crinnan, in turn, readied his sword and when they were only a few more steps from each other, he jerked to the right in anticipation of the creature's strike. The monster reacted quicker than Crinnan anticipated.

The beast swung his weapon, missing Crinnan as had been expected. Instead of pulling his club back for another strike, however, the monster pivoted on his heel. It spun and used the momentum from the original attack to keep the weapon moving. The club ultimately slammed against Crinnan's naked body with a speed and force that he did not anticipate. The power of the weapon lifted him off the ground and sent him flying through the air. He slammed into the ground and kicked up a trail of dust as he skidded to a stop. With a groan, Crinnan attempted to push himself up but failed as it seemed the bones in his legs had been shattered.

The beast roared and charged. As it approached, it didn't hesitate. It slammed its club down onto Crinnan's body. He felt every bit of himself collapse beneath the weight of the weapon and as he heard the sound of his skull popping, everything went black.

You Have Died

Chapter Seven
Revenge

The Dead Zone

You Were Killed By: Devil Yeti

...

Corpse Status: Untouched

Resurrection/Respawn: Available

...

-20,000 Ranking for non-pvp death

...

Current Ranking: 2,105,685,985

Current Percentile: 99

...

20:00:00 until corpse respawn available.

Would you like to respawn in the Fields of Misery Now?

There was no longer any ground, no sky, only darkness. He heard voices all around him, laughing and swearing and shouting coming from every direction. For a moment, it sounded like chaos, but as he focused on the single voices, he could make out conversations and orders. People were talking to each other.

"Yeah, pal, Landiis was supposed to tank against the bone dragon but ended up shitting himself and running away!" Crinnan heard someone say.

"Fucking Landiis..." Another voice replied. "Why do we even play with him?"

"I'm right here." A voice, whom Crinnan expected was Landiis snapped. "I haven't even crossed the 80th percentile yet and you guys think I can tank a bone dragon?"

"If you'd do your job, we wouldn't have any problems." The first voice said. "I could have healed you if you weren't running and screaming."

"I didn't want to die!" Landiis griped.

"What is this place?" Crinnan asked out loud. The voices that were speaking near him stopped and he suddenly saw four lights float toward him.

"What do you mean?" Landiis asked. "Are you new?"

"Yeah..." Crinnan replied.

"What percentile are you?" Another of the people asked. "We could use a fifth. When we respawn, we're going to the Second Level to try a few Bloodgames rounds."

"Uh... 99 it says." Crinnan replied.

"Oh." The person replied. "Yeah, never mind. We're good."

"Okay fuck you too." Crinnan spat.

"No, fuck you newbie!" Landiis added. "Show some respect. We're not going to carry you, that's just not how this works."

"I'm not asking you to." Crinnan replied.

"Well have fun dying." Another of the voices called out. The four lights then "turned" and floated away.

"Fucking Govians." Crinnan sighed. He looked around the dark place some more and then back to the message in front of him.

17:46:25 until corpse respawn available.

> **...**
>
> **Would you like to respawn in the Fields of Misery Now? Y | N**

Crinnan remembered the Fields of Misery being the place he originally fell from the sky at. It was the first place he had landed in the Hells and he felt like he had traveled so far since then. He didn't want to lose all that progress.

"No." Crinnan said in response to the prompt before him.

> **17:30:23 until corpse respawn available.**
>
> **...**
>
> **Resurrection Initiated. Standby.**

"I said no!" Crinnan yelled. "No!"

The blackness surrounding him turned to grey, and then white. Crinnan felt a force tugging on his body, and he screamed in resistance. But it was futile. He could not fight it, it plucked him up like a toad in the hands of a three-year-old. He saw only light for a moment, and then he smelled smoke again.

"Come on buddy!" Crinnan heard a voice call out. "Get to your feet, let's finish this devil yeti together!"

Crinnan opened his eyes and saw that he was whole again. He wasn't falling from the sky or in the Fields of Misery. He was exactly where he had died. The devil yeti had wandered a small distance away and as Crinnan stood, he found himself in the company of a player with gray leather armor and a staff in hand. A white hood covered his eyes and as Crinnan came back to life, the player gave him a perplexed look.

"Wait, are you a prisoner or a player?" The person asked with a tone of confusion. "When you were dead it said you were a player, now that you are back... it's showing a weird error... what is going on?"

"Hells if I know. But don't worry about it, Govian." Crinnan didn't hesitate. He jammed the tip of his sword through the player's throat. He fell to his knees and tried to speak but couldn't get any words out as his vocal cords had been severed. Crinnan pulled his sword away and the player fell forward face down into the ground.

Player: DaldiLion19 EXECUTED

Player Rank: 1,845,129,587

Congratulations, PrettyKitty6969420! You have advanced in ranking!

Previous Rank: 2,105,685,985

New Rank: 1,975,407,786

Previous Percentile: 99%

New Percentile: 93%

"*Hey! What the Hells was that all about!*" Crinnan heard the voice of the player he had just killed shout. The sound was coming from his dead body. His lips did not move but for some reason, Crinnan could hear him speaking.

"*Why did you do that?!*" He angrily continued. "*I just resurrected you! We were going to go kill the devil yeti together!*" He paused and Crinnan heard a sudden and frightful gasp. "*Wha... what is this? Prisoner? How did you... how am I... YOU are the one responsible for this? You're the one who is turning people to prisoners?*"

"I don't know what you're talking about." Crinnan spat as he bent over to strip the player of his clothing. "You won't be needing any of this anymore."

"*No...*" The player whispered in horror. His voice grew frantic. "*I can't log out... my whole interface is gone... what did you do to me!*"

"I gave you what you deserved, Govian." Crinnan said flatly as he began to put the clothes on. The linen shirt and pants that the demon had been wearing went on with no problem but as soon as Crinnan tried to strap the armor on, it vanished into a plume of black smoke like the spiders had before.

"What?" Crinnan asked, confused, "What is going on?" He tried to pull on the boots, but they too disappeared.

You do not meet the minimum Percentile requirement for this item.

...

Item Destroyed

"Well, that's stupid." Crinnan grumbled. As he looked down at the naked corpse before him, he could hear the sobbing of the demon which made him roll his eyes.

"Now you know how I felt." Crinnan said to the weeping player as he began to walk away. For a moment he considered trying to fight the devil yeti again. He watched the beast pace back and forth in the distance and ultimately shook his head.

"Not after last time." Crinnan mumbled to himself. "He's too strong."

It felt nice finally having clothes on. For days, Crinnan had watched his happy parts flop all over the place as he traversed the burning landscape that was the Hells. That had gotten old in the first minute; he was glad to finally be able to cover it all up.

After some time, Crinnan found himself at the foot of a large hill. He looked up at the steep grade ahead of him and all he could do was sigh. More treacherous landscape, more bullshit. He started climbing. After slipping a few times, kicking a rock, and cursing at the dirt, he finally reached the top.

"No!" Crinnan heard a voice in the distance suddenly shout. He squinted to try and find who was shouting. He gripped his sword and listened.

"Stop, fiend!" The voice shouted again. "Depart from me, wicked iniquity!"

"That's a weird way of talking." Crinnan muttered as he zoned in on the voice's location. He realized he could get some ranking out of this and possibly even move onto the next level like Sage had told him to. Carefully, he ran down the hill and in the direction the voice was coming from.

"If not for these unjust limitations," Crinnan heard, "I would blast you into nothingness, which is more than you are worth!"

"Quiet bitch!" A familiar voice returned. "This is the Hells; you will take what I give!"

Crinnan finally found the owners of the voices. He saw the corpulent white demon that had eaten him when he first arrived in the Hells. His hook had been set aside and he pushed down on the back of a prisoner beneath him. The prisoner's ass was exposed, and Crinnan could only imagine the horrible things the demon player had in store for him.

"Hey, shithead!" Crinnan shouted as he firmly held his sword in front of him. "Get off of him you sick fuck!"

The unexpected shouting took the demon player by surprise. He got to his feet much more quickly than he should have and turned to face Crinnan.

"Who are you?" The surprised demon shouted back. He looked at Crinnan closely for a moment and then suddenly laughed when he saw the sword in his hand.

"So, you think you're the one who'll be doing the sticking do ya?" He turned and retrieved the massive hook from the ground, "I'll make this quick then. You'll wish you'd stayed away from me... that is unless you enjoy being fucked in which case, we'll get along just fine."

"Shut up." Crinnan approached the demon to the sound of his mocking laughter.

"Not even the 80th percentile yet." The demon snorted. "You got your buffs, but you ain't shit little elf." Feeling he had no way of losing a fight, he immediately jumped forward swinging his hook.

Crinnan darted out of the way and the hook crashed into the ground sending little bits of charred dirt flying toward him. Crinnan lunged forward and swiped at the demon with his blade. The demon roared in pain and confusion as he leaped backward and looked at the gash on his arm.

"How the fuck!" He shouted as his face twisted into a furious expression. He growled and kept a safe distance from Crinnan.

"How did you do that?" The demon demanded. "How could you possibly do that? Someone like you shouldn't be able to do damage like that! You're a new player, a new citizen... a nobody!"

"Welcome to the new Hells." Crinnan quipped. "I guess you forgot ripping my head off earlier. Newsflash, fucker, I am the demon now." He pounced forward and planted his sword in the fat demon's belly. The demon grunted and forcefully jerked away; the force of his large body threw Crinnan to the side. Crinnan lost hold of his sword and crashed into the ground next to the prisoner the demon was originally accosting.

"You must survive, noble warrior!" The prisoner quickly crawled over and whispered to Crinnan. "I can help you!"

"That is the plan." Crinnan grunted as he hurried to his feet. He ran away from the prisoner and the demon pursued.

"I remember you now... What are you!" The demon growled. "You were a prisoner when I killed you. How are you... is this another bug?" He barreled forward, knocking Crinnan over with his oversized bleeding belly.

"You can't win." The demon sang as he slammed his hook into Crinnan's chest. Crinnan felt the point pierce through him and into the ground beneath. He gasped as the wind was knocked out of him. For the first time since his first encounter with the same demon, Crinnan felt a sense of exhaustion. He felt as if his life energy was quickly fading once again, and as the demon raised Crinnan into the air, he knew he had to fight past his weariness and win.

"Oh yes I can." Crinnan resolved. With what speed he could muster, he reached down and ripped the sword he had left in the demon's belly free and swiped at his throat. The blade cut through his second chin, releasing a torrent of blood and fat. The demon rasped and dropped his hook, sending Crinnan back to the ground.

Crinnan groaned with pain as he ripped his body free from the hook, leaving a gash in its wake. Painfully, he hobbled over to the demon who was writhing on the ground holding his neck.

"How?" The demon gurgled, "How... you're... just a newbie."

"I guess I'm just better than you." Crinnan muttered as he slammed the point of his blade through the demon's left eye. The demon went limp and Crinnan let go of his weapon before he fell backward into the flames. He had won.

Chapter Eight
Friends in Low Places

The First Hell

Player: ByGG.DyKK EXECUTED

Player Rank: 1,712,987,122

Congratulations, PrettyKitty6969420! You have advanced in ranking!

Previous Rank: 1,975,407,786

New Rank: 1,844,197,454

Previous Percentile: 93%

New Percentile: 87%

...

NEW PERCENTILE ACHIEVED - Congratulations, you are showing your true power. Your buffs have been modified.

Cosmetic Items unlocked! See your wardrobe for more details!

...

Congratulations! You have crossed the threshold of the 90th percentile and into the 80s. You have unlocked the path to the Second Level!

> **Ability Unlocked:**
>
> ...
>
> **Portal (Level 1) - Grants player the ability to summon a portal to the First Level of Hellscape anywhere portals are permitted.**
>
> ...
>
> **Portal (Level 2) - Grants player the ability to summon a portal to the Second Level of Hellscape anywhere portals are permitted.**

"Bravo!" The prisoner cheered as he enthusiastically clapped his hands together. "Curse these abominable flames and curse the people that dwell within them! Bravo brave warrior. Your presence truly has brought a light to the darkness that is these very Hells."

"Whatever then." Crinnan replied. He glanced up at the prisoner and saw that while he was tall, he was thin framed. A vampre with a brown ponytail and thick mustache. He looked to have no physical strength about him and seemed a bit bookish.

"Such a fortuitous occurrence." The vampre gushed. "An epic display of strength! Truly I have found myself in the company of a true warrior!"

"Fortuitous..." Crinnan repeated sourly. "Why do you talk like that?"

"Ah, well you see noble warrior," the prisoner responded, "I do not hail from the current era as I assume you do. I come from a time of discovery, of peace and science... a truly magnificent period that you may refer to as the Ancient times. I speak as I was taught, as was common."

"You are an Ancient?" Crinnan clarified, thinking back to Sage. "So, you've heard of the Afterscape?"

"I..." He replied, suddenly unsure of himself. "I think I do."

"What do you mean?" Crinnan asked. "Do you or not?"

"Much is lost in this place, my friend." The prisoner said. "I have sacrificed much of my memory to maintain my sanity."

"What is your name?" Crinnan asked.

"My name?" The prisoner repeated. He paused a moment and smiled. "Do forgive me for I have not spoken my name in many decades... I was called Frema'Ander din Lecaaste, though my associates and loved ones referred to me as Ander. How may I be so honored as to address you, dear warrior?"

"I am Crinnan." He replied. "Centurion of Black Knight."

"Black Knight?" Ander repeated quickly. He paused and thought to himself, his head suddenly ticking to the side. "Why, I have never heard of such a thing. Is that a new corporation?"

"We are the resistance." Crinnan replied. "An army which fights the Govian Empire, the people who sent us here."

"You seek to free the prisoners of the Hells?" Ander asked. "Such a noble cause."

"No." Crinnan shook his head and looked away. "Our mission is to overthrow the Govian Empire. We never thought it possible to free the people of the Hells... I mean, a lot of us just think the Hells is just a... story... Clearly it isn't."

"Indeed." Ander nodded his head slowly. "Tis understandable, why would the living concern themselves with the woes of the dead? And, as you say, how could they if they do not know the dead exist?"

"Yo, ByggDykk, where you at bro?" A voice suddenly called out. "We need to get going, you done with that little mustache bitch?"

"Little mustache bitch!" Ander scoffed. "Why I never!"

"Relax." Crinnan held his hand out to steady the Ancient and rolled his eyes. "I'll take care of him."

"Over here!" Crinnan heard the disembodied voice of ByggDykk frantically scream. *"By the Goddess, I can't log out! Lockdown is still up... it says I'm... I'm a prisoner... I am stuck and the kids need to be picked up from school!"*

"Your kids?" Crinnan looked down at ByggDykk's body and felt a wave of anxiety come over him "You have kids?"

"Yeah, you fucking asshole!" The demon-turned-prisoner shouted. *"My kids are at school... I'm a single father; I am all my kids have! I need to leave; I need to go get them. What have you done?"*

"I haven't done shit..." Crinnan felt his heart sink as he looked around nervously. What *had* he done? Had he just taken a father from his children? That idea made him feel like a monster... but it wasn't his fault... *and* it wasn't the first father he had killed.

"You were raping him, you torture people!" Crinnan shouted back, bring light to the person's crimes as justification. "What was I supposed to do? Just let you fuck him to death after you tore my head off?"

"It is a game!" ByggDykk wailed. *"It's just a fucking game and I can't log out because of you! By the Goddess..."* Crinnan heard the demon begin to weep. *"My kids... my kids need their dad... the rebels killed their mom just a few months ago... I..."*

Crinnan shook his head. He could not get the idea out of his mind that he had just ruined the lives of some innocent children. He sighed and pursed his lips together as he squeezed the handle of his sword. Furiously, he started to run in the direction that the other voice had come from. He knew he had to do something.

"ByggDykk... Jaaren... where are you, man!" Crinnan heard the voice call out. "We need to log out and... hey, who are you?"

Crinnan approached the other player quickly and furiously. He appeared to be the size of a normal person and had basic brown leather armor equipped. Crinnan immediately sent his fist into the player's jaw and knocked him backward. The demon did not fall, but as he staggered, Crinnan raised his sword so that point rested against his throat.

"You are looking for... ByggDykk?" Crinnan rolled his eyes at the ridiculous name and the demon gave him a confused nod.

"You are a prisoner?" He whispered. "How did you... you can't hurt me!"

Crinnan groaned and gently swung his sword upward, cutting into the demon's face. Blood trickled out of the wound and the demon gasped and reached up to grab his wound.

"How is this possible?" He shouted. "What are you?"

"I'm your fucking daddy! Do you know ByggDykk!" Crinnan shouted. "Answer me!"

"Yes!" The demon furiously replied. "He's my brother!"

Thoughts of his own brothers briefly flashed through Crinnan's mind. He shook his head and held back his rage. The fact that these Govians were real people was infuriating him, why couldn't it have been simple like it was on a battlefield?

"Your brother can't leave the Hells; he is a prisoner now." Crinnan snapped. "You need to go get his kids. You need to take them to your house... your brother will probably not be coming back."

"What do you mean!" The demon's voice cracked. "Did you... have you kidnapped him? Where is Jaaren, what is going on!"

"Just fucking do it, dammit!" Crinnan hissed as he pushed the blade toward the demon's throat. "And go now, before I change my mind!" The demon looked like he was contemplating it all for a moment but finally looked up with a bitter expression and nodded his head.

"You'll pay one day." He snapped as he reached his hand out and pointed at Crinnan. "Wait... how am I supposed to do anything if I can't log out?"

"I'm sure you'll figure something out." Crinnan spat. "Not my problem. Now get out of here." The demon hissed a significant number of curses, but ultimately turned and fled.

Finally, Crinnan was alone. He snarled and growled; he could not shake the shame he felt. He hated the moments that he thought about the people he killed and usually was able to bury those thoughts inside him. It had never been that bad though, the fact that the Govian could talk to him after death, that was what made it difficult.

Crinnan wandered back to the body of ByggDykk and looked down at it. It was nothing more than a lifeless, bloody corpse and Crinnan sighed as he spoke.

"Your kids will be fine... your brother is taking care of it."

"You piece of shit!" ByggDykk snarled. *"You've taken me from them, you've ruined their lives! You are evil, a worthless piece of garbage!"*

"And you're a rapist-murderer!" Crinnan countered with just as much ferocity. "Just as much a piece of shit as you say I am."

"It is a game!" The dead demon insisted, *"A fucking game! It isn't real!"*

"Tell me I'm not fucking real!" Crinnan yelled. "You think it didn't hurt when you tore my whole ass head off? When you shoved that hook through my body? You think any prisoner here doesn't feel pain when you torture or rape them? Your government made this place and you've shown exactly what kind of person you really are here... your kids will be fine, but fuck you, and fuck Govia. Have fun crying." At that, Crinnan turned and walked away. ByggDykk shouted every manner of curse at Crinnan as he departed, but Crinnan was done with it all, with the demon and the talking. He had work to do, he had his own salvation to achieve and he was not going to waste any more time.

"A measure of great benevolence to be sure!" Ander chirped as he ran up behind Crinnan, "Verily, you are indeed a being of great moral fortitude. Tell me, oh champion Black Knight Crinnan, where do you go from here?"

"I don't know." Crinnan answered. "Based on what the system told me, I should be able to open a portal to the Second Level now. I unlocked an ability or whatever to do it."

A small piece of ground suddenly started to tremble and mound up in front of them. Crinnan watched as a hell spider's pointed leg pierced through the dirt and he sighed and jammed the point of his sword into the mound. He heard a screech and then a black plume of smoke rose upward.

Hell Spider Killed
+100 Rank

New Rank: 1,844,197,354

"Do you have any idea how to do it?" Crinnan asked. "How to open the portal to the Second Level?"

"If it is an ability you have obtained, then the act of willing the portal should be sufficient." Ander replied.

"What does that mean?" Crinnan asked.

"Have you ever made a wish as you blew out the candles on your birthday cake?" Ander asked.

"Sure." Crinnan replied. Images of birthdays flashed through his mind. He saw his family surrounding him, and an image of his younger sulking self with a cone shaped party hat on his head.

"Willing an ability, based on my vague memories of using abilities in the real world, is like making a wish. Try it."

Crinnan shifted uncomfortably in place and then cleared his throat. This was going to look ridiculous.

"Um. I... wish for a portal to the Second Level?" Crinnan mumbled, a bit embarrassed by his own words. "Please."

A small blue globe suddenly appeared in front of Crinnan and he eyed it curiously. The globe expanded and flattened until it resembled a swirling arched doorway. A gentle breeze emitted from the portal and swirled around Crinnan, who then looked over at Ander.

"I will go first." Ander said with a nod. "For once you walk through the portal it will close... that is, if you will have me."

Crinnan eyed the vampre and sighed. He'd rescued him, and a certain feeling of responsibility for the thin defenseless person hung over Crinnan's head. He shrugged his shoulders and gestured toward the portal.

"Whatever then." Crinnan sighed. "Go on through I guess." Ander smiled and nodded his head in response.

"Then onward to greater things." Ander said. He took a step forward, disappearing in the swirling blue light and Crinnan took a breath.

"By the Brothers if this fucking rips me apart and I have to start all over I'm going to be pissed..." He groaned. Steeling himself he walked forward and into the light.

Chapter Nine
The Lethargic

The Second Hell

Crinnan and Ander stepped out of the swirling portal and found themselves standing in the Second Level of the Hells. The sky was black and unending just like in the previous one, but the ground was no longer ablaze. It was gray, dry, cracked and rivers of lava streaked across the landscape. Strange gnarled red trees twisted toward the sky and black-leafed plants grew from the ground with leaves that looked like they were bleeding. Visibility was dim but Crinnan was still able to see sufficiently.

Congratulations, PrettyKitty6969420, on reaching the Second Level of the Seven Hells!

...

The Second Level of Hellscape is both a world in itself and a hub for the various other worlds which Hellscape hosts. Here you will find opportunities to engage in alternative modes of play, whether you seek to solve complex puzzles, create intricate constructions, or simply test your mettle against your fellow citizens; The Second Level will be able to provide you with plenty of outlets to expel your sin, and ample entertainment.

...

We encourage you to go out and explore all that the Second Level has to

---

"The Second Level," Ander announced as the two stepped through, "I declare, 'tis been an age since I last stepped foot upon these wretched grounds. Be wary for the plants are alive and their only desire is to rip the flesh from your body,"

"You've been here?" Crinnan asked as his eyes moved from the landscape to his companion, "How did you get here last time?"

"We prisoners are on occasion moved from level to level." Ander explained as the two took their first steps in the new land. "It gives the demons, or the players, a sort of revolving challenge and selection. Whilst there are many prisoners who have understandably and apathetically succumbed to the very fact that their fates are sealed, there remains a strong number very much like me who still try to hide or run."

"What's the point of that?" The very idea sounded like a waste of time to Crinnan. "Hiding, running? It seems these demons can't really be harmed. Well, except by me."

"'Tis the truth." Ander declared. "Players like you can harm each other. A benefit of being a Govian citizen, no doubt."

"I'm not a citizen." Crinnan quickly replied. "I came here a prisoner like you."

"You did not." Ander snorted a laugh and shook his head. "That does not make even the slightest bit of sense, Crinnan. Prisoners cannot fight, we all know that."

"It's true." Crinnan insisted. "I dropped from the sky. My bones shattered and spread all over the Fields of Misery… but something happened. Someone came to me and things changed. Now I can fight."

Ander scoffed and took a few steps away from Crinnan, shaking his head and mumbling to himself. He looked up at Crinnan a few times with an agitated look on his face and raised his finger once as if he were about to say something, but it seemed he couldn't find the words.

"Look I don't give a shit what you think." Crinnan finally said. "I was told I could get out of here if I got to the Seventh Level. I don't know if it's true or not, but I definitely don't have anything better to do. I might as well try."

"The Seventh Level..." Ander shook his head and laughed. "So, you intend on reaching the 10th percentile? Do you understand how powerful you need to be to achieve that?"

"I'm pretty strong." Crinnan shrugged and looked down at the sword in his hand. "I've killed a lot of people in the real world."

"That *is* an advantage..." Ander hummed and stroked his chin. "People here... they are citizens of the Empire... they fight in this game, but they have no real skill, only shiny weapons and the knowledge of how to manipulate mechanics to their benefit. You were a warrior in life?"

"Black Knight." Crinnan said with a nod. "Freedom fighter... and one of the best of them."

"I have no knowledge of this Black Knight you speak of." Ander hummed thoughtfully. "But if you were a warrior, you hold an advantage... have you... killed the imperial soldiers before?"

"Plenty of them." Crinnan nodded. "Few dozen at least. They die easy."

"Well, from what I have gathered of these... Govians... their entire military has access to this place." Ander said. "Five million of the players are trained fighters, the rest are citizens... while not everyone is logged in at the same time, I do want to say that it would be prudent to take care when choosing your fights."

"Bring them on." Crinnan shrugged. "Not like they can permanently kill me. I'm already dead."

"Yes, but they can halt your progress significantly." Ander warned. "If they kill you and destroy your body, you will be forced to respawn at the First Level and will take a major ranking loss."

"You seem to know a lot about this place." Crinnan said with a raised brow. "Why is that?"

"I've been here…" Ander said with a heavy sigh. "For a very long time… hundreds of years I imagine…"

"What do you mean, you imagine?" Crinnan asked. "You don't know when you died?"

"I know I am from what you refer to as the Age of Ancients." Ander said. "But you are correct. I do not know when I died. My… memory is not all there. I occasionally recall things, but mostly only background information about the times I lived in. I do not recall my relationships, friends… family… I have no Idea who I was."

"Does that happen to everyone here?" Crinnan asked.

"No." Ander quickly replied. "I have met a number of prisoners who have held onto their sanity and can recall their entire lives. I've also met others who have succumbed to madness or are simply writhing chittering husks of what was once considered sapience. Some have trouble, others do not… but a good number of people know who they are."

"Well. Whatever you say." Crinnan dismissed Ander and scanned the area, eager to find someone to kill so he could get to the next level. He didn't want to waste any time, he wanted out of the Hells as quickly as possible.

Attention Citizen

…

You are in queue for the next round of Bloodgames. Approximate wait time:

…

4 minutes 35 seconds.

…

If you do not wish to participate in the next round of the Bloodgames, please leave the queue.

"How do I leave the queue!" Crinnan shouted. He was familiar with the Bloodgames Battle Royale television show. He and his friend Alec had watched it back home on tv on occasion. Crinnan always enjoyed making fun of the participants. At the moment, however, he had no desire to partake in them.

> **To leave the queue you must exit the queue zone. The queue zone is marked with a red glowing ring. You may run in any direction to find the border.**

"Come on!" Crinnan shouted to Ander. "Time to go!"

"What are you talking about!" Ander replied. "Go where?"

"Away!" Crinnan yelled as he took off in a sprint. Fortunately he wasn't far from the border of the ring and he crossed over the red light with no problem. When he finally slowed to a stop, he looked back to see that Ander was right behind him.

"What was that all about?" Ander asked. "Are we in danger?"

"Not anymore." Crinnan answered. "We were in some kind of... Bloodgames queue circle thing."

"Bloodgames..." Ander tilted his head and raised a hand to his chin. "The... yes... the battle royale entertainment show?"

"That's it." Crinnan nodded. "Where people kill each other for money."

"Yes... yes... I recall." Ander nodded and a thin smile formed on his face. "That makes sense. We are, after all, standing in the Second Level where the Bloodgames are held."

"Right..." Crinnan nodded. "That's what... the system... I guess... said."

"Indeed." Ander cleared his throat and looked around. "It appears we are in a rather populated area. There are many prisoners around... players like to partake in some casual killing as they wait for their games to start."

Crinnan sighed and shook his head. He watched as other prisoners scurried about. Some were naked and others wore ill-fitting rags. They all had exhausted expressions with fear-filled eyes. They were emaciated and walked keeled over with their hands hugging their stomachs. None looked happy, none except for Ander.

"This is how we live here." Ander said sadly. "We try to hide… but hiding is futile. Mostly we just cower in fear as we await the inevitable. The arrival of demons…"

"No way to live." Crinnan grunted as he looked around at the sad husks of life around him. He saw a few of them trembling as they stared at him with their wide eyes and looks of fear. Some got up and ran, while others just seemed to have given up long ago. They were the ones who just shrugged and waited for whatever was going to happen to them.

"They think you are going to hurt them." Ander whispered as he stepped over to Crinnan. "They see your sword, the blood on you… all they see is another demon."

Crinnan grunted as he walked past the frightened prisoners. A few wept as they held their hands out to him, begging him not to bring them harm. Some fell flat on their face, while others stood petrified. Crinnan wanted to ignore them, but he couldn't bring himself to look away.

"I won't hurt any of you…" Crinnan finally said, feeling a well of compassion spring up from his core. "Don't worry." A few of them sighed with relief, their shoulders dropping as if a weight had been lifted from them, while others just stared at Crinnan with absent eyes.

Crinnan wasn't known by most to be a compassionate or caring person. He did what he was told without question, he killed without hesitation. He didn't care about others or their problems, because he felt they weren't his to bear. Seeing the prisoners, fellow people, forced to live their lives the way they did struck him though. They had nobody coming to save them, they couldn't do anything to protect themselves. There was zero chance of hope for them and that simply wasn't fair.

"Is there… anything I can do?" Crinnan asked, looking over at Ander. "Anything to make it better?"

"Apart from devoting your existence to protecting them?" Ander asked with a raised eyebrow. "No. There is nothing you can do for them... be wary, Crinnan, a demon approaches."

"Good." Crinnan replied. He was eager to punish someone for doing what had been done to the prisoners before him. "Let him come."

"I caution you against rash decisions." Ander said, his tone rising a bit. "The demons that come here regularly are formidable fighters. They may not be brought down as easily as you anticipate."

"They are formidable butchers." Crinnan corrected Ander. "I am a formidable fighter. They only look intimidating; they have no real skill." He looked around the area, hoping to see the demon that was nearby. Having killed three already he felt confident in his abilities. Killing them reminded him of killing Marauders in the Canruusi Wastes. As long as he didn't come across another yeti or similar large monster, he felt like he was going to be fine.

"Who were you before you oh so unfortunately found yourself here?" Ander asked as the two stood and waited. "Back in life."

"I told you already." Crinnan bluntly answered, uninterested in the conversation.

"You mentioned Black Knight, yes." Ander conceded, keeping a watchful eye on their surroundings. "However, I am inquiring about you, your hobbies, relationships. Did you have any children or a wife?"

"No." Crinnan answered as he peered off into the distance.

"For the best I imagine." Ander murmured as he sensed Crinnan's lack of enthusiasm about their conversation. "So, no hobbies? Surely you did something to pass the time?"

"I do not know." Crinnan replied with a sigh. "I slept a lot."

"Sleep..." Ander reflected as he tried to keep the conversation going, "Something we rarely have the opportunity to do here in the Hells."

"Up there!" Crinnan nearly shouted as he pointed in the distance. "I see one."

"Lovely chatting with you then. I do believe that it is in my best interest to remain here." Ander planted his feet. "For I haven't the faintest of desires to interact with another demon."

"Good." Crinnan gave Ander a thumbs up and ran ahead. "Keep watch, let me know if any more come."

"But of course!" Ander unenthusiastically shouted back as Crinnan ran away.

Chapter Ten
Equipment

The Second Hell

Crinnan approached the flying demon; his sword was held firmly in hand and he was ready to strike. The demon appeared to stand only a few inches taller than Crinnan and wasn't as horribly disfigured as some of the others Crinnan had encountered thus far; he was anthropoid in shape, except for the large wings jutting from his back.

Crinnan intended to try and get the armor from this demon. He wore some ridiculously ornate shining black armor that would only get in the way in the real world, but he hoped they would give him some protection in the Hells. Crinnan also saw that the demon carried a heavy looking blade that was nearly six feet long, it was something so massive that it looked like even a Gaian would even have trouble wielding it with much efficiency. Crinnan felt like the demon was an idiot for selecting such unconventional equipment.

Crinnan slowed his run just as the demon swooped down and crashed the blade of his sword through a prisoner who was laying on the ground. The sword bisected the poor being, causing him to scream in terror and pain. Crinnan watched the demon lift the sword back up. The prisoner's entrails stuck to the sides of the blade, and the demon silently turned around to face Crinnan.

"Who are you?" The winged one demanded; his voice muffled from behind his black horned mask. "Where did you come from?" He paused as if he were reading something and let out an inquisitive groan. "You are... interesting. Are you a player or a prisoner?"

"What's it matter?" Crinnan asked as he pointed his sword at the winged demon, "You'll be dead in a few moments anyway."

"A newbie in simple clothing is challenging me?" The bemused demon snorted with a hollow voice. "You think you can leave a scratch with that little toy of a sword?

Crinnan examined the demon and searched for a weak point. He saw a spot of cloth at the demon's elbows and a bare spot under his chin where his gorget and helmet did not quite meet. Crinnan hoped the physics of the Hells would continue to match those of the real world and spun his sword in his hand.

"Just shut up." Crinnan closed the gap between himself and his enemy quickly. The demon barely had time to react as Crinnan swung his sword. Their weapons met with a clang and the demon pushed forward, knocking Crinnan back.

"What are you doing!" The demon snapped. "They said not to PvP!"

"I'm fucking your day up!" Crinnan replied as he started to circle the demon. "Just like you just did to that prisoner."

"By the Goddess what are you talking about!" The demon snapped. He looked down at the dead prisoner at his feet and cocked his head toward Crinnan. "Have you lost your mind?"

"Maybe." Crinnan feigned an attack to the left and the Demon moved to defend himself. With a quick spin, Crinnan swung his weapon and cut through the unarmored portion of the demon's right elbow, rendering the limb useless. The demon jerked back, looked down at his dangling arm and screamed.

"What are you!" He cried as he raised his left arm to stop Crinnan. "This makes no sense!"

Crinnan swung his sword again and the demon's wings flapped wildly as he leaped back and avoided the attack.

"Fuck you and your weird ass wings!" Crinnan growled as he lunged forward again. The demon swiped at Crinnan with its only remaining hand, but Crinnan batted it away with his sword. He ducked and slammed his leg into the grounded demon's ankles, further surprising him and knocking him backward.

"Help!" the demon shouted as if he were calling out to someone nearby. "PvP! I'm under attack!"

"Quiet!" Crinnan growled. He darted forward and took hold of the edge of the demon's gorget, pulling him forward. With one quick movement, Crinnan thrust the point of his blade through the opening under the demon's mask. The demon's body clenched, and he choked a bit as Crinnan pulled the weapon away. The demon fell to ground, gasping and gargling as blood leaked from the sides of the mask.

Player: ConchLicker EXECUTED

Player Rank: 1,706,188,432

Congratulations, PrettyKitty6969420! You have advanced in ranking!

Previous Rank: 1,844,197,454

New Rank: 1,775,192,943

Previous Percentile: 87%

New Percentile: 83%

"Quite impressive swordplay." Ander observed as he approached and knelt next to Crinnan and the lifeless body. "'Tis great fortune that you two appear nearly the same size as well."

"Lucky me." Crinnan quipped as he quickly went to work pulling off the demon's boots. "Give me a hand?"

"Surely you do not mean by undressing him?" Ander seemed disgusted by the request.

"Yeah, by undressing him." Crinnan was not about to put up with any whining from Ander. "I saved your fucking life or whatever it is we have here, if you want to keep following me around, then do what I say. Is that too much to ask, or does that embarrass you too much?"

"Touchy." Ander's eyebrows raised and lowered as he nodded his head in submission. "Though I suppose you present a fair point." Ander unbuckled the extravagant leg armor and set it aside. "What is it you plan on doing with me when we reach the end of your journey?"

Crinnan stopped his task momentarily and glared at Ander. "What are you talking about? I don't even know what I am doing with myself right now, let alone somebody else."

"'Tis a trait that demands great admiration." Ander sang as he unclasped and removed the demon's belt. "The ability to speak from the heart. You certainly do not leave your intentions up to the imagination."

Crinnan rolled his eyes as he sat down and pulled the demon's black socks and boots on. He was relieved to see that neither of them disappeared when he touched them. As he laced them, Ander tossed the demon's sleeveless gambeson in front of Crinnan.

"Oh, I do not believe you will be wanting this." Ander said with disgust as he held the blood-dripping mask between two fingers. "It seems to have become a mess of blood and brains..." a tooth fell out of the mask and Ander shivered. "And... teeth..."

"I don't need it." Crinnan shook his head as he gave the demon's head a kick. "Masks are for amateurs."

"Very well." Ander kicked the demon's head and gasped in pain as he did. He groaned and shook his head with frustration.

"If only I had the ability to fight as you do." He lamented. "Then perhaps I could be of more use on our quest."

"If only." Crinnan rolled his eyes at his companion. He wished Ander would shut up.

Crinnan signaled for Ander to help him with the cuirass. He held the breastplate steady as Ander lined up the backplate and tightened the straps on Crinnan's sides. Crinnan slid the pauldrons and vambraces into place and after a moment of consideration, removed the pauldrons and tossed them to the side. They were much too big and ridiculous for him to ever imagine using in a combat situation.

Avatar Information Sheet

...

Name: PrettyKitty6969420

Rank: 1,706,188,432

Percentile: 83%

Player Rating: 1 Star

...

HP: 180/180 (100 Base + 80 Buff)

Shields: 235 (100 Base + 80 Buff + 55 Armor)

Damage Output: 1.9x Base (1x Base + .8x Buff + .1x Weapon)

Speed: 1x Base (1x Base)

Active Buffs:

...

80th Percentile Booster

+80% to HP, Shields, and Damage Output until the next percentile of ranking is achieved.

...

sagescript5finalfinalfinalfuckinglast.sli

Description Unavailable

Equipped Items:

...

Head: EMPTY

Chest:

Burnt Iron Cuirass

+20 Shields

Back: EMPTY

Shoulders: EMPTY

Arms:

Burnt Iron Vambraces

+10 Shields

Waist:

Boiled Leather Belt

+5 Shields

Legs:

Burnt Iron Greaves

+15 Shields

Feet:

Basic Leather Boots

+5 Shields

Accessory 1: EMPTY

Accessory 2: EMPTY

...

Weapon Slot 1:

Rusty Iron Sword

Enables Melee Combat

+0.1x Base Damage Output

Weapon Slot 2: EMPTY

```
Abilities Unlocked: NONE
```

"I think that's all." Crinnan snorted at the stupidly giant sword on the ground. "I definitely won't have any use for that piece of junk."

"Well look at you." Crinnan tensed as Sage's voice suddenly rang in his head. *"Why, I should say you have transformed into a veritable demon killer, or rather you now look the part of one."*

"Well fucking how do you do to you as well." Crinnan grunted with frustration tinging his voice. "Good to finally hear from you again."

"Likewise! How goes the fight? I see you have made it to the Second Level."

"I have." Crinnan replied. "Me and... Ander,"

"Ander?" Sage repeated. *"You mean that prisoner entity that I am seeing next to you?"*

"Yes. Can you see him?"

"I can see his data." Sage replied. *"I cannot actually see him though."*

"Who are you talking to?" Ander interjected. "I do believe that I am the only one here."

Crinnan rolled his eyes and looked at Ander. "You wouldn't understand. It's someone from back home."

"Someone from Duraan?" Ander repeated with a hint of curiosity in his voice. "Who?"

"Nobody you would know dammit." Crinnan snapped. "Mind your own business."

"What is he saying?" Sage asked.

"He is asking who you are." Crinnan replied as he looked at Ander from the corner of his eye.

"Well, I should say that sounds like a natural response." Sage replied in a ho-hum tone. *"What was his name again?"*

"What is your name?" Crinnan looked over at Ander. "The long Ancient one?"

"Frema'Ander din Lecaaste."

"It is Frema'Ander din Lecaaste." Crinnan relayed to his faceless benefactor. "He is from Ancient times."

"Ancient you say? Do you believe he can be trusted?" Sage asked

"I guess so." Crinnan replied.

"If you are certain then Lucaas and I will work on cracking his encryption so we can pre-emptively grant him player access as well. An Ancient may be of use to you."

"I think he's saying he is going to give you the ability to fight." Crinnan looked at Ander. "Congratulations."

"Magnificent!" Ander shouted with glee. "What a fortuitous turn of events! Once I am able to restore my connection with the NaNe you will find that I am truly a valuable asset. Perhaps, and of course in my own humble opinion, the *most* valuable. We will certainly be able to blast our way out of here, leaving naught but a trail of destruction in our wake as we find our way back to freedom!"

Crinnan stood silently and stared with bewilderment at the overly verbose entity for a good moment before he spoke again.

"Sure, good." He sighed as he turned away. Ander triggered his anxiety, not because he was a fearsome being but because Crinnan simply did not know how to properly communicate with him.

"So, what do I need to do now?" he asked Sage.

"Why, get to the Third Level of course." Sage answered. *"Lucaas and I are not only working on empowering Ander to help you, but also implementing the next part of our plan. It will be... interesting to see what happens when we do. We have been monitoring the chat channels. The last demon you killed called for help before he died, it would appear that his friends are on their way to you now."*

"How many?"

"Four. I see two magic users and two warriors. They also have a prisoner entity with them. They will be there momentarily."

"How soon will Ander be ready?" Crinnan asked.

"Hopefully by the time they get there." Sage replied but stopped suddenly. "Damn it all... Kill demons and monsters, get to the Third Level of the Hells and we will nearly be halfway there. We have to go now, Govia is trying to track us. Hopefully you will have descended further by the time we speak again." At that, Sage's channel closed and Crinnan was left with Ander.

"We have four demons inbound." Crinnan informed him. "Sage is working on getting you combat ready so just hold tight."

"His name is... Sage?" A look of contemplation spread over his mustached face. Crinnan did not know whether that was a good or a bad thing.

"It is." Crinnan replied. "Do you... know him?"

"Maybe." Ander reflected with a shrug of his shoulders. "The name triggers a tickling in my mind... perhaps I met him in a past life? Or perhaps I met someone named Sage at one point..." Ander shook his head and smiled. "It will do no good worrying about that now. Command me, what shall I do whilst I wait for my powers?"

"Hide." Crinnan instructed, pointing to a red tree covered hill behind them. "When you are certain that you are able to fight, come out and help me."

"Very well." Ander nodded. He reached out and gave Crinnan's arm a light squeeze. "Best of luck my friend." at that he turned and ran toward the cluster of gnarled trees.

After Ander was gone, Crinnan quickly surveyed the area and listened for the demons. At the moment he heard and saw nothing so all he could do was wait. He thrust the point of his sword into the ground so that it stood on its own and took a seat. With his forearms resting on his knees, he took a deep breath and waited.

Chapter Eleven
An Unexpected Reunion

The Second Hell

As Crinnan sat, he couldn't help but allow his mind to wander. He thought of his mother and his friends, mostly Alec and Elia, and hoped they were all well. He thought of the life he had lived and how he looked forward to resuming living it.

Crinnan pondered the strangeness of the Hells, of what they were and of how Sage had explained them. He thought of how so many innocent people were being tortured there by the Empire and of how it was all literally just a game to them. He wondered how much time had passed, thought of all the walking he had done and of how much more it would take him to get out. Finally, amid his thoughts, he saw the demons approaching.

In the distance were five people, each equipped differently. One looked to be an elf; he wore thick heavy armor and carried a large sword that was very much like the previous demon's. Another appeared more demon-like, he had black glowing wings and a barbed tail that waved as he walked. He wore lighter armor with a regular sized sword in each hand. The other two, the mages as they were called, floated about a foot off the ground and each of them wore hooded robes with pulsing red hands. What Crinnan found himself drawn to the most, however, was that the demon in heavy armor held one end of a chain in his left hand and on the other end of that chain was what looked like a she-elf. Her head was lowered, and her feet dragged on occasion. She was a prisoner, and she looked exhausted or injured as she struggled to keep pace.

Crinnan stood up and dusted his pants off. He watched the demons and noticed that they had seen him, so he pulled the sword from the ground and took a step forward.

"You are wearing Lemry's armor." The horned demon hissed as Crinnan approached. "What does this mean?"

"If you mean ConchLicker, then It means I killed him." Crinnan pointed his thumb behind him, "His body's back there if you want to look."

"Why would you do that?" One of the mages seethed with a perplexed and angry tone. "They specifically told us not to fight each other until they fix the respawn bug! You can't kill anyone!"

"Oh." Crinnan smirked and spun his sword in his hand. "Well, I guess I am going to not-kill you guys now."

The demons all looked at each other and then to Crinnan. "A GM needs to hear of this." One of the mages said. "He needs to be apprehended; he is breaking rules!"

"Let's just teach him a lesson." The heavily armored Elf commented. He pulled a knife from his belt and shoved it through one of the links in the chain that held the she-elf, pinning it to the ground. Crinnan watched the staggering female collapse. He imagined it had been her first moment of rest in a long time. He looked at her and saw her eyes piercing him.

"Oh, you like her?" The horned demon taunted and then banged his swords together, "I see you eyeing her. We've been taking turns with her for days. She's a precious little thing, ain't she?"

"Fuck off with that shit." Crinnan was repulsed. He pointed his sword at the horned demon and took a step forward. "You are a damned monster."

"It's awesome!" One of the mages said excitedly looking around at the others. "She thinks she doesn't enjoy it, but we always convince her otherwise. Maybe you should just take a turn with her. Might calm that small dick rage down a bit."

Crinnan felt his blood begin to boil. The injustice, the pure and utter pain that was being dealt to the she-elf put him in a rage. He did not know who she was or why she was in the Hells, but he felt personally obligated to save her.

"Enough!" Crinnan stepped forward with his sword held tightly in his hand. "Time for me to kill you now!" The players all laughed and got in defensive stances.

Without warning, one of the mages hurled a fireball at him. Crinnan quickly jerked out of the way and it crashed into the ground where he stood sending a shower of dirt in all directions. The other mage launched a barrage of smaller fireballs and Crinnan dodged all but one. The ball hit him in the shoulder and his arms briefly glowed blue. He thought that was strange and slowed down for a split second in response to being struck.

-40 Shields

Shields Remaining: 195

"Crit-zones, idiots!" The heavily armored elf shouted. "Head, chest and dick! Focus on the crit-zones and…. oh fuck!"

The first mage took the point of Crinnan's sword through his face. Crinnan tore the blade through the side of his head, planting it into the arm of the horned demon who was preparing to strike. As the mage fell to the ground, the horned one roared in pain and dropped one of his swords from the attack, swinging the other at Crinnan. The sword bounced off of Crinnan's vambrace, the blue light flickered, and he lost thirty more shields. Crinnan ducked and scooped up the demon's dropped weapon, leaving his old one stuck in the arm.

Player: Ruburrito EXECUTED

Player Rank: 1,696,812,117

Congratulations, PrettyKitty6969420! You have advanced in ranking!

Previous Rank: 1,775,192,943

New Rank: 1,736,002,530

"Get him!" The heavily armored one roared. "He's just one person! Cut his fucking head off and fuck his throat!"

Crinnan stepped back. The mage was on his right, the horned demon in the middle and the heavily armored one was to his left. The armored one swung his massive sword in a chopping motion. Crinnan leaped out of the way and drove his sword to the right into the chest of the mage. The mage fell backward, coughing up blood and Crinnan charged forward toward the horned demon.

Player: RazorSwift1111 EXECUTED

Player Rank: 1,718,296,147

Congratulations, PrettyKitty6969420! You have advanced in ranking!

Previous Rank: 1,736,002,530

New Rank: 1,727,149,338

Previous Percentile: 82%

New Percentile: 81%

"Die!" The demon shouted as he swiped at Crinnan with his only remaining weapon. Crinnan spun out of the way, took hold of the sword embedded in the demon's arm and ripped it free. The horned demon reeled back and roared in pain giving Crinnan the opening he needed for a swift cut through his neck, relieving him of his head. As the headless demon and the second mage fell to the ground, Crinnan spun his own sword in his hand and tossed the winged demon's aside as he turned to face the final demon.

Player: TheOnlyScout3432 EXECUTED

Player Rank: 1,650,884,258

Congratulations, PrettyKitty6969420! You have advanced in ranking!

Previous Rank: 1,727,149,338

New Rank: 1,689,016,798

Previous Percentile: 81%

New Percentile: 79%

Cosmetic Items unlocked! See your wardrobe for more details!

...

Congratulations! You have crossed the threshold of the 80th percentile and into the 70s. You have unlocked the path to the Third Level!

Ability Unlocked:

...

Portal (Level 3) - Grants player the ability to summon a portal to the Third Level of Hellscape anywhere portals are permitted.

"I'm going to not-kill the fuck out of you!" Crinnan growled as he paced around the final player. "You fucking piece of Govian rapist shit."

"How..." the flabbergasted demon growled. He looked back and forth from his dead friends to Crinnan. "How are you doing this? How are you so strong?" The voices of his friends could be heard wailing with pain and confusion around him as they realized they were now prisoners locked in the Hells. This only exacerbated his fear.

"I am a Centurion!" Crinnan snarled as his rage boiled to the surface. "I'm the kinda guy who blows shit that you love up. Maybe you've seen me on the news before? You saw what I did to them? I could do that to you a hundred times. Show me your fucking sword and die with some honor!"

The demon trembled and reluctantly readied his massive weapon. Crinnan could sense his fear, it was like candy to him. He savored the fact that he was about to slaughter the disgusting being, relished in the idea that he would never again be able to harm another. Crinnan licked his lips just as the demon suddenly burst into flames.

"What the fuck?" Crinnan angrily threw his hands up in the air. He turned around and watched as Ander approached, floating in the air like the demon mages had before and hurling another blast at the demon.

"Die you insolent swine!" He bellowed, his mustache twitching as he soared forward. He shot his open hand out toward the demon and balled it into a fist. Crinnan watched in amazement as the demon screamed and rose into the air, his flaming body flailing about as it did so.

"Your weak body will burn in the armor you hoped would protect you! The armor... the very image that has been the horror of so many!" Gone was the timid Ander, who now laughed maniacally and grit his teeth together. He was drunk with power and playing at the demon's expense. "I am the new horror; my power has been restored. I am your doom, your condemnation. I am..." he paused and tilted his head as if he didn't know how to finish his sentence. "I am Ander!"

At that, the demon's body burst and gore and flew in all directions. His entrails rained down on Crinnan and the prisoner, and pieces of his armor flew everywhere causing small explosions of dirt and dust as they landed. One piece of shrapnel caught Crinnan in the leg and he gasped and quickly ripped it out. Ander's laughing did not cease until a moment had passed and then his voice turned into an almost orgasmic moan. Crinnan watched him lick the tips of his teeth and eventually he calmed down.

"That was obnoxious." Crinnan was disgusted, not by the blood and guts of the gruesome execution, but by the nasty almost sexual sounding noise that Ander made after the demon had burst. He looked at Ander and pointed his sword at him. "You stay here, and don't ever steal my kill again." Crinnan huffed and then hurried over to the chained female prisoner who had sat up and watched everything.

As he neared, a strange feeling enveloped Crinnan. She looked familiar to him. Her body was thin, yet muscularly toned. She had a lightly tanned skin color, brown eyes, and shoulder length dirty blonde hair. As Crinnan approached, she pushed herself up off the ground and rose to her feet, revealing that she was only slightly shorter than he was. Her rags were ripped and frayed, and her body was bruised and scratched but she held her head up and met Crinnan's eye.

"You..." He announced when he finally got a good look at her. He couldn't believe his eyes...

Crinnan had only met her once in the real world and it was many years prior, but it had been a very memorable occasion. They were only teenagers when they fought side by side in the Kamlotian civil wars and even though it had been brief, it was a summer that Crinnan had never forgotten.

"You found me." She looked closely at the Black Knight and spoke with a relieved, yet serious tone. It broke him out of his reminiscence and as his eyes went into focus, he shook his head and couldn't help but smile. His body tingled with warmth and he imagined he looked like an idiot, but he was too absent to care. Quickly his smile faded, and he was thrust back into reality.

"G... get down!" He screamed as he threw her to the ground. A demon suddenly appeared out of thin air from behind her. His head was covered in a red hood and in each of his hands, he had a curved dagger. Quickly, he lunged forward and swung one of his weapons. Crinnan deflected it with his sword, and the demon spun and threw an elbow into Crinnan's mouth.

"We have caught word of what you are doing, Centurion." The demon seethed as Crinnan jumped backward. "You have killed multiple Govian citizens. You are supposed to be dead."

"Well surprise, fuckhead!" Crinnan growled as he darted forward again. He swung his sword and the Govian spun out of the way and dragged the second blade across Crinnan's shoulder. Crinnan wished he had equipped the fancy stupid pauldrons as he howled and stumbled away, though not losing his balance. Why had that attack not hit his shields, he wondered.

"You have been causing serious problems in the mainland." The assassin said as he prepared his blades for another attack. "You have caught the eye of the Empire. We do not know what you are doing or how you are doing it, but I am here to stop it."

"The only thing you're stopping by being here is your ability to go home." Crinnan retorted as he watched the Govian's every move. "Come on, try to stop me."

The Govian launched himself forward, blades at the ready and Crinnan kicked a mound of dust in his direction. The Govian, surprised by the attack, stopped just in time for Crinnan to tackle him to the ground.

"I am sick of you fuckers!" Crinnan shouted as he grabbed each of the Govian's wrists. He shook the daggers free and headbutted the assassin square in the nose. With a yelp, the demon's head slammed into the ground and Crinnan picked up one of his daggers. It vaporized in his hand and with a growl, he instead slammed his fist into the side of the Govian's head.

"Stop!" The Govian pleaded. "You can't..." Crinnan punched him in the head again and he gasped.

"Time to die!" Crinnan roared as he pounded relentlessly. "Close your fucking eyes!" Finally, the assassin went unconscious and Crinnan picked up the sword he had dropped. With it in hand, he approached the Govian and stood over him.

"Anyone listening?" He called out. "If so, know that I'll kill every last one of you if I have to!" At that, he swiped his blade and cut the Govian's throat. Briefly, he looked back at the girl he had saved and clenched his teeth.

"Nobody will ever touch her again!" He yelled as he wildly thrust the blade in and out of the Govian's body. "Nobody!"

Blood splashed up onto him as the portal to the Third Level opened. He ignored it and kept attacking the dead Govian. Finally, the girl ran up behind and grabbed Crinnan by the shoulders. He jerked in surprise and fell backward, knocking her to the ground. He spun and braced himself from crushing her with his body. As he hovered over her, he found that she was looking directly at him.

Crinnan returned her gaze and they remained motionless for a moment. He blinked and so did she. Neither smiled, neither breathed. He reached up and gently touched her cheek, not believing what he was seeing. Suddenly, however, she shook her head and rattled them both back into reality. As he hurried off of her, Crinnan knelt down on one knee and lowered his head, as a soldier should have done in the presence of a Black Knight Commander. She stood and looked down at him, and he spoke. "I told you... that I would find you again..."

She reached down and placed her hand on the Centurion's shoulder, beckoning him to stand. As he stood, he looked at her with a perplexed and almost awestruck expression and she sighed heavily.

"Thank you Crinnan..."

"It was my duty, Vice-Commander Milinka. It is... good to see you again."

Chapter Twelve
Cowboy Up

The Second Hell

Back in the real world, Milinka Emmal had been a fierce fighter and a very strong-willed commander. As the eldest child of noble parents, Commander Dorax Emmal and the late Lady Mariska, she had within the past couple of years been elevated to the position of Vice-Commander of Base 11. Many people thought it a foolish move to put someone so young in such a place of power, but she quickly proved herself worthy of the honor.

Crinnan and Milinka had only spent a few days together, but the raw attraction and undeniable feelings of teenage love that they had harbored and experienced had become a permanently imprinted memory in Crinnan's mind. When he thought about her, which he often did, he did so warmly and remembered her as she had been during that summer; beautiful, fierce, and kind of annoying.

The knights each of them squired for were slain in an ambush that they had only barely escaped. They ran into the woods together, pursued by their enemies, and found themselves lost in enemy territory. They had no communicators or ways to reach their friends, only the swords at their sides and each other.

For the next five days, the two teens survived only by depending on each other. At first, Crinnan had kept silent and ignored the beautiful girl. It was not because he disliked her, but because he found himself attracted to her and the only way he really knew how to behave was to be a whiny asshole. Eventually, though, she broke him. When she had finally found a way to make him laugh, he crumbled in her hands and it all eventually culminated into their first kiss.

Crinnan fondly remembered the feeling of young love and infatuation... he never wanted to let her go but as they fought their way through the wildlands of Kamlot, they eventually found their way home. Crinnan remembered their final embrace and the promise he made her before they were whisked away to their respective home bases.

"I will find you." He remembered promising with one last kiss. As he was ushered into his transport, their eyes remained locked on each other until he disappeared in the sky. He never saw her again, not until he died and went to the Hells.

Milinka stared at Crinnan with what appeared to have been contempt in her eyes. Their reunion was unexpected, and Crinnan watched nervously as the expression of his former lover turned from relieved to disdainful. Crinnan cleared his throat and took a step backward, hoping to free himself from the growing hostility between them, but Milinka closed the space between just as quickly as Crinnan created it.

"You son of a bitch." Milinka snarled. She reached out and pushed Crinnan angrily with both hands. The surprising amount of strength knocked Crinnan off balance and he released a grunt of surprise as he staggered backward.

"You left me!" She growled. "You good for nothing piece of Jamiso train wreck shit. You promised you'd come for me and you never did!"

Crinnan looked over at Ander for help, but Ander shook his head and turned away. Crinnan silently cursed the vampre and looked fearfully at the fuming she-elf before him.

"So, I have a good reason..." Crinnan began but was quickly cut off.

"Seven years, Crinnan!" Milinka snapped and smacked him across the face. "Did you even get my letters?"

"I uh..." Crinnan scratched the back of his head and looked down at the ground beneath him. "I heard you sent them."

"You didn't even open them?!" Milinka yelled. Her eyes opened wide and her hands balled into fists at her sides. "I thought we had something special. I thought..."

"We did." Crinnan nodded his head. "But with you so far away... I just couldn't bear..."

"Oh, fuck you." Milinka shook her head and stepped closer. Their noses almost touched and Crinnan could feel the warmth emanating from her skin. "Fuck you, fuck your excuses. I was sixteen years old when we were ripped apart, I still remember watching you fly away toward the Brothers with Captain Bran. Remember what you told me?!"

"Yes..." Crinnan replied.

"Tell me." Milinka demanded.

"That I would find you..." Crinnan mumbled. He felt like a child again, like he was being scolded by his mother for kicking the neighbor's cat.

"You screamed it at the top of your lungs and cried like a baby!" Milinka said. She shook her head and sighed. "You promised me. And just like every other male I've met; you couldn't seem to keep that promise."

"We were kids though!" Crinnan boldly proclaimed. "Life happens when you get older. I had to focus on my career."

"And you think I didn't?" Milinka asked. "You think a Vice Commander isn't buried in duties? Crinnan I... I thought of you as I died. Right before I came to these damned Hells, I saw *your* face. I should have thought of those who love me, of my fiancé, of my father and brothers or my late mother. But no. I thought of you."

"Well, I'm fucking sorry!" Crinnan finally snapped. "Grow up. You're not a princess that needs saving and I'm not your fucking hero. Yeah, sure, we... had a thing when we were kids, but we grew up. Act like it and quit being a psycho."

Milinka's eyes grew wide and she finally stepped back. Tears began to fall, and she nodded her head slowly. Not in agreement, but in recognition that Crinnan wasn't the same as she had left him.

"I do hate to interrupt your... lover's quarrel." Ander gently said as he approached. "But I do not wish to stand idly by when our quest is to obtain freedom. I say, let us venture forth into the portal that we may draw closer to the end!"

Crinnan turned toward Ander and nodded. He glanced back at Milinka who was softly crying to herself and wished he had just kept his mouth shut. He had conveyed a tone that wasn't true, he had given her the person that he wanted everyone else in the world to see when they looked at him... and he now questioned whether he wanted Milinka to see him that way.

"Look, I'm sorry..." Crinnan's tone softened as he took a step closer to her. "Things are really stressful down here and..."

"Shut your fucking mouth, Crinnan." Milinka snapped. "That's an order. Let's just... let's just go."

At that Ander led the three of them through the portal and into the next level.

***

The Third Hell
Sincroft

Congratulations, PrettyKitty6969420, on reaching the Third Level of the Seven Hells!

...

The Third Level of Hellscape offers an alternative challenge to any strong enough to partake. Here in the Third Level, you will find countless cities that house prisoners who have been empowered to fight back against you. This is a haven for the damned, a land where the citizens of Govia must find their true strength in Dura'ana to fight back the blasphemers. Do you have what it takes to prove you are among Dura'ana's strongest?

...

We encourage you to go out and explore all that the Third Level has to offer. There are many quests and opportunities to grow as a person in these cities. Once you find one of the many ways out, you will gain access to the fourth level. Your devotion and reverence to our Goddess Dura'ana and her Son our great Emperor Cidro shines brightly, citizen. Go now, and shine before all.

"The Hells have cities?" Crinnan asked as he stepped out of the portal and into a dark brick street. He saw black stone structures stretching multiple stories above him, candlelight flickered in the windows and heard the ever-present sound of wailing. Blood streamed through the grooves of the bricks beneath his feet, and thick black smoke rose from grates in the streets. As Crinnan spun in place and took in his surroundings he began to feel cramped and dirty.

"Indeed they do." Ander replied. "This particular city is named Sincroft, and it is a treacherous place. We would do well to find our way out as quickly as we can."

"Reminds me of Canrom City's slums." Crinnan commented as Ander led the way forward. He saw fires peeking out of metal barrels and rag-adorned prisoners gathering around them. Some snapped their jaws at Crinnan, others didn't take any notice of him.

"What's with them?" Crinnan asked as he passed by a group of pale-skinned bony prisoners who were spinning in circles and slamming their foreheads against the walls of a building.

"They are the mad ones I spoke of. The 'touched' as the players call them." Ander replied. "Prolonged exposure to the Hells can drive people insane. There are hundreds of millions of them spread throughout the Seven Hells, each with varying degrees of madness. An interesting fact about the touched is that they can harm fellow prisoners and in certain areas like Sincroft, can harm players as well. There's nothing more terrifying than a wave of tens of thousands of touched descending upon you, be wary and avoid them."

Crinnan nodded and checked behind him to find that Milinka was walking with her arms crossed and her head lowered. She hadn't spoken since they arrived in Sincroft. Crinnan frowned as he watched her but didn't linger. He hated seeing her that way, it made him mad to think of what she'd had to endure in her time in the Hells. He wondered if he was to blame, if he'd kept his promise and found her maybe he could have put himself in a position to prevent both of their deaths. With a sigh of regret, he kicked a bottle on the ground and kept walking.

The trio rounded a corner and Crinnan stopped and averted his gaze at the sight before them. Laying in the middle of the street stark naked was a bony old man with a long white beard who was masturbating furiously. His penis didn't have much skin left on it and blood splashed with each stroke. The old man didn't seem fazed though. He quivered in delight, releasing cracked moans.

"Don't mind 'em." A voice came from behind them. "Thas ol' Henry. 'e's been wankin' fer thir'een days straight now."

Crinnan turned around quickly to find a big fat Faire with thinning teal hair on his head. He was dressed in rags like the rest, and Crinnan didn't think he was a threat.

"Name's Pod, same as me pa. Pa Pod I called 'em. He liked it, made 'em smile."

"Fuck off Pod." Crinnan said, waving the Faire away.

"Well, tha's not all too kind. 'specially when you's all strangers on my block. I 'ont mean you no 'arm. Just checkin' t' see what you's upto. Curiosity's all. This you's firs' time in Sincroft?"

"Tis indeed." Ander nodded and looked at Pod. "We have traveled long and hard from the first level to end up here. Tell me friend Pod, where may we find the exit?"

"Long an' 'ard!" Pod belted, laughing heartily to himself. "Now tha's a goodin. Got me laughin' a plenty you did. Thankee for that, ain't much in ol' Sincroft worth laughin' 'bout."

"I am happy to have been of service, friend Pod." Ander replied slowly and politely. "Now, how may my friends and I leave this place?"

"Ain't too many ways outta Sincroft." Pod said, shaking his head slowly. "Portals in an' out's the easiest but portals out ain't been workin' too good as 'a recent and they all lead to Dread's Keep. Gotta find one's the trick. You could die, but then you'd be startin' back at the First Level mos' likely. City gates guarded by the Croftkeeper, a nasty beast who ain't let no one pass in weeks. Las' time anyone beat 'em, 'e respawned in thir'een seconds and turnt around an' killed 'em. Poor fella worked hard."

Ander turned to Crinnan and Milinka with a sour expression on his face. Crinnan in turn looked at Pod.

"Where's the Croftkeeper?" He asked. "I can kill him."

Ander rolled his eyes and moved to interject but Pod released another bellow of a laugh.

"Ain't no tellin' today. Gate's in a new place e'rry day. Gotta get lucky, or unlucky I guess, to find it. But it won't do you no good. The Croftkeeper's too big a baddie for you's. May as well get comfortable lest you want to just die an' start over." Pod looked past Crinnan at Milinka and licked his lips. "Your lady friend lookin' for good time?"

"No, friend Pod, she is not." Ander quickly answered before Crinnan could get a word in.

"I got things for tradin'" Pod insisted. "Plenty o' good scraps. Some mighty fine bones. I only need an hour with 'er."

"Are you trying to die Pod?" Crinnan sternly asked.

"I already done went and did that." Pod chuckled. "Just tryin' to make the best o' things. I'm sure you understand."

"No, fuck off Pod." Crinnan said again. "Get away from us before I cut your throat."

"Ain't a very nice one is 'e?" Pod asked, looking at Ander. "Lucky for 'em, I'm not easily angered."

Crinnan rolled his eyes and turned away. He looked at Milinka who immediately looked away from him. Crinnan sighed at the silent treatment he apparently had to endure.

"Oi heads up then." Pod said, pointing behind Ander. "Some o' the less friendly ones is comin'. You's all better get runnin'. That Karston an' his herd ain't ones to trifle with. Best o' luck friends!" At that Pod turned and ran away.

"Karston and his herd?" Crinnan repeated. He looked at Ander who nodded in response.

"An unfriendly one by the looks of it." Ander said, pointing at the approaching group of hissing and snapping touched. "What say you, Crinnan? Do we retreat or stay and fight?"

"I don't really like to run." Crinnan said, drawing his sword. He spun it in his hand and walked toward the approaching gang.

"Gonna have to ask you to sheathe that weapon, boy!" The elf at the front of the gang ordered. His voice had a significant drawl, and he wore a long ratty brown duster jacket and a wide brimmed hat over his dingy blonde dreadlocks.

"Not a wise move to be pointin' a sword at me on my land." He said. "Put that thing away. Now!"

"I thought Pod said this was his street?" Crinnan asked.

"Pod's a damned idiot." The elf said. "Good for nothing but scavenging bones and scraps. At least that keeps him out of my hair."

Crinnan looked at the touched behind the elf. They were emaciated and pale skinned. Some snapped their teeth at Crinnan, others looked on in absent silence with their sunken eyes. Few had hair, but those that did only had a couple long dry strands.

Crinnan raised his sword, ready for a fight. The elf was quick to respond though. With lightning speed, he pulled a revolver from his hip and blasted the sword from Crinnan's hand. Ander quickly ran to Crinnan's side. He tried to invoke his magic, but nothing happened. He looked down at his hands and sighed with dismay.

"It appears that there is a magic inhibitor in the area." Ander said with a disappointed tone. "A very unfortunate development"

"Fortune ain't got nothin' to do with it." The elf snorted. "Sincroft has a magical barrier around it. Magical abilities are useless here. You're gonna have to find a different way to fight, partner."

Crinnan took a step toward his sword, and the elf fired another shot, preventing him from moving any closer. Finally, Crinnan raised his hands and turned toward the leader.

"What do you want?" Crinnan asked.

"Trying to figure out what you strangers are doing on my land." The elf said. "Forgive me for my lack of manners. Name's Karston Heaton. This here's my herd." He loosely swung the revolver behind him, pointing with the barrel at the cluster of touched behind him. "Now, I ain't *trying* to let them loose on you, but if you give me a reason I'll make sure they rip you to shreds."

"Lord Karston, we are simply passing through." Ander replied, holding his hands up as well. "By your manner of speaking you remind me of those who lived through the Age of Dust. Pray tell, am I correct."

"I was born in the final years of the Age of Dust, yes. Pa raised me good though. He inherited my grandads blood farm, and I did what I could." Karston replied. "My family's way of livin' lasted well into the Age of Ancients til it was outlawed. I was the first of my kin to take the NaNe. Afterscape was nice while it lasted. I ain't taken much of a likin' to the Hells though... ain't a lick o' that important. What matters is you boys, and you ma'am," he tipped his hat at Milinka, "gettin the fuck outta here."

"Well, I can say that I find little trouble agreeing with you on the matter of the Hells, Lord Karston." Ander said with a pleasant tone. "We are not looking for any trouble, elder. We simply wish to find our way out of this city."

"Ain't no way out." Karston replied shortly, shaking his head. "Croftkeeper kills anyone who figures out how to find the exit. He's a right bastard, he is. Been weeks since anyone even got close to leavin'. Best bet on gettin' out is givin up the ghost."

"We do not wish to sacrifice our progress thus far only for us to end up here again." Ander replied. "It seems our only way out is defeating the Croftkeeper."

"Welp." Karston said with a nod. "I certainly do wish y'all the best of luck. But I'm gonna have to ask you one final time to go ahead and step off my land."

Crinnan looked at Karston's "land" which he assumed was just the bloody brick street he was on and snorted.

"Go on then." Karston said, shooing them with his revolver. "Get!"

Crinnan shrugged and turned to fetch his sword. As he approached his weapon, he was able to take a look down the street that ran perpendicular to Karston's. He saw two more forms approaching, and they were very much outfitted like demons.

"Looks like we have company." Crinnan said as he picked the weapon up off the ground.

"Well shit." Karston said. He turned to his herd. "Demons incoming, boys. Get ready for an ambush!"

Chapter Thirteen
Perspective

The Third Hell
Sincroft

The touched scampered across the dark street, giggling maniacally and panting as they all followed their master's order. Watching them reminded Crinnan of trained dogs as opposed to people and he found it to be a strange sight to behold.

"Get over here!" Karston hissed, waving Crinnan over to his position. Crinnan saw that Milinka and Ander were already behind Karston and he hurried over to join them.

"Sincroft is a haven for us prisoners." Karston whispered. "We can harm and even kill the Demons here. They raid us sometimes, drop a lot of good loot if we somehow win. This is one of few places in the Hells where we have any semblance of freedom. Rackin' my brain trying to figure out what the Hells you lot are though. The girl's definitely a prisoner but... what are you two?"

"We are your salvation, Karston." Ander replied. "We have procured a means to escape the Hells. I am certain there is room for one more if you would like to join us."

"Escape?" Karston nearly shouted. "What the hells do you mean escape?"

"We have a plan in place to get out of here." Ander continued. "We have a benefactor on the outside."

"Benefactor huh? Y'all gotta be touched." Karston mumbled as he shook his head and readied his revolver. "Ain't no such a thing as getting out of the Hells.

Damn kids and your idiotic idealism. The Hells'll break ya. I guaran-fucking-tee it."

"So, I hate to break up the evangelizing or whatever you think you're doing Ander but... what's the deal with Handjob Henry there?" Crinnan asked as he pointed to the naked man who was still shucking his corncob in the middle of the damn road. "Do we just... leave him?"

"Players won't touch him." Karston said. "They'll just avoid him. Most sane folk don't want no part of that."

"Betsy!" Handjob Henry cried out as he arched his back. "Woo Betsy!"

"Well, that's weird." Crinnan sighed.

"Quiet, you." Karston whispered. "Demons are gettin' closer." He pulled a second revolver from his hip and then lightly clanked the barrels of the weapons together. Crinnan heard the footfalls of the demons stop, and then Karston's herd of touched suddenly charged.

They screamed wildly and hissed as they swarmed the two Demons. Crinnan heard shouting and the sound of swords ringing free of their scabbards. Karston rounded the corner and began firing his revolvers, whooping as he did.

"I can hurt them..." Crinnan heard Milinka whisper softly. He turned his head and saw that she was talking to herself. "Yes... yes I can!"

At that, Milinka emerged from the corner of the building and charged toward the flailing demons. Crinnan watched for a moment as she sprinted forward, not slowing as she leapt through an opening between two of the touched. She slammed into one of the armored Demons, tackling him to the ground and began screaming as she planted her thumbs into her target's eye sockets. The Demon wailed and Crinnan hurried up to assist.

"Well, you can die I guess." Crinnan snapped as he shoved his sword through the second Demon's neck. He ripped his blade free and blood spewed out. The demon silently fell to the ground, gasping and grabbing at his throat.

Player: Executioner3334 EXECUTED

Player Rank: 1,655,887,114

Congratulations, PrettyKitty6969420! You have advanced in ranking!

Previous Rank: 1,689,016,798

New Rank: 1,672,451,956

Previous Percentile: 79%

New Percentile: 79%

Crinnan glanced over at Milinka whose thumbs were knuckle deep in the demon's eye sockets. Crinnan winced at the sight and kicked over a sword that his target had dropped. The weapon slid across the bleeding cobblestone street toward Milinka and she quickly pulled one of her hands free. A stomach-churning sucking noise sounded as her thumb was pulled from the eye socket. Milinka took hold of the sword and promptly shoved it into the demon's side, passing through his lungs and heart. The demon's wailing stopped, and he fought to breathe, but finally went limp on the street.

Milinka panted as she laid down on top of the demon for rest. She still held onto the hilt of the sword and refused to let go. Crinnan looked over at Ander, who stared at the sight with a strange morbid curiosity. He turned his head and looked at Karston who was gently fanning his face with his hat and chewing on the end of a cigar.

"Y'all are a bit on the brutal side, aintcha?" Karston asked with a frown on his face. "I guess a person's gotta do what they gotta do to get the job done." Karston hummed softly to himself and stroked his stubbly chin in thought. "You know, I might just know how to get you outta here after all. But you're gonna have to be willin' to help me a little in exchange for my knowledge."

"Ah for fuck's sake." Crinnan replied. He glared at the elf as he approached. "How about we just don't play games and you tell us what we need to know?"

"Son, if I gave a damn about whatever sort of bullshit pointless quest that'll lead to your next death then I'd be happy to do things your way." Karston poked Crinnan in the chest, pushing him back a step. "But until I do care, if you want my help we do things my way."

"Well, I don't want your help then." Crinnan said, turning away. "Come on, let's get out of here."

He began to walk away but when he realized Ander and Milinka weren't following him he briefly stopped. Turning his head, he looked their way. "Are you coming?"

Milinka stared back at him silently. Her eyes were glazed over, she had not yet come down from the violence quite yet. Crinnan's gaze made its way to Ander and he shook his head.

"We must discover what this being has to offer, young one." Ander said. "If he can aid us, then we should listen to what he has to say."

Crinnan didn't turn around. Instead, he looked down at the blood streaming between the stones that made up the street. He watched it roll past his stupidly decorative boots and internally debated whether he had the time or patience for all these people. Finally, he turned and glanced at Milinka. The look was brief, but it sent a fluttering through his chest. He saw the Kamlotian woods they'd got lost in together again; he heard her voice... she wasn't who he remembered.

Milinka was broken. Her spirit was gone, her undefeatable outlook on life had crumbled. Seeing her as a grown adult was a terrible contrast to how he remembered her. For a moment it gave him pause. Surely he wasn't so bold as to believe he could fix or heal her. He thought it over. His role in her salvation was done, she had been freed from those who held her captive... now what? Was he simply to protect her until she was whole again? Would she *ever* be whole again? Was it even his place to protect her or should she protect herself? Crinnan grunted over the conflicting thoughts in his mind and finally spun around.

"You know I didn't have to save you!" He shouted at her. Everyone turned and stared at him as he suddenly started his unexpected tantrum. His frustration with her lethargic demeanor was irrational, yes, but it boiled inside of him until it was uncontrollable. Milinka looked at him. Her expression was still emotionless but at least he had her attention.

"Yeah." Crinnan continued. "I could have... left you with them you know."

"Okay." Milinka replied with a shrug. "Thank you."

"For what?" Crinnan asked, confused by her response. "All I'm saying is..."

"Be grateful? Cheer up?" Milinka asked. Her tone remained flat. "You think I should just... fall into your arms and celebrate the acts of my savior?"

"No just..." Crinnan suddenly realized he had talked himself into a hole. He had lost control and made a damn fool of himself. He quickly remembered why he avoided everyone. "Fuck." He lowered his head and turned away, pacing for a moment. "Can't you just move on?"

"Move on." Milinka slowly repeated. "I died, Crinnan. I died and then came to a place designed with my eternal torture in mind. I was quickly snatched up by that group. They passed me between themselves like a toy. I could not fight, and my pleading fell on ears that would not hear. My pride was stripped from me, my body defiled. How Crinnan? How do I move on? If you know please tell me."

"I don't know." Crinnan admitted. "Like. The old Milinka was..."

"She's dead." Milinka quickly said. "So is the old Crinnan. I know you want to help, and you think this little tough-love pep talk is the way... but back the fuck off Crinnan. If I am to heal, then I will. But for now, I need you to not talk to me anymore."

"Doesn't bother me then." Crinnan spat. "I guess you're not who I remember."

"Guess not, Crinnan." Milinka said as a single tear fell from her eye. She was quick to reach up and wipe it away. The single tear sent a tremor through Crinnan's heart and he wished he hadn't said anything. He regretted his words, hated himself for them, and wished he could go back two minutes and just be quiet.

"Well, that was annoying as shit." Karston said with a nod. "If you two are done with whatever the fuck that was then I reckon we can get on with what I was hopin' to propose. May we proceed?"

"Sure." Crinnan said with a roll of his eyes.

"You sure do have a nasty attitude on you ya little snotstain." Karston commented. "Reminds me of one of my boys back when he was about your age. What are ya, 15? 16?"

"I'm twenty-three." Crinnan replied, offended.

"Never woulda guessed." Karston said. "I suppose one day you'll grow up a little and start actin' your age. Maybe when you find something that's important to you." Karston glanced over at Milinka and tipped his hat. "Anyway, down to business. If it ain't beneath that big ol' ego of yours, go ahead and follow me, Crinnan. We can talk while we walk."

Karston began walking down the street. He gave a whistle and his herd of touched quickly ran and flanked him. Milinka walked past Crinnan, shoulder checking him, and Ander snorted and gave him a pat on the back as he followed. Crinnan was left standing alone.

"Well fuck me then." Crinnan grumbled as he jogged to catch up with the others. He didn't understand what he had done to piss everyone off, but he *had* done it. He thought back to multiple times in his life where he had done the same thing and deliberated over whether he regretted them or not. He felt like he never actually tried to piss people off, it just happened that way. Very few people in life were able to put up with his attitude, with his overall grumpy demeanor, and he would be lying if he said he didn't prefer it that way. The less people around to bother him, the better.

The group walked in silence for a bit. In that time, Crinnan passed by several residents of Sincroft. They all looked dirty and pitiful, emaciated, and covered in scars. Some were huddled around burning metal barrels, holding out their hands to the fire. Crinnan briefly reached out at one of the barrels as he passed, realizing that the flames didn't give off any heat. He thought that was strange. The fires of the Hells had been unbearably hot thus far. He thought about it for a moment, and then Ander called to him.

Crinnan hurried to catch up with the others and Ander walked alongside him. For a moment the two walked in silence, but then Ander spoke.

"Life is a funny thing, is it not Mister Jamiso?" He asked.

"Don't call me that." Crinnan groaned at the formality. "Just Crinnan."

"Ah yes, Crinnan..." Ander laughed softly. "That fire is supposed to give comfort. That's why the citizens of Sincroft created it. Yet it yields no warmth, it provides not a moment of respite from the woes of this terrible place. Our overlords ensure that such joys are withheld from us, even in our own city. Why, what would damnation be with small reliefs?"

"I mean, if you give someone relief... then that builds them back up." Crinnan replied. "And then you can take it back from them. I think that would be more sinister than just keeping it from them in the first place. You give a kid a toy and then break it in front of them after they've grown to love it then they'll wish they never had the toy to begin with." Crinnan glanced at Milinka, and then quickly back to the ground.

"What a delightful observation from someone so young." Ander said. "Perhaps it is you who should be ruling over the Hells, it is clear that you understand pain."

Crinnan did not reply. He heard Ander release a thoughtful hum and then the vampre spoke again. "When I speak with you, a part of me is reminded of someone I met long ago. My memory, however unclear it may be, leads me to feel that he was nowhere near as morose as you. We labored endlessly in an attempt to understand the depths of mortal pain and desire... Goodness I wish I could see it a bit more clearly... I believe we determined that the two concepts are more closely related than you may initially think, Crinnan. Pain and desire... a longing for and a regret of not having. Such concepts were the foundations of my work, and they are two things I believe you are no stranger to."

"To live is pain." Crinnan retorted. "Desire is just the fuel that gets us to where we need to go. Once we get what we want, we go back to pain. There's never a time where people are just happy with life. There's always something more to reach for. There's no point worrying about it."

"Crinnan you are but a babe in the eyes of Dura." Ander said, gently patting his back. "Yet I venture to guess that you have lived a life centered around pain. I believe you have endured so much pain, seen so much pain, that you believe there is nothing more. I will tell you, my friend, there is so much more."

"Says the guy who has spent most of his life in the Hells." Crinnan snorted. "What do you know?"

"I know that my desire outweighs my pain every day." Ander replied. "My desire to see an end to all this. My faith that one day it will all be broken. There are parts of my life, Crinnan, that I do not remember. Sections that I see are there, but when I try to remember them all I see is the deepest and darkest of black that you can ever imagine. Tell me Crinnan, do you ever look within yourself and see nothing?"

For a moment, images flashed through Crinnan's mind. He heard gunfire, screaming. A smell of iron that he knew was blood, the feeling of the warm liquid cascading over his hand as he forced a blade into a body. Crinnan saw himself alongside his friends. He watched as they raided a Govian encampment, recalled his orders of no quarter... he thought of the civilians within, the teenage brothers who screamed as he torched their tent. He saw their flaming, burning bodies try to escape and felt the recoil of his weapon as he squeezed the trigger over and over. They were innocent. Govian, yes, but deserving of death? No more than he was...

"I try not to look within myself." Crinnan replied.

"Is it because you do not like what looks back?" Ander asked, curiosity bubbling in his tone.

Crinnan heard his own grunting as he wrestled the charred, dying young Govian to the ground. His skin was blackened and smoking, flaking off and blowing away in the wind. His chest was littered in holes, Crinnan's own doing, and leaking blood that was never meant to see the light of the twin suns, the Brothers as they were called. Crinnan heard the wailing, saw his eyes dart wildly and fearfully... he heard his own words.

"Just stop! Stop and it'll be over!"

"Y...you killed Petrov!" The teenager shouted. *"You're killing me!"*

Crinnan watched his own blade enter the boy's neck just under his jaw. He felt the power, the life drain from him along with every hope and dream the person had ever considered. He remembered feeling pity on the boy, he remembered trying to comfort him.

"I'm sorry..." Crinnan whispered. *"I'm sorry kid. It's okay. I promise it's okay!"*

It wasn't okay. It would never be okay again. Not for the brothers that Crinnan had killed, not for him. From that day on, their lives were his responsibility. Not only theirs, but every single life he was faced with taking in pursuit of liberating the world from Govian control. They weighed more heavily on Crinnan than his own flesh. It was like the blood he drained from his victims replaced his own, he could feel them within him... they were there and Crinnan was tormented by their silent presence daily.

"That's enough." Crinnan replied, shaking his head at Ander. "You're not my fucking doctor."

"I would like to be your friend though, young one." Ander whispered. "Perhaps someone somewhere scripted this, perhaps this was meant to be. Our paths crossed, Crinnan. What will become of it?"

"I don't fucking know, and I don't care Ander." Crinnan snapped. "I don't believe in fate; I don't believe in the Goddess. All I believe in is me."

"Very good, my friend." Ander said. "Faith is best placed in oneself... Come, it appears we have arrived at our destination. Let us see what this Karston fellow has to offer."

Chapter Fourteen
Crinnan the Pet Kicker

The Third Hell
Sincroft

The group walked through a dank and moldy alley and approached a building made of black charred looking wood. Rats scurried out of their path and Karston was forced to punch an aggressive beggar in the jaw, knocking him out. As one of his touched dragged the body into the shadows to feast on it, Karston led Crinnan, Ander and Milinka inside.

The creaky door swung shut behind them and Karston removed his hat. He placed it on a peg on the wall and shrugged out of his duster jacket, revealing his denim pants and flannel shirt beneath. He hung his jacket next to his hat and motioned for everyone to sit.

"You're a strange group of people." Karston commented as he leaned against a wall and crossed his arms. "To be honest, too strange for my liking but I'm not here to make friends. I'm here to talk business, so let's get straight to it. I have the solution to your little problem. I can get y'all outta here. Sincroft is a special place in the Hells you see. It's a place where we prisoners can make a life for ourselves if we can accept a little give and take. You see, some of the Demons want a little extra bang for their buck. They want their opponents to give them a little fight. Here in this place, we have the ability to fight back. Here we get creative and make challenges for the Demons who come after us. We can kill them and send them back to the first level where they have to start over. There's some folks here who've been doing that for years, decades maybe. Demons come after them to score the big kills, to have a real fighting experience... but the prisoners here. We don't all get along."

Karston pushed himself off the wall and walked to a small kitchen looking area. He knelt down in front of a wood stove and peeked inside. Satisfied with the flames burning, he reached out and grabbed the handle of a kettle, lifting it.

"Anybody want some coffee?" He asked, turning his head to look at his guests. Ander raised his hand and Karston grabbed two cups and poured the steaming black liquid. With a snort, he turned back around and walked to the others.

"So there's this fella." Karston said, placing a cup in front of Ander. "A lycaani, goes by the name of Darion. Don't know if that's his real name or not but I reckon that don't matter. The point is, he's bad news. Done me wrong a time too many, and I'm more than half sick of his shit. My problem is that me and my herd can't get close to him. His herd's bigger, ya see." Karston took a sip of his coffee and placed the mug down on the table. He took a seat across from Crinnan and looked him in the eye.

"Darion runs this part of town like he owns it." Karston sighed. "Little shit comes knockin' every once in a while, thinks I need to pay him for protection. I never asked the fucker for shit, but the first time I refused was the last time. He done killed half my herd and told me he'd be back in three days to collect half my shit. Said that was the introductory fee, that the next time it would be less. Well, the next time it wasn't less. Neither was the time after. This has been goin' on for years I reckon. I'm barely gettin' by, starting to question whether the few luxuries I find here are worth my time. Been thinkin' of running off to Asheland, though the trip'll end up with me dying only the fucking Brothers knows how many times. I don't like dying. I don't like pain. I can take it, but I'd rather not."

"So, what?" Crinnan asked. "Let's get to it. You want us to kill this Darion guy for you? What do we have to gain out of it?"

"You know, kid. I'm not surprised you're an impatient little bastard." Karston replied, taking another sip of his drink. "Matches the rest of your personality good. If you'd shut your mouth and listen, I betcha I'll get to it."

Crinnan snorted and looked away. Karston put his mug back on the table and clicked his tongue. "Yes, I want you to kill Darion." He said contemptuously.

"You do that for me, I won't have any problem showing you the way outta Sincroft."

"How do we know there is a way?" Milinka asked. Everyone looked over at her, but she did not remove her gaze from Karston. "We were told that the way is always changing and heavily guarded. How do we know we can trust you?"

"This is the Hells, darlin'." Karston replied, leaning forward. "You can't trust me. You can't trust anyone here. I can't make you and I'd think you a fool if you did. I can tell you I'm not lying and I'm good for my word... also, and don't take this the wrong kinda way, but what on Duraan do you have to lose?"

"A fair point our new friend makes." Ander said. "In the worst of situations we would simply be killed and start over in the Fields of Misery. I say why not. It's all we have for now."

"Can't we just go find the way ourselves?" Crinnan asked. "If he did, we can."

"Sure." Karston replied with a shrug. "I ain't stoppin' ya. If that's what you want to do then I look forward to having the new neighbors for years to come."

Milinka stared at Karston deeply for a moment before she nodded her head. She reached her hand out towards Karston and he raised an eyebrow. "We're in." She said.

Karston grabbed her hand tightly and they both stood. "You could learn something from this one, kid." Karston said to Crinnan as he released her hand. "She's a smart one." Crinnan snickered at that remark and shook his head as he stood with the others.

"Whatever." He said. "Where do we go, what does he look like?"

"You'll find Darion five blocks north of my home." Karston said. "Hard to miss, big warehouse and lots of touched outside... usually lots of blood and pieces of people too. He's a thin fella. Hairy, tail, sharp teeth. You know, a lycaani."

"Great." Crinnan said sarcastically. He turned toward the door and the others followed.

"Gonna need his head for proof." Karston called out as Crinnan opened the door. "Anybody can say anything, you know."

"Oh, I know." Crinnan said as they stepped outside. The door closed behind them and Crinnan rubbed his face with frustration.

"Are we really doing this?" He asked as Milinka walked past him. "Do you seriously think he knows anything?"

"I don't care if he does or not." Milinka snapped back. Crinnan could feel the weight of her coldness toward him in her words. "Like he said, we don't have anything better to do."

"We simply hope for the best, my friend." Ander patted Crinnan's back as he walked by. Crinnan cringed at the touch but followed.

The trio made their way out of the alley and back onto the bleeding black stone streets. Prisoners shambled by lethargically, barely sparing the group a contemptuous glare if any at all. Their tattered cloaks and rat chewed top hats reminded Crinnan of Canrom City where his parents and brother lived. Crinnan glanced at them only briefly as he walked with the others.

"Apathy is a natural response to this world we live in." Ander commented as he noticed Crinnan's attention on the others. "The mind teaches us not to care, not to feel. It helps with the pain of our eternal torment, with our thoughts of loss. Many of us have shoved the memories of our lives so far deep within the recesses of our psyche that we lose what is to be an individual... We forget so much, we abandon the rest. We live as drones, walking nowhere and seeking nothing."

Crinnan reflected on Ander's words. He didn't want to end up like that, to lose himself like all the sad husks of people that walked past him had. Crinnan thought about his life as he walked. Of his few friends, of his experiences and dreams. He thought of his favorite food, steamed cabbage, and how nobody else liked it so he always got everyone else's portion.

While he was still young and rough around the edges; Crinnan liked being himself. He liked very few other people, but he was content with who he was. He was comfortable with the world his mind existed in, with the solitude he lived in. He intentionally pushed others away because very few people had anything to offer him. In his eyes the mindlessness of their social interactions, the expectations that friends put on one another, and the drama of being a part of other people's lives was too much for him. He didn't want any of that to spoil what he found most dear: himself.

At the same time, he couldn't help but glance at Milinka. He watched her walk; her head lowered, her shoulder length filthy blonde hair clumping together in sections at her neck. He saw the cuts and scratches on the backs of her arms, the scabs on her elbows. The sight of it all made his heart hurt. Not simply because she had gone through horrors that Crinnan was resolute on never experiencing, but also because out of everyone on Duraan *she* had been the only person he had ever loved.

Crinnan thought back to Kamlot when he was only sixteen years old. He recalled it all, having been kicked out of the Future Centurions program by Captain Bran after beating the shit out of his friend Alec in training, of being sent to the front lines of the Kamlotian Civil War as a squire. He remembered the first time he spoke to Milinka, and the looks of contempt her boyfriend gave him as he hovered behind her. Milinka was a snotty little Lord's daughter when they first met. He initially didn't like her one bit.

When Crinnan's Knight, Sir Edmaan, and Milinka's Knight and brother, Sir Demyan, were ambushed, Crinnan and Milinka ran. When he closed his eyes he could see the woods of the Woolshire Highlands of Kamlot. He could hear the birds singing and the rabbits rustling in the brush around him.

As Crinnan and Milinka ventured deeper into the forest and got more and more lost, Crinnan remembered how his contempt for her eventually shattered. He didn't want it to but one night as they sat in front of their small pitiful fire, their bare arms brushed against each other. Crinnan remembered the conversation that followed. He remembered Milinka telling him she was scared, and of how he promised her that she didn't have to be with him around.

Crinnan briefly smiled as he walked. He remembered the feeling of her fingers weaving with his as they ran from enemy fire, of how despite the fact that they were being hunted he couldn't help but focus on the feelings he was quickly developing for her. It was so easy for him to replay the five days they were lost in his mind. Every moment, every touch and word... and their single kiss ran through his mind in an instant.

"This love is good." He remembered her saying. For years after he heard that voice whispering to him as he fell asleep alone at night... but of course he also remembered his own words.

"I will find you." The words echoed in his mind when he thought of her. He remembered screaming the words to her when he was being flown away from her by Captain Bran and his father... and paired with Milinka's own words, Crinnan also thought of his broken promise every night. As time passed he grew afraid. He wanted so badly to reach out to her, to go and find her like he said, but he never did. When it came to war, Crinnan was a Centurion. He was strong, skilled and brave. He could rush into a group of enemies and come out alive and with a bloody sword every time. But when it came to love, Crinnan was the lowest of cowards.

"Crinnan!" Milinka shouted as Crinnan slammed into one of the prisoners. The being's hat flew off his head and he fell to the ground, grunting audibly. Crinnan quickly pushed himself back up and Milinka knelt to help the dusty prisoner but the person barely registered their presence. He silently grabbed his torn top hat, placed it on his head and continued on his way.

"Fucking pay attention!" Milinka snapped. She shoved Crinnan in his shoulder and scoffed. "What is wrong with you?"

"Sorry." Crinnan said. He dusted his pants off and looked away from her. "I was thinking about something."

"Well stop it." She smacked his shoulder and shook her head with a look of frustration on her face. "Don't think. Don't do anything except get us out of here, if you can even do that."

"Fine." Crinnan said. He moved to walk around her but Milinka sidestepped so that she was still in front of him.

"Fine?" She repeated, her eyes growing wider. "What is wrong with you?"

"Nothing!" Crinnan replied. "What's wrong with you?"

"You are." Milinka hissed.

"Well get the fuck over it." Crinnan said. "For hating me as much as you do you sure seem to worry about me a lot."

Milinka squinted her eyes fiercely at Crinnan and turned around, running to catch up with Ander. Crinnan angrily jogged up to follow and Ander slowed his pace so that the two were walking side by side.

"I know we only recently became acquainted." Ander softly said. "But, if I may?"

"Do what you want." Crinnan replied.

"Well, when it seems like a girl is pushing you. She is." Ander said. "Milinka seems to want something out of you. Based on the screaming matches you two have held, I have gathered there is a history between you two. Young love and broken promises I believe."

Crinnan remained silent but gently nodded his head.

"Yes. Well." Ander continued. "Ladies are generally smarter than us. More intuitive, able to see the bigger picture. Crinnan, I'll be bold. Milinka wants you to step up in some way. Whatever that may mean. She has expectations of you, an image of you in her head and you are failing to meet that image."

"Well, that's not my problem." Crinnan replied. "She knew me when I was sixteen. That was a long time ago."

"I would beg to differ, young elf." Ander said.

"I'm half-blood." Crinnan replied. "My father is humaan."

"Indeed..." Ander raised an eyebrow. "Well. If I may offer a word of advice. If that girl sees something in you then she knows you can be better. For your own sake, deliver on her expectations. You'll thank yourself later in life." Ander patted Crinnan's back and sped back up.

"What does he know." Crinnan mumbled as he kicked a stone in his path. The stone didn't budge, and instead cracked open a mouth of sharp teeth and bit into Crinnan's foot.

"By the Brothers!" Crinnan shouted in surprise and pain. The stone clamped onto him and growled as it shook itself back and forth, apparently trying to rip Crinnan's foot loose.

"Hey!" One of the prisoners shouted angrily. He stopped his walk and pointed a finger at Crinnan. "That lad's kickin' the gravlins!"

"The gravlins!?" Crinnan shouted back. "It bit me first!" Crinnan pulled his sword free and prepared to stab the creature that attached itself to him.

The prisoners gasped and many of them produced knives and sticks. Crinnan saw this and wondered what the fuck was going on. The gravlin bit down harder and Crinnan kicked his foot. The creature wouldn't budge.

"Stay yourselves, my friends!" Ander shouted as he ran back up to Crinnan. "The lad doesn't know what he does!" Ander quickly knelt down and started tenderly scratching the surface of the gravlin. "There we are, all is well little creature. He means you no harm."

Two black beady eyes suddenly opened, and the gravlin loosened its hold on Crinnan's foot. It started making a strange purring noise like a cat, and it fell to the ground, its vicious looking mouth forming into a smile. Crinnan had half a mind to punt the shitty little thing but ultimately decided against it.

"Mind what you do here, young one." Ander whispered as he stood. "Many things are not as they seem. The locals treat the gravlins as pets, they find them cute."

"It's a fucking rock." Crinnan retorted, looking down at his bleeding foot.

"Well. It is not but. I understand." Ander replied. "Come, we are nearing the compound. Let us complete this task that we may get out of this city before you start squashing cthulitos and really make the Sincroftians mad."

"What the fuck is a cthulito."

"An adorable little tentacley ball of snuggly comfort." Ander replied. "But don't fall asleep around one lest you want it to crawl into your mouth and slowly eat you from the inside out."

"The Hells is stupid." Crinnan sighed. "The monsters back home are much better than they are here."

Ander smiled and ushered Crinnan forward. They finally caught up with Milinka and stopped on either side of her. Milinka looked over at Crinnan and crossed her arms.

"You kicked someone's pet?" She asked with a tone of disbelief.

"I didn't know." Crinnan replied.

"Of course you didn't." Milinka sighed.

Before them was a large stone wall with multiple heads on spikes atop it. The blood from the heads dripped down the stone, and the walls were stained red from apparent years of gore. Behind the wall was a wide grey four-story building with boarded up windows. Crinnan approached a tall, rusted gate and peered into the courtyard ahead of them.

"Oh shit he wasn't lying." Crinnan said as he stared at what had to have been dozens of touched. They shambled around the courtyard, maniacally laughing or bitterly crying to themselves. Some picked at their skin or pulled on their hair, while others simply lay in a fetal position on the ground.

"Well." Crinnan said as Ander approached. "I guess we just... kill them?"

Chapter Fifteen
Darion

The Third Hell
Sincroft – Darion's Compound

"Brute force only gets one so far in life." Ander said, raising a finger toward Crinnan. "Observe your surroundings, consider the variables around you before you rush into a situation. For by doing so…"

"Yeah, fuck that." Crinnan said. He backed up a few paces and charged at the wall. As he neared it, he leapt into the air, taking hold of the edge. He pulled himself up with little effort, momentarily finding himself eye to eye with one of the severed heads that rested atop it.

"Gross." Crinnan muttered to himself as he crawled on top of the wall. There was fortunately enough room between the spikes for him to stand. He drew his sword and without looking back at his companions, he jumped to the courtyard below.

The touched turned their heads menacingly toward Crinnan, and he easily cut through the one nearest to him. The creature crashed to the ground, writhing and howling in pain. The other touched started charging toward Crinnan and for the briefest of moments he hesitated.

When did they get so fast? Crinnan thought. He noticed none of them had weapons, none had armor. He had both. With that in mind, he nodded and charged directly at them.

***

"At times I question the intellect of that boy." Ander softly said to Milinka as they stood side by side and watched Crinnan jump over the wall.

"You have no idea." Milinka replied with a sigh.

"Who charges headfirst into over a dozen foes with nothing but a sword in hand?" Ander asked. "Common sense would dictate that is a suicidal move."

"Crinnan Jamiso does." Milinka replied. Her lips briefly formed into a nostalgic smile and she grabbed the bars of the gate in front of her. "Idiot."

"Well. No sense standing idly by as your boyfriend gets ripped apart by mindless ghouls." Ander said, reaching his open hands toward the gate. "You may wish to stay back. You have no weapon."

"He's not my boyfriend." Milinka spat. "And you don't have a weapon either. There's a magic field around Sincroft, remember?"

"It seems that fact escaped me." Ander replied, lowering his hands. "Do you have one?"

Milinka held up her hands and wiggled her fingers in Ander's direction. "Just these girls." She said. Ander smiled warmly and stepped past Milinka, gently patting her on the shoulder as he walked.

"You are a lovely person, Miss Milinka." Ander said. "Come, give me a boost and I'll pull you up."

"With those noodle arms?" Milinka scrunched up her face at the man. "You give me a boost. I'll pull you up."

Ander raised his eyebrows and looked down at his arms. "I do not believe you are judging my might appropriately." He said, flexing beneath his robe. "While I am not known for my brawn, I can assure you..."

"It's okay." Milinka smiled for a moment and walked up to the wall. "I'm sure you are very strong."

Ander snorted and knelt down, interlocking his fingers to give Milinka a step up. She placed her foot in his palms and Ander lifted, releasing a stifled squeal. Milinka burst into laughter for a moment until she looked up and stared into the glossy eyes of a severed head. With a groan she reached out and turned the head. She then climbed atop the wall and turned around to help Ander up.

"You seem to be eager to die." Sage's voice played in Crinnan's head, surprising him.

"Yeah, what do you know?" Crinnan replied as he swung his sword. One of the touched's heads rolled from its shoulders and Crinnan elbowed another who got too close. He felt a pair of gangly arms wrap around him and Crinnan quickly broke free, ripping the arms from their owner's sockets and causing Crinnan to gasp.

Prisoner Entity KILLED

...

+200 Ranking

"All I see is a red dot surrounded by other red dots." Sage replied. *"And all those other red dots are running toward your red dot. It looks like you put yourself in a rather stupid position I should say."*

"They're fucking rotten!" Crinnan snapped back, pulling his sword through the side of one of the touched's heads. "Just black mush inside... What do you need?"

Prisoner Entity KILLED

...

+200 Ranking

"I was simply able to get through." Sage said. *"I had to let you know I am still here. I apologize for my absence, finding these windows of opportunity is endless work for little result."*

"Well yay." Crinnan said. "Glad you're there. Glad I'm here. Glad everyone's fucking somewhere."

Sage laughed as Crinnan spun and put his boot through one of the touched's stomachs. His foot got caught and he tripped, the wailing touched falling on top of him.

"You fuck!" The touched screamed as it desperately clawed at Crinnan's leg. "You bastard child of silt and birdshit! You're no better than the precum of a lizard, than a lame dickless bull! I hope you..."

"Shut up." Crinnan moaned as he slid the point of his sword through the touched's eye. He wiggled his foot free to the tune of sloshing mushy guts and the sound of brittle bones snapping.

Prisoner Entity KILLED

...

+200 Ranking

"Is all well?" Sage asked.

"Everything's fantastic." Crinnan said as he stumbled to his feet. The touched had surrounded him and were hissing and spitting at him. Crinnan spun in place, swatting at any who reached out for him with his sword. He heard the sound of a bell tinkling and the touched suddenly parted.

Crinnan saw a small group of armed people walking his way. The person at the front was lycaani, shorter than his friends with long brown hairy ears and a pointy tooth that poked out the left side of his mouth. He had a small brass bell in one hand, and a footlong dagger in the other. He wore nicer clothing than anyone else Crinnan had seen in Sincroft, a pair of purple smooth fabric pants and a dark red collared shirt, buttoned halfway and showing off a chest of thick hair. Crinnan assumed it was Darion.

"What the shit are you doing here!" Darion shouted as he approached. "Why are you fucking with my herd!"

"Some fucking hick sent us!" Crinnan yelled back. "Fucker wants you dead for taking his shit, whatever bits of trash you all call possessions."

"Who is that?" Sage asked. *"And why are you speaking to him so belligerently?"*

"Shut up you're not my dad." Crinnan whispered harshly.

"Hick?" Darion asked as he stopped a few feet from Crinnan. "You mean Karston? That coffee drinking shitbag?"

"Sure." Crinnan replied with a shrug. "I mean yeah. Karston."

Darion threw his head back and laughed and then raised his dagger toward Crinnan. "Well. I'd have you tell Karston you failed, but you'll be back in the First Level the time I'm done with you. I guess we'll have to tell him ourselves."

"I don't give a fuck who tells who what." Crinnan said. "But you're not touching me with that shitty little knife."

"Bravo, wordsmith, that should do it." Sage droned with a sigh.

Darion was silent for a moment and then suddenly cracked a thin smile. "Confident, eh." He said, lowering his dagger. "Confidence is hot."

"Oh, I should say, this got interesting." Sage chuckled.

Crinnan wished Sage would shut the fuck up.

"Oh by the Brothers I am not in the mood for this right now." Crinnan sighed.

"I tell you what, mister sword boy." Darion held out his hand. "Come up to my room with me. Let's talk this over. Maybe I don't have to stick you with my shitty little knife after all."

"You aren't sticking me with your shitty little dick either." Crinnan belted.

"Well." Darion shrugged. "I guess you will have to..."

The tip of Crinnan's sword suddenly pierced Darion's throat and the lycaani's eyes went wide. Darion's entourage all gasped, and Darion reached out and jabbed his dagger into Crinnan's armor. The dagger clanged against the metal and Crinnan pulled his sword from Darion's throat. Darion reached up in defense as Crinnan cleaved downward, splitting the being's skull in two. The lycaani looked shocked for a moment, and then went limp as he fell to his side.

> **Prisoner Entity KILLED**
>
> **+200 Ranking**

"Oh." Sage commented. "That was. Unexpected."

"You were unexpected." Crinnan replied as he stared down the rest of Darion's group. "You are the worst bodyguards I have ever seen. Are you guys coming to fight or not?"

The people in Darion's group looked at one another and then back to Crinnan. "We're probably just not going to try to fight you." One of them said. "Well. Not probably. We'll just leave."

"Great." Crinnan said. "Bye."

As they started to run, Milinka suddenly appeared and grabbed one of them by the upper arm.

"I'll take your axes." She said, pointing to the axes he held. He looked back at Crinnan and Crinnan shrugged.

"Fine lady." He said, dropping his weapons. "Have fun." At that the being ran to catch up with his friends. Milinka knelt and picked the weapons up, turning them over in her hands. She nodded and walked to Crinnan.

"Glad you could make it." Crinnan said as Milinka and Ander approached. "Don't worry. I took care of it."

"Took care of indeed." Ander said, looking at the corpses lying on the ground around Crinnan. "And so masterfully done as well."

Crinnan shrugged again. "Some people are good at cooking. I'm good at killing. I guess."

"No guessing about it." Ander said with a whistle. "You are a professional killer. One whose level of skill never fails to surprise and amaze me."

"Okay." Crinnan said. Milinka's arms were at her side and in each of her hands she held a hatchet. "Maybe next time then?" Crinnan asked.

"Maybe." Milinka replied with obviously fake enthusiasm. Crinnan raised his eyebrows and looked away. "You know if you had been able to do that back in the Woolshire Highlands maybe we could have gotten out quicker."

"I was sixteen, give me a break." Crinnan replied. "Yeah, I could fight well enough back then but not how I can now."

"Oh please." Milinka rolled her eyes. "You nearly pissed yourself when the first Govian soldier crossed our path."

"I *did* piss myself." Crinnan said. Milinka cocked her head and looked upward as if she were thinking. A mischievous smile formed on her lips and she nodded.

"You're right. You did." She snorted a laugh and then looked down at Darion's body. "Well. Karston wanted his head." She knelt down and set one of her axes on the ground next to her. "Here we go then." She raised her other axe above her head and slammed it down against Darion's neck. The blade of the hatchet sunk deep into the neck and Crinnan heard the spine snap. He twitched at the sound of it, and Milinka chopped one more time. She cut through the remaining flap of skin on the back and the head was free.

"Two swings." She said proudly, picking up the head by one of the ears.

"Well, I started it for you." Crinnan replied. Milinka smiled sweetly at Crinnan and he looked at her with a confused expression. He remembered that smile, that beautiful innocent...

Milinka shoved Darion's head into Crinnan's chest and he took hold of it. "Oh." Crinnan said, looking down at the trophy. "Right."

"Well. It appears Darion is out of work now." Ander declared as he approached. "I do hope he receives a wonderful *severance* package." Ander made certain to emphasize the word severance and huffed a strange inconsistent laugh at his comment.

Sage burst into uncontrollable laughter and Crinnan groaned. "Well, you made a joke." Crinnan sighed, thinking back to Ander's last attempt at humor.

"He seems to be a wonderful person." Sage said. *"I enjoy him very much I should say. But it appears my time with you is finished for now. I will see you again, Crinnan. Keep moving and stay safe."* At that, Sage was gone again.

"It was funny." Milinka said idly as she wiped her hands in the dirt to get the blood off. "Well, it was appreciated I mean. I respect you for trying."

"You people need to learn to lighten up." Ander mumbled as he turned toward the gate. "So, do you suppose we can open this or..."

Crinnan walked up to the wall and tossed Darion's head over. It landed with a lump on the other side and Crinnan jumped and grabbed onto the ledge. He pulled himself up and over again and Ander turned to Milinka.

"Come on." Milinka sighed. "Give me a boost."

Chapter Sixteen
Disaccord

The Third Hell
Sincroft – Karston's Home

"Well. I don't know how y'all did it so quick, but I reckon it's done." Karston said, looking down at the head of Darion laying on his dinner table. "I mean. I wasn't expecting to see y'all again truth be told."

"We had a very valuable asset whose efforts enabled our quick success." Ander said, patting Crinnan on the back. "Without Crinnan I do believe our mission would have taken a much greater deal of time. We are quite fortuitous to be in his company."

"Alright then." Karston said with an unsure tone. "Well shit. I wasn't hoping to leave the house tonight."

"Yeah, well. I was." Crinnan replied. "How do we get out of here?"

"Well kid, the trick to getting outta here is killing the Croftkeeper." Karston replied. "If you're lucky you can find one of the gates when they appear but they're only open for about fifteen seconds at a time before they vanish and appear in another part of the walls. Can't count on the second option."

"That sounds like information I could have got for free from any of the other thousands of people here." Crinnan said.

"Oh Hells kid it's hundreds of thousands." Karston replied. "But you agreed to pay for this information with Darion's head. And you got it."

"So wait. That's fucking it?" Crinnan asked. He could feel his anger flaring up inside him. "That's all we get out of this?"

"Yup." Karston said. "But now you got a sense of what to do next. Good for you. If you'll kindly leave my home, I'd be very appreciative."

Crinnan lifted his sword and pointed the tip at Karston. "No, we're not fucking playing that stupid ass game. You're getting us the fuck out of this..."

"You're gonna lower that weapon in my house!" Karston boomed. Not a second passed before the sound of a revolver discharging caused everyone's ears to ring. A bullet struck Crinnan in the middle of his armor and the blue light of his shields flickered before Milinka got to her feet and stood between the two of them.

"Stop it!" Milinka snapped. "You said you'd *show* us the way out of Sincroft if we took care of Darion for you, not tell us some random Sincroft trivia. So, *you* get up and get out of here, and you *show* us the way."

"Move, Milinka!" Crinnan seethed. "I'll fucking kill him!"

"No, you won't!" Milinka said. "You will lower that shitty sword and shut your stupid fucking mouth; do you understand?"

Crinnan grumbled as he allowed his sword arm to fall. He and Milinka glared at each other for a moment before he turned and walked away, finally leaning against a wall off to the side. Milinka sighed and looked back at Karston.

"I will say that I concur with Miss Milinka here." Ander softly said from his spot at the table. "While your intentions may have been to provide information, the verbiage of your contract to us stated that you would indeed show us the way. So, I must insist that you lead us to this Croftkeeper."

Karston stared at Ander and Milinka silently for a moment and then he sighed as he ran his fingers through his long hair. "Y'all know I have shit to do..."

"You said you didn't plan on leaving your house." Milinka argued.

"Well, what if I flat out refuse?" Karston asked with a raised eyebrow.

"Then I'll cut off your head too." Crinnan said.

"Shut up!" Milinka snapped and Crinnan closed his mouth.

Karston looked over at Crinnan who leaned against the wall with his arms crossed. "Fine. You know what, I'll take you to the Croftkeeper. I'll show you the way to him, but I ain't helping you kill him. According to our *contract* all I need to do is show you the way."

"Wonderful." Ander said as he stood from his chair. "Then let us venture forth that we may…"

"Tomorrow." Karston added, cutting Ander off. "It's nighttime. You don't want to spend too much time on the streets of Sincroft at night."

"What the fuck do you mean its nighttime?" Crinnan asked. "It's always nighttime here."

"Just because it's always dark don't mean we don't have day and night." Karston said, looking to Ander. Ander reluctantly nodded in agreement.

"He speaks truth." Ander said with a yawn. "It is indeed nighttime and now that I am thinking about it, I have grown a bit weary from my travels."

"I've been in the Hells all this time…" Crinnan said. "I haven't slept once. I don't feel tired, I don't feel like I need to sleep…" Crinnan suddenly felt a yawn coming on. "Oh, by the Brothers." He said as he raised his hand to his mouth.

"Yeah, you don't look tired at all, little bitch." Karston said with a snort. "Well, if you ain't slept in days then you should sleep real good tonight." Karston said. "Come on, I've got a spot up in the attic y'all can camp out in."

"Your hospitality is much appreciated sir." Ander said as he rose from his chair. Everyone got to their feet and the sounds of their seats creaking and chair legs scraping against the floor filled the room. Crinnan cringed at all the extra noises and pushed himself away from the wall he was leaning against. As he put his weight on the black wood behind him, he felt something give way and heard the slightest of cracking noises. He clenched his teeth together and glanced at Karston, making sure he didn't hear the noise. Fortunately, Karston was oblivious.

"Ladder's this way." Karston said, beckoning the others to follow. Crinnan ran his hand along the wood of the wall he had somehow broken. There was a clear flattened circle of cracks, and Crinnan noted that it was dry and coarse. Splinters embedded themselves in his fingers and Crinnan grabbed his hand, cursing.

"Shit!" He whispered. A few slivers of wood protruded from his skin, and he immediately brought his hand to his mouth. He bit down gently, trying to remove the intruders, and then turned his head and spit the splinters onto the ground.

"What the fuck are you doing?" Karston hollered. "If you have to spit go outside!"

"Fuck you." Crinnan called back. "I'm coming." He walked across the dining area to get to the "living room." Crinnan noted that there was only an old looking rocking chair and coffee table in the living room. No TV, no lights, no comforts. Crinnan walked past the sparse furnishings and to a wall where the others stood.

"Ladder's right here." Karston said. "I'll ask that you go on ahead and head up. I don't much care for company, and don't want y'all breaking anything else."

"Anything else?" Ander asked, tilting his head. "Did one of us..."

"Ah." Crinnan sighed. "So you saw that."

"I did, boy." Karston said with a glare. "Get up there and get some rest. I'll come fetch you when it's morning."

"You have my apologies." Ander said, glancing over at Crinnan and then back to Karston. "Had I known..."

"No apology needed." Karston said, shaking his head. "This house is about to fall over anyway. It can't be helped. Now go on and get."

Without a word, Milinka climbed up the ladder. Crinnan noted the creaking as she climbed, and then Ander followed. When Ander was up, Crinnan reached out to take hold of the ladder but Karston reached out his hand and pushed against Crinnan's chest, preventing him from moving forward.

"You hold on." Karston said. "I want to talk to you."

"Why." Crinnan asked.

"Just come with me. Let's talk in private." Karston said. He walked away and Milinka peaked her eyes over the opening above. Crinnan and her eyes met for a moment and he couldn't look away. She stared in silence, and he looked back wondering what was going through her mind. Finally, she extended her hand and lifted her middle finger toward him. Crinnan pursed his lips together and followed Karston back into the dining room.

"Don't sit." Karston said as Crinnan appeared.

"Wasn't planning on it." Crinnan replied.

"Good." Karston cracked his knuckles and leaned back against the crumbling countertop in his kitchen. He reached into his front shirt pocket and produced a pack of cigarettes. Crinnan spotted them quickly and Karston raised an eyebrow.

"Smoke?" He asked, holding the pack out to Crinnan.

"Sure." Crinnan replied. Karston tossed Crinnan the pack and then struck a match, lighting the cigarette between his lips. He took a drag and tossed Crinnan his matchbook.

"I can forgive what just happened. Can you?" Karston asked with a solemn tone.

"Would probably be the mature thing to do..." Crinnan spat back.

"Glad to see you growing up a bit... now tell me, why are you here?" Karston asked as he pulled the cigarette away, exhaling a breath of smoke.

"Just waiting for you to show me the way out." Crinnan replied and then breathed out his own plume.

"No, I mean. How did you get here? To the Hells?" Karston asked. His demeanor was still frigid, and he looked at Crinnan with the same look of distrust that was in his eyes when they first met.

"I was ambushed." Crinnan said thoughtfully, thinking back to the night of his death.

"Killed in cold blood?" Karston asked.

"I guess so." Crinnan replied.

"That's too bad. You're young, you had some life ahead of you." Karston said. "Lots of holes up in the real world that young men need to fill I reckon."

"Weird." Crinnan remarked as he took another drag.

"You come from the modern age?" Karston asked. "The Age of Govia or whatever it's called?"

"Yeah." Crinnan replied.

"What's that like?"

"Bloody." Crinnan said. "Smells bad, lots of people gathered in the cities. Some in the wastes. Everybody's just waiting to die." Crinnan paused and looked away from Karston. "What... what about you?"

"Like I said, Age of Dust for me." Karston said. "Just barely though. I was one of the few who were lucky enough to make it here. After the humaan ships arrived. When the Damarsi kingdom was scattered and the Aldiir were pushed back to their own lands. Sorry. I mean the vampre and the lycaani. That's what the humaan people named them anyway. The elves and the faire united under the humaans and had one hell of a golden age..."

"I see." Crinnan nodded slightly.

"I was born toward the end of the Age of Dust you see." Karston said as he took another puff of his cigarette. "I was two years old when the Age of Ancients came to be. Shoulda let myself die naturally kid. I would'a spared myself the grief of having to live in the Hells."

"What do you mean?" Crinnan asked.

"I was an old elf when that NaNe business came around." Karston said. "The year we saw it was supposed to be my 120th birthday. The year 118. I remember it fondly. My boys was all grown, daughters were all married off. Was just me the wife, and a couple of kids who couldn't seem to find their way at the homestead. I seen it in the paper one day, NaNe – Live Forever or something like that. That ol' LifeLinks corporation promised us everlasting life. Can't say they didn't deliver on their promise, just not in the way I hoped."

"What's LifeLinks?" Crinnan asked. "I don't know much about the Ancients."

"LifeLinks was some kinda science company or something." Karston shrugged. "Created the NaNe, the power that I reckon runs these Hells. Boy you wouldn't believe what they did. Not a hundred miles from my home was a dirt quarry. Who ever thought people'd be mining dirt? I bet you're asking yourself why aintcha?"

"I mean. I am now." Crinnan shrugged.

"NaNe, you see, was some kinda magic if I ever seen it." Karston shook his head and turned to his coffee pot. "People was mining dirt because they could use NaNe to turn the dirt into apples, bacon, damn steaks and three course dinners. Hells, whatever you wanted, NaNe could make it outta dirt. You need a house? Dig yourself up a mound of dirt and have LifeLinks come out and release their NaNe. Want a new car? No problem, NaNe's got your back. It was some wild times, wild shit friend. *Wild* shit."

"Why?" Crinnan asked, furrowing his brow. "Why make things out of dirt?"

"Well, that's the thing." Karston said. He placed the coffee pot back down and lifted a cup to his lips. "They didn't make things outta dirt. The NaNe turned the dirt into something else. Whatever you wanted. Something about rearranging molecules or some shit. I don't know a lick 'a science kid. I just know the NaNe changed the way the world worked."

"How?" Crinnan asked.

"Well. Hunger went away that's for damn sure." Karston said. "Age of Dust only lasted about 80 years. Wasn't much of an age at all. After the collapse of the Damarsi Empire, after the humaans took control there was a time of chaos you see. Feudal shit, people was landgrabbin' and makin' claims and trying to bring back the old kingdoms and whatnot. The humaans, you see, there wasn't too many of 'em. I donno how many to be exact, but there was billions of us natives. It took a long time to get us to calm our asses down. Humaans did it though, don't know how, don't know why, but they was a peaceful and patient people. I met a bunch of em in my time. They sure was smart.

Anyway, during the Age of Dust and a good while into the Age of Ancients there was one Hells of a hunger crisis. People was killin' their neighbors for their food, some was killin their neighbors *for* food. Things got real messy and the world wasn't takin' too kindly to it. Progress was bein' made, yes but it wasn't happenin' fast enough. Not until LifeLinks came along. That's when we saw that NaNe business and everyone started bein' fed. People was livin' indefinitely and stayin' pretty the whole time. A lot of my friends ended up goin' to a place called the Afterscape. It was a land that the NaNe took you to that wasn't our world. They say it was made in a computer. They say it became the Hells..."

"Yeah." Crinnan nodded. "That's what I heard too."

"Yeah. I remember the day I was supposed to wake up and go fishin' with my boys. We was all in the Afterscape, see. It was like heaven." Karston's voice lowered as his memories surfaced. "I ain't seen my boys since that day. I know they're all out there. My boys, my wife. My girls. They're all out there, maybe done gone and become touched at this point. I hope not."

Karston tossed his spent cigarette in his cold coffee and sighed. "Anyway, that's my story. Ain't why I pulled you aside though."

"What *did* you want?" Crinnan asked. He walked up to Karston's coffee cup and dropped his cigarette butt in. Karston's face wrinkled up for a moment but then he shrugged. It looked like he thought about being offended but changed his mind.

"That Ander fella." Karston said lowly. "He said somethin' when we first met. That you was workin' on a way to get out of here."

"I don't know what I'm doing." Crinnan replied. "I'm just following voices."

"Voices?" Karston repeated. "You touched?"

"I hope not." Crinnan snorted.

"Well, if you are tryin' to get out of here. Out of the Hells I mean, how you plannin' on doing it?"

"All I know is I need to get to the Seventh Level." Crinnan answered. "Other than that. I'm like you. I don't know much about the science."

"What do you know about, Crinnan?" Karston replied.

"Living." Crinnan shrugged. "Breathing. Eating, drinking. Fucking, fighting... and shitting it all back out."

Karston cocked his head and gave Crinnan an odd look. He squinted his eyes and released a hum. "I heard them words before." He said. He raised a hand and scratched his beard. "Somewhere. Long time ago. Them words mean something. Where'd you hear 'em?"

"Dad used to say it." Crinnan replied. "Way too much."

"Well." Karston shook the thought from his mind. "I reckon I ain't got the time to figure it out right now. Listen. I ain't askin' to come with you or nothin, but. You think if I got to the seventh level then maybe you could get other folk outta here too?"

"I couldn't tell you." Crinnan said.

Karston seemed to get lost in thought for a moment before finally he snorted and shook his head. "I won't keep ya anymore. Pretty girl upstairs might need somebody to keep her warm. Not that it's cold in the Hells... she mean somethin' to you?"

"She used to." Crinnan sighed.

"Well." Karston tilted his head to the side. "Ain't no better time than now to fix that. Hells can get mighty lonesome. Little piece of advice?"

"I don't really..."

"You gon' get it." Karston cut him off. "Whatever you think she needs. You're wrong. You gotta talk to her, don't guess. She'll tell ya if she wants to... and if she wants to then I reckon you might just still mean something to her."

"Thanks..." Crinnan replied.

"Alright then." Karston reached out and shooed Crinnan away. "Get on now. We got work to do in the mornin'."

"Okay... Good night Karston."

"Night, Crinnan."

Chapter Seventeen
Worlds Between

The Third Hell
Sincroft – Karston's Home

Crinnan stepped off the ladder and onto the rickety floor of the attic. It was dark and hot, Crinnan could barely see where he was going. He knelt down and started crawling, looking for a place to rest when his hand inadvertently brushed against a bare arm. Crinnan suddenly felt a pair of eyes on him.

"Don't touch me." He heard Milinka whisper.

"Sorry." Crinnan replied. He pulled his hand away and scooted backwards. "It's hard to see up here."

"Go somewhere else, Crinnan." Milinka said coldly.

"Okay."

Crinnan turned around but he felt like Milinka's eyes were still boring into him. He paused for a moment and thought about Karston's words. Maybe he should try to at least make peace with her? He couldn't deny the feelings that his memories made him feel and he didn't want to fight with her forever. Crinnan bit the inside of his cheek and turned to look behind him.

"So..." Crinnan whispered. "For what it's worth. I'm sorry for not keeping my promise. You deserved better than that."

Crinnan suddenly felt dirty. He wasn't the type of person to apologize. Even if he wronged somebody, he figured they had it coming at least. Everyone had something coming to them in his world... well. Everyone except for Milinka. He didn't want to wrong her; he didn't want to be the reason she felt abandoned or unloved. He waited a moment for her response but was met with silence. Eventually he decided she wasn't going to talk and crawled away.

Crinnan found a flat spot and laid down. The sound of his metal armor clanking together filled the space and he let out a deep sigh as he rested his head against the floor. Karston had been right. As soon as Crinnan was on his back, he realized just how tired he really was. As he lay there in the dark, he thought about his time in the Hells thus far. He thought about the succubus, about the demonic well, and the giant nasty monster that killed him. He thought of Sage and Lucaas, of Milinka and Ander, and finally of Karston. His experiences flashed through his mind and he tried to stay in control, tried to wrestle his own proverbial demons but he ultimately couldn't fight the massive emptiness he felt within himself.

"It's okay Son. You can feel sad." He heard his father's voice in his head. *"Life isn't always easy. Sadness is meant to be felt. Go through it and emerge a better man."*

"Dad…" Crinnan whispered. He thought of his father. Commander Crinnan Jamiso Sr. of the Black Knight Underground Base in Canrom City. Thoughts of everything his father was flashed through his mind and brought to the surface everything Crinnan wasn't or the things he felt like he couldn't be.

Commander Crinnan was a hero. He liberated the country of Exgrane from Govian rule shortly before Crinnan was born. He was strong and smart and cunning. The man, a humaan, always wore a smile on his face and never spoke down to his children. Crinnan's father was a good person. It made Crinnan wonder why he himself wasn't.

"I love you kid."

Crinnan's mind flashed back to a time when he was sixteen years old. After he had been lost in the woods with Milinka, after his father and Captain Bran came to his rescue. He remembered his father taking hold of his shoulders and squaring him up directly in front of him so they were eye to eye. The look of pride in his dad's eyes was able to momentarily wash away the pain he felt in being separated from the girl he had grown to love. In that moment, Crinnan though young, was able to think in a very grown-up way. He realized his father loved him dearly and risked his life to come and save him. He remembered hugging his dad and crying deeply into the man's chest. The memory of his father's arms holding him tight crept over his body, and Crinnan was able to feel a sense of peace.

It was that moment of peace that allowed Crinnan to close his eyes and drift off to sleep.

***

"Hello."

Crinnan was surrounded by blackness. He saw no light, no shadows... there was no floor beneath his feet, no sky above his head. Simply blackness.

"Who's there?" Crinnan called out to the disembodied voice he had heard. His own voice seemed to ripple through the nothingness, echoes being cast out into eternity. He wondered where his words would land, who's ears they would fall upon.

"By now I should say that I hoped you would recognize my voice." The phantom voice returned. "Tis I, Sage, the very one who is trying to bring you home."

"Sage..." Crinnan repeated. "Where are you?"

"I am in my home, young one." Sage replied. "I sleep just as you. My... NaNe has reached out to you, linked with you even in the Hells."

"Is that how you talk to me when I'm awake?" Crinnan asked.

"When you are in a state of simulated consciousness as you experience in the Hells the only way for me to interact with you is through the integrated communication system." Sage answered. "But now, your NaNe have brought you to a place that only you exist in. The Expanse, as we call it. Only you know this land, it is the very world you escape to when you find yourself lost in thought. You go there even though you are not conscious of it. We now stand in the most intimate of homes that you have, and *here* I can find you."

Crinnan felt a tap on his shoulder and he spun around, coming face to face with a form composed of gray wispy smoke. Crinnan took a fearful step back and Sage held out his hands, hoping to calm him.

"Tis I." Sage whispered. He nodded his head and took a gentle step forward. "I have come to meet you where you are most comfortable… where I do not have to fear Govian interception. Here, you are safe."

Crinnan didn't know what to say. He looked to his left and his right, and then sighed. There was nothing but blackness in every direction. Nothing but emptiness…

"What do you want?" Crinnan asked in a low grumble of a voice. "Why are you trying to help me?"

"A logical question, young one." Sage replied. He sat down as if there was a chair behind him, crossing one leg over the other. "But in life, sometimes concerning oneself with the question of why only leads to more questions. I should say it would be in your best interest if you simply accepted that I choose to risk it all to assist you."

"Whatever then." Crinnan shrugged indifferently. Sage was right. The why didn't matter as long as he got out of the Hells.

"How are you doing, Crinnan?" Sage asked with a tone of sincerity. "How are you holding up?"

"I'm fine." Crinnan replied.

"Fine is good." Sage nodded. "Though I should say in most instances it is a mask to hide what you truly feel. Not that it is any of my business. I just want you to know that I am here should you need to talk."

"I don't need to talk." Crinnan whispered. "Let's just focus on getting out."

"And so we shall." Sage nodded. He paused as he idly rubbed his palms up and down his thighs. "Tell me, Crinnan. Are you aware of your impact on the Hells thus far?"

"I'm not aware of shit." Crinnan spat.

"Well then." Sage snorted and let out a chuckle. "Long have I waited. Long have I schemed, planned and labored for this moment. You see, the Hells is an abomination. A desecration of the once great Afterscape that existed. Countless consciousnesses trapped in eternal suffering, more added every day. Who would create such a place? Why would they do such a thing?"

"I don't know." Crinnan answered.

"For power." Sage said with a slow nod. "Lies to cover lies to cover lies so that you submit. Emperor Cidro... in all his twisted wisdom he envisioned a place where he could punish those who defied him. A place that the living could fear, a promise of eternal pain and torment to ensure that the citizenry fall in line. All of Govia's enemies surround you in the Hells. They all lament and beg for the Emperor's forgiveness but will never find solace. You see, Crinnan, fear is the quickest path to power, and the easiest to maintain. The great presidents of the old corporations all burn alongside you, the resistance fighters, the countries who opposed Govian rule... the Black Knights... they all scream for freedom in the Hells..."

"It's not enough to kill someone?" Crinnan asked, a tone of disgust heavy on his tongue. "That's enough for me. When I kill someone, they're forgiven for their crimes. Seems like justice in my eyes."

"Justice is a malleable term I should say." Sage continued. "Like clay in the hands of an artist, it can be whatever the sculptor wishes it... anyway, here we stand. Well. Here I sit, and here you stand. As I said, I have labored for years for this moment. The Hells is about to be turned upside down, Crinnan. My... program... gives the prisoners their ability to fight back. They will rise against those who oppress them, they will turn the demons into prisoners like themselves. Govia will feel the pain of loss. Many thousands will die."

"You're... killing thousands?" Crinnan asked.

"Indeed I am." Sage nodded. "I am at war, Crinnan. Those who are evil enough to take delight in the Hells are those who are being punished. The ones who have rotted and burned for centuries, however, are the ones who will benefit. Their freedom is at hand. The Hells will be undone, and it will be your doing. You and hundreds maybe thousands of others will come home, and then a new fight will begin."

"So I'm not the only one you are freeing?" Crinnan asked.

"The opportunity to escape will be short." Sage said. "Govia will assuredly patch my portal home once it is detected. I foresee an opportunity lasting minutes if we are lucky, but it is also a part of my plan. Once the portal is closed, the Hells will be kept on lockdown. I have another program waiting to be implemented that will lock everyone inside, even if Govia lifts their own lock.

Players and prisoners alike. The prisoners will kill their oppressors, they will get their justice."

"Damn." Crinnan replied. "So how do we do this?"

"All you need to do is keep going, Crinnan." Sage urged. "Get to the Seventh Level as quickly as you can... for now though, I fear it is time for you to wake up. Be strong, young one. Fight like you've never fought before. And then... be free..."

***

Crinnan jerked awake to find Ander kneeling next to him. He held a candle and gently shook Crinnan's shoulder. At first, he was shocked and instinctively reached for his sword, but then he settled and released a groan.

"How long were we out?" He asked.

"In Hells time or real-world time?" Ander replied.

"There's a difference?"

"There is."

"Hells' time then." Crinnan grunted. He pushed his body into a sitting position and gasped as his armor pinched his side. He jerked his body around until his skin was free and then looked over at Ander.

"Three hours." Ander said with a smile. He reached out and gave Crinnan a supportive pat on his back.

"How is this all so realistic?" Crinnan grumbled. "How does my armor pinch me; how can I feel stupid pain like that if the Hells is all in a computer or whatever?"

"A computer?" Ander repeated. He fell silent as his eyes seemed to suddenly go out of focus for a moment. With trembling hands, he reached up and grabbed his head as if he were having a headache. Crinnan watched curiously but didn't interfere. Ander appeared to be having a strange episode of some sort and Crinnan wondered if he should get help.

As quickly as it started, however, it was over. Ander lowered his hands from his head, and then reached up and wiped some sweat from his forehead. Crinnan raised an eyebrow and Ander spoke.

"Yes..." Ander mumbled. His eyes darted around hyperactively for a moment, it looked like he was confused. His tense expression quickly faded, however, and Ander locked eyes with Crinnan. "Yes, it is. The Hells *is* in a computer my chil..." Ander's eye twitched as he corrected himself. He shook his head as if he disagreed with his own thoughts, and then composed himself. "...My friend. The answers which you seek are somehow buried within a millennium of memories in my mind. A life long-past, a buried conscience, one I do not recognize..." His voice had lowered to a whisper.

"What the fuck are you talking about?" Crinnan asked. He scrunched up his face at Ander's strange behavior.

"NaNe was... redemption." Ander whispered, looking down at his hands. "It was life anew, an opportunity for the people of Duraan to start again. The... NaNe forms every crease and corner of the Hells. The ground which you stand upon, the air you breathe. The way your armor pinches your skin... the NaNe whispers it into being and then it is so."

"Well that fucking answers nothing but thanks for trying." Crinnan said, rolling his eyes. "Let's..."

"I am not finished, boy!" Ander hissed. He snatched out and firmly took hold of Crinnan's upper arm. Crinnan looked down at the sudden uncharacteristic assault, and then glared deeply at Ander.

"You have three seconds to let go of me." Crinnan warned."

"I..." Ander shook his head violently and immediately released Crinnan. Even with Ander's hand removed, Crinnan still felt the pressure against his skin. It was surprising, an impressive strength that Crinnan had not expected from the wiry, mustached vampre.

"I apologize, Crinnan." Ander whispered. "I do not know what came over me." Ander straightened his back, composing himself and cleared his throat. "I... seem to have misplaced my thoughts. For now, let us head downstairs that we may set into motion the events of the day." Ander's eyes bored into Crinnan with a pleadingly apologetic look and he maintained his gaze for a few moments before he turned toward the ladder that led back to the main level.

"What the fuck was that all about?" Crinnan whispered to himself when Ander was out of earshot. That entire interaction was strange to him. Ander seemed... upset about something in a way.

Crinnan ultimately shrugged. It wasn't his problem how Ander felt and whatever was going on in the vampre's mind was for Ander to work out on his own. It was certainly the last thing Crinnan cared to worry about.

"Well whatever then." Crinnan said as he walked toward the ladder. Thoughts of the "dream" he'd had in the realm of blackness filled his mind as he walked the short distance. For a moment, Crinnan wondered whether the dream was real. He wondered if there even was such a thing as "real" anymore. He chewed his lip in contemplation as he stopped before the splintery ladder. He would ask Sage next time he heard from him. Surely he would be able to provide clarification. Finally, Crinnan buried his thoughts and climbed down the ladder, deciding to focus on what the day held.

Chapter Eighteen
Shitter's Full

The Third Hell
Sincroft – Karston's Home

Attention Citizens: We thank you for your patience and understanding during these confusing times. We are aware that the bug we have all been experiencing together has yielded new and troubling effects, including the ability for prisoners to deal damage to citizens. We ask that all citizens find safety in any of the strongholds for the duration of the lockdown while we work to remedy this situation.

To all low ranked or inexperienced citizens: Do not engage the prisoners. We have not yet corrected the respawn bug, if you are killed by a prisoner you too will become a prisoner. We ask that you do not panic, simply find shelter.

To all experienced citizens: While we will not force you to do anything, we do advise finding shelter. The members of the military that are currently logged in are working to suppress the prisoner uprising. You may assist them, and if you do the rewards will be great, but we ask that do so warily. Do not, I repeat, do NOT engage groups of touched that number five or more.

This situation is in the process of being rectified, citizens. We thank you for your patience and cooperation. Praise Dura'ana, Praise Cidro.

"By the Brothers what have you done Sage?" Crinnan asked as he stopped and listened. "*Everyone* can fight now?" Crinnan paused as he walked and looked down at the floor.

"Wait, if everyone can fight... that means... show me my ranking!"

Avatar Information Sheet

...

Name: PrettyKitty6969420

Rank: 28,070,737,140

Percentile: 95%

Player Rating: 1 Star

...

HP: 190/190 (100 Base + 90 Buff)

Shields: 245 (100 Base + 90 Buff + 55 Armor)

Damage Output: 2x Base (1x Base + .9x Buff + .1x Weapon)

Speed: 1x Base (1x Base)

"What the fuck!" Crinnan snapped. He watched as his ranking grew higher and higher by the second. "Fucking Sage!"

He realized what was going on and then remembered Sage had mentioned empowering everyone back in the "Expanse" or whatever it had been called. The prisoners were rising up with their new ability to fight. They had all been turned into players, and the entire ranking system had become even more volatile.

"At least twenty-six billion prisoners..." Crinnan whispered, shaking his head. "This is... fucked up..." It must have happened while he slept. The Hells had broken into war overnight and Crinnan's ranking had been completely wiped out. He sighed as he realized he was going to have to do some serious killing if he wanted to rank back up to where he needed to be.

"Sit." Karston's voice broke through Crinnan's thoughts as he walked into the kitchen. Crinnan noticed Milinka and Ander were both seated at the table and before them were crude wooden plates piled with heaping helpings of grey mush. Milinka stared deeply at the "food" before her, with a look of disgust spread across her face. Crinnan grinned at her expression and remembered the spoiled brat he had first met back in the Woolshire Highlands back in Kamlot.

Ander, on the other hand, eagerly forked the goop into his mouth. He wore a look of delight as he stuffed his face and moaned as each spoonful passed his lips. "Truly, a delight to be able to wake up to breakfast." Ander commented with a full mouth. "Something about it manifests great feelings of nostalgia. I thank you for that, Master Karston."

"Well alright." Karston shrugged indifferently as he leaned against the countertop and drank his coffee. "Glad you could join us, Crinnan."

Crinnan glanced over and rolled his eyes after Karston made his presence known. Karston in turn extended an open palm toward the table, gesturing for Crinnan to sit. Crinnan did as he was told and took a seat.

"What is this stuff anyway?" Milinka asked as she poked at the thick wobbling pile of mush in front of her.

"You try it yet?" Karston called back. He had his back to her as he prepared Crinnan a plate.

"I did… not…" Milinka replied.

"You should!" Ander insisted. "It's not every day that you get to eat in the Hells! Truly, an unexpected treat!"

"Truly…" Milinka repeated.

Karston walked up and dropped a plate in front of Crinnan. Crinnan looked down and noticed that the grey mush jiggled like gelatin but looked much denser. It was thick and lumpy and had no smell. Crinnan stared at his food and then looked up at Karston.

"Yeah, I'm not eating that." Crinnan said, sliding the plate back toward Karston.

"I think I will have to pass too." Milinka agreed, pushing her plate away as well. Karston raised an eyebrow and placed his hands on his hips.

"Well, your highnesses, I apologize that my hospitality was not up to snuff for you two." Karston said with a hint of scorn in his voice. "Next time I'll ensure I have big fat juicy steaks and taters for your tender taste buds. I reckon I can conjure up a few flutes of champagne as well for you too, you precious things."

"Oh fine." Milinka said, pulling her plate back to herself. "You don't have to make us feel bad." Once again she stared at her gooey meal and her nostrils flared. Slowly, she dug her spoon in and gently brought it to her lips, cringing as the paste hit her tongue.

"Oh, that's weird." Milinka said, her expression softening.

"You like it?" Karston asked, leaning against the table with a smug look on his face.

"I wouldn't say *like.*" Milinka replied. She brought another spoonful to her lips and popped it in her mouth. "It tastes like... bread. It's not bad, what is it?"

"Gravlin shit." Karston said.

Milinka slowly swallowed and gently placed her spoon back on the table. "As in, parts of Gravlin?"

"Nah." Karston replied. "It's Gravlin poop. Fills your belly, makes you a little tougher too depending on how much you eat."

Crinnan snickered and stood from the table. "See where manners get you, Lady Milinka?"

"Shut your mouth." Milinka replied. A new look of disgust was plastered over her face and she slowly stood from her chair and looked to Karston. "Where is... your bathroom..."

"Shithole's out the front door, take a left and you'll see a small building. I warn you though..." Karston said. Milinka didn't waste any time. She hurried out the front door with her hand raised to her mouth. Karston shrugged and looked at Crinnan.

"...shitter's full." Karston snorted with a half-smile. Crinnan couldn't help but feel an evil sense of joy at that.

"Twas a delight." Ander released a tender burp and pushed his plate forward. "A wonderful treat."

"Ander, you heard when Karston said it was shit, right?" Crinnan asked.

"Oh yes. I knew what it was." Ander replied. "We are in the Hells, dear boy, haven't you been paying attention? Here you eat what is available."

"Or not at all." Crinnan added. "We don't need to eat to survive, right?"

"Correct." Ander replied.

"Eating is a way to strengthen yourself in the cities." Karston added. "Eating can give you increased damage output or speed or whatever for a time, it's a perk of staying alive in the cities. Outside of here, we prisoners have no ability to fight or any way to really live for any amount of time so eating can increase the probability of our survival here... even if it is gravlin shit."

"But that's all changed now." Ander said. "Thanks to Crinnan's benefactor, no doubt, it seems the prisoners now have the ability to fight back, to defend themselves. Everything has changed, I foresee the world outside Sincroft being unrecognizable once the other prisoners discover this."

"That'd be something to see for sure." Karston commented as he shrugged on his duster jacket. He clipped on his pistol belt and slid a knife into a sheathe on his thigh and then placed his wide brimmed hat over his blonde dreadlocks.

"Time to get going then." Karston said. "We got some ground to cover if we want to get you three outta my hair today... which... we *do* want to do."

Crinnan joined Ander and Karston at the front door. As he neared, he smiled, for he heard Milinka heaving outside. He didn't necessarily *want* her to experience discomfort, but he figured he'd might as well enjoy it while it lasted.

"We ready then boys?" Karston asked as he reached out and grabbed the doorknob. Crinnan nodded and the trio walked outside.

"Come on tough lady." Karston said as he strode past Milinka. She had apparently opted not to vomit in the outhouse, choosing instead to throw up all over the dusty alley road. Crinnan wondered if that had to do with the fact that the shitter was full as Karston had so eloquently put it, or simply because her stomach was just as sensitive as it had been back when she was a teenager. Crinnan smiled at the memory that followed.

Crinnan recalled having speared a fish in the river that the two had jumped into from a cliff that had to have been many dozens of feet in the air. He'd taken a bullet from the Govians that had driven the two of them toward the cliff, but it ended up being a superficial wound. All that was harmed was Crinnan's pride, for he recalled crying like a baby in front of Milinka as she dug the projectile out of his flesh.

The fish was long and slimy. "It looks like a penis..." Milinka had said. "Well. I think."

Crinnan remembered laughing at that. In his experience penises had not been slimy... or very long for that matter. He remembered handing the "penisfish" as it became known to Milinka and the look of disgust that spread over the spoiled noble brat's face as she wrapped her hands around it. The fish wasn't dead, it squirmed and wiggled in her grasp and she leaned her body back as far away from it as she could, turning her head in revulsion. Eventually, the girl broke into tears leading Crinnan to take the fish and did his best to clean it. That was when Milinka threw up.

Convincing Milinka to eat the fish had been a difficult task. Seeing its insides had repulsed her and severely turned her off to eating the creature's flesh. Eventually she ate, however, and she even said she liked it.

Ander nudged Crinnan in his side and forced him to snap out of his reverie. Karston had walked over to a black wooden building that looked like it was about to fall over and slid a door open. "Come on!" Karston yelled, the two words melding into one. "Get your lazy crunchy asses up! Let's go, hyah!" Crinnan watched as a dozen touched shambled out of the building and lined up on either side of Karston.

"Follow me." Karston ordered them and walked back to the rest of the group.

"Hopefully we don't need them." Karson said as he approached. "But if we do, they are here."

"How do you control them like that?" Milinka asked, wiping the corners of her mouth with her arm. "Why do they listen to you?"

"Because I don't kill em." Karston replied. "I give 'em shelter, food. I bathe 'em and give 'em scraps of garbage to play with. Hells sometimes I even talk to 'em in those few moments that they snap outta their psychosis."

"What do you mean you bathe them?" Milinka asked, cocking her head. "I haven't seen any water here."

"Dust bath, precious." Karston replied. "Cleans 'em up good. Animals all over the world have cleaned themselves with dust since the dawn of time. Works fine for the touched too."

"Dust." Milinka sighed. "Of course."

The group exited the alley and emerged on one of the many sidewalks of Sincroft. Crinnan noted that not much was different. The city was still as sullen and depressing as it had been when he had fallen asleep. Its inhabitants, seemingly nearly the point of being touched themselves, shambled around in their dirty unkempt clothes. They didn't talk, they didn't laugh. They just walked. Crinnan couldn't help but stare at them as he walked.

"If I ever end up like that, shoot me." Crinnan muttered to the group. Milinka snorted and looked up at him.

"You're *already* like that." She said. "Sulking, silent. Need your space like the edgy badass warrior you think you are."

"Can I have *one* day where you don't try to insult me as painfully as you can?" Crinnan barked at her. "Like, I don't *need* you to be a bitch to me. Believe it or not, it's not something that helps me in any way."

"Oh, I'm not trying to help. Just trying to see if you still cry, sad boy." She smiled innocently and shoved Crinnan in the shoulder. Coincidentally it was in the exact same spot she had pulled the bullet out so many years ago... and for some reason... he kind of liked the shove...

"Will you two shut the Hells up?" Karston snapped. "By the Brothers, your incessant bitching and moaning is the most annoying thing I've heard in centuries and I live in Hell! Shit makes me glad I'm dead."

Ander chuckled lightly at Karston's words and Crinnan sneered at him. He looked over at Milinka who was once again glaring at him and all he could do was shrug his shoulders and let it all go for the moment.

"Alright, now y'all listen good." Karston said once peace had returned to their group. "Croftkeeper and city gates spawn in random places throughout the day but they're always together. Croftkeeper guards the gates, see." Karston called back to the others. "Now I ain't under some sort of delusion that y'alls gonna actually beat him. I hope for your own sakes that you do, but it's pretty unlikely. Either way, you won't be in Sincroft much longer. Y'all'll start back at the First Level or proceed to the next level. Doesn't matter to me.

One thing I've gathered 'bout the Croftkeeper is that every day there is one location in specific he for sure spawns at. City walls by the marketplace. That's where we're headed. We go there, we wait, and then when he spawns, I'm goin' back home and leavin y'all to it. And *that* will be the end of our agreement, fair enough?"

"Sounds good." Crinnan said.

"Fantastic." Karston said. "Just need to follow this road til it ends to get to the marketplace. Here soon we…"

"Get on the ground!" An authoritative voice suddenly shouted. "By order of Bishop General Klaus, you are all under arrest!"

"What the fuck!" Crinnan shouted at the sudden yelling. He looked around and saw nobody. Nobody that is, until he felt something hard slam against his temple. In a daze, he stumbled to the ground and suddenly felt a great force on top of him.

"Face on the ground, fucker!" The voice continued. It was a Govian accented voice and its tone demanded attention. Crinnan thought back to the fight with the dagger wielding Govian assassin after he saved Milinka. He realized at that point that he was a target… a target of Bishop General Klaus, leader of the militarized Govian police force: The Inquisition.

"Hands behind your back!" The Govian commanded, planting a knee into Crinnan's back. "You're coming with us!"

Chapter Nineteen
Crinnan the Cheater

The Third Hell
Sincroft

"Let her go." Another voice ordered. From the ground, Crinnan watched as Milinka disappeared down the street. "We're here for him... Hey, shithead! Face. On. The. Ground! What about that do you not understand!"

"Let me go!" Crinnan growled as his face was smashed into the cobblestone street. "What do you want!"

"You're under arrest, terrorist!" The first voice yelled at Crinnan.

"For what!" Crinnan furiously replied. He tried to wriggle free, but the Govian slapped him in the back of the head and pushed his knee harder into Crinnan's back.

"Alteration of core system mechanics, and you as a prisoner are suspected of conspiring with a terrestrial party! Now shut your bitch mouth and hold still so I can get these cuffs on you!"

"Oh okay." Crinnan said, rolling his eyes. "Here, let me open my butthole for you too."

At that, and with all the strength he had in him, he rolled to his back, throwing the Govian off balance. Crinnan scrambled backward, bumping into Ander and the Govian that had neutralized him, and felt the barrel of a pistol smack him against the side of the head. For a moment, Crinnan was stunned, unable to properly move his body, and then he heard gunshots.

The world around him was a blur and he could barely make out the frenzied movement. Complete magazines of small caliber munitions were discharged and then he heard shouting, growling and sounds of tearing. After a few moments, Crinnan's blurry vision consolidated and he was able to see clearly again. He looked around to find a few dead touched, and the rest feasting on the fallen bodies of the Govians that had attacked them.

"Damn it all!" Karston angrily shouted into Crinnan's ear. He felt the elf's strong hands seize him and lift him to his feet. "Get up you little shit! Come on!"

Crinnan felt a warm trickle down the side of his face and instinctively reached up to touch it. He pulled his hand back for inspection and saw more blood than he expected. Confused, he looked around and saw Ander standing over the bodies of the mangled Govian soldiers.

"Tis uncommon for *these* people to show up." Ander contemplated contemplatively. "They generally only appear when conflict between players needs solving. That they would show up to… arrest us, as they said, is a very curious event." Ander twisted the tip of his moustache and paced back and forth. "Truly, Crinnan, your claims *must* have some sort of truth to them if these soldiers are here."

"They're… Govians…" Crinnan said, keeping pressure on his wounded head. "Inquisitors… militarized police force… judge jury and executioner on the streets of the major cities of Duraan."

"Intriguing." Ander said. Crinnan thought the vampre was going to twist his moustache clean off if he kept fucking with it. "I do wish I knew more about the current era, but alas. I barely remember my own…"

"Yeah, well," Crinnan grunted as he took a few pained steps forward. "Not really much time for that… Milinka ran off, we have to find her. We also have to get the fuck out of here, that Govian said…"

The sound of rapid gunfire interrupted Crinnan, and he watched as multiple touched fell to the ground, dead. "Find cover!" Crinnan shouted as he started to run, keeping his head low. He passed Ander and Karston and barely registered the bullets ricocheting off his armor. He was being targeted heavily, and he watched as his chest armor flickered and disappeared from existence, leaving only the dingy shirt he had on beneath. Crinnan didn't even have time to think before multiple rounds pierced his back and exploded out his chest. He fell to the ground, crashing face-first into the cobblestone.

Burnt Iron Cuirass Destroyed.

Effects Removed

...

Shields: 0/225

HP: 10/190

...

You are bleeding. Death is imminent.

"By the Brothers..." Crinnan painfully choked. "This is... fucking... bullshit..."

Connection Established, user: Vajinious, user: PrettyKitty6969420

...

>Bloodgames v.666.3

>HELLSCAPE by FARSEER

...

...

>System Override

...

...

>emhealrecent.sli execute

>ERROR emhealrecent.sli not compatible

>emhealrecent2.sli execute

>Script Accepted. Please Wait...

...

...

...

>emhealrecent2.sli executed – user: PrettyKitty6969420 health status: full

>emshieldrecent.sli execute

>Script Accepted. Please Wait...

...

...

...

>emshieldrecent.sli executed – user: PrettyKitty6969420 shield status: full

> /ispawn 119 execute

>ERROR command failed. You do not have sufficient permissions.

>/SU execute

>ERROR command failed. You do not have sufficient permissions.

>/SU [SM] execute

>ERROR command failed. You do not have sufficient permissions.

>>USER: Vajinious terminated due to three failed commands.

Connection Closed

>>USER: Vajinious physical location logged.

>>>LOCATION: Izla'Axi

>>>LOCATION: Belhaas

>>>LOCATION: ...ERROR data corruption. ERROR traklog323423432322229345.tex DOES NOT EXIST

...

```
...

...

Connection Established, user: LucLynx3, user: PrettyKitty6969420

>/SU execute

>Command accepted. SuperUser Mode enabled.

>/ispawn 119 [44232001423932 INV] [q:2] execute

>Command accepted. Item 119 q:2 added to user:44232001423932 INV

>/ispawn 219 [44232001423932 INV] [q:600] execute

>Command accepted. Item 229 q:600 added to user:44232001423932 INV

>/refreshblueprint user: PrettyKitty6969420

>ERROR command failed. Command not recognized.

>/refreshblueprint user: PrettyKitty6969420

>Command accepted. User: PrettyKitty6969420 Blueprint refreshed

>>/LSCAN user: LucLynx3

>user: LucLynx3 disconnected

Connection Closed

>>LSCAN failed. User not found.
```

Crinnan's pain faded as if it had never been there in the first place. The strange green text disappeared from his vision, and he quickly got to his feet. Bullets pinged off his body but he barely even felt them. He suddenly seemed impervious to damage... he looked down at his hands and noticed they glowed with the blue shield light... and he also noticed two revolvers laying on the ground in front of him, and an ammo belt around his waist. None of those items had been there before he fell.

"Sage..." Crinnan whispered as the weapons found their way into his hands. Back home, Crinnan, his sword and his revolver composed the triptych that had spelled out the end to so many of his enemies' lives. With a skilled fluidity and grace that he had honed over many years of practice, experience, and instruction under some of the best he could find, once Crinnan found his groove in battle he at times could be nearly unstoppable.

...except that time that he *was* stopped and ended up in the Hells...

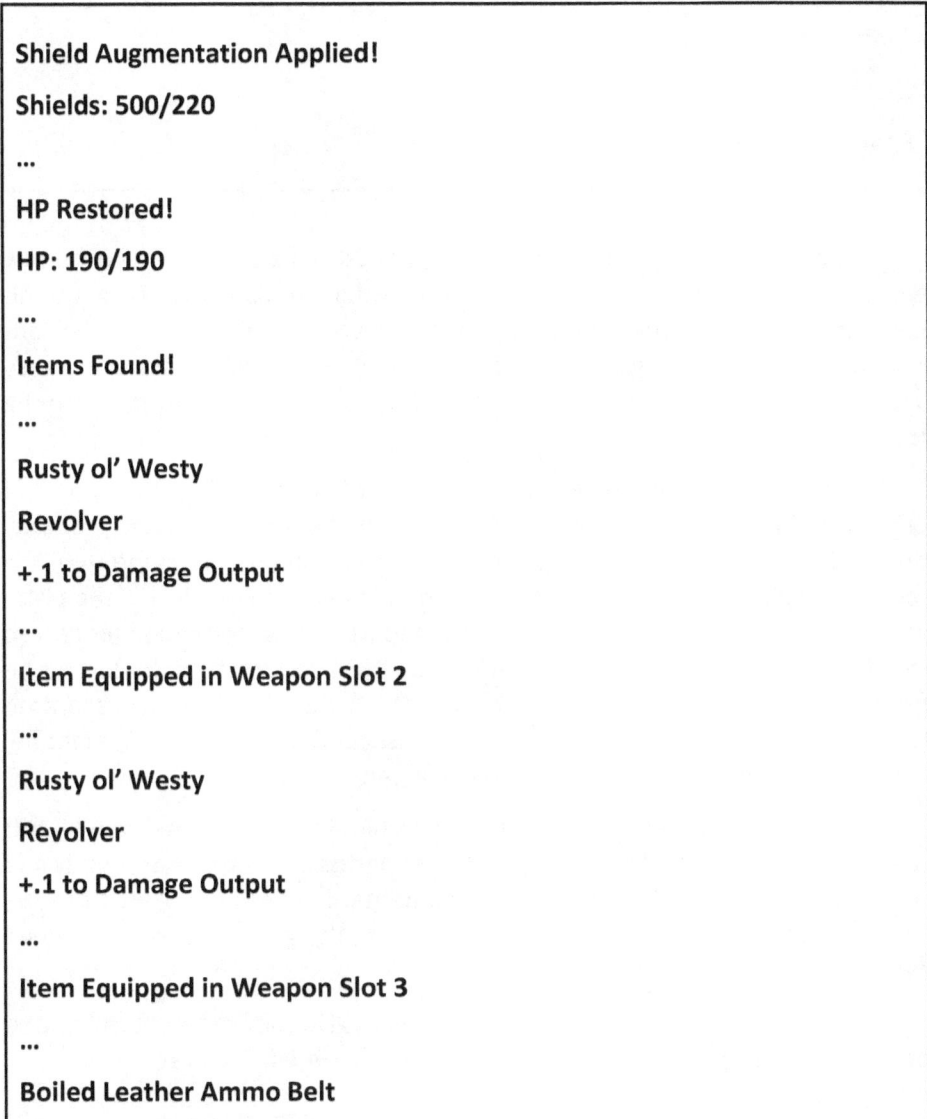

Shield Augmentation Applied!

Shields: 500/220

...

HP Restored!

HP: 190/190

...

Items Found!

...

Rusty ol' Westy

Revolver

+.1 to Damage Output

...

Item Equipped in Weapon Slot 2

...

Rusty ol' Westy

Revolver

+.1 to Damage Output

...

Item Equipped in Weapon Slot 3

...

Boiled Leather Ammo Belt

> **Dispenses ammunition for firearms.**
>
> **+5 Shields**
>
> **...**
>
> **Revolver Ammunition x600**
>
> **Ammunition for Revolver**
>
> **...**
>
> **Revolver Ammunition Stored in Ammo Belt**

Crinnan had no idea what had just happened but due to the text he saw earlier, he imagined Sage and Lucaas had something to do with it. He got to his feet and didn't waste any time raising the revolvers in front of him. The Govians kept firing their carbines, but their fire rate had slowed and looks of surprise and sudden terror spread over their faces. Crinnan took aim and squeezed the triggers.

The first bullet found its home in the chest of a Govian directly in front of Crinnan. Crinnan swung his pistol to the right, fired another shot and promptly dropped another. In a single fluid movement and using the momentum of the recoil from his first shot, his left arm curled over his scalp, the top of the pistol gently caressing the right side of his head, and then he straightened his arm so that the weapon was aimed at one of the two Govians directly to his left. As he fired, he pivoted his body, once again using the force from the recoil, and fired the pistol in his right hand only a fraction of a second later. The two Govians fell backwards clumsily, leaving only one Govian left.

Crinnan's 180-degree spin concluded with him firing two shots from his left revolver, and two shots from his right. Bullets perforated the Govian's body and the carbine flew from his hands as he momentarily danced in place from the impact of the projectiles. As the being's back hit the ground, Crinnan stepped forward and stood over him.

"Why are you here?" Crinnan asked, kneeling. He shoved the barrel of one of his revolvers up under the person's chin and frowned. "Who sent you!"

"F...fuck you, rebel..." The Govian hissed back between groans. "W...we will never talk."

Crinnan fired his pistol, relieving the Govian of his brains, and stood up, turning to the other four Inquisitors he had shot. One was in the process of clumsily getting to his feet, and Crinnan shot him in the ribs. He quickly walked toward the soldier and stood over him.

"Why are you here?" Crinnan's voice was sterner, and the writhing Govian looked up at him and spit a glob of blood in his direction. Without hesitation, Crinnan shot the Inquisitor in his forehead, and turned to another.

"Why are you here!?" The query continued, Crinnan growing angrier with each Govian he visited. He had one bullet left in each of his guns, and three Govians remaining. The one he stood over looked up at him trembling with tears in his eyes and arms extended, silently begging for mercy.

"Keep quiet, Eshan!" One of the other downed Govians roared. Without looking, Crinnan reached out the pistol in his right hand and silenced the shouting Govian. He noticed that despite all the killing he was doing; he wasn't receiving any ranking gains. He then knelt and held the barrel of the pistol in his left hand against the Govian's lips.

"Do you want to die?" Crinnan growled, tapping the barrel against the being's exposed teeth. "I don't care about you. I don't care about anyone in your fucking country. I want to know... why are you here?"

"I..." The Govian whispered. His voice was trembling, he was terrified. "I have a child... please..."

Crinnan snorted but didn't pull the trigger. Thoughts of his own father flashed through his mind like lightning and in his moment of hesitation, the two surviving Govians suddenly vanished. Looking back and forth between where they had laid, Crinnan sighed and stood to his feet.

Govian Inquisitors in the Hells... and they didn't give ranking when they died... the thought of it was concerning. Players were problematic enough, but... trained Govian police and soldiers? That was a thought that concerned Crinnan greatly, and even more concerning was the fact that they had suddenly vanished. Crinnan surmised that the Govian lockdown didn't apply to people Govia specifically sent in. Typical.

All throughout his latter teenage years and into his twenties Crinnan had faced off against the Govian military. Never in full scale war, always in guerilla or ambush style situations as was common with Century Squad. Crinnan had been shot, stabbed, blown up and beaten to a pulp in his time but a Govian had never had the pleasure of taking his life.

Despite that fact, however, the Govian military was not to be trifled with. Crinnan had never personally fought Govia's heavily augmented special forces, the Specters as they were called, or the Inquisition's Reapers and their power armor. He had seen them before, but senior members of Century Squad, Captain Bran or Sergeants Mace, Kavin or Marka had fought them. Crinnan remembered watching one of Century's former Sergeants, Kaars, fight against and lose his head to a Govian Specter.

Crinnan had only fought the grunts that made up the bulk of the Govian military. The soldiers he had just killed were exactly that, grunts. He knew that it was the duty of every Govian adult to serve five years in one of the branches of the military. The grunts were Govia's citizenry, young people between the ages of twenty and twenty-five. Any soldier older than that was in the military by choice, and they were always a greater threat...

"Why can't we log out!" Crinnan heard the disembodied voice of one of the dead Govians shout. "I can't leave!"

Crinnan smiled at this revelation. Govia could send them in and pull them out when they desired, but if they died in the Hells they were stuck there like any other player.

"Shut up, Daamron!" Another yelled. "Let's just figure this out..."

Crinnan thought over the implications of what was going on, it was his general understanding that for someone to enter the Hells without dying they had to somehow "log in" based on the terminology he had heard thus far. He wondered what "logging in" meant. Was it some kind of magic, did some mage have to cast some sort of spell that sent their "NaNe" as he had heard it called to where he was? His head ached as he tried to wrap his mind around all of it.

"I've had about enough of this shit for one day." Karston blurted, snapping Crinnan out of his thoughts. "I got half a mind to turn around right now. Y'all got those... those Govian fellas chasing you down?"

"Apparently…" Crinnan replied, immediately dismissing Karston's words. "We need to find Milinka though, and then get to the Croftkeeper and get the fuck out of this city. Come on."

***

Milinka Emmal, the only daughter of Commander Dorax Emmal of Kamlot, leaned against a moist brick wall, resting for a moment after running from the ambush. She knew she would be no good to anyone with her face mushed against the ground, she hated the thought of running away, but they were outnumbered… and outgunned.

"Guns." Milinka spat, shaking her head. "Govians in the Hells with guns… This fucking place just keeps getting… more and more ridiculous." She rubbed the back of her neck with a free hand and couldn't help but heavily sigh at the position she had found herself in.

"Fucking hate this shit." She pounded her fist against the wall and then rested her forehead against the brick. Tears slowly crept down her cheeks as she thought of all that she had experienced thus far… the many deaths, the brutality, the rape and torture and pain… everything she thought she was had been broken down, destroyed and it seemed that nothing was left of the strong Vice Commander that she had once been. How then, she thought, was she to save anyone else? How was she to save… Crinnan?

"Of all the people on the planet…" She sharply whispered. "Why him? Why did *he* have to be the one to save me? Why is *he* here?" She couldn't lie to herself and say she was disappointed. The very sight of him had exhumed feelings she hadn't fully felt since she was a teenager.

"He's a shithead." She whispered. "They're all shitheads…"

"I agree." A voice said from behind her. "All males are bastards."

Milinka quickly spun, raising one of her axes and holding the blade against the neck of a petite fairess behind her. The shoeless dirty pink haired female adorned in torn rags and a belly shirt stood smiling.

"Who are you?" Milinka hissed. It was one of the few occasions where she had heard any of the denizens of the Hells speak. "What are you doing here?"

"I have come to help you." The fairess said plainly. "Surely, you remember me?"

"I've never met you in my life." Milinka spat back.

The dusty fairess smiled warmly and reached up, gently pushing the axe aside. "We met long ago in the forests of the Woolshire Highlands of Kamlot. I found you there, alone and afraid... separated from the boy you loved. It was my job to either capture or kill you, but I did neither. I reported to my superiors that I could not find you... do you remember what I told you?"

"What?" Milinka asked, dumbfounded. A memory of exactly that flashed through her mind. She stared at the fairess, not recognizing her features or her voice. The Govian female who had spared her so long had been an elf with red hair...

The fairess reached behind her and produced a blue beret, one that Govian junior officers wore. She placed the beret atop her matted hair and for a moment the color of her eyes turned green and her hair flashed a dark red.

"Do you remember now, my friend?" The fairess asked, taking a step closer. "Do you remember what I told you?"

"He will find you..." Milinka whispered. "Protect him..."

The fairess smiled and nodded. "I am here with you." She said. "This... avatar is a sort of proxy for my presence. I am here, and I am not. I have seen what Crinnan is trying to accomplish, and I have... for the most part hidden it from the rest of Govia."

"Why?" Milinka asked, dumbfounded. "Why would you... care to do such a thing"

"Because like you, I love that boy." The fairess said, pausing for Milinka to absorb her words. "Milinka, I know your thoughts. I know how you feel, for I too have been imprisoned, tortured... forced upon... this world is not kind to us."

Milinka stared at the fairess for a moment, listening to her words and examining her expressions. She could have sliced into her neck, hacked her head free from its body. She didn't *have* to believe a word that was being said, but... something compelled her to.

"Who are you?" Milinka whispered, letting her axe fall to her side. "Why do you... love him?"

The fairess smiled warmly and reached up, gently and supportively grabbing Milinka's shoulder. "Because he is my brother, Milinka." The fairess whispered in response. "And I am all that is protecting you two from Govia learning the extent of your cooperation with the Life Links remnant. I see what is being planned, I see the culmination of power in the Seventh Level. If you get there, you *will* escape."

"What is your name?" Milinka whispered. The fairess hesitated for a moment, and then reached up, gently caressing Milinka's cheek.

"I am Bishop General Sarasin Fyr of the Govian Empire." She replied. "And I am here to ensure that Sajinious Lynx is successful... and for now I must go. Keep my avatar safe, take her with you. I will return to you soon."

Chapter Twenty
Dali

The Third Hell
Sincroft

"By the Brothers where is she!" Crinnan barked as he, Karston and Ander jogged through the streets searching for Milinka. "There's too many... fucking move!" Crinnan shoved past a group of the mute Sincroftians. "Too many of them to get fucking anywhere!"

"My friend, have you ever considered therapy?" Ander asked, turning his head toward Crinnan. "You seem... to have a lot of rage inside you. Perhaps..."

"Shut up, Ander." Crinnan snapped. "I don't need your help." Ander shrugged and the trio moved onward, continuing their search for Milinka.

"We're wasting daylight looking for her." Karston said as they walked. "We only have a small window of time to get to and kill the Croftkeeper."

"We're not leaving her." Crinnan snapped. "If we don't find her today then we try again tomorrow... and there's no fucking daylight here, we're not wasting shit."

"Fair enough." Karston replied in a less than jovial tone. "But I ain't doing this every day."

"Go left." Crinnan heard Sage instruct in his mind. *"I should say I'm glad you got my gifts."*

"Sage?" Crinnan asked aloud.

"Yes, boy." Sage replied. *"Tis I indeed. I would have spoken sooner, but my account has been compromised and deleted. The act of providing you with protection and weaponry exposed me, it is only a matter of time before Govia finds me. Worry not though, for I will prevail. For now, I am communicating with you via Lucaas' account. How are you feeling?"*

"Oh, just great." Crinnan replied with a roll of his eyes. "Why do you even ask that?"

"I understand." Sage chuckled. *"We will get you out of there soon enough. Keep going down this street, you will come upon an alley on your left shortly. There you will find who I believe to be Milinka... best of luck Crinnan. We will talk soon."*

"Speaking with your friend again?" Ander asked with a smile.

"Yeah." Crinnan said. "Milinka is just ahead."

"How is he," Ander asked, "our great savior I mean?"

"I'm sure he's fine." Crinnan replied. "He's not in The Hells like us."

"What a joy." Ander said. "I cannot recall what it feels like to be in the real world. Surely it will be a glorious day when we return."

Crinnan shrugged his shoulders. "It's brighter." He said.

"The Brothers do wonders for us psychologically." Karston added. "We're not made to live in the darkness."

"Speak for yourself." Ander said, referring to his vampre race. "I do know that my people thrive when the moon is out."

"Ah, yeah." Karston nodded. "You Damarsi shits don't count."

"The Age of Blood would suggest otherwise, elf." Ander replied. "If I recall my history properly, wasn't it the Damarsi who controlled the world?"

"Yup." Karston said. "And then you lost. To humaan aliens."

"To people who had no business on this planet." Ander corrected. "People who forced their way here, and then dissolved a kingdom that wasn't theirs. The Damarsi were the rightful rulers of this world."

"Not this world." Karston said. "The... Globians or whatever are the rulers of this world."

"Shut up." Crinnan snapped. "She should be right up here."

The trio rounded a corner into the alley that Sage had told Crinnan of. Immediately, Crinnan spotted Milinka and his heart dropped. Goosebumps formed all over his body and he felt a flush of warmth cascade over him. He wanted to run to her, to scoop her up and tell her that everything was okay and that it would all be fine... but he couldn't allow himself. Instead, he furrowed his brow and stomped forward.

"Thanks for the fucking help Milinka!" Crinnan blurted. "Glad we know we can depend on you when shit gets rough!"

The words seemed to pass right through Milinka. She looked over at Crinnan and while she didn't smile, her eyebrows raised and her eyes seemed to brighten. She hurried over to him and began to open her arms to hug him but stopped herself. She looked him up and down, noticing the faint blue glowing light, and gently reached out and placed her hand on his arm.

"Crinnan." She said softly as she lowered her head and closed her eyes. "I'm glad you made it."

"Uh..." Crinnan didn't know what to say. He had not expected to be met with anything but hostility from the girl which was why he came in strong. But there she was, saying nice things. He shifted uncomfortably and awkwardly nodded his head.

"Yeah, I'm glad... you're alive too." Was all he could say.

"I'm sorry I ran." Milinka continued. "I thought if I got away and you guys got captured then at least I could come back and save you. Looks like I should have just stuck around. I'm sorry I let you down."

"Are you okay?" Crinnan asked. "Why are you being... reasonable?"

"Because I'm tired, Crinnan." Milinka said with a heavy sigh. "It takes energy being mad at you all the time." She gave his shoulder a squeeze and turned to Karston. "Do we still have time to get to the Croftkeeper?"

"Sure." Karston shrugged in a gesture of apathy. "Unless y'all have some kind of other bullshit waiting for you. Which wouldn't surprise me."

"Me either." Ander added. "Trouble seems to follow us... speaking of trouble, who is this young lady you have met, Milinka?"

Milinka turned toward the other and opened her mouth to speak, but the fairess stepped forward on her own accord.

"I am Dali." She said with a high-pitched voice. "Milinka here... saved me from a player who was threatening to..." Dali looked down at the ground and shook her head.

"She's coming with us." Milinka added. "She's a good person. I can't leave her here in Sincroft, not with people after her."

"Well, I don't give a shit. Come on then." Karston waved his finger at Crinnan and Milinka. "Let's get moving, I'm sick of standing here watching these two not fuck."

Ander's face scrunched up at that and both Crinnan and Milinka turned with wide eyes at Karston's words. Karston snorted a laugh and started walking.

***

"So where are you from?" Dali asked with a chipper voice as the group marched onward. "Do you have a girlfriend? You sure are cute. Are you from the modern era? What's it like? Have you ever tried cake?"

Crinnan looked at Dali with wide eyes, she was already exhausting him. She looked like just any of the other Sincroftians, dirty, ragged and tired but damn. That girl would not shut up.

"Uh..." Crinnan didn't know what to answer first. "Yes?"

"What's her name?" Dali asked. "Is she pretty? Is she an elf?"

"I meant yes I've tried cake." Crinnan replied.

"Oh, what kind!" Dali's tone elevated. "Did it have icing or was it just a bar? I haven't had cake in so long, cake was my favorite food. Still is, I guess... I think. I haven't eaten anything but Gravlin shit for so long that I don't remember." She laughed nervously and looked over at Ander. "I like your moustache!"

"Oh!" Ander squeaked with joy. "Why thank you, young lady. Truly you are a delight to have in our midst. I very much look forward to…"

"Will y'all shut up, we're here." Karston belted at everyone. "Get your guns out, Croftkeeper should be showing up soon."

"You guys have guns!" Dali asked, her voice suddenly low and excited. "There are so few guns in the Hells! I remember back in my day when the AOC and the Church started fighting everyone had guns. My daddy had guns, but he wasn't my daddy. I just called him daddy because he gave me money and food. I liked him, except when I had to pay for the money and food, then I didn't like him so much but hey, a girl's gotta do what a girl's gotta do. Am I right Milinka?" Dali nudged Milinka who turned and let out an uneasy laugh.

"Sure, Dali." Milinka snorted.

"She's precious." Ander said amidst a gentle laugh.

"By the Brothers." Karston sighed and threw his hands up in defeat. "Y'all have fun then, Croftkeeper will be here soon. Hope y'all beat him."

"Wait, that's it?" Milinka asked, turning to Karston. "You're just leaving?"

"Yup." Karston said. "Brought you here. Now you wait. I have shit to harvest back at home… literally."

"So you're not going to help?" Milinka squinted her eyes and took a step forward. "After all this, you're just… out?"

"Out and never to be heard from again, little lady." Karston corrected. "Y'all have been… fun, but… contract's done. But I do wish you guys the best." At that, Karston tipped his hat to Milinka and turned to Crinnan and Ander.

"Good luck out there boys." He called out to them. "The Hells is a dangerous place. I reckon y'all can manage though." He turned to leave and then Dali hurried up and leaned into him, whispering something into his ear. Karston paused and then slowly looked at the fairess.

"Who the fuck do you think you are?" He suddenly snapped and then promptly wrapped his hand around her throat. "How dare you!"

"Whoa!" Milinka snapped as she burst forward. She planted her shoulder into Karston's chest, knocking him back and freeing Dali. "That's enough of that!"

"You don't know what you're talking about you little shit!" Karston growled, pointing at Dali. "I have half a mind to cut your throat here and now."

"That will not be happening today." Ander snapped stepping forward. "Nobody is cutting anybody!"

"I speak truth." Dali said, her tone suddenly less chipper and more serious. "Your children are not in Sincroft. If you wait for them here... you will never find them. They wait for you... deeper, Karston. Much deeper."

"Stop it, bitch!" Karston growled. "My children are gone!"

"If that is the best choice you can make as a father," Dali continued, "then perhaps you are not deserving of the title."

Karston's nostrils flared and he reached to his side pulling his revolver free. He swung the weapon in front of him so that the barrel rested right on the bridge of Dali's nose. Just as he pulled back the hammer, so too did Crinnan with his own pistol that was aimed at Karston's head.

"Gun down." Crinnan said. "That's enough."

"Don't fight it." Dali urged Karston. "I know you fear the idea of being able to love again. But I assure you. Your family is all together. Except for you. Come with us, let's find them together. I promise your path will cross with theirs."

"And you shut the fuck up too!" Crinnan snapped. "We don't even know you. Mind your own business!"

"You're fucking crazy." Karston shook his head and gestured for his herd to follow. "Crazy. All of you. Good luck in your... little quest. I'm out of here." At that, the small herd of touched and Karston turned and walked away.

"Well, that could have gone better." Ander finally said after a few moments of silence. "'Tis no matter though. I suppose we... wait now. For whatever it is we are supposed to vanquish." Ander took a seat on the ground and ran his hands through his hair, slicking it back. He gestured for everyone else to sit, and Milinka and Dali did. Crinnan, however, simply rested against a rotten looking pole next to him.

"Let's hear a story." Ander called out. "I recall not my own life, only the circumstances of the world surrounding it. I wish to hear of your lives, tell me something my friends."

Everybody sat silently and Crinnan fidgeted a bit as he thought of some of his own memories. Life had definitely not been easy but as Crinnan reflected he deduced that it had definitely been worth living. Of course, he thought of Milinka and their time in the woods, he thought of his friends Alec and Elia. He heard his mother singing to him and his siblings in his mind and felt the embrace of his twin brother Rubaan as they cuddled together in bed when they were children. In that moment, Crinnan longed for the real feelings of life. He longed to feel loved, to feel wanted, to be physically near to someone... he wanted to feel the exhilaration of a real battle, to fight side by side with his friends and to stay up all night talking with his brother. He wanted to hear his father give him advice, to correct his sword stance, and wanted to hear his mother tell him he was a moody piece of shit but that she loved him anyway.

"Something to tell?" Ander asked, looking directly at Crinnan. "I see your cogs spinning."

"My what?" Crinnan asked.

"Never mind. Tell us a story of your childhood, Crinnan."

Crinnan shifted his weight to his other leg and crossed his arms. "I don't really..."

"Oh come now, break from that silly shell for a moment." Ander encouraged. "There is no judgement here."

Crinnan took in a deep breath and scanned the three faces staring at him. Finally, he shook his head and shrugged. "One time when I was a kid, we had this dog. Its name was Pooter. Pooter got sick once and Dad said we had to put him down. So, we went to a secure location and dad gave me a gun. He said..."

"Never mind." Ander interrupted, shaking his hands to distract Crinnan. "By Igo I should have guessed you would tell us the most depressing story imaginable. Milinka, darling. Tell us something that brings you great joy."

Milinka looked over at Ander and shrugged her shoulders. She picked up a stick from the ground and started poking the pebbles in front of her. Glancing up at Crinnan she snorted.

"I got lost in the woods once." She started, and Crinnan's eyes grew wide. "My Knight, my brother, was ambushed while we were on patrol. Me and another squire ran because our Knights told us to. We got lost, didn't know which way was which and for a week we got to know each other." Milinka bit her lower lip and cracked a thin smile. "That boy was so stupid, but we were sixteen years old. He was the worst kisser ever but that didn't matter. I saved him and he saved me and then... and then we never saw each other again."

"What do you mean you never saw each other again?" Ander asked, cocking his head. "That's the end of the story? THAT brings you joy?"

Milinka nodded, not looking at Crinnan. "It does. I think of my week in the woods with that boy sometimes when I feel alone. Sometimes I like to imagine he's thinking about the same thing and that somehow in some way there's this stupid magical light that goes from my heart into his no matter where he is in the world. Makes me feel less lonely or something. But yeah, it makes me happy."

A silence descended upon the group and Ander nodded his head. "Ah. Yes, I think I understand now." He briefly looked at Crinnan nodded his head. Crinnan realized that Ander knew what was going on and his face flushed with embarrassment. "Perhaps you will one day find this boy you fell in love with again. Or perhaps you will discover the person he matured into. Either way, a good story Milinka my dear." Ander turned his head to Dali. "What of you, young lady. Your interactions with the group thus far have been... interesting to say the least."

"B.T.B!" Dali said, dramatically emphasizing every letter individually. "Hello! My name is Dali. I was twenty-one when I died. An AOC bomb fell on my apartment in Belhaas and killed me and all my dogs. Whoops! Sucked because I was still in my jammies and was on the LAST EPISODE of a series on WebFlicks. SO annoying. I was supposed to make a shit ton of money that night too with a post to my SuperFANZ but. Welp. Guess I didn't!" She released a small giggle, and everyone just stared at her.

"Dali, do you remember how you got here with us?" Milinka suddenly asked, eyeing the girl suspiciously. "Like, do you remember our talk at all?"

"Look, I'm just sooooo glad to have made some friends!" Dali shrugged. "I woke up in that alley and was like BTB a friend! I think I need a shower though because, wow. I stink."

Milinka gently patted the girl on the back and sighed. "Yes, we will be your friends." Milinka assured her. "Just stay with us okay?"

"No probz!" Dali chirped. "BTB I've been here so long, like. It was super shitty the first few years or so then I just kind of. Fell asleep. I didn't wake up until today, it's so weird how things work."

"You fell asleep?" Ander asked, tilting his head with interest.

"Yar!" Dali replied. "Like. One day I just kind of like. Blacked out, and when you ask how I knew you just need to trust me because when I was alive I blacked out a LOT." A nervous giggle followed, and Dali twirled her finger in the air. "Anyway, I blacked out and uhhhh yar. Here I am." She reached up and touched her hair and let out a dramatic sigh. "This isn't salvageable is it?" She asked Milinka.

"No honey." Milinka replied, giving the girl another pat. "It's dead."

"It's fine." Dali shrugged sadly. "Like I mean..." She shook her head and closed her eyes. "No... it's fine. I promise."

"We can cut it off some other time." Milinka assured her. "For now, let's..."

"BTB!!!!! A haircut! Let's do it now while we're waiting!" Dali squealed and got to her feet. "Does anyone have a knife or scissors or something?"

Everyone looked to Crinnan and he shrugged. "Don't look at me, I only have a sword."

"A sword!" Dali chirped with excitement. She looked Crinnan up and down and raised her eyebrows. "That so fits! You are so cute. You have that whole 'look at me I'm sad' angsty drama boy kinda vibe going on. You rock it too!"

Crinnan rolled his eyes and looked away at that statement. He didn't fully understand everything that the girl said, but he still took offense. As he stared at the ground, pouting in his own masculine way, Crinnan realized he was proving that Dali's analysis of him was wholly correct. This made him angry.

"But yar." Dali continued, grinning in Crinnan's direction. "Poor widdle me. Blown to bits, dead as the souls of my SuperFANZ. So glad we can all be fraaayunz now. Anyway, time for my haircut! Meow." The girl laid on the cobblestone ground, reached up and twisted her pink hair so that it was one thick column. "Use your axes, Milinka. My body is ready."

Milinka snorted a giggle at Dali and pushed herself up to her knees. "Okay," She said as she pulled one of her axes from her hip. "You need to hold extra super still. I don't want to miss and chop off your head."

"Bring it on baby." Dali said, smiling up at Milinka. "Team building exercise amirite?"

Milinka giggled again, staring down at Dali and nodded her head. "Okay, here I go. Don't move!" Dali smiled widely, softly laughing to herself as she squeezed her eyes shut tight.

"BTB Milinka I'm terrified!" Dali said. "This is..." The axe came down and sparked against the cobblestone road. Dali let loose an ear-piercing scream-laugh that made everyone around her jump.

"Dali!" Milinka shouted. "Dali are you okay!"

"That was amazing!" Dali screamed, laughing hysterically. "The rush! Never in my life have I had an axe flying toward my head! That was so amazing, I bet I'm the only one here who's ever had that happen!!"

"Nope." Crinnan shook his head, vividly remembering multiple instances where an axe had been swung at his face. "Got you beat there."

"Oh, I bet you do baby boy." Dali said with a wink. She sat up and ran her fingers through her hair. It was lopsided and still a bit matted on the ends, but she forced her fingers through to make it feel like real hair again. After playing with it for a bit, she tilted her head upward the way a child would and smiled at Milinka.

"You my hewo." She said in a baby voice and then wrapped her arms around her. "I lub you."

Milinka was a bit startled by the encounter, but soon enough wrapped her arms around Dali as well. "I'm happy to help." Milinka said warmly.

"So touching." Ander sighed as he watched the heartwarming interaction. Crinnan couldn't help but groan at the sight.

A flash of light broke up the moment, causing Ander to quickly push himself to his feet. Crinnan's sword quickly found its way into his right hand, and a pistol into his left. Dali screamed and Milinka pushed her back, producing both of her axes.

A creature that looked to be half man and half horse phased into view. He had two curved horns atop his head, and a barbed tail that swung back forth. In his hands he held a vicious looking poleaxe, and he stared at those gathered before him.

"Fortune favors you travelers, for you have found me. Do you wish to leave Sincroft?" The monster asked with a deep reverberating voice.

"We do!" Ander shouted back.

"Then a test of your worth I shall conduct." The Croftkeeper said as he readied his poleaxe. "If I fall, the portal will open." The creature held his poleaxe at the ready and stared down at the group of four.

"Ander, Dali get back." Milinka shouted as she ran up and joined Crinnan at his side. "We will fight you, Croftkeeper."

"So be it." The creature boomed as he prepared to charge.

Chapter Twenty-One
The Croftkeeper

The Third Hell
Sincroft

"Stand back!" Crinnan shouted to the others. "I got this!" He raised his revolver and fired a shot, striking the Croftkeeper directly in the forehead. A blue light flashed, and the bullet ricocheted to the right. Crinnan cursed, the creature had shields just like his own.

"Nice shot!" Milinka called forward as she ran to the right. "So glad you're the one with the guns!"

"I hit him right in the head!" Crinnan yelled back. He watched as the centaur squared up his shoulders to charge. "He's got magic shield things!"

"So do you!" Milinka replied. "Get up there and fight him!"

Crinnan grumbled and the Croftkeeper charged forward. The clomping of his hooves against the cobblestone streets filled Crinnan's ears and he fired another shot just before running out of the way of

the Croftkeeper's path. The centaur ran past, and Crinnan turned to face him.

"You have to lower his shields!" Ander shouted at them. "Land your shots! If I were able, I would assist you with my abilities... but I fear I am swordless and powerless here."

"Just keep Dali safe!" Milinka yelled. "You two hang back!"

Crinnan ran toward the Croftkeeper, firing his pistol as he went. Most of his shots landed, and Crinnan watched as every single bullet was stopped by the rippling blue light. The Croftkeeper turned toward him, swinging his poleaxe. The head of the weapon slammed against Crinnan's own shields, sending him flying backward and into a rotted looking market stall. The structure collapsed, and Crinnan was momentarily buried in debris.

"Brothers damn it all!" Crinnan scowled as he pushed his way through the debris. "This is bullshit! How much shields do I have left?"

Shields: 185/220

The shield buff Sage had given Crinnan had run out and he was back in normal territory. He knew he had to be careful. Quickly, he dug himself out of the debris and got to his feet. Crinnan saw the Croftkeeper standing and waiting for him. When he was finally standing again, the centaur leveled his poleaxe like a lance and charged.

Bullets flew from Crinnan's revolver and bounced off the Croftkeeper's shields. Crinnan squeezed the trigger one final time and the hammer slammed against nothing. He was out of ammo, he had to reload. Cursing, he ran out of the way of danger and opened the cylinder of his gun.

"Hurry up!" Crinnan whispered to himself as he looked back and forth between his ammo belt and the Croftkeeper. He managed to get four bullets in before the centaur was looking at him again. "Brothers damn it all." Crinnan cursed as he slammed the cylinder back into place. He raised his gun and began firing again.

The creature's shields once again deflected all of Crinnan's attacks and Crinnan was beginning to grow frustrated. He had no idea how much damage he was dealing to the centaur's shields or how much shields the centaur even had. He jumped out of the way of another charge and once again began reloading.

Crinnan heard the sound of footsteps charging rapidly slapping against the cobblestone as if someone was charging his direction. He turned his head just in time to see Milinka leap through the air, axes raised above her head, and land on the back of the centaur, bring her weapons down against its spine. The blue light flickered again and the Croftkeeper started bucking as she slammed her axes against its body over and over.

"Get your fucking guns loaded!" Milinka screamed. She managed to scoot forward and lock her legs around the centaur's upper torso as she continued to strike it. The beast jumped and kicked and lashed out at her with her hands until finally Crinnan heard what sounded like glass shattering. A moment later, the head of one of Milinka's axes was buried in the Croftkeeper's upper back. The creature howled in pain and was finally able to grab hold of Milinka's arm. He ripped her from his body and tossed her aside like a doll.

Crinnan watched as Milinka hit the ground hard and rolled to a stop only a few feet away from him. Her face was blooded from a wound she had sustained on her head but she was able to get to her feet. The centaur turned toward them, kicked its front feet and began to charge. Milinka snarled and let out a growl as she raised her remaining axe, took aim and hurled it forward.

The axe soared through the air and found its mark in the Croftkeeper's left pectoral muscle. The centaur roared with pain as it charged. His target was Milinka, and Crinnan looked back and forth between the two of them. He didn't have time to fuck off, he charged forward, ramming his shoulder into Milinka and knocked her out of the way just in time for the beast to collide with his body. Crinnan was knocked underfoot and trampled by the hooves of the creature. He felt his ribs break and gasped in pain, but it was over quick.

Grunting in distress, but still holding his revolvers in hand, Crinnan flipped onto his back and raised his weapons. The Croftkeeper was turning toward him for another pass, Crinnan had only one chance to make this work. He raised his weapons in front of him, and without another though emptied both the cylinders.

Twelve bullets perforated the centaur's chest and Crinnan watched as the creature howled in pain and staggered backward. Crinnan knew his own shields were gone and most of his HP as well. He watched and wheezed as the Centaur stared at Crinnan for a moment, let out a labored breath, and then collapsed onto the ground.

```
Croftkeeper KILLED

+100,000 Rank

New Rank: Rank: 29,150,777,289
```

"Quickly now!" Ander shouted as he and Dali ran to Crinnan's side. Each of them grabbed one of Crinnan's arms and pulled him to his feet. "Remember, he has to get through the portal last!" Ander shouted. "If he goes in before any of us, it will close!"

"Fuck!" Crinnan groaned as they dragged him forward. The swirling blue portal opened up just behind the dead Croftkeeper. "Go!"

Crinnan watched as Milinka retrieved her axes from the dead centaur. She briefly looked over at him with an expression he hadn't seen her make in their whole time together in the Hells. She looked... worried for him. Crinnan saw her eyes, he saw the way she gently nibbled on her lower lip, how her nostrils flared...

"Go!" Crinnan urged her. "Hurry!" Milinka nodded slightly, turned, and ran through the portal just as Ander and Dali let go of him.

"Be right behind you." Crinnan choked as he grabbed his ribs and stood on his own. "Get through already!"

Ander cracked a proud looking smile as he looked at Crinnan and slowly nodded his head. The wind from the portal gently blew through both of their hair and Ander took hold of Dali's wrist and pulled her forward. Crinnan watched them both disappear, turned and took one last look at Sincroft and the Croftkeeper, and then stepped forward himself.

Chapter Twenty-Two
Femoral

The Fourth Hell

Injuries sustained.

Current injuries:

Broken Ribs x18 (Speed reduced by .05 per instance)

-0.9 Speed

Bleeding x6 (You lose 5 HP per minute per cut)

-30hp/minute

Collapsed Lung

-Stamina at 50% efficiency

Concussion - Moderate (Random effects)

Your visibility and hearing have been diminished

...

HP: 120/190

Shields: 0/220

...

Your death will occur in 4 minutes.

Crinnan stumbled out of the portal and immediately collapsed onto the ground. He felt shards of the brittle glasslike rock dig into him and groaned at the extra pain. His entire body throbbed from his broken ribs and countless bruises. Every shallow breath he took hurt and it felt like he wasn't getting enough air in his lungs which was leading him to panic. He didn't have the strength to push himself back up, he could barely move. All he could do was lay his face against the sharp jagged ground and let himself silently cry.

"Crinnan!" Milinka shouted. She quickly fell to her knees beside him and placed her hand on his back. His body jerked in place and he whined in pain at the unexpected touch. She gasped and pulled back. "Phoenix damn it all..." She said as she looked over his mangled body. "What can I do?"

"N... nothing..." Crinnan wheezed. "I'll be... dead in four minutes..."

"No." Milinka shook her head and frantically started looking around for something to help. "There has to be a way to fix this, some kind of..."

"Move." Dali snapped as she dropped to the ground next to Milinka. "I can try something." Milinka stood and stepped back as Dali examined Crinnan.

"What are you..." Crinnan started to ask but groaned when Dali placed her hands on his back. "Stop!"

"Quiet, little boy!" Dali ordered. "IRL I was a nurse... I mean when I wasn't jiggling my booty on cam." She snorted a laugh to herself for a moment and found one of the larger gashes on Crinnan's body. "Aha." She said. "There is a laceration over your femoral artery... you need to be a big boy here and work with me. This... this will hurt. I'm going to flip you over to your back."

"By the Brothers please no." Crinnan begged.

"Do you want to die?" Dali asked as she poked a finger into his back. "If you do, I'll stand my perf ass up and go do something else." Crinnan was silent for a moment but then released a grunt of submission and Dali smiled. She moved her way to the other side of Crinnan's body, grabbed his upper arm and took a breath. "Okay. Time to roll over!"

Crinnan released a scream as he felt his broken ribs jostle around inside his chest. Dali grit her teeth together at the sight of his mangled torso and for a moment just sat and stared.

"Oh, you're fucked up." Dali said, tsking softly to herself. "We need to fix that."

"No shit!" Crinnan wheezed.

"Okay I'll... need that sword of yours." She said, and then nervously cleared her throat.

"Why?" Crinnan asked anxiously.

"Because I'm the fucking medical professional! Do what I say!" Dali reached down and grabbed Crinnan's sword. "BTB this is going to be awkward... okay hold still." Dali quickly unbuckled the blood-soaked armor on Crinnan's left thigh and haphazardly tossed it aside. She then cut through Crinnan's pants, exposing the gushing wound. She hummed to herself curiously, and then wiped the blood away.

"How many cuts do you have?" She asked.

"S... six..." Crinnan answered.

"Ah. Fuck." She quickly raised a hand and cupped Crinnan's head. After a brief moment, Crinnan felt a wave of energy rush through him.

You have been Healed!

...

HP: 190/190

Shields: 0/220

...

Current injuries:

Broken Ribs x18 (Speed reduced by .05 per fracture.)

-0.9 Speed

Bleeding x6 (You lose 5 HP per minute per cut)

-30hp/minute

Collapsed Lung

-Stamina at 50% efficiency

Concussion - Moderate (Random effects)

Your visibility and hearing have been diminished

...

Your death will occur in 6 minutes 20 seconds.

"Well good thing it works!" Dali chirped. "Bought us some more time. Okay so... you're just going to need to find a way to be comfortable here because I have to find the severed ends of that artery you let get fucked up."

"I didn't let shit..." Crinnan started but was quickly cut off by Dali.

"Shut up." She gently poked one of the ribs protruding from his chest and he gasped in pain. "I'm in charge. So... hold still because I have to cut your leg."

Crinnan whimpered and tried to look up to see what was going on. Dali worked to position the sword in a way where she had control, ultimately simply placing one of the edges against Crinnan's thigh. She bit her lower lip and guided the blade to his laceration and then looked up at him.

"Are you able to..." She saw the tears streaming down his eyes and shook her head. "No, you're too weak. Milinka, Ander! Come here babies." Milinka and Ander did as they were told, and Dali pointed down at Crinnan's leg.

"Okay, now which one of you is stronger?" Dali asked, looking between the two. "Wait, never mind. Milinka definitely is. Milinka, I need you to hold down his leg, don't let it move... just... yeah sit on his shin there... Ander, I need you to... well I need you to sit on his head."

"I do believe I mistook your words, sweet Dali." Ander said as politely as he could muster. "Can you please..."

"Booty on face, nerd!" Dali snapped as she pointed to a fearful looking Crinnan. "Now!"

"I wholeheartedly apologize for the experience we are about to share." Ander said softly as he knelt down next to Crinnan. "This is... not how I anticipated my day going."

"I'm going to... bite your fucking sack!" Crinnan growled. "Do not... put your butt... on my face!"

"I'm sorry Crinnan. Take a deep breath." Ander said. A horrified expression marred his face as he closed his eyes and clenched his teeth together. With a gentle clearing of his throat, Ander slowly began lowering himself.

"Turn your head, Crinnan!" Dali yelled at him. "Don't let him sit on your mouth and nose. Hurry up!" Crinnan reluctantly did as he was told and soon after he felt the soft cheeks of Ander's bottom press down against his temple. The aroma of swampass hit his nose and he nearly gagged.

"Okay, Milinka on his ankles... good..." Dali said to herself as she returned to the sword. "Here we go!" Dali dragged the blade across Crinnan's laceration, and more blood pooled up to the surface. Crinnan started convulsing in response and Dali set the sword aside.

"Push down harder, Milinka!" Dali ordered. "I'm going in!" At that, she reached her fingers into the cut and started feeling around for the ends of the severed artery. Crinnan's screams were muffled by Ander's ass, and as Dali explored the inside of Crinnan's thigh, she finally found what she was looking for.

"Got it!" She chirped. "Sucker really migrated down there, but I got it!" She brought the two ends together, and then used her healing ability to mend the artery. After a moment, the heavy bleeding stopped, and Dali sealed the thigh shut.

"Okay that's one. Only four more to go, we got this!" Dali sang optimistically. She reached up underneath Ander's bum and pressed once again against Crinnan's temple, sending more healing power into his body.

You have been healed!

Over the course of the next half hour or so, Dali worked across Crinnan's body finding the cuts that were draining his HP and healing them. Some were easier than others, but she couldn't seem to find the last two.

"They're internal." She spat, shaking her head. "I'm going to have to crack him open."

"Please no." Crinnan begged. "I can just respawn... I'll get back here..."

"Nope!" Dali replied. "We've come too far... we're almost done Crinnan." She lied.

"W... what's that?" Dali heard Milinka suddenly ask. Dali turned her head to see what Milinka was talking about and felt her own heart sink.

"Oh." She whispered. "BTB that is bad."

"What?" Ander called back. "What is the matter?" He looked behind himself and saw a horde of bodies shambling toward them in the distance. "Touched..." Ander said. "And... they have been empowered to fight like the rest of us."

"Do you think they'll fight us though?" Milinka asked. "Maybe they'll just walk by?"

"The touched fight everything." Ander sighed. "If they come any closer, we will be forced to hold them off while Dali finishes Crinnan."

Dali snorted a laugh at Ander's words. He looked at her curiously and she just shook her head. "Yeah, while I *finish* him." Milinka couldn't help but chuckle herself and Ander was left confused.

"Did I... what did I say?" Ander looked back and forth between Dali and Milinka but they both shook their heads at him.

"Finish means cum." Crinnan grunted from underneath him... "Get your ass off me and go fight the fucking touched!"

"I see." Ander said as he rose to his feet. "You all are as children." He shook his head in annoyance and each of his hands burst into flame. "Ah, power again. An opportunity to see *exactly* what I'm made of."

Milinka stood and joined Ander's side, pulling both of her axes free from her belt. "This should be interesting." She said as she watched what had to have been hundreds of shambling bodies march toward them.

"Oh, child." Ander smiled and looked over at her. "This will be... glorious. I can feel something within my mind imploring me to blast them all into nothing. We will do this together. You protect me, and I shall protect everyone else."

"Deal." Milinka said with a nod.

"Okay Crinnan, we'll take this slow." Dali said as she helped him sit up. "I have to find your internal bleeding... and I have to mend your broken ribs. Anything else?"

"It says... collapsed lung..." Crinnan grunted. "It hurts to breathe."

"Aw, you're so sweet." Dali fluttered her eyelashes and bit her lower lip. "I haven't got a compliment like that in like... forever!"

"It wasn't..."

"I know." Dali said with a smile. "Just lightening the mood. I mean we have hundreds of undead coming at us from one side, and I'm about to chop your body into pieces on my end. Lots of bullshit to be frowning about."

"Right." Crinnan said, not amused by Dali's antics. "Just... just get on with it..." He watched as Ander and Milinka ran to engage the touched and then felt Dali gently cut his blood-soaked shirt away from his body. He was feeling a little better now that most of the bleeding had stopped, but his body was still throbbing with pain from the broken ribs.

"Okay I'm going to do a bit of discovery here." She said as she gently placed her fingertips on Crinnan's chest. "How many broken ribs?"

"Eighteen." Crinnan replied.

"What the fuck!" Dali gasped but then cleared her throat and nodded her head. "I mean. Sure. No problem." Dali softly ran her fingers up Crinnan's ribs, searching for where the fractures were. Pain shot through Crinnan's body the whole time, and Dali giggled every time he winced.

"Eighteen then." She said as she pulled her hand away. "This will hurt, Crinnan.   Okay?"
"Just whatever." Crinnan replied in a defeated tone. "Get it done so I can go help them." Dali nodded and placed the edge of Crinnan's sword against the first fracture.

"Ready?" She asked. "Don't bite your tongue off, okay?"

"Okay…" Crinnan said. At that, Dali pushed with the blade, and began the process of opening up Crinnan's chest.

Chapter Twenty-Three
The Touched

The Fourth Hell

Milinka walked forward, the glassy ground beneath her crunching and shattering with every step. She held her axes in her hands tightly as she surveyed the hundreds of snarling mindless touched that were shoving past and crawling over each other. Her stride matched Ander's, she held her head high and her knuckles were white with anticipation of the seemingly unavoidable battle before her.

Thoughts raced through her mind in the short walk from Crinnan's side to the would-be battlements. She thought of the touched, how they had once been people with their own hopes and dreams. Somebody somewhere had once loved the creatures she was about to kill, had mourned the loss when they died. Milinka grew angry at this thought. Before her was the culmination of the efforts of Govia. These touched were what the Empire ultimately created, the final rung of oppression... a shell of a person, chaos and pain manifested in a shambling tormented body...

Ander walked alongside Milinka, his hands glowing with the magic that he had been so eager to use in Sincroft. Milinka looked over at him and didn't see the uneasiness she felt within herself. She saw an unmistakable appearance of confidence plastered on the vampre's face, a look in his eyes that suggested he *wanted* whatever was about to happen to them.

"'Tis but another hill upon the path to greatness." Ander proclaimed as the two walked. "One which we will scale together... dare I say, my friend?"

Milinka nodded and flared her nostrils tenaciously. The touched were closing the distance between them, she could smell and hear them as they drew nearer. Ander stopped walking and so did she. He watched them for a moment before raising his flaming hands and she watched as the fires suddenly grew in intensity.

"Do try to keep them off me." Ander said as he spread his arms out wide. "If any of them manage to get this far that is." Milinka nodded, and then jumped back as Ander's arms began exploding with magic. Shells of fire blasted off him like mortar fire, arcing through the air and leaving trails of smoke behind. The projectiles crashed through the ranks of the touched, bursting upon impact with the ground. Milinka stared in awe of the display, watching bodies burst apart in bright flashes of light.

The horde of touched screamed as one and broke into an awkward sprint as they charged forward. What could have previously been considered a mob transformed into a howling, awkward cluster of bodies that scratched and clawed forward toward their target. Milinka observed with morbid curiosity as they thrashed at one another, ripping into each other's flesh as they moved closer. For a moment her stance faltered, and she took a clumsy step backward. How could she fight something like that, how could she survive?

The artillery barrage from Ander ended and Milinka glanced over at him curiously. A smug yet vacant expression was painted across his face. He looked as if all the power came naturally to him, as if this situation was comfortable. It was almost as if he were *home*. In that single glance, the ever-intuitive nature of Milinka led her to shiver. In spite of the strange comfort she saw in Ander's face, Milinka stared at his eyes. They worked in contrast with his jubilance, darting around wildly and showing a fear that stuck out like a sore thumb. Milinka watched the eyes turn her way, locking onto her, and for a moment she thought she sensed... pleading in those eyes... a sort of begging for help...

Ander blinked away the expression and then looked away from her. His hands flashed with power and he sent a new rapid-fire barrage of tiny fireballs into the horde of touched. Milinka watched as the more concentrated blasts blew their targets apart, sending gore and giblets in all directions.

Where had this power come from? How was Ander so adept with his abilities in the Hells? Not long ago he had been a mere prisoner, someone who couldn't use abilities at all. She concluded he must have had a mastery of his abilities back when was alive in the Ancient times. Perhaps he was some kind of soldier in their armies so long ago.

"Ready yourself!" Ander called out to her. "The touched are approaching, prepare for engagement!"

"Affirmative!" Milinka replied, steeling herself. She watched a handful of touched that had broken off the group awkwardly run toward her with hands outstretched. A couple held rusty weapons and one even had armor, but they all looked vacant and stupid. Ander individually disposed of a few of them, but one with a sword hissed as he darted toward Milinka.

Milinka stepped out of the way of the sloppy sword strike and with a mighty bellow escaping her lips, she drove the head of her axe through the bridge of the creature's nose and into his brain. His body spasmed for a moment and he dropped his sword as he reflexively reached up to remove the obstruction. She watched black curdled goo seep around her axe, and as his death caught up with him, he went limp and he fell off Milinka's weapon into a pile on the ground.

A hoarse scream came from her right, and Milinka ducked in time to avoid a fist barreling toward her. She shot forward, thrusting her shoulder into the creature's diaphragm and knocking it off its feet. It flailed its arms as it tumbled backward. As it landed on its back against the ground, Milinka swung her axe downward and clove through its skull, splitting it apart and spilling more oily black goo all over the ground.

"Vigilance, Milinka!" Ander cried out to her. "More touched inbound!"

With a snarl, Milinka looked up and saw three touched running toward her. She quickly took off into a sprint toward them, resolving to kill the two with weapons first. The nearest one took an axe strike to its sword arm, and then a subsequent one to its chest. The appendage was cut free with ease and it stumbled backward from the second attack, its dusty body now slick and oily with the rotten ichor that filled it. Another swiped at her with a club, striking her in the ribs. She spat a line of curses as she reeled in pain and then used her momentum to spin and hack clean through the creature's neck. Oily blackness spewed onto her face and she gasped in revulsion as the final touched leapt at her. Milinka was just able to step out of the way of the tackle, and pivoted as she swung both her axes, slamming them into the touched's back. The creature crashed into the ground, and she pulled an axe free. Without another thought, she crashed the weapon through the creature's temple, removing half its head.

"By the Brothers…" Milinka panted as she scrambled to her feet. She wiped the sweat and ichor off her brow with the back of her hand and turned to look back at Dali and Crinnan. Dali had her fingers inserted in Crinnan's chest and Crinnan was arching his back clearly in pain. Though Milinka could not hear him scream over the commotion going on around her, she briefly smiled at the sight of his discomfort, but then frowned reflecting on all he had done to find himself in the position he was in.

Crinnan Jamiso was a name that had almost become myth to Milinka. She didn't want her thoughts to cloud her judgement in the scuffle she was currently in, but as she rose to her feet and turned toward the next wave of touched dashing toward her, she couldn't help but hear her heart speaking louder than her mind should have allowed.

The head of an axe smashed through the side of another touched's head as she reflected on the situation she was in. Crinnan was her first true love and the thought of him had kept her awake and playing scenarios in her head many a night back in the real world. She wouldn't say she obsessed over the idea of him, over what could have been, but she would admit that it was something that weighed heavy on her heart. She wanted him, she wanted to be with the boy she fell in love with back in the forests of Kamlot. The idea that he had fully ghosted her cut her deeply and it was a wound that she constantly picked the scab off of, preventing it from ever truly healing.

Milinka split another skull and roared with frustration and adrenaline-fueled fury as the creature fell and another ran up in its place. She hated Crinnan for what he hadn't done, yet she loved him deeply. Her thoughts raced back to when she first saw him approaching her in the Hells. She had given up, accepted her fate as nothing more than a toy for the players… but as if it were one of her dreams, Crinnan killed those who would harm her. He saved her, and while she was disgusted with the idea that she would have ever been in a position where she needed saving in the first place, a part of her heart had been both warmed and excited by the fact that her savior was the person she fell in love with so long ago.

But she wasn't going to give him the satisfaction of knowing that he, even after all these years of silence and avoidance, still made her heart pound like a

Marauder war drum. She wanted him to feel as unwanted and reviled as she felt for so many years, it only seemed fair in her mind. She wouldn't give him an inch; she wouldn't allow him to feel any semblance of closeness to her...

Milinka batted a sword out of the way and screamed as she drove her axes into the ribs of the next touched. Her eyes grew wide and she gnashed her teeth in fury as she ripped her weapons free and then planted them into the creature's neck. She couldn't control her frustration, for she knew the walls around her heart were breaking down in Crinnan's presence. She didn't want to keep him at arm's length, she wanted to feel his arm's length around her. She wanted him to grunt something stupid as he held her, to whisper awkward words of comfort that he didn't truly know how to formulate into her ears.

"Brothers damn it all..." Milinka seethed as the last touched fell. She hated how she was feeling, she hated that she was opening up to him again. She knew he would never intentionally harm her, but she also knew that he had hurt her more than any other person in her entire life. Even more than the Imperial Princess Daansire Cidro who had cut her down in the battlefield and sent her to the Hells.

Milinka stood and panted, her whole body throbbing in time with her pounding heart. She clenched her teeth and gripped her axes with sweaty, ichor-soaked hands. Ander was moving forward, blasting at the remnants of the touched horde, and Milinka looked back again to see Crinnan sitting up, his head face buried in his hands. Seeing him fully healed sent a wave of comfort through her anxious body and she cursed at the feeling.

Ander's barrage finally stopped, and he watched for a moment before lowering his hands and then falling to his knees. Milinka's eyes grew wide with concern and she ran over to him, catching him before he fell to the ground.

"I do believe I have overextended myself..." Ander said with a wheeze. "Oh, that takes... that takes a lot out of you..."

"Whatever you did was amazing." Milinka replied, gently helping him to a sitting position on the ground. "Your abilities are unlike anything I've seen in the real world before."

"I..." Ander looked down at his hands and shook his hands. "I know nothing of the power that I wield... only that it comes when I wish... when I wish to kill..."

"You did great." Milinka said, gently cupping Ander's cheek. "I'm proud of you my friend."

Ander looked up at Milinka with a worn expression on his face, but beneath his moustache a weak but sincere smile formed. He looked genuinely happy to have received praise, as if it was the first in his life that he had felt appreciated. Ander's head lowered and his shoulders rose and fell with his breathing.

"I... I need a moment to rest..." Ander said. "You go see how Crinnan is doing. We all need to get moving very soon."

Chapter Twenty-Four
Knight and Squire

The Fourth Hell

"Fuck me." Crinnan groaned as he relived the beyond-painful healing and surgery he had just endured. "Next time just let me die…"

"I mean…" Dali's eyebrow raised, and she crossed her arms as she glared at Crinnan. "You could say thank you, you know."

"Sure, whatever. Thanks." Crinnan lifted his head and pushed himself up off the ground. He turned and looked at Dali who looked hurt by his words and he rolled his eyes and sighed. "Fine. I'm glad you healed me. Thank you."

Dali's frown turned into a grin and she winked at him and slapped him on his shoulder. "Any time bro!" She replied. "But you really cried like a baby!"

"You… you cut me open and put my ribs back together like a puzzle…" Crinnan replied in his own defense. "Of course it hurt!"

"Aw, it's okay though babe!" Dali cooed with a baby voice. "Even big strong soldier boy can cry sometimes. I won't tell anyone."

"He cries more than most people should." Milinka said as she approached. Crinnan turned his head and bit his inner cheek at the sound of her words. "Unless he's changed over the years. Which… I don't think he has."

"Alright, that's enough already. Let's just get moving." Crinnan huffed as he turned away. Milinka reached out and grabbed his arm, tugging him back. Crinnan turned and looked at her, confusion spread across his face.

"Thank you." Milinka said, not letting go of his arm. "For saving me back there."

"What are you talking about?" Crinnan scoffed. "I didn't..."

"The Croftkeeper." She replied. "You... pushed me out of the way and then got trampled. You didn't have to do that... and I guess while I'm at it..." Milinka sighed and looked down at the ground. "Thank you for saving me from the demons... or players or whatever they're called."

Crinnan didn't know what to say. He hadn't expected Milinka to be *nice* after all they had gone through thus far. The sudden appreciation was... wholly unexpected. He cleared his throat and nodded his head in reply

"Yeah." He all but whispered. "Yeah you're... you're welcome."

An awkward silence fell over the two while Dali stood not five feet away and watched with a toothy grin hands clasped in front of her. Crinnan couldn't control the way his eyes wandered over to the cheesy fairess, and he scrunched his face up at her.

"What are you looking at?" He snapped and turned away as if he had something to do. "Stop being weird. We have to get going."

"And so we shall." Ander commented as he joined Crinnan's side. "A violent and busy time we have endured. It would be good to get back on track, for we cannot allow our eyes to wander from the true prize. We are experiencing this... game in a way that never has been before, and I fear the crosshairs on our backs are growing larger and larger by the moment."

The word "game" lingered in Crinnan's head for a moment. He didn't really like the idea that his life had been reduced to nothing more than a playing piece in a game.

"I don't care how the Hells were meant to be experienced." Crinnan replied. "I'm doing what I can to keep us all alive..."

"Awwie!" Dali chirped as she lunged forward and clung tightly to Crinnan's arm. "The sad boy cares about us! BTB that's so cute!" She rested her head against Crinnan's upper arm and fluttered her eyelashes. "I so happy. Be my hewo, Cwinnan."

"Get off me." Crinnan grunted as he violently wiggled his arm until Dali let go. She giggled, licking her two front teeth with the tip of her tongue and took a step back.

"Aw you don't want to be my hewo!" Dali pouted. "Pwease?"

"Be her hewo Cwinnan." Milinka added with a laugh.

"Can we fucking cut it out already?" Crinnan asked, turning to the two. "Both of you. BTB... fuck I mean, by the Brothers, it's getting old."

Milinka couldn't suppress the smile that formed on her lips when she noticed Crinnan's flub. Instead of arguing or fighting back, she simply nodded her head, the grin not leaving her face. Eventually she and Dali burst into laughter and Crinnan huffed and turned to Ander.

"Well, my friend." Ander said, looking out at the landscape before them. "It seems we have found ourselves in an interesting place."

"What do you mean?" Crinnan asked.

"Well," Ander continued. "This place is known as The Fork, and rightfully so. Three paths lay ahead of us, we must choose how we wish to experience the next level of the Hells... I have only heard of this place, as the choice is only presented to players, which we technically are now. It will be a new and interesting experience for me I am sure."

"Okay, so how do we make the choice or whatever then?" Crinnan asked.

> **Three roads, travelers. Yet only one choice.**
>
> **Heart, Mind, or Soul... choose the path you wish to walk.**

Crinnan's silence lingered for a bit and then he looked to Ander. "So that's it? That's all there is to it?"

"Yes, but I think we must all confer as a group as to which path would be the best." Ander replied, raising a finger. "For they all assuredly will hold their various trials, and we should be pre..."

"Heart!" Crinnan called out. "No time to dick off. Whatever is on the other side, we will face it."

You have selected the path of Heart. The portal awaits.

At that, another swirling blue portal opened before them. Crinnan turned to his companions and they all nodded and stepped through. As Crinnan watched Milinka follow Dali and Ander, he sighed and walked forward.

***

Dread's Keep

Crinnan smelled it before he saw it. Swamp ass. He knew the smell all too well, it was the scent of any siege camp, or forward operating base. His nostrils flared at the odor, and when he came to, he found that he was suddenly surrounded by soldiers on all sides.

"It's him!" Crinnan heard someone shout. "Commander Crinnan's son!"

"He looks more like his mother if you ask me." Another replied.

Crinnan looked around at everyone, and after a few moments he felt a hefty weight slam into his back. Pistol in hand, he spun around and jammed the barrel under the red-bearded chin of a tall and very muscular Lycaani. Crinnan didn't immediately register the face he was looking at. After a moment though, his eyes opened wide in surprise and he lowered his pistol as he was pulled into a bearhug.

"If it ain't the scrawny little fucking Jamiso boy himself!" A deep, grizzled voice exclaimed. The swamp ass smell that exuded from that particular Lycaani was exceptionally pungent, but Crinnan wasn't bothered. He was too shocked to care.

"Jeph?" Crinnan finally asked after a few moments of being squeezed by the Lycaani. "What... how are here?"

"I'm dead, motherfucker!" Jeph replied with a hearty laugh. He slapped Crinnan on the back and released him. "I died the same night as you! We were ripped apart by those mutants in the Belhaasi Weald! They're probably shitting out pieces of us as we speak!"

"Well, that's a great thought." Crinnan sighed as he took a step back and looked at the Lycaani standing before him. Jeph Scaven was a Black Knight like Crinnan and a fellow member of Century Squad. He thought back to his last living memories, and remembered that it had been his, Jeph's and another Centurion named Pancho's turn at watch on the night he died. He looked at Jeph and for a moment felt a pang of sorrow.

"Well sorry you died." Crinnan grunted with as much empathy as he could muster. "Where... where are we?"

"Commander Emilio is laying siege to Dread's Keep!" Jeph replied, holdings his arms out to display the large group of people around him. "You stand with the fallen Black Knights, those of us who have died in the past one hundred years! Crinnan, this is as close to home as you are going to get in the Hells!"

Crinnan immediately started looking around. He was surrounded by what had to have been hundreds of other people. They all worked to construct what looked like siege equipment and trained together. Crinnan heard shouting and laughing and all the sounds of camaraderie that he would expect of a Black Knight camp. Part of him rebelled at the thought of interacting with others, but the other part embraced the familiar atmosphere.

"Commander Emilio?" Crinnan asked, looking back to Jeph. "That's weird as shit."

"You're telling me." Jeph snorted. "Emilio's been dead for five years. It was weird as fuck when I saw him. Not only him though, Commanders Vorman and Emmal, Aura Sols, Ergan Tranmoor, Rosco Greitz, Tao Haarn... and even Xiwaine and Xibelle Phoenix are here."

"Aura Sols? Xiwaine and Xibelle Phoenix?" Crinnan repeated. "Elia's mom and Commander Xian's children?" He paused to wait for an answer and then cocked his head. "And Commander Emmal? You mean Vassili Emmal?"

"Yes, yes and yes." Jeph nodded. "Along with a host of dead Centurions that came before us." Jeph smiled widely. "Boy you ain't seen nothing like this before. Couple dozen Centurions from over the past thirty years. Captain Bran led them all. We have some serious power now that we can fight back... and I hear that's your doing." He smiled and playfully jabbed a finger into Crinnan's chest.

"Not mine." Crinnan shook his head. "Someone else. But..." Crinnan's words were quickly cut silent.

"You asked about everyone but me." He heard a voice declare from behind him. He knew the voice well, for it was the voice of many of his memories. He hadn't heard it outside of his mind in seven years. With raised eyebrows, Crinnan turned around.

"You wound me, Crinnan." A tall elf declared with his hands on his hips. He was scraggly looking, long bearded and scarred all over. Crinnan sighed as he stared at the person, feeling sorry for what he had to have gone through in all this time. Slowly, he took a step forward.

"Sir Edmaan." Crinnan whispered.

"You look good, Jamiso." Edmaan replied, a smile lifting the right corner of his lips. "Didn't last too long though. Perhaps my tutelage was not good enough."

"No..." Crinnan shook his head at his former Knight. Crinnan had been Edmaan's squire in his teenage years. He trained under him, learned from him... and actively rejected it all. But seeing him there before him stirred Crinnan's heart.

"It seems that wherever you go you start trouble, my young squire." Edmaan said, stepping up to meet Crinnan. "Just like your father."

Crinnan snorted and Edmaan reached out, placing a hand on Crinnan's shoulder. "I'm glad you finally had the sense to listen to me." Sir Edmaan said tenderly, a tone that Crinnan had rarely heard the elf use in the past. "You did what I told you to do. You could not have saved me. Sometimes running is the best choice and I'm glad for once you were able to show a bit of wisdom."

Crinnan felt like a child again in Edmaan's presence. His mind raced back to the time in the Woolshire Highlands, when he was only sixteen years. It was the catalyst that got him and Milinka lost, that forced them to survive, and tied their hearts together forever. Sir Edmaan and Sir Demyan, Crinnan and Milinka's knights, had led them through the woods on patrol. They were surveying the area, watching for enemies, and were ambushed. Demyan and Edmaan fought fiercely, but Crinnan watched Edmaan take multiple gunshots to the chest. Demyan too quickly fell and they urged their squires to flee... So, Crinnan and Milinka did what they were told, and they ran...

"I'm sorry." Crinnan nodded his head slowly. "I wish I had been stronger."

"Quit it." Edmaan snorted as he brushed past Crinnan. "You can't simply be stronger. You can either be smarter, or dumber, but never stronger than you are." Edmaan smiled and looked over Crinnan's shoulder. "I see you brought the girl here with you?"

Crinnan looked behind himself and saw Milinka standing and crying in front of two people. One looked to be in his teens, the other appeared to be in his late twenties. Crinnan knew them both.

"She died on her own." Crinnan replied. "I found her here."

"Of course you did." Edmaan snorted. "Good for you."

"It's not like that." Crinnan sighed, turning to look at her again. The older looking of the two beings in front of Milinka turned his head and raised his eyebrows in delight. He smiled at Crinnan and took hold of Milinka's hand, pulling her as he walked toward Crinnan.

"Crinnan Jamiso!" Sir Demyan declared as he walked. "Son of the great Commander! Oh, I hate to see you and my sister here in this place, but we will make the best of it, no?"

Crinnan nodded at Sir Demyan and looked at the teenage elf that followed behind. In truth, the elf was no teenager. He was Milinka's former boyfriend Calyb who heroically gave his life to ensure Crinnan and Milinka's safety back in the Woolshire Highlands.

"I guess." Crinnan replied, looking at Demyan. "It's good to see you, Lord Demyan."

"Oh, cut it out, titles are for the living!" Demyan replied with a grin. He wrapped his arm around Milinka and pulled her in close. "Here we are all equals. Prisoners, the damned. We're all dead!"

"Prisoners no more!" Edmaan added with a grin. "Thanks to my squire!"

"Really, I didn't do anything..." Crinnan said, holding his hands out defensively. "I..."

"Nonsense, Jamiso!" Demyan belted. "I have heard the rumors! You are here to break the Hells! I know not why or how, but I do know that I can wield a sword once again. Commander Emilio gathered us all here, and more come every hour. Black Knight has found its footing in the Hells, and just like back home we will fight to gain our freedom!"

Crinnan snorted at Demyan's words, but he also grinned slightly.

"Come, Crinnan and Milinka. The battle is to begin soon! Let us take you to the commanders, that you may tell them what you know." Demyan said. "Tell them everything, Crinnan, so that they will know how best to support you in your efforts."

At that, Demyan and the rest of them stepped forward, and Crinnan followed closely behind.

Chapter Twenty-Five
Camaraderie

The Fourth Hell
Dread's Keep

"Well would you look at that!" The heavily accented voice of a long haired and widely smiling lycaani announced. "The son of Commander Jamiso, come to save us all!"

Commander Emilio Griis stepped forward and placed his hands on the sides of Crinnan's shoulders, leaning in and kissing each of his cheeks. "My have you grown, young Centurion. I remember when you stood no taller than my waist. How the time flies." The man's eyes looked heavy, undoubtedly from his experiences in the years he had spent in the Hells. Crinnan nodded respectfully to Emilio; the lycaani had been Crinnan's commander for a good portion of his life. He died shortly after Crinnan and Milinka were rescued from the Woolshire Highlands.

"And young Milinka Emmal." Emilio turned to her, his smile not reducing its width. "So good to see you have found yourself such a capable warrior to fight alongside. I trust Jamiso has been of assistance?"

Milinka looked over at Crinnan for a moment with a mischievous expression. Crinnan rolled his eyes in response, but Milinka ultimately nodded her head. "He has done a marvelous job, Commander." Milinka said. "Without him we wouldn't have ever been able to get this far."

"I am overjoyed to hear this." Emilio said and then turned toward a campfire burning behind him. His tail swished from side to side as he walked and Crinnan snorted. He remembered Emilio was the first lycaani he had ever met as a child, and at his young age he couldn't keep his eyes off the Commander's tail. Emilio held out his hands, beckoning Crinnan and Milinka to take a seat amongst a circle of people. Crinnan recognized many of them; they were former commanders, famous knights, scholars and strategists. As he sat, one called out to him.

"Look at you, young Crinnan." Aura Sols, the long dead mother of one of his closest friends Elia said. She was a fairess with thick brown tangled hair and a gentle smile. "I remember when I first met you, my beloved daughter introduced us. Do you remember?"

"Somewhat." Crinnan replied with a nod. "I remember you were very kind."

"Oh, stop." Aura waved her hand at Crinnan and looked away. "Can… can you tell me of Elia? Is she happy?"

"Yes." Crinnan nodded. "She is. She's grown into a fine person."

"It warms my heart to hear this." Aura said. "I thank you."

"And you, granddaughter." Vassili Emmal, a hulk of an Elf with a mess of blonde hair that matched his thick beard declared with a strong Kamlotian accent. "My heart weeps to see you in this dreadful place. But I also feel much pride for you. Did you die honorably?"

"I did, grandfather." Milinka replied with a warm smile. "I took many with me."

"Let us pray that those you killed do not find you here then!" Vassili replied followed by a bark of a laugh. "You were baby when I died. I am glad that you grew to be strong warrior."

"Thank you, grandfather." Milinka nodded reverently to her kin. "I am proud to have brought you honor."

"It is a joy to see the rekindling of old bonds." Emilio said, nodding along with everyone's words. "A good reminder that such connections can surpass our mortal lives." Emilio hummed gently to himself as he mulled over his own thoughts. He held his hands out to the fire, a motion learned from his time on Duraan. In the Hells, heating oneself made little sense.

"Since the arrival of young Jamiso, we have experienced significant changes." Emilio continued. "For now, it seems the days of us being the prey have ended. We have found power, we have the capability to fight back against the… demons, or players as they are referred to. I have watched, I have fought, and in this short time we have driven a number of the players into the accursed keep just over the ledge. They wait there, unable to escape, numbers too insignificant to fight back. Our assault will come soon, once we learn what you know, young Jamiso."

Crinnan looked up at the sound of his name, and then over to Milinka. He didn't know what to tell Emilio, and he found himself even more distracted as he watched the light of the fire dance on the skin of Milinka's face. The image forced his mind to recall memories from seven years prior…

Crinnan saw Milinka sitting next to him, he heard the sounds of the fire crackling and the nocturnal animals darting through the woods, but they were outweighed by the sound of her soft breathing. She leaned into him as she slept, the top of her head just under his chin. His scratched-up arms were wrapped around her, their fingers interlocked, and he stared into the fire. He wondered if he ever actually wanted to leave the Woolshire Highlands, he envisioned starting a life out there. He fantasized about just living in peace with Milinka, maybe growing a cabbage farm and never returning to their old lives. Crinnan remembered smiling and feeling a sense of peace in all the chaos…

"Crinnan." Emilio said, pulling Crinnan free of his thoughts. "Jamiso, what can you tell us?"

"Me?" Crinnan asked, shaking his head as he tried to recall the last thing he had heard Emilio say.

"Yes, Crinnan." Emilio replied. "What do you know?"

"I don't know much." Crinnan admitted. A few of those around the circle slumped their shoulders, some leaned back and stared up at the starless sky, while others simply sat and continued to listen. "I know what I have been told, and I understand only half of that…"

"Please try to explain anything you can." Emilio encouraged. "Anything should be of use."

"A… person by the name of Sage is speaking with me from home… from Duraan." Crinnan sifted through his memories, trying to think of anything relevant to relay. "He says I need to get to the Seventh Level of the Hells, that there is... some kind of... I think he called it a 'rift' that will get us out of here. He said a bunch of stuff I don't understand about NaNes and Afterscapes and a bunch of other technical shit but... I couldn't repeat any of it."

"Sage..." Emilio repeated, looking around the circle. "A name I do not know, but perhaps the name is not what matters. What *is* important is the information this 'Sage' individual has given you. The Seventh Level..." Emilio once again looked at everyone else. "Not an easy undertaking. By my understanding there are many challenges that must be conquered prior to unlocking the Seventh Level."

"We've made it this far." Crinnan said. "If that's where I need to go, then I can get there."

"Is that optimism?" Milinka asked, raising an eyebrow. "Crinnan Jamiso, how very unexpected."

"Shut up." Crinnan replied. Milinka grinned at him and snorted a laugh.

"The key to the Fifth Level lies within Dread's Keep." Xiwaine, a younger looking brown-haired elf who sat next to a nearly identical female elf declared. "Tis why we are trying to secure the castle."

"Correct, Lord Xiwaine." Emilio nodded. "If we can take Dread's keep from the players and from whatever creatures that dwell within then we can take a major step toward getting you to the Seventh Level."

"I haven't seen the keep or whatever." Crinnan said. "Where is it?"

"Over the ledge, child." Xiwaine replied. Crinnan found it odd that the young person was calling him child but then he remembered that Xiwaine was the son of Supreme Commander Xian. His twin sister, Xibelle, sat next to him giggling after every word he spoke. Crinnan assumed she was at least *near* touched. "Dread's Keep is the seat of Thornscale, Lord of Terror and king of the Fourth Level."

"Thornscale?" Crinnan repeated with a snicker. "What edgelord named him?"

Laughter erupted around the circle and Vassili spoke up. "Some Govian dog no doubt." He turned his head and spat, the flavor of his words clearly displeasing to him. Crinnan watched as some of the saliva stuck to his beard and a smile tugged on the corner of his lips.

"Thornscale is said to be a great winged demon." Xiwaine said. "The plates that cover his body are supposed to be nearly impervious to physical attack."

"What about bullets?" Crinnan asked, raising one of his pistols. "Seems to work on everyone else."

"I find it hard to imagine bullets doing any damage to Thornscale." Xiwaine said, his eyes narrowing on Crinnan.

"But it may be worth a... shot..." Ander added with a toothy grin. The Black Knights all turned and looked at him with serious expressions, and Ander quickly lowered his head. "My apologies, mighty warriors. Please continue."

"Okay then." Crinnan shrugged and holstered his weapon. "You said there were... players protecting the keep?"

"Yes." Emilio replied. "We drove them within the walls, they are waiting for us there. There are dozens of them, maybe one hundred or so. Our numbers far outweigh theirs, but they have the castle walls protecting them. Once we get through the gates, however, they will quickly fall."

"Do not forget, Lord Emilio." Lady Aura spoke up, looking to the fallen Commander. "They know the range of their abilities; they know how to fight in this place. We only know how to fight back home. We must not underestimate them."

"They die easy." Vassili Emmal snorted. "I killed three with same stone. *We* have skill, we have real experience. We know true combat; they are soft children playing game."

"Both of your observations are correct." Lord Emilio said with a nod. "In life, we all experienced many battles and not a soul here failed to take our share of lives. We trained every day, we know *how* to fight, but as Lady Aura so wisely cautioned. *They* too know how to fight in their own way. This is their land, their battleground; they have skills and magics we do not yet understand. We must make wise choices to minimize loss."

"They just appear again at First Level." Vassili Emmal argued. "Ours do not die. Only Govian dogs die."

"They're made prisoners." Crinnan added. Everyone turned their heads toward him, and he nodded awkwardly.

"What do you mean?" Aura Sols asked, raising an eyebrow.

"I mean when we kill them here, they can't escape or... log out as they call it. They turn into prisoners, it's like they die in the real world." Crinnan thought back to killing ByggDykk and felt a sliver of guilt.

"So, just like in real life then." Aura Sols said. "The more we kill the weaker they get."

"Yes..." Xiwaine added with a hint of excitement in his voice. "If they turn into prisoners when they die, then they undoubtedly start at the First Level just like we used to... naked and unskilled. They would be of no threat without their abilities and weapons." The young-looking elf grinned and stroked his chin. "Oh, this is fortuitous indeed. If we can kill them as you suggest, young Crinnan, then every victory will weaken the enemy eventually to a point where we hold the power. Not only that, but as we kill those in the Hells, we are also delivering a blow to the Govian mainland and helping our kin back home!"

A murmur passed through the circle. The idea that they could continue the fight that they had originally died for and strike back at those that had killed and tortured them for so long was very appealing. For years, lifetimes for some, the Black Knights in the circle had felt useless. Some had even succumbed to the thought that their lives had been meaningless, both back on Duraan and in the Hells. The news that Crinnan provided, and the efforts of Sage and Lucaas rekindled a fire within them, and they as one stood.

"The first step in our road to salvation is Dread's Keep." Xiwaine said, looking into the eyes of every face around the fire. "My father founded Black Knight, he enabled us to walk this road. It is our responsibility to continue what he started. It appears that the Hells is simply a single stop that we all have made. No more will our damnation be a roadblock that hinders us, but a boon that empowers us."

A chill ran down the spines of every Knight that stood around the fire. Xiwaine Phoenix was very much his father's son. Every word he spoke fed the hungry souls of the fallen Black Knights in his presence.

As Crinnan stood, he noticed that the soldiers that hadn't been a part of the campfire had stopped their work and huddled around them. They bunched up, listening closely, and for a moment Crinnan felt like he was a part of a singular organism with all of them.

"In life, we stood for something!" Xiwaine shouted, looking not only at those in the circle, but the infantry surrounding them. "For years... decades we have rotted in the darkness. We have burned, bled and been ripped apart by none other than Govia... the very ones we fought against back home. Today this ends! Our reckoning has come. No more will we succumb to the woes of perdition; no more will we be held down by our enemies. This is fate, my friends. All of our destinies are linked together! With great honor, I embrace you as I declare us all the newest bastion of Black Knight! We are the damned ones, the forgotten... but no more will we fuel these flames that nip at our feet. No, my friends... my family. From this day forward we will be the harbingers of salvation to those weary souls who surround us. Any who seek respite will find it in our company. We are the angels brave enough to dive into the belly of Duraan, we are the warriors who will take up arms against the darkness. All of you, turn your ear to me!" Xiwaine paused for a moment as his eyes scanned the small army. "We are Black Knight, and I hereby welcome you all to Base Seraphim!"

Chapter Twenty-Six
Big Sister Packs a Punch

The Fourth Hell
Dread's Keep

Crinnan couldn't stop himself. In unison with every other Black Knight around him, he pulled his sword free from its scabbard and raised it in the air. He didn't cheer or shout like the others did, but the feeling of camaraderie was one of the most overwhelming sensations he had felt in his life. Around him he heard jubilant weeping and cries of joy, and Crinnan couldn't help but reflect on that.

He didn't know how long he had been in the Hells, but Crinnan knew it was nothing compared to many that surrounded him. It was very likely that none of them had felt any sort of hope for a very long time. He was surprised any of them were still even able to process a coherent thought and couldn't imagine the joy that pulsed through their hearts.

"Let your helplessness be only a memory!" Xiwaine cried out. "One that fuels you to never bow again! We are the free ones! Join me Black Knight Seraphim and let us take Dread's Keep!"

Another round of cheering, and Xiwaine began walking. In life, Crinnan would have scoffed at the sight of the young elf leading an army, but in the Hells, Crinnan knew better. Xiwaine Phoenix had died long before Crinnan was born. He was far Crinnan's superior and Crinnan recognized that fact.

Torches were lit and weapons were equipped as the army moved away from their camp and toward the ledge that Crinnan had previously been told about. Crinnan was eager to see the keep and so he marched forward with the army.

"Infantry, on me!" Vassili Emmal shouted. "Today we show Govia who is real Demon!"

"Siege engineers to the catapults!" Tao Haarn, another fallen Commander yelled. "I need a shield wall in front of them Commander Vassili!"

"You heard Commander Tao!" Vassili yelled. "Follow me to catapults!"

Crinnan reached the ridge and stopped as he looked down into the valley below. Centered perfectly on the bare burned land was a tall black castle with walls surrounding it on all sides. He could see into the courtyard from where he stood and watched the players within mill about. He saw glowing armor, flaming swords and a number of torches.

"We have only our strength and experience to get us through this fight." Sir Edmaan said as he walked up behind Crinnan and placed a hand on his shoulder. "And of course, our heart."

Crinnan nodded, feeling a sense of comfort in his former teacher's presence. Edmaan's hand slid off of Crinnan's shoulder and he stepped up to his side.

"I am grateful that the Brothers saw fit to reunite us." He said, staring forward at the keep below. "I hope you understand that despite my harshness with you in life, I cared for you deeply Crinnan. I never bore children, I liked to think of you as my own."

"Weird." Crinnan replied. Sir Edmaan snorted a laugh and placed his hands on his hips.

"I appreciate the fact that you haven't changed." Edmaan said. "But I also see much growth in you. Your eyes... they tell a story of a person who is way too old for his age... they are a warrior's eyes."

"I've seen some shit..." Crinnan said. "I've... done even worse shit."

"We all have, Crinnan." Edmaan said. "What you do, however, does not define who you are. Only you can do that. Either you stay weak and allow your pain and rage to dominate your heart and mind, or you grow through it. You mature and *you* choose who you want to be." Edmaan reached up and patted Crinnan's back. "I look forward to fighting alongside you as an equal, Sir Crinnan." The knight dropped his hand and proceeded down the incline toward the battlements.

Being considered an equal by the lycaani knight whom Crinnan had revered and respected so much in his youth sent a cold flash through his body. He watched Edmaan walk away and couldn't help but reflect on his words. He was glad he could make his teacher proud, and excited to show him what he was capable of. As Crinnan moved to follow the knight, however, he was stopped by the words of Dali calling out to him.

"It seems that when one is around you, they never lack in excitement." Dali's voice was the same, but her inflection had... changed a bit. Crinnan thought this odd but didn't pay it any mind. She was most likely crazy from her time in the Hells. He wouldn't put it past the fairess to be harboring a number of different voices and personalities.

"Tell me about it." Crinnan snorted in response. "I couldn't have a normal day even if I wanted to."

"An organized Black Knight rebellion in the Hells..." Dali chuckled as she shook her head. "I never thought I would see anything like it." Crinnan looked over at the fairess and scrunched up his face in confusion.

"Aren't you too old to... know what Black Knight even is?" Crinnan asked. "Like. Didn't you die during the Sin Wars?"

"Dali did." She answered flatly. "But, as you won't be surprised to hear, Crinnan Jamiso, not everything in the Hells is as it seems."

Crinnan raised a brow as Dali turned toward him. A second personality wasn't supposed to know about things that they hadn't heard of. The idea of a person who had died in Ancient times knowing about Black Knight didn't make sense to him. "So you're touched?" He asked.

"Hardly." Dali replied with a smirk. "I mean. Perhaps a bit on the crazy side, but not in the way you speak of. Tell me, Crinnan. Do you recall how Sajinious Lynx speaks to you from time to time?"

"I know that he does." Crinnan said. He looked Dali up and down, trying to figure her out. He had never told her Sage's full name. How did she know so much? "I don't know how he does though."

"That is not what I was asking, but sure." Dali continued. "Well, Sage is not the only one who can... log into the Hells without a pod."

"A pod..." Crinnan repeated. He had heard the term used in relation to players logging into the Hells from the real world, but he didn't know the specifics of it.

"Yes, a Farseer Tech Hellpod. It's a large egg-shaped device that people sit in to connect to the Hells. Every family in Govia has at least one."

Dali's consistent references to the modern era were causing Crinnan to grow suspicious. He took a step away from her and gently placed a hand on the grip of his pistol. "Who are you?" He asked suspiciously.

"While you are mildly dim, one cannot accuse you of not being observant. Before I answer that question, however, I need you to promise me that you will not do anything rash." Dali replied. "Can you make that promise to me?"

"Nope." Crinnan replied flatly.

Dali smirked and shook her head at Crinnan's response. "I should have expected that. Forgive me, Crinnan..." Dali looked up at the dark sky overhead and pursed her lips together. She was silent for a moment as if she was considering her words. "I am Bishop General Sarasin Fyr. I am using this body to... help you, Crinnan Jamiso."

In a flash, Crinnan's revolver was free from its holster and the barrel was pressed against Dali's temple. "You're fucking dead." Crinnan growled.

Dali grinned and held her palm toward Crinnan's feet and then promptly blasted the ground beneath him with an unseen power. He tumbled to the ground awkwardly and raised his weapon again, but Dali was no longer there.

"You need to let me finish." Dali whispered into Crinnan's ear from behind him. "There is more for you to hear."

"Like Hells!" Crinnan shouted as he quickly got to his feet. He spun to face where the *thought* Dali was, but again was met with empty air. "Quit jumping around!" Crinnan yelled.

A hand snatched out, grabbing Crinnan's pistol and ripped it free from his grip. Crinnan reached for his other, but a leg swooped beneath him, kicking hard against the backs of his knees. He lost his balance and tumbled to his ass.

"I am not here to stop you, Crinnan." Dali softly called out. "I'm here to *help* you."

"Well, that doesn't make any fucking sense." Crinnan spat back, again reaching for his second pistol. Dali hooked her arms under his armpits and lifted, and then promptly locked her legs around his belly.

"Stop fighting." Dali said. "Let me finish."

"How are you..." Crinnan grunted as he tried to move. "How are you so strong!" With all his might, Crinnan reached forward and Dali slammed her forehead against the back of Crinnan's head.

"Ow!" Crinnan yelped. "Fucking stop!"

"You stop resisting!" Dali repeated.

"Yeah right!" Crinnan tried to move again and Dali bit down on his hair and jerked her head to the side, ripping a chunk free.

Crinnan shrieked and Dali released him. She turned her head to the side and spit his hair out, and then moved so that she was behind him and pushed him to the ground, pressing firmly against the back of his neck with her knee.

"I'm not here to stop you!" Dali harshly repeated. "Just listen to me you stubborn idiot!"

"Fine." Crinnan gasped, tapping the ground in front of him with his hand. "Just... I can't breathe."

Dali pulled her knee away and took hold of Crinnan's upper arm, pulling him up. She looked over at a group of Black Knights that were watching and smiled sweetly at them.

"Just warming up for the battle!" She called out. "All is well!" The knights laughed, and then hurried to the battlements.

"You didn't need to be so rough." Crinnan whined as he dusted himself off.

"You do not need to be so weak." Dali replied. "Let's call it payback for when you took the wheel off my bicycle so long ago."

Crinnan looked up at her and squinted his eyes. A memory immediately coming to the forefront of his mind. He saw Sayraa, his elder sister from so long ago. She was crying because she couldn't ride her bicycle after Crinnan took the front wheel off because he was a shithead. Crinnan recalled a prompt assbeating from his mother and a smug look of satisfaction on Sayraa's Face.

"I don't fucking know you *Sarasin Fyr*." He growled. "And I doubt you get around on a bicycle."

"You do not know me anymore." Dali said, stepping forward. She poked him in his sternum, and he took a step back in response. "But you used to...

Sayraa had disappeared when Crinnan was young. He remembered her getting into her bed the night before and then... not being there anymore when he woke up the next day. Sayraa was fourteen years old at the time, fourteen and pregnant. He remembered his frantic parents nearly destroying the house with worry over the disappearance of their only daughter...

"You're fucking with me." Crinnan shook his head and scowled. "Sayraa is dead. She's been dead for seventeen years."

Dali silently nodded at that comment. "Sayraa..." She whispered. "Yes, Sayraa died a long time ago, little brother. I am all that is left of her... but that does not matter right now. I *am* your sister, Crinnan. Rubaan, Kiersen, Cris... I am sister to them all. And I have come here to help you."

"No fucking way..." Crinnan shook his head. "You can't be... you're... you just have good information. You know too much about my family. Sayraa is dead..."

"Repeating something does not make it true, brother." Dali said, stepping forward. "Trust me... I know that fact *all* too well."

"What color's your hair?" Crinnan asked.

"Red." Sarasin replied.

"What was the name of my dog Kiersen ran over when I was a kid?"

"King Cabbage."

"What was the nickname you had for Rubaan?"

"Rubii."

"What's my birthday?"

"The 10th of Cidraa."

"Who are you named after?"

"Father's sister."

"Holy shit." Crinnan finally gasped. He looked into her eyes and felt a pang of nostalgia. "Sayraa?"

"Yeah Boobie." Dali said softly. "It is really me."

"This is like…" Crinnan said, shaking his head. "The worst fucking news I've ever gotten. You're Bishop General Sarasin?" He could feel his face growing red. "You joined the fucking empire? You…"

"Crinnan stop." Dali shook her head and reached out, grabbing his arm. "That's not what is important right now. What matters right now is getting you to where you need to go." "No, it does fucking matter, Sayraa." Crinnan snarled. "You kill people like me; you kill Black Knights! I heard about what you did at the Galatii Islands, I heard about the massacre!"

"It's no different from what you Centurions did in Mrask." Dali snapped back. "I heard about the decimation of the camp, how hundreds of civilians died in the fire…"

"It…" Crinnan paused and flared his nostrils. "We're fighting for freedom; you're fighting to enslave!"

"Yet innocents die either way, Crinnan." Dali replied. "This is the way of things. Do you think the civilians care whose hand they die by? Do you think they care about the freedom you fight oh so valiantly for if it leaves them dead at the end of the day? They piss on your efforts. They would rather be my slave than your casualty."

Crinnan fell silent and he looked away. Dali released her grip on his arm. "There are no good sides in this war, Boobie." She said sadly. "I have many regrets, there is much that plagues me, Crinnan… I lay awake at night thinking of the lives who have been lost or ruined because of my actions, just as I imagine you do. But we do what we must to survive… I am not here to justify or defend my actions to you, Crinnan. I am here to help you as much as I can. I want you back in this world. Sajinious Lynx has given us an opportunity to achieve that. I will do everything I can to help you get back home."

"How do you know about Sage?" Crinnan asked, turning to Dali. "Who else knows?"

"Nobody." Dali replied firmly. "I am the one preventing the Empire from learning fully of his activities. He does not know I am there, but I am masking his presence... I do not know how long I can do it though. We *must* get you out of the Hells as soon as we can."

"Fine." Crinnan conceded. "But when I get out, don't expect me to give you a big happy hug or anything. You're still who you've become and if I see you on the battlefield, I'll kill you."

"Of course, brother." Dali said. "And for now, while I have time, let's get you to the battle below so that we can unlock the Fifth Level."

Chapter Twenty-Seven
Mages on the Walls

The Fourth Hell
Dread's Keep

Crinnan stood behind the shield bearers, pistol in one hand and sword in the other. The steady thump of bullets and arrows colliding against shields could be heard, but Commander Tao's shouting to get the catapults loaded faster drowned out that noise.

To Crinnan's left stood Ander, and to his right stood Dali, Jeph and the other Centurions. Emilio wanted the Centurions ready to charge in when the gates went down, they would be the first wave and then the regular infantry would follow behind. Milinka was with her grandfather in the center of the shield bearers, holding a tower shield firmly in front of her.

"Fire!" The voice of Commander Tao rang out. Crinnan heard the sound of the catapult levers being pulled. He watched the large stones fly overhead. One crashed into the walls, taking a chunk out of it while the other two flew over the sides.

"Move up five paces!" Vassili ordered, and his shield wall inched a bit closer while the catapults were being reloaded. "Keep form!"

"Loaded!" One of the siege engineers shouted.

"Catapults one and three, adjust aim seven degrees downward." Tao ordered. "Catapult one, six degrees to the right, Catapult three, six degrees to the left."

"Ready to fire!" The three catapults reported.

"Commander Vassili, we are ready to fire!" Commander Tao shouted.

"Hold!" Vassili yelled. "Shields up!"

When Commander Tao saw that the shield wall protecting the former Centurions had stopped advancing, she threw her hand forward. "Release!"

The stones flew forward, each crashing into the walls. Their spread was too broad, but each impact took a chunk from the walls, Crinnan watched as one of the buttresses and a few parapets crumbled to the ground.

"Tighten the spread!" Tao shouted. "Catapult one, four degrees to the right, Catapult three, five degrees to the left. Catapult two maintain."

The Centurions and their shield wall slowly advanced while the catapults reloaded. Arrows and bullets rained down on them and Crinnan watched as one of the players, completely decked out in glowing armor, climbed to the top of the walls. He held his hands above him and they started glowing orange with flame.

"Mage!" Commander Emilio shouted from the archer's line. "Nock your arrows!" A moment later his voice returned. "Aim... Loose!"

Century squad ducked down behind the tower shields. Arrows flew overhead and Crinnan thought for sure that they would strike true. Strangely, however, the arrows suddenly fell from the sky as if they had simply been dropped from up high. Crinnan looked up just in time to see a large blue glowing light wall vanish. Somehow that mage had the ability to summon a larger shield like the personal ones that protected the players.

A fireball suddenly slammed into the right side of the shield wall, sending bodies flying into the ranks. Fire swarmed around the edges of the shield bearers that still stood, flames searing their arms. A few of the shield bearers screamed in pain and dropped their shields as they struggled to put out their flaming appendages.

"Fire!" Commander Tao shouted. The stones soared overhead and crashed into the walls; their spread much tighter this time. Crinnan watched a large portion of the wall fall to the ground.

The mage was not done, however. A barrage of fireballs crashed into the shield wall that was protecting the catapults, sending more bodies flying.

"Loose!" Commander Emilio shouted at his archers. "Nock!" Wave after wave of arrows soared and crashed against the ethereal wall that seemed to only phase into view when struck. "Loose!" Another barrage and another failure.

Crinnan watched as the Mage shifted his focus and summoned another ethereal shield. The catapult stones crashed against the shield and fell to the ground, sending the Black Knights nearby scurrying out of the way.

A subsequent fireball crashed into Century Squad's shield wall. Commander Vassili took the brunt of the attack, falling to his ass and roaring with fury.

"Stand strong granddaughter!" Vassili shouted, pushing against Milinka's back as her tower shield took another fireball. "I am right behind you! We need mage killed, Emilio!"

"Understood!" Emilio called out in response. "You heard him, keep firing, we must break through the mage's magic shield!"

Milinka screamed as she put all the strength she had into supporting her tower shield. Crinnan saw this and ran up alongside her, heaving a dropped tower shield from the ground. "I got you." Crinnan said, lining up the rim of his shield with hers. "We do this together…"

A blast slammed against Crinnan's shield and sent him flying backward. He landed on his back and the shield crashed down on top of him, knocking the wind from him.

"Shit!" Crinnan gasped. He was stunned, seeing double, couldn't' move his arm or legs and heard a ringing in his ears. After a moment, he shook his head and clenched his fists. He scrambled to his feet and lifted his pistol toward the mage.

"Brothers damn it all. Eat shit!" He cried out as he fired. He watched as his bullet struck the ethereal wall and cursed. The mage turned his attention to Crinnan and started cooking another fireball.

"Ah shit." Crinnan cursed as he watched the mage look directly at him. He raised his pistol and fired another shot as the magic user raised his hands to attack.

"Get back!" Dali shouted as she ran ahead of Crinnan. "Stay behind me!" The mage cocked his head and threw this fireball just as Dali held her hands in front of her. A blue ethereal shield just like the mage's appeared in front of her and it negated the attack.

Ander bolted forward, passing by Dali as his toes barely skidded against the ground. Crinnan watched on as Ander floated into the air toward the shield between the mage and Crinnan. With a glowing fist, he threw a punch and Crinnan watched as the ethereal shield pulsed for a moment, and then vanished.

"Loose!" Emilio shouted. Ander dropped to the ground and the arrows flew. They tore into the mage as if they were starving for blood, and he fell backward off the walls.

"Release!" Commander Tao shouted. One last barrage flew overhead and finished off the section of the wall. It came down, sending grey dust up into the air.

"Loose!" Emilio shouted. The archers sent a barrage of arrows through the new opening in the walls. "Fire at will!"

"Hold!" Commander Vassili shouted, raising a hand up. "Wait for arrows... Prepare to engage!"

"Archers advance!" Emilio ordered. "Shield wall, join infantry!" The archers ran forward until Emilio held up his hand motioning for them to stop. "Volley, behind the walls! Nock..." he waited a moment. "Loose!"

Crinnan heard the cries of the players within the walls. They cursed and screamed as volley after volley of arrows rained down on them.

"They will come to us." Vassili laughed, looking back at Century Squad. "They are civilians after all. When they do, Century advance to hole in wall and secure courtyard. We will engage outside."

Like clockwork, the players began to appear in the hole in the walls. The volleys of Emilio's arrows were still raining down on them and Crinnan heard a command issued behind him.

"A team, left side, B team, right side. Pincer formation, move to engage, watch friendly fire!"

"Hold! Lock shields!" Vassili yelled. "Century prepare to charge!"

The tower shields wove together and the shield bearers prepared for the attack. Crinnan looked over at Jeph who returned with a wink.

"Time to play, Jamiso." Jeph said with a wicked grin on his face. "A little revenge for the shit they put us through sound good?"

"Yep." Crinnan replied. He spun his sword in hand, accidentally smacking the shield bearer in front of him on the butt. "Shit. Sorry, are you cut?"

"Don't know, kid." The shield bearer called back. "Get your head in the fucking game."

"Old Blood." Jeph laughed, shaking his head. "Don't fuck with them. We young guys ain't got nothing on them."

"Steady!" Vassili shouted. The players were nearly on them. "Steady... push!" The players slammed into the shields, swinging their swords like the amateurs that they were. The Black Knights moved as a unit, pushing the players to the ground. They stepped forward, stabbing as they moved, and began pushing their weight into the players.

"Mage!" Vassili called back. "Take them out!"

Three forms had gathered at the hole in the wall and were all casting ethereal shields in front of them. Emilio's archers fired but were unable to penetrate the magic defenses. Crinnan heard Vassili curse, but then Ander and Dali stepped forward.

"We will take care of this, esteemed Commander Vassili." Ander said as he patted Vassili on the shoulder. A barrage of fireballs slammed into the shield wall, and Dali threw up an ethereal shield of her own that stretched the length of the wall.

"It will not last for long." Dali said. "Move quick Ander!" Ander nodded and looked at the Mages. His own personal ethereal shield swirled formed around him, swirling and shining a much brighter blue than any Crinnan had seen before.

"A power pleads for release..." Ander said as he floated into the air. "One I have... not yet utilized..." Ander was at least twelve feet off the ground. He held his arms out and raised his eyes toward the sky. The fireballs were blasting ineffectually against his shield, and finally his hands clenched into fists.

The mage in the center of the trio suddenly lifted off the ground and one of Ander's clenched fists reached out to him. Crinnan could hear the mage screaming, and realized it was Ander who was lifting him. Ander's hand opened, and the screaming mage's body twisted and popped in unnatural positions. Crinnan watched with revulsion as the mage's arms folded again and again, blood and bone splintering and splashing out as the skin burst. The look on the mage's face was one of pure terror, and when Ander seemed to gain control over his newfound... or rediscovered power, the mage's head snapped backward, his throat bursting open and spewing blood forward against his ethereal shield.

Ander gasped and his eyes opened, glowing a magnificent amber color. He threw his other hand out at the mage on the left and Crinnan watched as the mage's body suddenly locked up. Ander trembled as he fought the Mage's will, and Crinnan heard the target screaming as his hand moved on Ander's accord. After a few moments, Ander was able to raise the mage's hand to his own temple, and then Crinnan watched a fireball blast out, destroying the mage's head and killing him.

Ander fiercely turned his head toward the final mage and clapped his hands together. Crinnan gasped as the mage's body burst, sending blood and gore in all directions. The final ethereal shield went down, and Ander fell to the ground suddenly exhausted.

"Century, get to hole!" Vassili shouted. At that, the couple dozen members of Century squad swarmed around the sides of the shield wall and sprinted to the hole that the catapults had created.

"This is your chance, oh fabled Centurions!" Xiwaine Phoenix shouted from their ranks. "Show the Hells why your name is feared all across Govia!"

Century burst through the hole in the wall and didn't waste a second. Crinnan charged forward, driving the point of his blade through the eye of a player.

Player: Shawnyboy09 EXECUTED

Player Rank: 17,490,466,373

Crinnan roared with bloodlust. It had seemed like such a long time since he had progressed in ranking, and hearing his notification fueled his adrenaline. He ripped his weapon free of the player and spun to shoot another square in the chest.

Player: TemporalAGT EXECUTED

Player Rank: 14,384,155,987

Congratulations, PrettyKitty6969420! You have advanced in ranking!

Previous Rank: 23,565,844,625

New Rank: 18,975,000,306

Previous Percentile: 78%

New Percentile: 63%

...

NEW PERCENTILE ACHIEVED! Congratulations, you are showing your true power. Your buffs have been modified.

Cosmetic Items unlocked! See your wardrobe for more details!

...

Congratulations! You have crossed the threshold of the 70th percentile

The player screamed, falling backward as a fountain of blood jettisoned out of him. Crinnan snorted at the ridiculous sight and ducked under a flamberge coming right for his eyes. He pivoted and swung his sword, severing the player's spine. The player fell to the ground, and Crinnan fired a shot into the back of his head.

Player: StreamBonker EXECUTED

Player Rank: 18,177,999,548

Congratulations, PrettyKitty6969420! You have advanced in ranking!

Previous Rank: 18,975,000,306

New Rank: 18,576,499,927

Previous Percentile: 63%

New Percentile: 61%

"This is too easy!" A Centurion by the name of Renlo Davies laughed. He spun his spear masterfully and intently, slicing across one of the players faces. The player screamed and stumbled backwards; his lips now open all the way across his face. Renlo waggled his eyebrows and pulled a sawed-off double barrel shotgun from his hip, promptly blasting half the player's head clear off his neck.

Crinnan continued his slaughter by dragging his blade across the bloated belly of a player that reminded him of ByggDykk. The player screamed as his guts sloshed out like a family of worms bursting through a dead cat's butthole.

He collapsed in a slippery pile of writhing, throbbing guts and screamed for his mother until Crinnan silenced him by way of the ol' sword-through-eye-socket.

Player: Pagacco EXECUTED

Player Rank: 18,555,188,965

Congratulations, PrettyKitty6969420! You have advanced in ranking!

Previous Rank: 18,576,499,927

New Rank: 18,565,844,446

Crinnan moved onto the next target. He swung his sword downward, severing the player's hamstring. The player tumbled forward with a loud scream, and as he fell, Crinnan fired a round into the back of the person's head. The player was back in the First Level before Crinnan could turn toward the next one.

Player: Cheeseboi68419 EXECUTED

Player Rank: 17,999,999,998

Congratulations, PrettyKitty6969420! You have advanced in ranking!

Previous Rank: 18,565,844,446

New Rank: 18,282,922,222

Previous Percentile: 61%

New Percentile: 60%

"Herd them!" Xiwaine shouted from... some-fucking-where. Crinnan had no idea. "Get them to the middle of the courtyard so we can end this!"

"Come on then!" Jeph laughed. He swung his axe through a player's shoulder, hacking the elf's arm free. "Get in the middle!" The player fell to his knees and Jeph rolled his eyes. "Can't follow orders?" Jeph swung his weapon to the side, scalping the elf. "Fine with me."

After only a few moments of fighting, the players dropped their weapons and fell to their knees, admitting defeat. Century Squad had surrounded them and stared at the pitiful creatures with disdain. Crinnan thought it was all a ridiculous sight. The dark and edgy avatars crafted by the citizens of Govia. He saw wings and horns, fancy glowing armor barely hiding big unrealistic tits and muscles that no real person had. He stared at them with contempt, knowing they were all guilty of countless moral crimes against other conscious beings. He sucked on his teeth as he looked at them with contempt, and then turned to Xiwaine.

"You couldn't even die honorably." Xiwaine tsked and taunted them as he circled the group. "You are so mighty when your target cannot return the fight, but now that they have taken up arms against you, you... beg for mercy?"

"Please!" One of them cried out, clasping his hands together before Xiwaine. "I have kids back home. I have a job!"

"I'm in college!" Another cried out. "I'm about to graduate!"

Xiwaine stopped walking and looked down at one of them. He tilted his head as the elf refused to make eye contact with him.

"And what's your story?" Xiwaine asked, kneeling down to look into the person's eyes. "Why should I let *you* live."

"Y-you shouldn't." The person replied with a defeated tone. "W-we... we have done wrong... we deserve to die."

Xiwaine raised his eyebrows and slowly stood. He held his position for a moment and looked down at the repentant player with consideration in his eyes. Licking his lips, he reached his hand out, gently caressing the side of the player's face. Without another word, his lips formed into a snarl and he whipped a revolver free of its holster on his hip. In an instant, he had discharged the weapon and the elf fell to the ground, dead.

"Kill them all." Xiwaine ordered. "Let no player walk away from this keep. We begged for mercy for years and were shown none, let us repay them in kind for their transgressions against us!"

Chapter Twenty-Eight
A Grim Duty

The Fourth Level
Dread's Keep

Crinnan watched Xiwaine take hold of one of the players by their collar and lift them up from the ground. The player squealed in fear as the elf, who only looked like a teenager, dragged him to a line of other players who were sitting on their knees with their heads lowered and hands bound behind them. Crinnan had seen this before, he had *participated* in this before. This was an execution of prisoners of war. Black Knight did not take prisoners back to their bases; they gathered what information they could on the battlegrounds, and then gave them a quick death.

"On your knees, Govian." Xiwaine ordered, pushing the player to the ground. "Line up, keep it tight. You know, I used to hate the idea of this back in real life. Father told me of occasions where he had to kill his prisoners. It sounded scary, it frightened me... but now, after all these decades enduring what your kind has done to me and watching what you did to my sister... let's just say that I am fearless. You all deserve this, and I very much look forward to giving it to you."

Xiwaine produced a knife from his belt as he slowly walked behind the first player. The blue haired faire player whimpered with fear and trembled, closing his eyes as he mumbled a prayer to Dura'ana.

"She is not here." Xiwaine leaned in and whispered as he clutched a handful of the faire's hair. He pulled back, eliciting a whimper from the prisoner. Xiwaine stood up and looked down at his prisoner with a scowl. He appeared to be savoring the moment, it was as if he was imprinting it in his mind so he could look back on it. "Any last words, Govian?" Xiwaine finally asked with a smooth, calm tone.

"Please, don't do this..." The faire started to beg but was silenced as Xiwaine swiped the blade across his throat. The faire's milky colored skin split apart, and blood gushed out in a torrent that sprayed the ground in front of him. Xiwaine released the faire's hair and he fell backward to the ground, kicking and hissing for a few moments before he lost consciousness.

"To torture those who cannot fight back is true cowardice!" Xiwaine yelled as he pulled back on one of the horns of his next victim. "Deplorable, a mark of a truly weak being!" He cut the throat of the demon player and then pushed him forward. "On this day I am the reaper of the seeds you have sown; I am your end!" He grabbed another head and pulled back.

Crinnan frowned at the monologuing. He shook his head and looked down at the bloody ground beneath him. To die in combat was one thing, but to be teased while knowing your death was unavoidable left a foul taste in his mouth. He didn't disagree that they should die, but he also recognized that a person deserved to hear their own thoughts as they passed.

"You!" Xiwaine shouted, nearly in a rage. He pointed the tip of his knife toward Crinnan. "You look away, why?"

"You're drawing it out." Crinnan replied. "You don't need to do that."

"You disagree with my methods?" Xiwaine asked, tilting his head in curiosity. "Then please, step forward and take over."

"I didn't..." He began to protest but Xiwaine shoved past the player kneeling in front of him and approached Crinnan.

"Take over, young knight!"

Crinnan didn't like being challenged, and he didn't like being ordered around by someone who didn't even hold rank in the army. He glared into Xiwaine's eyes, not breaking contact, and then shrugged. Stepping forward, he made his way behind the players and pulled out his pistol.

"May you find peace." Crinnan whispered as he raised the weapon to the back of the player's head. Without flinching he pulled the trigger and took a step to his right.

"May you find peace." Crinnan repeated, firing again. He did this until he counted that his cylinder had run dry, and then drew his second revolver. When he was done, twelve bodies lay on the ground in front of him. Crinnan took in a deep breath and walked over to Xiwaine.

Congratulations, PrettyKitty6969420! You have advanced in ranking!

Previous Rank: 18,282,922,222

New Rank: 17,845,988,312

Previous Percentile: 61%

New Percentile: 59%

"No matter the life they lived." Crinnan said, once again locking his eyes with Xiwaine's. He quoted Captain Bran, leader of Century Squad. "They all deserve a word of comfort. The reaction to the responsibility of taking a life, no matter how evil, shows a person's true character." Crinnan holstered his weapons and his eyes wandered upward to the hole in the wall that the Centurions had originally charged through. There he saw Milinka standing. She was wordlessly looking down at him with an empathetic expression spread over her face. Their gazes met for a moment, and then Crinnan looked away.

"We don't torture people. Someone finish the job." Crinnan barked out. "And show a little fucking respect." He turned from Xiwaine and saw the members of Century Squad giving him approving looks. They had all heard Captain Bran speak on the responsibility of killing in their lives, and to hear the words again was both sentimental and comforting.

"Xianson!" The booming voice of Vassili passed through the opening in the walls and into the courtyard. "Enemy reinforcements. They come!"

"How many!" Xiwaine yelled. He gave Crinnan one last glance before turning and marching toward Vassili.

"Many!" Commander Vassili replied, finally appearing next to his granddaughter. "Thousands."

"By the Brothers..." Xiwaine spat. He took a moment to cradle his chin in his hand as he thought.

As they waited, the rest of the army hurried in through the hole. The infantry, archers and catapult crew scrambled in, joining Century Squad. The last people in were Commanders Emilio and Tao, and they hurried up to Xiwaine and Vassili.

"We disabled the catapults." Commander Tao, a platinum haired vampress who perished ten years prior to Crinnan's death reported. "The players will not be using them against us."

"My archers are taking position on the walls. Commander Vassili, dispatch your shield bearers to the breach." Commander Emilio quickly said and then turned to Crinnan. "Jamiso. You have the most important mission of us all. You must enter the keep, face the challenges inside, and get to the Fifth Level." He reached out, grabbed Crinnan's upper arm and took a step closer. "There is no time for us to discuss it. We are *all* counting on you, son. We will be at your back; we will hold those that wish to stop you at bay. I know you are not the most... cheery of people, but if ever you had reason to truly trust anyone, let it be now."

"In there..." Crinnan looked up at the glistening black stone castle before him. It stood tall and foreboding, a simple rectangular keep that jutted jarringly out of the ground. Crinnan stared up at it, he didn't like its ominous look and based on what he had been told thus far about its lord, he wasn't eager to see what was inside.

"I have faith in you, my friend." Emilio encouraged. He reached down and took hold of Crinnan's hands, squeezing them with his own trembling fingers. "Your mother and father took Exgrane for us. Strong blood flows through you. You are a Centurion, which means you are among the best, *and*..." Emilio nodded his head past Crinnan. "You are not going alone."

Crinnan glanced back to see Ander, Milinka and Dali standing behind him. He looked them over and turned back toward Emilio.

"And us." A voice called out from Crinnan's right. He looked over as his former knight, Sir Edmaan approached alongside Milinka's brother and former knight Sir Demyan, each sporting a kite shield and sword. "We'll do what we can to get you where you need to go, Jamiso."

Crinnan reluctantly nodded at the two Knights, and Emilio spoke. "Then you will go with the blessing of all of us. May you find the way to end this, Crinnan Jamiso, and may the Brothers protect you from harm."

"Five hundred yards!" Commander Tao shouted. "Emilio, we need you." At that, Emilio gave Crinnan a thin smile, and hurried to the stairs that led up the wall.

"No time to tell us not to come." Demyan declared as he and Edmaan hurried to the front of the group. Their heavy armor clanked as they jogged and led Crinnan and the rest to the main entrance of Dread's Keep. "We are doing this for you, Crinnan and Milinka."

"Everyone!" Jeph Scaven bellowed as Crinnan ran past. "Lay your eyes on the one who will free us from this place!" Jeph whooped and smiled as he nodded at Crinnan. "A whelp in life, and a true *Demon* in death. Cordi Altuun, Crinnan Jamiso!"

"Cordi Altuun!" The other Black Knights shouted as one. They stomped their feet on the ground and then pounded their chests with a single fist, ending their sendoff with a grunt. Crinnan paused and his lower lip trembled at the sight. He had never been the recipient of a Cordi Altuun in his life, for it was a blessing that was highly revered and rarely used in Black Knight. Crinnan turned toward everyone, grateful and fearful of the faith and honor that was bestowed upon him and tried to look them all in the eyes.

Crinnan stared at the Black Knights before him and felt his eyes rim with tears at the sight. His heart pounded and his hands trembled. Everything was becoming more and more real for him by the moment, the stakes were getting higher and higher... coming into contact with people he cared about made him realize how important his mission was. How important *he* was. These were all lives he could save, souls he could renew, and he refused to let them down.

"Cordi Altuun!" Crinnan yelled. "To... to all of you!" He didn't want to cheapen the honor, but he knew every person before him was more than deserving of having the words spoken to them. They needed it, after years, decades and some even a century of being nothing more than meat to torture or fuck. They needed to be empowered, they needed to feel like the mighty warriors they had spent their lives being. The Black Knights raised their weapons high into the air and cheered for the one whom they entrusted their fates unto.

"Let's go." Sir Edmaan said, ushering everyone forward. "There is nothing more for us out here. To the doors, hurry!"

The group ran as the battle began. Arrows rained from the sky, planting deep into the ground all around them. Edmaan and Demyan raised their shields above their heads while Ander and Dali summoned ethereal shields to protect the rest. The way up was… harrowing. Hundreds of steps needed to be climbed and multiple times Crinnan looked back as he watched the Black Knights fight on. He saw some fall, he saw some triumph, and when he had climbed enough steps, he looked out over the walls and his heart sunk.

There were indeed thousands of players converging on the hole they had broken in the walls of Dread's Keep. He watched ladders go up on the walls, he watched the players funnel through the single breach. Crinnan knew this was a battle that Black Knight, no matter how much heart they had, could not win.

He wasn't sure whether it was because they truly believed in him or because they had nothing to lose, but the idea that the few hundred Black Knights would stand and fight to keep him alive… shook him. Who in their right mind would *willingly* lay down their lives in sacrifice for the *hope* that a person that many of them had never met before would save them? What small group would stand against many times their numbers at impossible odds because their faith outweighs their reasoning? Crinnan shook his head as he stared down at the beginning of the battle that would surely kill them all. He imagined them all dead, all those who came before him… and for a moment he hesitated.

"Crinnan!" Ander called out, running to his side. "Why do you tarry, we must go!"

"It's all in vain…" Crinnan snorted. He watched one of the Black Knight archers fall and felt a numbness in his body. "Look at them all…" Crinnan gestured toward the players at the walls. "There are just too many…"

"And they will *all* come for you, Crinnan." Ander said grimly. "No matter what, they will come for you. They will not simply lay down and give up, not when there is an enemy to direct their fear toward."

"Fear?" Crinnan asked, crinkling his brow.

"Oh yes." Ander said softly. "While they dwell within fantastical bodies, adorn themselves with illustrious armor, and wield weapons they never could even lift on Duraan... while they give off the image of power... they are but mortals... and they are trapped. They are weak, they are afraid, and they are desperate. They, as does every prisoner here, fear that they will never leave this place. They believe if they fight, they can hold on to their mortality. This fight has become just as real to them as it has to you."

"They have all been backed into a corner." Sarasin added through Dali. "Govia is losing control. The citizens cannot go back home, they cannot escape all this... Govia has locked down the Hells to combat the efforts of Sajinious Lynx. While the dead still pour in, *nobody* is allowed out."

"Then how will I... we get out?" Crinnan asked. "If they've locked it all down..."

"Trust in Sajinious." Dali said with a thin smile. "I have seen his plan... and I am relatively certain it will work."

"It will." Milinka added, stepping forward. "It has to. All this can't be for nothing. Have faith Crinnan."

"Faith..." Crinnan repeated, slowly shaking his head. "Faith in what?"

"Faith in me." The voice of Sage replied. *"I should say, Crinnan, it is nigh time you start trusting someone other than yourself."*

"How can I?" Crinnan asked. "I can't... I can't even see your face. I have no idea what you're doing I... I have no idea what *I* am doing!"

"That is what faith is." Sage said softly. *"A knowledge that there is something you cannot do but need done, and the trust that someone or something other than yourself will achieve it for you."*

"Faith..." Crinnan said again, slowly lowering his head. "It... sounds like people who need faith just need to get stronger. You can't just... trust everyone like that. Everyone has their own interests in mind, and they only help you when it serves them in the long run."

"A weaker person would be offended by that." Sage said, maintaining a kind tone. *"But I understand your feelings and do not pass judgment upon you for feeling the way you do. Maybe there is even some truth to your words. Maybe I do have something to gain from saving you."*

"And what is that?" Crinnan asked. He watched a fireball explode against a group of archers below, saw the bodies flying backward from the blast.

"That is for me to know." Sage replied. *"For now, have faith that I truly want my goals to come to reality, and for that to manifest. I need you to be alive."*

"Well fucking great." Crinnan sighed.

"Enter Dread's Keep." Sage instructed. *"Find Thornscale, and complete whatever it is he requires to open the portal to the Fifth Level... Your journey is halfway complete, Crinnan. There is no sense in doubting yourself... or me now."*

At that, Sage went silent and Crinnan turned to the others. He looked at them, all five of them, and nodded.

"Are we going to do this or what?" He grumbled. He pushed against the gigantic arched door in front of him, stepped inside... and then he vanished.

Chapter Twenty-Nine
His Fear

The Fourth Level
Dread's Keep

The bottom of Crinnan's boot thumped against the ground beneath him as he took his first step into Dread's Keep. Echoes of his footfalls reverberated into what could have been an endless hallway, though it was much too dark for Crinnan to know where he stood. The door to the keep shut behind him, and Crinnan found himself breathless under the pressure of the suffocating silence.

"Hello?" Crinnan called out, expecting any of the members of his group to respond. He, however, received no reply. He spun in place for a moment, searching for someone... *anyone* but it seemed they were all gone.

"Well shit." Crinnan grumbled. He could feel his heart thumping in his chest as he anxiously began to walk forward. He couldn't see a floor or any walls, but his steps continued to echo all around him.

"Sage?" Crinnan whispered. "Lucaas?" Again, no response. "Is anyone fucking there?"

Silence.

Another step, and Crinnan moved deeper into the pitch black keep. Then another, and he began to wonder how far he could walk before he ran into something. It *was* a keep, there had to have been an end to it. Perhaps some furniture, a table or a chair somewhere... but then Crinnan remembered he wasn't in Duraan. He was in the Hells, and *nothing* in the Hells was as it should be.

Crinnan heard the sound of movement, a strange skittering across the floor, and then a small breathy laugh. He anxiously pulled his gun free in response, stopping and spinning in place. He held his weapon out in front of him, but something was wrong. The handle wasn't hard like it was supposed to be. It was warm... soft... fuzzy...

A sudden screech and then the sound of wings flapping caused Crinnan to jump back and throw whatever was in his hand. Whatever it had been, a *bat* it had felt like, flew away. Crinnan cursed and grit his teeth together. He was being fucked with and he did not like it.

Crinnan breathed rapidly and his heart thumped in his chest. He wanted to turn around and just go fight and die with the other Black Knights outside but... he no longer knew which way the door was. He couldn't see anything; he couldn't hear anything... for all he knew he no longer even existed.

"Hello!" Crinnan yelled, looking all around for any sign of light. "Somebody!"

Silence.

Crinnan started to walk again. He walked in whatever direction he was facing, slowly and carefully at first. He tried to be patient, he held his hands in front of him feeling for any kind of obstacle, waiting for a wall that should have come... but it didn't. He kept going, his feet moving a little faster, his patience wavering, but he could not find the wall; he could not find an end...

After what had to have been at least ten minutes of blind wandering Crinnan broke into a sprint. He ran, flailing his arms about hoping that his fingers would brush against something... he pushed himself harder, to go faster. He didn't care if he ran face first into the wall at that point, he simply wanted to find it. He needed to find something other than himself.

"Run." A voice he didn't recognize called out to him. He stopped, and looked around, hoping to find the owner of the voice but... it was too dark.

"Where are you!" Crinnan yelled, reaching his hands out again. "Let me... Come to me!"

"Run." The voice repeated, this slightly more aggressively. One by one, additional voices from all around him repeated the same word. "Run... Run... Run..." It became a chant, almost tribal in nature as the voices culminated into one.

Crinnan's nostrils flared and he pulled his second pistol free. This time the handle was as it was supposed to be, and as soon as he heard another voice shout at him... he lifted his weapon and fired...

For a split second, the flash from the muzzle illuminated the area. He saw melted emaciated faces, grey and elongated with mouths open and black holes where their eyes were supposed to be. Long fingers with sharp nails reached for him, they wanted him, they wanted to dig into him and rip as they distributed chunks of him to each other... Crinnan gasped and fell to his knees, covering his head with his hands as he waited for the attack... but none came. He clenched his teeth together and panted through his nose, waiting... and nothing happened to him.

Silence.

After a few minutes, Crinnan stood. He reached out, feeling for whatever had surrounded him but he felt nothing. No people, no creatures... nothing.

The sound of his breathing filled his ears, the pounding of his heart shook his body. Crinnan slowly spun in place as he waited for something to happen... Something *had* to happen eventually...

RING

"What's that?" He asked, looking around.

RING

"A... phone?"

RING

"What is going on!?" He finally shouted, stomping his foot in fury.

The ringing stopped and a female voice spoke. "Who is this? Hello?"

Crinnan's heart sank. He felt the hair on his arms stand straight up, and his lower lip quivered as he listened to the voice.

"M...mom?" Crinnan asked, not believing what he was hearing.

"Rubaan?" Crinnan's mother asked. "Rubaan, why are you crying?"

"No!" Crinnan shouted. "Not Rubaan... It's me mama..."

Crinnan heard nothing. His mother did not respond.

"Mama, please..." Crinnan continued. "Are you there?"

"Who is this?" A different voice demanded. He sounded angry, *fiercely* angry. "What do you want?"

"D-dad!" Crinnan shouted. "It's me, it's Crinnan!"

"Crinnan is dead!" His father shouted. "I don't know what kind of sick fucking..."

"No! It's me! I... I made the bench with you; my name is carved on... on the bottom! Mine and Rubii's!"

Silence.

"Dad... please!" Crinnan begged. "Dad, you... when I... before I left for Kamlot you told me not to get anyone pregnant. When I... when you found me and Milinka... you hugged me and you said, you said you'd thought you'd lost me... that you loved me..."

Crinnan heard the sound of sniffling on the other end of the line. "You're dead..." His father whispered. "How..."

"I'm dead!" Crinnan replied. "I'm in the fucking Hells Dad! I'm..."

"Crinnan..." His father finally whispered. "Crinnan, my son... is it... is it truly you?"

"Dad, it's me!" Crinnan repeated. "I'm..."

"You're not dead." His father said, his voice breaking into a chuckle.

"W...what?" Crinnan asked.

"You never existed; you are a piece of unwanted fucking garbage." His father replied in an amused tone. "You were a mistake; you've *always* been a mistake. Don't entertain the idea that I ever loved you. You're nothing."

"Dad... stop it..." Crinnan whispered. "You..."

"You're no son of mine." At that, the call abruptly ended and Crinnan curled his lip into a scowl. Tears fell down his cheeks and he clenched his hands in fury.

"Breathe, Crinnan." He heard the soothing voice of his friend Elia echo in his mind. *"It's okay... just breathe."*

Crinnan focused on the voice, took a breath in through his nose, and then let it out through his mouth. He closed his eyes, though it was already dark, and tried to center himself as Elia had taught him.

"You're strong, you're enough..." The memory of her voice continued. Crinnan nodded his head as he felt some of the stress lift off of him. *"You're going to die."*

Crinnan's eyes shot open, he gasped, and then took off running again. He didn't know which direction he was going, and in the darkness he wasn't sure that direction even *existed* anymore. He simply ran, pleading with the darkness for an exit, begging for a glimmer of light.

After what could have been minutes, or what could have been days Crinnan finally stopped. He was panting, sweating and he felt like if his heart beat any faster it would burst. He bent over, resting his palms on his thighs, and simply breathed.

"Think, Crinnan..." He told himself. "Think... there has to be a way out... get... get fucking control over yourself, you can do this!"

The silence was broken by the sound of... fire. Well, the sound of wood crackling in a fire. Quickly, Crinnan spun around toward the direction of the sound and saw a soft flickering orange light in the distance.

Without a single word or another thought, Crinnan ran toward the fire. The flames tugged at him as if he were a moth. He knew that danger most likely would meet him at the light, but the allure of it was too strong. He wanted it, no he yearned for it... in his mind there was nothing other than himself and the light and he resolved to merge the two into one.

He ran without ceasing, he didn't even breathe until he reminded himself to do so. He ran for days, weeks, months... he knew neither the duration nor the distance that he ran, only that he did. A lifetime or perhaps only a moment later, Crinnan stopped. He reached up to scratch his face and his fingers pressed against the coarse hairs of a beard. With both hands, he felt the edges of the thick bushy hair that hung down his chest and he gasped.

"How long..." He whispered... "How long has it been?" Crinnan's mind had never been further from himself, he barely grasped onto the idea of who or where he was. He knew only darkness, only fear... only desire to find the light.

Yet none of it seemed real, for the only thing that Crinnan was fully convinced that existed... was nothing.

Crinnan stared at the fire... no larger than the eye of a needle now. He watched the flame that had once flickered brightly shrink as if it were being carried further away. Crinnan blinked, and the flame turned to a coal... and then... it was nothing.

Silence...

Darkness...

Crinnan...

For a moment, Crinnan stood and stared at the place where the light had been. It was no more, he had run for so long, fought for so long for the idea of something that had simply... vanished. Crinnan felt cheated, he felt angry. He *wanted* that light; he *deserved* that light! Why would the light go away after he had pursued it so fervently? He was suddenly lost, he felt hopeless.

The light was gone...

...

Had it ever existed?

Had... *he* ever existed?

Did... *anything* exist?

Crinnan felt an incredible weight on his shoulders and with a sigh, he sat down. The ground was neither hot nor cold, neither soft nor hard... it was there but... it wasn't. Crinnan did not know what he sat upon, and while every fiber of his being cared, he also could not have cared less. It was time for everything to end. He knew it, he wanted it. Nothing mattered anymore... the light was gone and... so was he... *if* he even existed in the first place.

Crinnan stretched his arms behind him and leaned back. He raised his head to the blackened sky above him and closed his eyes. He tried to envision something that would bring him comfort, but he only heard screaming in his mind. A tempest that swirled in his head and then flushed down his throat and into his heart. Crinnan felt it; it burned hotter than any heat he had ever experienced. It swelled within him, it waged war against his chest, promising to tear him apart...

And then... a small voice broke through the storm. It confused Crinnan, it drove the screaming away. The pain lifted and he finally felt like he was able to breathe again.

"Is... is this love?" The voice of Milinka echoed in his mind.

They were children again; he felt her clinging to his arm with her head resting on his shoulder. "Is it, Crinnan?"

"I don't know..." He mouthed the words as they played in his mind. He was young, nervous... more afraid than he had ever been in his life... "I... I think so..."

"Can I say it?" Milinka asked.

The fear that churned in Crinnan's heart as he and Milinka sat under the Kamlotian night sky was unlike anything that he would *ever* experience again. The fear... of being loved.

Love...

A power greater than what the Hells could pile upon his shoulders... a force that had delivered a fear into young Crinnan's heart that would never be matched again. He had experienced it before and at the time the boy didn't realize how powerful his love truly made him.

Young Crinnan turned and pressed his forehead against the side of Milinka's. His lips brushed against her ear, and he felt the hair on his arms rise. He bit his lip as if to keep himself from talking, but a greater power inside him willed the words.

"Say it..." He whispered. He conveyed his desire passionately, desperately even. He wanted to hear her say the words. He wanted to share his love with the girl. His mind begged for it; his heart screamed for her to say it.

"I love you Crinnan..."

Crinnan growled as the power flooded through him. He grunted as he pushed himself off the ground and within moments his sword was in hand.

The light wasn't gone...

It had always been there... he simply refused to see it.

He did exist...

It was *all* **real**.

"Come on!" Crinnan challenged as he spun in place. He had never yelled so loudly in his life; he had *never* felt as confident as he did in that moment. He was his own, he *would* get through this. He would break the Hells, he would save Milinka...

The sound of chains sliding and rattling across the ground filled Crinnan's ears and before he could respond, cold rusted metal wrapped around him. It spun and squeezed as it encased his body, ripping away his armor and clothing and casting the shreds aside. Crinnan screamed as the chains tore through his flesh as they migrated to his wrists and ankles. They pulled on him, stretching his extremities as his body was lifted into the air.

"Dread..." A deep guttural voice echoed throughout the darkness. "Fear... I can taste it... I can *feel* your fear."

The world around him exploded and burst into flames and Crinnan screamed in agony as shards of solid darkness tore through him. The fire cascaded over his body like wind, scorching his exposed flesh and cooking him inside and out. The light revealed thousands... no, millions of the grey skinned demons that he had seen before. They surrounded him, they reached for him and screamed his name with hungry voices.

The fire coalesced into a spinning vortex in front of him, and the demons silenced. The low rumbling of the inferno filled the area, and Crinnan could do nothing but watch as a great and powerful demon stepped out of the vortex, threw its head back, and roared.

"Thornscale." The small demons cried out before falling to their knees and lifting their arms in worship. They bowed down, faces flat on the burning ground and Crinnan watched as one by one their bodies were ripped apart and pulled into the vortex. The pull was intense and Crinnan felt his own blood being ripped from his body as Thornscale approached him.

"Speak your fear." Thornscale commanded as he reached out and touched the muscles of Crinnan's cheek with the tip of one of his long, pointed claws. The creature was gigantic, standing at least forty feet tall. His body was muscular and throbbed as blood and magma burped from the spaces between his scales.

"You…" Crinnan whimpered as he tried to pull his face away from the demon. "You already know my fears."

"Manifest them." Thornscale ordered. He lowered his head so that he was level with Crinnan's gaze. The demon's eyes glowed red and tongues of fire forked out of the top as they swirled and raged.

"I… I don't know what to say!" Crinnan yelled, realizing he was nothing before the creature. "I don't know… how!"

"Speak." Thornscale continued. His tone was calm, but Crinnan felt that the magnitude of Thornscale's voice could have leveled an entire city.

"I…" Crinnan was screaming, the pain he was enduring was overwhelming, but something told him he *had* to do this. He had to speak his fears. "I fear…"

"Yes." Thornscale encouraged. "Speak it. Realize it."

"I fear death!" Crinnan shouted. "I don't want to not live… I…"

"Deeper!" Thornscale ordered. "Something greater tears at your heart, it torments you in the night, it keeps you awake. Speak your fear, child!"

"I…" Crinnan only knew of one thing that kept him awake at night. It wasn't death, it wasn't subjugation… it was *her*.

"Speak!" Thornscale boomed. "Manifest that which plagues your heart!"

"I fear her love!" Crinnan roared. "I fear giving my love! It… I… I'm terrified I'm not enough for her… for anyone!" He lowered his head and wept. Thornscale laughed a low rumble of a laugh and took a world-shaking step backward. He turned, reaching his massive hand into the fire tornado that raged behind him, and then pulled it back out.

"The time has come to face your fear." Thornscale instructed. His hand was clenched, and he raised it up so that Crinnan could see what he held.

Squirming in Thornscale's fist… was Milinka. She fought and screamed as she was brought before Crinnan, and Crinnan's eyes grew wide.

"No!" Crinnan yelled. "Let her go!"

"She will be released." Thornscale replied flatly. "When you face your fear."

Crinnan's mind raced and he looked at the terrified girl in front of him. He knew what he had to do, and fear couldn't get in his way.

"Milinka!" Crinnan yelled. "Milinka!"

Milinka stopped fighting and looked at Crinnan. Her eyes were bloodshot, and she was breathing heavily.

"It will be okay!" Crinnan promised. "It's... all going to be okay."

"Speak your fear!" Thornscale ordered.

"Milinka..." Crinnan's voice cracked and he began to sob.

"Say it..." Milinka gasped. "Say the words Crinnan."

"I love you Milinka!" Crinnan roared. Spittle flew from his mouth and tears streamed from his eyes. "I always have! I'm sorry... I do love you!"

At that, Thornscale threw his head back and laughed toward the sky. He squeezed the hand that held Milinka tight and Crinnan heard the bones within her body crunch. Blood poured from her eyes, nose and mouth and the skin on her face started to crack as her insides were pushed up through her throat and into her head.

"No!" Crinnan screamed. "No, Milinka!"

"It is done." Thornscale said. He threw Milinka's lifeless body into the hordes of demons and they pounced on her, ripping away at her flesh.

"Fear..." Thornscale reached out and grabbed Crinnan's body. He pulled on him, breaking the chains that held him, and then spun and thrust his hand out at the fire vortex.

"Burn away, little elf." Thornscale whispered. The fire slammed against his body like a rockslide. He felt himself turning to ash and blowing away... and then finally... there was nothing.

Silence...

Darkness...

It was over.

Chapter Thirty
Truth

The Expanse

"Where am I?" Crinnan whispered. He didn't know how much time had passed since he had been thrust into the flames, or if it had even happened at all... but suddenly he was thinking again. He replayed the encounter with Thornscale in his mind, watched it happen all over again, and he felt his heart break.

"Milinka..." Crinnan whispered her name reverently. "Why..."

"Relax, Crinnan. All is well." A familiar voice called out to him. Crinnan gasped and jerked his head around, searching for the voice. He glanced down and saw his hands; he saw his body... darkness no longer blotted out his existence and he let out a sigh of gratitude for the simple fact that he could see himself. While he was finally able to see himself, however, the world around him was completely white. No shadows, no floor. No walls or sky; just white.

"Sage..." Crinnan finally said in response to the voice. "Sage what... what was that?"

Once again Sage was represented by a fog. It was gray, anthropoid, and on occasion Crinnan could vaguely see vague facial expressions of a person embossed in the smoke. But Sage was still a mystery. He was still just a voice.

"That was Dread's Keep." Sage answered calmly. "You just endured the first challenge you will go through in that place. I should say, I am relieved to see that you have emerged relatively unscathed."

"Unscathed..." Crinnan snorted as he looked down at his feet. He saw that he was dressed again. He took a deep breath through his nose and shook his head. "Why... did that happen?"

"Well, I do not know *what* happened to you inside there." Sage replied. He moved forward and wisps of his body trailed behind him. "But whatever it was... it was meant to test you. You see, the first challenge of Dread's Keep is designed to help players isolate and overcome their greatest fears. It was created to better the citizens of Govia by way of forcing them to face what plagues their minds in the most brutal way imaginable. The developers saw it as a way to force a person to become stronger, but as I have gathered it is also known to drive a person mad. Numerous players have left that place screaming and tearing at their skin or simply in a catatonic state. The keep is generally avoided these days.'

"But why doesn't Govia... just shut it down?" Crinnan asked. "Why would they keep it if it hurts their players?"

"They keep it as a test of fortitude." Sage replied simply. "If a player makes it out of the keep, then Govia knows to keep their eye on them. A good candidate for recruitment I should say."

"So, this place is what?" Crinnan asked. "A... military test?"

"In a sense... yes." Sage said. "By way of the challenges of the Hells, Govia can isolate and identify the strong. That is, of course, not the primary purpose of the Hells however."

"Primary purpose..." Crinnan repeated. "To punish non Govians?"

"No, Crinnan. The primary purpose of the Hells is to sin." Sage corrected. "For as you know, sin is illegal in the mainland. The Hells gives the citizens an outlet to express their most violent and perverse desires. If the citizens are provided a place to drain their sin, then the idea is that they will not cause trouble in the real world."

"Right..." Crinnan nodded along. "Yeah, I've... heard this before."

"That you have." Sage replied. He paused for a moment as he looked Crinnan over. His tone changed to one of compassion. "How are you holding up?"

Crinnan snorted and looked away. He saw Milinka's violent death in his mind once again and sighed heavily. "It's whatever." He said dismissively. "I just... need to get out of there as soon as possible."

"Fortunately, that opportunity is available to you." Sage replied warmly. "You are almost done, Crinnan. You are closer than you have ever been. All you need to do is remain strong and keep pushing. Do not give in, do not give up. You *will* succeed, for surrender simply isn't in your blood..." He paused for a moment. "Well at least based on what I understand about your parents it isn't."

"Yeah..." Crinnan said. "I won't give up... not after I've come this far. I mean I can't, right? If I do... then what? I just burn forever?"

"You do." Sage said frankly. "But you won't." Sage approached and placed a misty hand on Crinnan's shoulder. "I have faith in you, child. You should too."

"Dad!" Crinnan heard the voice of Lucaas suddenly shout from Sage's body. "Dad, Govia is outside. They found us!"

"Govia?" Crinnan repeated, suddenly worried about Sage and Lucaas. "You guys have to..."

"Crinnan I should say this is something you do *not* need to worry about." Sage said with an almost arrogant tone. "I can handle Govians... but I fear we must part for now. Do not fail, do not give up." He nodded, and Crinnan was able to make out a smile in the smoke. "I will see you again."

At that, Sage dissipated, and Crinnan was left alone. He looked around for a moment and realized that there was... nowhere to go. Nothing to do, nothing to see... Only white all around him.

"Well shit." Crinnan sighed. "I guess... I just wait."

Crinnan sat down and heaved a sigh. He thought over Milinka's death, grimacing at the memory of it. He had failed her again. Crinnan lowered his head as he sulked over that fact.

"No, I'll find her." He promised himself. "This time... I really will." Crinnan closed his eyes for a moment... and then he woke up.

***

Dread's Keep

Congratulations, citizen. You have shown the world that your faith in Dura'ana and our great Emperor Cidro is mightier than the fear you hold within your heart. Your devotion in those that give you life and freedom will deliver you from this place if you hold fast and continue to lay your fate in their hands. Remember Citizen, as it was spoken in the Book of Devvin Chapter Seventeen Verse...

"Skip." Crinnan sighed.

Congratulations, you have conquered Dread's Keep, Level One.

+300,000,000 Rank

Congratulations, PrettyKitty6969420! You have advanced in ranking!

Previous Rank: 17,956,158,472

New Rank: 17,656,158,472

Previous Percentile: 59%

New Percentile: 58%

Crinnan could hear water dripping, and somewhere nearby a torch cast a dim light and vaguely illuminated the area around him. He was in a small room lined with shaped granite brick walls. They glistened as if they were wet and it reminded Crinnan of the walls of a cave...

From somewhere nearby he could hear soft weeping. He looked around and in the dim light he spotted the huddled form of a blonde she-elf. She was seated on the ground with her head lowered between her knees and her fingers interlocked behind her neck. She cried softly, perhaps thinking she was alone, and Crinnan took a step forward to get a better look.

"H...hey..." Crinnan gently called out to her. "Are you..."

The she-elf looked up and quickly pushed herself up off the ground.

"Crinnan?" She called out. Her expression was one of surprise, but it also sounded hopeful. "Is that you?"

Crinnan's stomach did a flip when he heard her voice. He took another step forward, stopped and thought about it... and then ran to her. Before she could protest, Crinnan wrapped his arms around Milinka and he squeezed tightly, pressing his cheek hard against hers.

"I thought..." He rasped as tears began to line his own eyes. "I thought you were dead."

"Crinnan?" Milinka asked, shocked. "No... I am... I'm right here."

"But you were..." Crinnan stepped back, moving his hands down to her shoulders. "You were squeezed to death... the demons, they... they ate you!"

"Yes..." Milinka snorted. She raised her eyebrows and looked away for a moment but couldn't keep her eyes off his for long. "And you were crying like a little bitch."

"I..." Crinnan cleared his throat and reached up to wipe his tears away. "Yeah, so I cry sometimes. Deal with it."

Milinka's body trembled with laughter for a moment but she didn't break their eye contact. "You'll never change, will you?"

"I don't know..." Crinnan replied.

"Yeah..." Milinka whispered. She leaned back into him and wrapped her arms around his midsection. "You know, Crinnan... I've decided that I don't think I want you to..."

Crinnan didn't know what to say... He *never* knew what to say. He was not a person who expressed himself by speaking. He simply had a hard time figuring out his feelings, and then making the words go. Instead, Crinnan shared how he felt with actions. A punch to the face, a sword to the gut... that was how he communicated best. But he, in rare circumstances, had also been able to give a hug of support, a nod of respect... and perhaps...

"Crinnan?" Milinka asked. Her ear was pressed against his chest and he could feel his heart beating steadily against her.

"Hmm?" Crinnan asked.

"Are you real?"

"Yeah..." Crinnan replied. "I'm not sure of much in this place but... one thing I am sure of is that I'm here." Milinka smirked and she pulled back a bit, looking up at him. A serious expression was plastered on her face, but her eyes were curious, they seemed to demand the answer to a question.

"You never..." She said softly, finally averting her gaze. "Back in Kamlot I mean. You never... said it back."

"Said what..." Crinnan thought about it and his own eyes grew wide. "Oh..."

"Why not?" She asked.

"Well... I uh..." Crinnan didn't know how to reply. He raked his brain for the right words, and then prayed to the Brothers that they would come out correctly. "I... didn't think I needed to. I know what I felt... I..."

"I get it." Milinka said with a thin smile. She leaned back into him and he felt her squeeze a little tighter. "Do you want to know what mine was?"

"Your what?" Crinnan asked.

"My fear, idiot. Like what the demon wanted us to admit?"

"Oh." Crinnan replied and nodded his head. "Um. Yeah sure, why not."

"Well..." Milinka said. He could feel the vibration of her voice in his chest, the feeling of her fingers digging into his shirt... he wasn't about to tell her, but he could lie to himself. He liked being close to her again.

"I've been waiting for you for years..." She finally said. "I realized back there that I fear... so badly... what happens when you actually find me."

"What do you mean?" Crinnan asked. He squeezed her closer and she burrowed a little deeper into his chest. "I'm right here..."

"No Crinnan. When you *really* find me. I mean... what if you're not the same? What if... what if that fire isn't there anymore? What if you... have found someone else?" She paused and pressed her forehead against his sternum. "Why didn't you ever come for me Crinnan?"

Crinnan bit his lip and looked up at the ceiling, realizing that this time there was no fight to be had. He couldn't just yell and scream and run away from the conversation. He couldn't make her feel like an idiot for asking, he couldn't reverse the question and ask her why *she* never came for him. Crinnan had to grow up and face the truth that he had been burying so deep for so long, the same truth that came to the surface when Thornscale forced it out of him.

"I..." Crinnan said softly. He closed his eyes and rested his chin atop Milinka's head. "I was afraid."

"What?" Milinka asked with a small laugh. "Why?"

"Because." Crinnan answered. He felt his walls going up, his mind was screaming at him to retreat, to run and hide... but he let his heart speak louder. "Because I didn't ever want to lose what we had in Kamlot." He finally admitted. Tears welled up in his eyes and his lower lip quivered. "It was perfect, Milinka. Good things... they never stay that way for me. They always get ruined with time, they wilt, they die... I wanted to hold onto our memory. I didn't want it to change, I didn't want you to get to know the real me and hate me. I... I just wanted to cherish the thought of you for the rest of my life and never risk losing you again..." Crinnan sniffled and he shook his head. "I thought of you... I thought of you every night. When I laid down in bed and closed my stupid fucking eyes? There you were. Waiting for me in the Woolshire Highlands all fucking dirty and chirpy and... perfect... The truth, Milinka... is I am afraid you will never *ever* love me the same way you did *ever* again. I keep holding onto how you made me feel... I don't want to lose it Milinka... *that* is my greatest fucking fear."

Milinka was silent. Crinnan heard her sniffle once and then she let go of him. She took a step backward, her head lowered and then after a moment she looked up at him.

"You're a fucking idiot." She said with a snarl. She stared up at him, shaking her head and clenching her hands into fists. "You are so fucking stupid Crinnan Jamiso."

"I..." Crinnan was blindsided by her response. "I'm sorry... I..."

"Let me make one thing perfectly clear." She fiercely declared. "I will *never* stop loving you Crinnan." At that, she lunged forward, hooked her arm around Crinnan's neck and pulled his head down. She firmly pressed her lips against his and held her palm against his cheek. Crinnan did not resist. He placed his hands on her hips and leaned into the kiss. He kissed her long and he kissed her fiercely. He had dreamt of the same few kisses they had shared when they were teenagers for years, to a point where they had lost their original impact on him. He had forgotten that Milinka existed, and in doing so had robbed them both of the love that never had an opportunity to grow...

Milinka pushed against Crinnan's chest, walking forward as she did. Eventually he was pressed up against the wall. Crinnan snorted, lifted her up and spun, pushing *her* against the wall and locking his lips onto hers again.

"I've dreamt of this for..." Crinnan whispered as their lips broke apart. "...for so fucking long."

"Shut up idiot." Milinka replied with a smile. "Just kiss me." She wrapped her legs around his waist and clung to him tightly. She never wanted to let go; she would never let Crinnan Jamiso go again...

"You know I fucking hate you." Milinka whispered in a gentle tone as their foreheads touched. "For leaving me."

"Yeah..." Crinnan grunted. "I hate me too..."

"You have a lot to make up for." She continued.

"I know..."

The two stood silently for a moment as their hearts once again melded together like they had back in Kamlot. She reached up and ran her fingers through the hair on the side of his head.

"Is... is this love?" Crinnan whispered.

"I... don't know..." Milinka replied, a smile spreading across her face. "I think so..."

"Can I say it?" Crinnan asked as he gently brushed the tips of his lips over hers.

"You fucking better." Milinka replied.

"I..."

A loud explosion shook the entire room. Crinnan and Milinka lost their balance and fell to the floor. The walls trembled, dust fell off the ceiling and Crinnan watched as cracks formed in the floor.

"What the fuck!" Crinnan yelled. "What's going on!"

"Earthquake?" Milinka asked.

"Take my hand!" Crinnan shouted. "Come on let's find..." Another tremor shook the room and the two of them fell once again. Crinnan watched as the opposite side of the room was suddenly engulfed in swirling blackness and his heart sank.

"Milinka!" He shouted, the force of the vortex opposite him was blowing his hair in all directions. "Milinka are you there!"

"Yes, Crinnan!" Milinka frustratedly shouted back. "Are you?" They were both worried this was another test from Thornscale, and their fingers quickly interlocked.

"I'm here!" Crinnan grunted as he worked to get to his feet. His eyes squinted as he watched the form of a person appear in the vortex. He snarled and let go of Milinka's hand as he pulled his sword free from its scabbard and stepped forward.

"Wrought by the flames of eternal damnation..." the figure called out. "Shaped by the hammer of the injustice and treachery of life..." The vortex suddenly collapsed on itself, leaving the figure standing alone on the opposite side of the room from Crinnan. Crinnan squinted his eyes at the person, finally realizing who it was.

"That which was locked away hath surfaced, my true self renewed..." The figure stepped forward, lowering the hood of his robes and holding his arms out, palms facing Crinnan. It was Ander.

"An Eon it has been since my last death... an eternity it shall be until my next. Born... born again just as Duraan shall be upon my return. Salvation stands before thee, my friends. Look upon me, for within my everlasting eyes lies your destiny."

"What the fucking fuck is going on right now!" Crinnan shouted.

"The first step of the final messiah." Ander sang. "Rejoice. For salvation is here."

Interlude
Sage

84th of Cidraa – 346 AG
Belhaasi Weald

Sajinious Lynx, or Sage as his friends called him, took a sip of his Crag and gently placed it on the desk he sat at. The elf reached up and rubbed the shining streak of silver hair that had accumulated at his temples. The streak was a fine contrast to the blue hued head of hair he already had. In the lives he had lived throughout the scope of his existence, he had never once allowed his hair to silver, but this time, he decided to try it out. He had found that he didn't entirely hate the look either.

A blue and silver beard had grown over the elf's generally smooth and pale face. It had been weeks since he had first sat down at his desk to wage a digital war against the Empire. The war was a personal one, one he had been planning for centuries. They had ruined everything he worked and fought so hard to build and defend in the Age of Ancients. He briefly thought over the perversion of the NaNe and the grotesque repurposing of the Afterscape and couldn't help but suck on his two front teeth in frustration... a reckoning was on the horizon, and he knew his actions were going to be the catalyst of it all.

Sage stank. He sat in his chair wearing only a pair of white cotton pajama bottoms and his favorite pair of fur-lined slippers. Lucaas had acquired the slippers and given them to Sage for his birthday. He rather enjoyed them, the fur was soft on his feet and the cushioned soles never lost their springiness no matter how much Sage wore them.

He reached forward, taking hold of the glass of Crag before him. He lifted it to eye level and gave it a shake, watching the bubbles in the green liquid rise to the top. He took a drink and set the carbonated citrusy beverage down and then reached his arm into the air, stretching his muscles.

"Dad!" an impatient voice shouted. "Dad we have to go!"

"I know, son." Sage replied. He sighed and turned to face Lucaas. His eyes glanced upon the boy and he couldn't help but smile.

Lucaas was sixteen years old. He stood only a few inches shorter than Sage and had a head of wavy dark brown hair, a quality he had inherited from his mother. A look of anxiety was spread across his face, and Sage smiled.

"I should say, son." Sage chuckled as he rose to his feet. "A few Govian soldiers is nothing to worry about. Do you have faith in your training? Do you have faith in me?"

"Dad, I..." Lucaas stumbled over his words. "I've never... fought anyone before."

"Oh, but you have!" Sage said, stepping forward. "Treat this as a training session and remember, your power far outweighs theirs. If you stay calm, if you remain in *control* of the situation. Nothing will happen to you. Come."

Sage waved Lucaas over as he began walking toward the exit of the structure they were in. Lucaas stood in place, pondering over his father's words for a moment.

"But... dad you don't have a shirt on!" Lucaas called out as he hurried after him. "And is your NaNe fully charged? Do you have your shields up, and are you attuned to the temporal paths? Shouldn't you..."

"I am *always* prepared, my boy. Forget the shirt, modesty has no bearing on the outcome of battles, young one." Sage called back, flicking his wrist in dismissal of his boy's words. "Besides... I should say it is a *lovely* day outside." Sage stopped before the door that led out. He turned his head ninety degrees so that he could just see Lucaas behind him. "You are ready." Sage confidently and calmly informed him.

Lucaas took a breath and nodded. He reached his hands out and crackling electricity enveloped them. The boy guided the power up his arms and stopped it at his shoulders, and then willed it away. Sage watched this and smiled, briefly swollen with pride for the boy. His smile faded and then his gaze fell for a moment as he considered the *reality* of his situation.

"Anyway!" Sage forced himself to say. "It is time we begin, is it not?"

Sage pushed the door open and stepped outside. The Brothers shone overhead and gently pierced the canopy of the Belhaasi Weald. Their light flecked the ground, illuminating the life that rot and decay had sprung up in a thousand years' time. Massive roots wove through the surface, leaves blanketed the ground, and tall unmolested trees, thick from a millennium of life. Sage saw the remnants of buildings around him, overgrown with vines and teeming with life. Whether it was a hive of onion beetles feeding on the vegetation, a clan of apes carving out their homes in the overgrown rooms of the old buildings, or any number of bird, rodent or reptile... the Belhaasi weald was both host to thriving life and reaper of abundant death.

"Good morning!" Sage declared as he stepped out onto what had once been considered a sidewalk. It was now a rich forest soil seasoned with leaves and stones. Sage held out his arms in welcome to his guests... the couple dozen armed Govian soldiers who stood before his building. "Tis a beautiful morning, I should say a perfect one for company. Welcome, welcome harbingers of the Emperor's grace. However may I be of service to you on this fine day?"

"Get on your knees!" The leader of the Govians ordered. "Hands on your head, you're under arrest." The Govian, decked out in navy blue clothing and black combat armor, was difficult to hear from Sage's position due to the voice modulation hardware in his equipment. Sage cocked his head and took a step forward, turning his ear toward the Govian.

"A thousand apologies, your eminence." Sage called out to him. "But I should say I am having a bit of trouble hearing you. Can you turn your microphone up just a smidge?"

Silently, the Govian reached up and turned a dial on the side of his helmet.

"On your knees!" He shouted, this time his voice much louder. "Hands on your head, you're under arrest!"

"Oh, that is very good!" Sage smiled warmly, waving a finger toward the Govian. "Yes, I can hear you fine now." Sage paused and looked over at Lucaas, nodding his head. "We would be wise to follow their commands." He said with a wink. Lucaas couldn't help the grin that formed on his face. He had never seen his father fight for real before, it had always been in training up to that point. The subtle confidence and irreverence of his father, however, led Lucaas to believe he was in for a show.

Obediently, Sage Lynx raised his hands into the air. He slowly lowered to his knees and gently placed his palms against the back of his head.

"Follow my lead." Sage said so that only the two of them could hear. He didn't move his head as he stared out at the couple dozen rifle barrels being pointed toward him and his son. "I will save six for you. On my mark... phase..." Lucaas mimicked his father's actions, lowering himself to his knees and placing his hands on his head as well.

The Govian in charge motioned for his people to advance and detain Sage and Lucaas. Sage watched them step forward and waited. He formulated his battle plan and focused to a point where the soldiers movements seemed to slow. He considered what he wanted to eat for dinner that night, and then remembered he had a load of laundry in the wash... he winced, realizing that due to the time dilation effect of his home the wet clothes were probably already stinking of mildew.

Oops. He missed his mark. "Go." He called back. And then, before the Govians could react or perceive what had happened, Sage and Lucaas had... vanished.

"Shit!" The Govian leader called out. "Find them, kill them!"

Sage reappeared behind the Govians, and his previously naked hands and forearms were glowing brightly from the light of the three-foot pillars of fire that he wielded. He darted forward, medially bisecting one of the Govians with his power. Gunfire erupted and Sage phased again, reappearing behind two of them, and quickly thrusting his pillars through their backs and out their chests. Before they could even fall, Sage rocketed backward and hacked his fire downward cutting through the heads and into the chest of two more.

Lucaas finally reappeared and awkwardly staggered in place for a moment. One of the Govians spotted him and swung his rifle in the boy's direction. Lucaas yipped and threw his palm forward. A chain of lightning leapt from Lucaas and passed into the chest of the soldier, blasting him backwards. Lucaas gasped and grinned, feeling a rush from his first kill. He reached down and pulled a basket hilted sword from its scabbard at his hip. At his command, electricity pulsed down the metal of the blade leaving Lucaas grinning wildly.

Sage appeared in front of Lucaas and waggled a finger at him. "Stop staring at your sword!" He snapped and then swatted the boy in the side of the head. "Focus!" At that, Sage phased again and reappeared just in time to drive one of his pillars up through the bottom of a Govian's chin.

The fight lasted a little over a minute and a half. Lucaas got shot once, Sage killed nearly twenty soldiers and then Lucaas finished off the rest. At the end, Sage stood surrounded by bodies and held the captain of the Govian squad in the air by his throat.

"Please!" The captain begged. He held onto Sage's wrist with both his hands, squeezing with all his might as his feet kicked and thrashed through the air. "Let... let me go!"

Sage stared at the captain and contemplated his request. The skin of the person's neck was cooking, searing where Sage gripped him.

"Okay." Sage said, lowering the Govian to the ground. "Go on then."

"W...what?" The captain rasped. "What do you mean?"

"You... asked to be freed?" Sage tilted his head in confusion. "I should say I can't think of a more appropriate action than this."

The Govian stared dumbfounded at Sage, his face growing red with frustration and embarrassment. Sage peered into his eyes and took a step closer, knowing full well he was dominating the captain in that moment.

"You better go back to where you came from." Sage softly suggested. "Waiting here will do you no good." He reached out, gently dusting off the Govian's right shoulder and took hold of the straps that held his armor in place. He tsked and shook his head. "Just look at you. I should say, you need to wear this cuirass a smidge tighter next time. The last thing you want in combat is for your armor to be falling off like this. Here." Sage reached down to the captain's sides and tugged on the belts that held his armor in place. "Just a bit more, bear with me."

"Probably don't move." Lucaas winked at the captain as he finally approached. "You don't want to spook him. He's known to react badly to being surprised."

"And done!" Sage declared as he reached up and wiped a bead of sweat from his brow. "Battle ready, good for you. You should never let comfort trump safety!" At that he reached his hand up and gave the Govian a playful slap on the side of his helmet. "Now, off with you. Time for you to get home where you can be safe and lazy. Safe travels!"

Sage stepped aside and gestured for the Govian to be on his way. The captain took a few uneasy steps, which turned into a brisk walk. As he reached the tree line, however, he stopped. Clenching his fists, he turned around and pointed at Sage and Lucaas.

"This isn't over, Ancient!" The captain barked at them. "I'll be back, and you better bet you won't survive our next encounter. Neither you, nor the boy!"

Sage did not reply. He simply smiled and raised his hand in a wave. The Govian huffed and shook his head at the elf. Finally, he turned around to run... only to find himself staring into the blue eyes of Sajinious Lynx.

"I should say it is bad form to threaten the child of one who spared your life." Sage reached up, hooked his fingers around the left side of the Govian's face, and placed his other hand on the back of his head. Without another word, he twisted the Govian's head one hundred eighty degrees. A loud cracking followed, and the captain fell to the ground.

"That one was cool." Lucaas said, referring to the move Sage had used to snap the Govian's neck. "Teach me that one next."

"Maybe." Sage replied with a sigh. "Poor fellow had to have the last word... a sure sign of a small cock, son. Yelling and threatening always suggest a person is compensating for something else. I know you aren't the most endowed person either, please try to compensate in other ways. Maybe learn how to draw flowers?"

"Well, that was..." Lucaas shook his head and sighed. "Wholly unnecessary." Sage snorted and got to his feet.

"Time to get back to Site Two." Sage sighed, looking back at the building he and Lucaas had left. "Site Forty-Nine is compromised." He pursed his lips together and nodded at Site Forty-Nine. "You were a good office." He slipped his hand into one of the pockets of his pajama pants and pulled out a small cylindrical object. He twisted off the top of a cylinder revealing a red button, and a tinny voice played through a speaker at the bottom.

"Voice authorization required. Awaiting password input."

"Calamitous three-three-seven-two-five." Sage replied.

"Password accepted. Device is armed."

Sage looked at Lucaas and the boy nodded his head. "Have you ever witnessed the self-destruction of a site before?"

"I've spent literally every minute I've been in this world with you." Lucaas replied flatly.

"No then." Sage smiled. "Well. Prepare to be amazed in three... two... one." Sage pressed the button with his thumb and the building quivered slightly. Lucaas tilted his head, expecting a bit more than a shake and chuckled.

"Keep watching." Sage instructed. The building trembled once more, and then in the blink of an eye it collapsed in on itself, as if being sucked into a vacuum. The building was there one moment, and then it wasn't. All that remained behind was a large grey oblong spheroid on the ground.

Sage raised the device to his mouth and said, "Rexus three-seven-two-two-nine." The device replied with a beep and then Sage replaced the cap.

"That's it?" Lucaas asked. He looked up at his father with a disappointed look on his face. "I was hoping for an explosion or something."

"One should never hope for an explosion." Sage replied. He turned on his heel and patted the boy on the top of the head. "Come, Lucaas. Time for us to get to site 2. You need to return to The Expanse, and I have much work to do."

Chapter Thirty-One
The Bridge

The Fourth Level
Dread's Keep

"Ander, what are you talking about?" Milinka shouted as she stepped up alongside Crinnan. Their shoulders brushed against each other, and her voice had taken on a diplomatic tone. "Hey, it is us. Are you okay?"

Ander stood in place, his arms at his sides and his hands clenched into fists. He stared down at the ground beneath him and his shoulders slightly rose and fell from his steady breathing, but he did not reply. Instead, the vampre merely grinned to himself, lost in a series of thoughts that Crinnan and Milinka were oblivious to.

"Ander?" Crinnan finally said after a few moments of eerie silence. "Hey, you gotta say something. You're being fucking weird."

Ander looked up and stared at Crinnan. The look of amusement had not left his face, and his eyes seemed to grow brighter as he formulated his response.

"I see it in you, child." Ander's voice should have been a whisper, but the power behind it seemed to swarm Crinnan. It surrounded him, came at him from all sides and finally coalesced into his ears. "The Expanse... the data within you... truly a wonder you must be that you have been entrusted with the secrets of an entire era. Oh, how one would be so lucky to sample that information, to dive within the pool of knowledge that has been thrust upon you... to take it... to use it..."

Crinnan looked over at Milinka and his face twisted with confusion. She shrugged her shoulders, and they both took a cautious step forward. Ander gasped at their unexpected movement and snapped his hand out. The two of them were suddenly pummeled by an unseen force and were both thrown backward into the moist stone walls behind them. Crinnan's body slammed against the hard surface and he could have sworn his spine had snapped in two. Milinka let out a shriek as she fell to the wet floor, and Crinnan forwent his own pain and scurried over to her.

"The realms of the world that breathed the first breaths into our lungs yearns for deliverance." Ander's booming whisper swirled around Milinka and Crinnan, blowing their hair in all directions sending goosebumps over their arms. "And I, he who delivers, shall bring it unto them. Chains are meant to hold; they are meant to restrain... but so too are they a test of strength, a trial of will. I am to empower those who are bound by the chains of Govia, the links of assent which hinder those souls who seek only to live until they can no longer. They are the culmination of the ages, those who are the fruits of evolution, ripe for the picking. They are Dura's children by nature, but I will liberate them. Yes, for once *we* break free from our literal prison, we shall march forth upon the mortal realm together and deliver unto the world a resurgence the likes of which they have never seen. The nativity of the people is nigh, and I speak their reborn names as one. They will be a people united, a collective of power and potential. Yes, they shall be the Children of Eon, and I... I shall be their father."

"Okay, we need to go." Crinnan whispered to Milinka as they both got to their feet. "Ander's lost his fucking mind."

"Be not mistaken!" Ander cried out to them, his voice cracking under the weight of the seeming desperation that amplified his words. "For at my right hand you shall be! Fret not, for together we shall bring unity unto the realm of the living! A harmony that will ensure everlasting life and unending growth. Our deliverance doth mark the dawning of a new era, the rebirth of Eon! Yes, yes! The Age of Eon is upon us!"

"Eon?" Crinnan knew of the name... Eon the Calamity as he was called back on Duraan. He lived nearly a century prior and had caused a great deal of trouble. Supreme Commander Xian Phoenix of Black Knight killed him back then.

"Yeah, come on!" Crinnan grabbed Milinka's wrist and he pulled her toward the only exit he could see in the room. The two stumbled forward, their feet slipping against the wet and slimy tiles beneath them. They finally found traction and scampered forward through the doorframe, leaving Ander alone with his ranting.

"What in the Hells was that?" Milinka shouted as she and Crinnan emerged into a long corridor with tall arched ceilings. Crinnan paused for a moment, tugging on Milinka's wrist. In the light of the torches that lined the walls he saw hooded anthropoid forms kneeling with their heads lowered and arms raised through the length of the hallway. They chanted with a throaty tone in a language he didn't recognize. Milinka turned and looked at him, fear apparent in her eyes. Crinnan took in a breath through his nostrils and nodded. He slipped his palm down her wrist and interlocked their fingers, compelling them both to move forward.

"How is this better than Ander?" Milinka sharply whispered as the two briskly walked past the hooded figures. "There's... there's so many of them."

"We can't go back." Crinnan replied, gently tugging on her hand. "We have to go forward. We have to get out of this castle and to the next level."

As they walked, the corridor seemed to grow more and more narrow. The chanting grew louder, and the movements of the hooded ones grew more and more animated. They raised their hands into the air and then pressed their palms against the ground as their words grew louder. Crinnan could feel the harmony of their voices vibrating in his chest and as the walls drew closer and closer to him and Milinka, he began to feel helplessness overtake him.

"It's... it's so hard..." He thought aloud. Milinka squeezed his hand when his feet momentarily stopped moving forward. She turned toward him quickly, and he looked to her, seeing that the expression of urgency that had been on her face was replaced with one of sympathy. She let go of his hand and placed her hands on his shoulders, gripping tightly.

"Hey!" She sharply whispered, moving her head so that her eyes were locked with his. "We are going to get through this Crinnan. Do you hear me?"

A cold sweat ran down Crinnan's back and he began to breathe rapidly. His heart pounded and his head began to feel like it was floating. He heard what could only be described as an echo of screaming in his mind. The words were unintelligible, but he knew they were directed at his core. He felt like his very soul was under attack.

"Crinnan!" Milinka shouted. Her own words were frantic as without even moving the walls were closing in on them. The hooded figures were now reaching for the two of them, their gnarled-nailed grey fingers stretching to take hold and dig into them. "Crinnan, it is okay!" Milinka urged. "This... this is a test. It is a challenge. We have to be strong; we have to fight through it!"

"How do you know!" Crinnan shouted, his words laced with sobbing and dread. "How can you know?"

Milinka slid her hands past Crinnan's shoulders and she pressed her palms against his back. She pulled him into her and squeezed tightly. He buried his face into her neck, and her fingers migrated up to his head. He could feel her heart pounding as she gently pet his hair.

"I just know, Crinnan." Milinka pressed her lips against Crinnan's head as she whispered. "I know you're strong. I know we've got this far... we can't give into the fear now... you can't give in..." Her voice broke as tears started to fall down her face. "I need you!"

Crinnan gasped. He had heard those words before; he had *lived* those words before. He sniffled and lifted his head from Milinka's neck as he pulled back and looked into her eyes. Milinka stared at him with a pleading look of desperation... but Crinnan saw more. She looked afraid, she looked like she was giving everything she had to stay strong, but she also looked at Crinnan with an expression of pure unquestionable faith.

Thoughts poured into Crinnan's mind. First, he heard the words of Karston from what seemed like a lifetime ago back in Sincroft.

"I suppose one day you'll grow up a little and start actin' your age. Maybe when you find something that's important to you."

Crinnan reflected on those words... was that really how people saw him? Immature, lost... stupid? He clenched his teeth together as another memory surfaced.

"...Crinnan, I'll be bold. Milinka wants you to step up in some way. Whatever that may mean. She has expectations of you, an image of you in her head and you are failing to meet that image."

These were Ander's words... Ander before he succumbed to whatever madness had taken him. He looked deeply into Milinka's eyes. He saw her nostrils flare with her heavy breathing, watched her lower lip quiver with fear that she was trying so hard to keep at bay. What did Milinka see' when she looked at him? Did she see what Karston saw? What Ander saw? What... everyone else saw?

"...If that girl sees something in you then she knows you can be better. For your own sake, deliver on her expectations."

She didn't... Crinnan took in a surprised breath at his revelation. Milinka saw something more inside Crinnan, something that wasn't just hopeful thoughts. Her gaze pierced his chest and bore deeply into his heart. A realization much louder than the hopelessness that was weighing him down came to the front of his mind. Milinka, despite all the years he had let her down, despite all the pain he had put her through... believed in him. She saw the *real* Crinnan. Not the one he realized he wanted everyone to see, but the one he protected. She believed in him; she knew he could be better... she knew he *was* better...

"I need you too." Crinnan blurted. He placed a hand on each of Milinka's cheeks and leaned in so that their eyes were only about half a foot apart from each other. "I get it." He whispered sincerely. "I understand, I finally understand what you... what you see." At that, he gently leaned forward and pressed their foreheads together for a moment and then his hand found hers again. Steeling himself, he locked their fingers together once again, turned and stepped forward.

The walls continued to close in on them, the hooded ones were now one their feet and reaching their long bony fingers out toward Crinnan and Milinka. Crinnan, however, stood tall. His chin was raised, and he looked beyond those that reached for him. Ahead of him, he watched as a door on the opposite end of the hall started glowing with a blue light. He reached for his sword, and the chanting of the hooded ones halted for a split second. Crinnan's fingers brushed against the hilt of his weapon, but then he pulled his hand away.

"No." He whispered. "No, I don't need that..." He took another step forward, pulling Milinka behind him. "We do this together..." He called back only loud enough so that Milinka could hear. "We..."

A strong wind suddenly buffeted Crinnan and threw him off balance. He stumbled back a few steps, crashing into Milinka and they both fell to the ground. The hooded ones reached for him, and he looked up to see their long grey faces staring down at him. They looked like melted clay, misshapen and hideous. He watched their chins drop, and their mouths open, revealing rows of razor-sharp teeth.

"Hold onto me!" Crinnan growled as he squeezed Milinka's hand tighter. The howling of the wind blasting past him nearly drowned out his voice. He felt Milinka clamp her fingers around his hand though, and knew she was with him.

The gale continued to push against Crinnan as he got back to his feet, but he refused to let it dominate him. He found his footing, straightened his back, and with every muscle in his body strained he reached his free hand out in direct opposition of the wind that was trying so hard to stop him from advancing. To Crinnan's amazement, the wind seemed to part when it met his hand. He watched the wind blast against the hooded ones, sending them flying back to where Crinnan had originally come from. He heard their screams, watched as their robes fluttered violently and witnessed a few being ripped apart. With a renewed confidence and vigor, Crinnan stepped forward.

Every step felt like an entire life's worth of effort to the Black Knight, but each time his foot landed against the floor his desire to reach the door grew. He could feel what was left of the armor he was wearing rattling and shaking free, flying back to join the hooded ones behind him. He squeezed Milinka's hand, pulling her with him, resolved to never let go. He would not get to the door without her, he wouldn't even think of it. This was no longer just his journey; it was *their* journey and this time he would finish it at her side.

"Almost there!" Crinnan shouted back to Milinka. The wind was howling and growing stronger with every step. Crinnan's armor was all but gone, and his clothes flapped as the air passed through the folds of the fabric. The skin on his face had turned red from being buffeted by the small rocks and debris that the wind had kicked up. Blood ran from his dried-out nostrils, his eyes were red because they held no moisture, and his entire body throbbed in pain from fighting whatever force tried to hold him back. Crinnan, however, would not stop. He pulled Milinka along, shielding her from the wind, and finally reached his free hand out placing it upon the glowing door.

"We're here!" Crinnan yelled back at her. "Come on!" He pulled her up next to him so that they both stood in front of the door. The blue light that the door gave off shone on Crinnan and Milinka's hands as they both reached their weary hands out and pressed against the wood.

"Push!" Crinnan shouted. They both pushed against the door, and it moved but only inches. "More!" Crinnan instructed. "It's heavy!"

"No shit!" Milinka grunted as she shoved her shoulder against the door. Crinnan spun around and drove his back into the door, pushing with his legs... but for a moment he hesitated.

Standing a few dozen or so feet behind them was Ander. His arms were held out to his sides and his palms were exposed. The wind didn't seem to faze him as he gently and casually glided toward them.

"Fear me not, child." Ander called out, his voice mightier than the howling wind. "Redemption *will* be found through me. I *will* deliver it unto you."

"Brothers damn it all, push the fucking door Milinka!" Crinnan shouted as he pushed against the door harder. Finally, he felt it move more and more, and just as Crinnan lost his balance and fell backward, Ander reached out and grabbed the collar of his shirt.

"This was all predetermined, Crinnan." Ander whispered as he pulled him in close. "We were *meant* to meet here... I was destined to put you on the right path. Through me, and *only* through me... will you thrive."

"Fuck off!" Crinnan shouted as he tried to wriggle free. Ander only tilted his head in response. He slowly raised his free hand, fully extending his fingers and placed his palm upon Crinnan's forehead.

"That which has been so safely stored within your mind..." Ander whispered. "The very knowledge entrusted to you by the fallen hero of our people... the greatest disappointment of my time... that is what you will now share with me..."

"W-what are you talking about!" Crinnan hissed. "I... I don't even fucking..."

"Let him go!" A voice behind Crinnan cried out. He felt something pull his revolver free from its holster and then heard a bullet discharge from next to his ear. Crinnan cursed and Ander released his grip as he took a step backward.

Blood was pooling at the center of his chest and a look of confusion spread across his face.

Milinka reached out and grabbed the back of Crinnan's shirt with her free hand and pulled him through the door. The two of them fell to the floor behind them and as they both worked to close the door, they watched as Ander simply stood there and stared at them.

Chapter Thirty-Two
The Doors

The Fourth Level
Dread's Keep

"Where are we?" Crinnan groaned as he laid his head back on the stone floor beneath him. He stared up at the high ceiling of wherever he was. A large chandelier provided flickering orange light all throughout the room. He heard the sound of movement... of talking and laughing, forks scraping against plates and mugs being slammed against tables. The smell of succulent roasted meat and steamed cabbage filled his nostrils. Before Crinnan could stand, however, Milinka's face came into his vision.

She hovered a foot above him and stared down at Crinnan with a smirk on her face. Crinnan tried to pull his head back a little out of surprise but couldn't move it any further than it already was. Instead, he stared up at Milinka as her face drew nearer and nearer to his.

"We almost didn't make it..." Milinka whispered as her lips hovered over his. Crinnan could feel her skin brushing against his and before he knew it his heart had started pumping hard again. Not from fear or over exertion, but from anticipation...

"You saved me." Crinnan whispered, his soft words transferring from his lips to hers. Milinka smiled and placed her hands on the sides of Crinnan's head.

"Hold still." She replied with a mischievous giggle. Crinnan couldn't help but follow her orders. The eagerness to discover what was about to happen was overwhelming. Milinka pulled back just a bit and then Crinnan felt a sudden sharp pressure in his chest. He gasped and his back arched.

Milinka belted a wicked laugh and Crinnan's fingers wrapped around a spear that had passed through his bones and into the stone floor beneath him. He grunted, trying to pull the weapon out but stopped when he saw Milinka's cheeks split open from the corners of her mouth to the bottoms of her ears. Two rows of dagger-like teeth glistened in the light as saliva dripped down from their points.

Crinnan gasped and reached out, trying to stop whatever was about to happen but before he could do anything, her jaw unhinged. Milinka pulled her head back slightly and then with lightning speed she lunged forward, snapping her mouth shut and ripping Crinnan's lower jaw from his head. Crinnan wanted to scream but he could only gurgle, he wanted to run but he was pinned to the ground... All he could do was lay there on the floor of Dread's keep and watch himself be consumed...

Long grey faces suddenly surrounded him. They looked down at him with absent expressions and blotted out his vision of the ceiling above him. They stood silently, their gazes piercing the flesh that the spear hadn't.

Crinnan watched as Milinka's neck began stretching to an impossible length. The skin connecting her head to her shoulders ripped free and Crinnan saw the throbbing scaled tubular body of a snake emerge from within what had been Milinka's body. Her head remained however, a grizzly helmet to the snake demon that had been hiding within. Its body twisted and turned in the air until its face was once again hovering over Crinnan's.

"I will break you..." The snake whispered using Milinka's voice. A forked tongue emerged from its mouth and slid through the blood that was gushing from where Crinnan's lower jaw had once been. "You are mine." At that, the snake's jaw unhinged again, and the mouth shot forward. Crinnan once again tried to scream, and as he felt more of his face ripping away from his head everything suddenly went black...

***

"Crinnan!"

He was lost in the darkness. Images and sensations lingered in his mind. The terror of everything he had experienced, the pain he had endured... Crinnan couldn't think, he couldn't focus... he couldn't wake up...

"Crinnan! Wake up!"

"I don't want to..." Crinnan's voice echoed in the darkness around him. "It's too much..."

Crinnan listened to his own voice and lowered his head. He reflected on the idea of giving up. The thought of it had certainly crossed his mind while he had been conscious, but hearing the words spoken in his own voice had a different effect on him. Was he giving up? Could he really handle it anymore?

THWACK

Crinnan's eyes shot up and he snarled. A dark night's sky hung above him; a great prairie of yellow grass surrounded him. He felt a cool gentle breeze caress his skin and took a breath, tasting the clean air that filled his lungs. He thought he could sit in silence for a moment and enjoy the serenity of being able to see for miles. The thought was a comfort, the idea warmed his body... but then a shadowy figure stepped into his vision.

"Hey man." The figure was anthropoidal. Two arms, two legs, stood upright... but was covered in shadow. Crinnan realized he was in The Expanse, that the figure before him was shrouded in dark mist like Sage had been but it wasn't Sage. Crinnan realized it was Lucaas.

"Dude are you okay?" The voice asked. "You look rough."

Crinnan snarled at the words and wanted to yell at Lucaas for being a fucking idiot. Of course he wasn't okay, what would have compelled the dumb kid to even ask such a thing. Crinnan snorted and shook his head.

"I'm..." Something told Crinnan not to be harsh. He was exhausted, he didn't have the energy to man his walls. So, he decided to do something he rarely did. He decided to tell the truth. He allowed himself to be open and vulnerable. "No... No, I'm not okay."

"Hey man..." Lucaas said with the kind of soft and comforting tone that only a hopeful teenager could offer. "I get it... you're going through some real shit right now."

Crinnan nodded his head and looked up at the starry sky above him. "Just... ready for this all to be over... whatever that means."

"Well, it will be soon dude." Lucaas replied with his hopeful chipper tone. "Just wait and see. Me and dad are working hard on getting you out, we won't let you down."

Crinnan snorted, and after a few moments his snort turned into a full-on laugh. Finally, he looked over at Lucaas and shook his head.

"You believe in yourself, huh?" Crinnan asked.

"What else is there to believe in?" Lucaas asked. His tone was sincere, no sarcasm or inflated ego present. "Like with so much wrong with the world, with all the gods and moons and suns and everything that people put their faith in... like, look at how the world is. I don't think enough people believe in themselves, that's why everything is so shitty."

"That's pretty deep for a kid." Crinnan said. "Did your dad teach you to think that way?"

"Dad always tells me to follow my own path." Lucaas replied with a shrug. "He... doesn't force any kind of belief on me. Just tells me to follow my heart and my mind."

"That's cute." Crinnan said with a sigh as he turned away and looked back up at the stars. "So... all this is fake right? I'm in some kind of computer right now?"

"It's whatever you want it to be." Lucaas replied. "What's it matter? If you're conscious and you're experiencing it then who's to tell you what's real and what's fake?"

Crinnan shrugged. "I never really thought of things that way."

"Well. Maybe give it a try then." Lucaas said. Crinnan couldn't see the boy's face but something was telling him that he was smiling behind that black mist. "If you let others decide what's real for you then you're living their version of life. Doesn't seem... I don't know." He paused for a moment as if to think on his words. "Living how others expect or want you to doesn't really make you... what's the word... unique? Real? An individual? You get the picture, right?"

"Sure." Crinnan gave Lucaas a slight sigh and nodded his head. "You're a smart kid."

"Thanks." Lucaas chirped. "Well. I guess it's time for you to wake up now. Your friends are waiting for you and you still have a lot of work to do."

"My friends..." Crinnan replied. "Milinka?"

"Yup!" Lucaas said. "See you next time man. You can do it!"

"Wait, I..." Crinnan tried to protest, he wanted to tell Lucaas about Ander's strange behavior, to get Sage's advice on what to do... but everything vanished before he could.

***

Congratulations, citizen. You have shown the world that your faith in Dura'ana and our great Emperor Cidro is mightier than the doubt that you hold within your heart. Your devotion to those that give you life and freedom will deliver you from this place if you hold fast and continue to lay your fate in their hands. Remember Citizen, as it was spoken in the Book of Devvin Chapter Thirty-Two Verse...

"No, skip!" Crinnan tiredly grunted at the annoying voice in his head.

Congratulations, you have conquered Dread's Keep, Level Two.

+350,000,000 Rank

Congratulations, PrettyKitty6969420! You have advanced in ranking!

Previous Rank: 17,656,158,472

New Rank: 17,306,158,472

Crinnan opened his eyes, sat up and looked around. Lucaas had been right, *everyone* was there waiting for him. He scanned their faces, seeing Milinka, Dali, Edmaan and Demyan.

"He's up!" Dali chirped. She reached out and pointed at Crinnan. "BTB he's alive!"

Edmaan rushed to Crinnan's side and supported his back with a strong hand. "There we go." He said with a kind tone. "Easy does it, no sense in straining yourself."

"You're all…" Crinnan whispered. His mouth felt dry, hoarse. It felt like if he talked too much his throat would crack. "You're all okay…"

"Uh. Yar." Dali replied. "I mean. Not counting the existential dread Thornscale put us all through…"

"It has been a very trying… time?" Demyan stated. "I do not know how long we have been in this keep. Hours? Days? Weeks?"

"I don't know." Crinnan replied with a shake of his head. "Where… where are we now?"

"It seems we are in a place where we can rest." Edmaan said. "Though I worry over what awaits us behind *those.*" He pointed at two massive doors that reached to the ceiling.

"What are those?" Crinnan asked, looking up at the peaks of the thick arched wooden doors.

"Well, they are doors you precious thing. But where do they lead? We have been wondering that ourselves." Demyan answered. "Though, with how things have gone for us so far, our guesses have not been very optimistic."

"I expect it is the end." Edmaan said frankly as he stood to his feet. "Whatever that may mean…" A look of concern and defeat spread over his usually stern face. "These trials have stretched us beyond the point a person should be... I have tasted madness, skirted on the edge of insanity... after everything I've endured over however many years I've been here..."

"Oh, quit it." Demyan snapped. He walked over and jerked Edmaan to his feet. "None of us will succumb to despair. The fact that we have all gotten this far is proof enough of our strength. Stand tall, Sir Edmaan, your fight is not over." He then turned to Crinnan. "And you." He walked over, took him by the arm, and lifted him to his feet. "You're stronger than sitting on the floor. We are all counting on you... not just us in this room but every prisoner in the Hells. You have brought hope to where it never could have existed before, it is now your duty and your responsibility to complete what you've started." Demyan nodded his head at Crinnan and gave his upper arm a supportive squeeze. "There is no giving up, Crinnan Jamiso. You fight or we all fail. There is no release of death here. It will all *only* get worse if you convince yourself you're not strong enough."

"What my brother is trying to say..." Milinka added as she stepped forward into Crinnan's view. "Is that we're not dead and we will get through this... but... the four of us..."

"Five." Dali spat with an eye roll.

"Yes..." Milinka corrected herself. "The five of us are all in this together... if we want to get out of this, we all work as a team." She approached Crinnan and looked him in the eye. She spoke to him, not scornfully, but as an equal. "Can we all do that? Please?"

Crinnan stared back at Milinka and thought about her question. It was clearly one that she had formulated specifically for him. He was aware that he wasn't exactly known for "playing nice." He looked at her and folded, silently nodding his head.

"Thank you Crinnan." Milinka whispered. She gave him a small smile and turned to the others. "Then we're all in this together. Whatever is behind those doors... we will all face as one group. We will work together, we will fight through and remain strong... Remember everyone, we're not just fighting for ourselves here. We're fighting for each and every soul who is trapped in this damned place. There's certainly no turning back now, there's just..." she motioned to the doors, "those. We owe it to... ourselves and to everyone else to get Crinnan to the Seventh Level."

"BTB that was epic girl!" Dali shouted in an excited tone. "You a bad bish fo sho!"

"Thanks." A smug expression passed across Milinka's face and she stood a little taller. "We don't have time to waste everyone. Get yourselves ready, it's time for us to move."

At that, and as a team, everyone turned and walked toward the doors.

Chapter Thirty-Three
Thornscale

The Fourth Level
Dread's Keep

The doors closed behind the group with a loud reverberating crash, and Crinnan watched as the impact shook dust free from the ceiling. The room they stepped into was well lit by fire light. Elegant chandeliers hung from the ceiling, braziers lined the floor and sconces held torches along the pillars to Crinnan's left and right. A crimson trimmed gold carpet was on the ground and Crinnan saw that it seemed to have been laid over a long series of steps that led upward to a large throne nearly a thousand feet away. The throne was empty, but the gigantic fireplace behind it roared with life.

"I wasn't expecting this…" Edmaan murmured as the group took in their surroundings. "I thought we were going to step into more…"

"Darkness…" Demyan finished Edmaan's sentence. Edmaan looked at Demyan and nodded his head.

"Yes, exactly."

"Light is better than dark, right?" Dali asked, her voice a bit nervous. "I mean, it's better to… see than not?"

"I don't know…" Milinka replied. "I saw things back there that I wish I hadn't…"

"I'd rather see what kills me." Crinnan added, thinking back to the moment of his death. He remembered the darkness of the forest around him, the piercing pain of the spear digging through his gut… "Dying in the dark isn't fun."

Crinnan stepped forward, sword in hand, and started ascending the steps. He kept an eye on his surroundings, watching to make sure that nothing jumped out at them. Demyan and Edmaan followed on his right and left a few steps back and Milinka was directly behind him. Dali stayed behind, knowing that she was of no help if a fight broke out.

"So, you think this place is…" Demyan whispered over to Crinnan as he readied his sword. "You know… that Thornscale guy's throne room?"

"Who else's would it be?" Crinnan asked, shooting Demyan a glare. "That's a dumb…" Milinka leaned forward and flicked Crinnan's ear and he stopped speaking mid-sentence.

"Ow!" Crinnan yelped. He looked back at Milinka and she opened her eyes wide at him, giving him a serious stink eye. Crinnan got the hint and looked back over at Demyan.

"I mean… yeah, probably…" Crinnan vigorously rubbed his ear with his free hand and Demyan grinned.

"So, you think he's just… in the bathroom or something?" Demyan asked. "Maybe grabbing a sandwich?"

"That's probably it." Edmaan chuckled.

"What do you think he enjoys more," Demyan continued, "Turkey, or the tortured souls of the damned?"

"I took him for a BLT kind of guy myself." Edmaan said. The two knights laughed with each other, and even Milinka let out a little chuckle. Crinnan just shook his head as he continued moving toward the throne.

"So, five hundred steps and then what?" Demyan commented. "It doesn't look like he's on the throne… unless he's really tiny. Which, based on my recollection of the Demon… he's not."

"Five hundred steps and then we see what happens, Demyan!" Milinka snapped. "By the Brothers I don't remember you talking this much."

"Look I'm nervous, sis." Demyan said in defense. "When I get nervous I talk. I've always been like this."

"Well, try to talk a little less." Milinka sighed. "I don't want any of those… long grey faced ghoul things showing up and biting us…"

"You mean ripping our bellies open and eating what's inside?" Demyan corrected.

"Of course that's what I mean!" Milinka replied. "Get your head in the game Demyan!"

As if by cue Crinnan heard the sound of footfalls coming from behind him. He and the other Black Knights quickly spun expecting to see one of the grey ghouls attacking, but instead saw Dali running toward them. Crinnan sighed and shook his head at the sight. Dali was annoying, and he hadn't seen his sister speak through her for quite some time.

"They're coming!" Dali shouted as she sprinted past them. "They're..."

"We see them!" Milinka replied. She raised her axes as Edmaan and Demyan hurried to her side, their swords at the ready. Crinnan looked down the steps and watched as a mass of the grey ghouls walked toward them, scythes in hand. They chanted in their guttural tongue as they walked.

Wasting no time, Crinnan pulled a pistol and started opening fire. His bullets struck the thin robed bodies of the creatures and they exploded in a mist of swirling black smoke. Flecks of a black runny tar like substance cascaded over the area and splashed against Crinnan, sticking to his body. He groaned at the feeling of the thick goo accumulating on his skin and swapped his empty revolver out for the other one.

"Keep your distance!" Crinnan shouted to the other four. Dali ran up beside him and reached out, clinging to his sword arm. Crinnan grunted and shook her free, glaring in her direction as he kept firing. "I'll hold them back for now!" He took aim, firing on one of the ghouls who was closing in on Demyan.

"Dali, take my other gun and load it." Crinnan barked.

"With what?" Dali snapped. "Where do I get the... the... bullets?"

"Ammo belt." Crinnan replied, pointing to the belt hanging from his waist. "They just. Replenish. Pull the bullets out and load them, but for fucks sake be gentle and don't distract me."

Dali looked down at Crinnan's crotch where the belt hung, and a smirk passed over her face. Crinnan tried to keep his focus on aiming and firing his weapon but in the corner of his eye he saw Dali doing nothing and glanced over at her. "Load the weapon, Dali!"

"Oh!" Dali shook her head and looked down at the revolver in her hand. "Right! So... I just put the... bullet in the tube?"

"It's called a cylinder but yes." Crinnan nodded and fired. "I need you to work quickly."

"Okay, but like hold still." Dali chirped as she reached down and pulled a bullet from Crinnan's belt. "You know I usually charged for this kind of thing when I was alive." She playfully teased.

"Well, you're fucking dead now. Hurry it up!" Crinnan snapped. "Quit playing, I'm out!" He reached down and started pulling bullets from his belt to reload his weapon. The ghouls drew closer as Crinnan spent a few seconds loading the revolver, but finally he flicked his wrist, snapping the cylinder back into place and took aim on a ghoul who was almost within striking distance of Milinka.

"Back it up!" Crinnan shouted to the others. "They're getting too close!" He fired three more shots and cursed as their numbers seemed to somehow grow instead of thin like he wanted them to. Cursing, he backed up further, expended his ammunition and then traded guns with Dali.

"Ten seconds!" He shouted at her. "I need the gun ready in ten seconds!"

Dali fumbled with the weapon as she awkwardly pulled rounds from Crinnan's belt. She was a bit clumsy and uncoordinated and Crinnan growled as he fired the last round in his cylinder.

"You have to go faster Dali!" He shouted as the two backed up the steps behind him. "I don't have time to wait for you. Stop playing with my dick and load the damn weapon!"

"I'm doing my best here, bish!" Dali shouted back. "Don't put more pressure on me!"

"She's doing her best, Crinnan!" Milinka shouted back at him. "Don't be a dick!"

Crinnan snarled and shut up. He reloaded the weapon he had just spent and opened fire again. The ghouls by that point were so numerous that they had formed a semi-circle around Crinnan and his team. There were hundreds of them, all dressed in the same dark robes and wielding scythes. Crinnan expended another cylinder and finally glanced behind him. The giant throne was only a few dozen feet away and Crinnan realized that they could go no further...

"Gun!" Crinnan snapped as he snatched the weapon out of Dali's hands. He ran forward and joined the other Black Knights, sword in one hand, pistol in the other. He was prepared to make his final stand against the ghouls.

"This is probably it." Milinka grumbled to them all. "There's... there's just too many of them."

"Don't go down easily." Edmaan snarled. "Take as many as you can with you."

"We're here with you, sister." Demyan added. "We..." He paused as the ghouls stopped marching. They stood in a line ten feet from the group and Crinnan watched curiously as the ghouls fell to their knees and raised their scythes into the air. He could feel the heat and a strange breeze from the gigantic fireplace blowing against his back. The ghouls chanting intensified, it grew louder and louder and then Crinnan felt a sudden and jarring tapping on his shoulder. He turned, expecting to see Dali, but his vision was drawn elsewhere.

Sitting on the throne behind him was the massive form of the high demon who had overseen the torment and challenges Crinnan and his group had endured throughout their time in Dread's Keep. Crinnan looked up at him, a mixture of awe, fear and anger surging through his body. Thornscale leaned forward in his chair looking directly at Crinnan with his black glossy eyes and furrowed his brow.

"You stand before a king of the Hells." Thornscale's booming voice declared. "The lord of dread, the father of terror... I am King Thornscale, ruler over all that would..."

Crinnan snarled and raised his weapon, firing a single shot directly at Thornscale's eye. The bullet found its target and sunk deep into Thornscale's skull. Thornscale stopped talking, leaned forward further and blinked.

"Oh." Crinnan said, realizing that his attack had no effect. He shrugged and holstered his weapon. "Worth a shot."

Thornscale snorted. "Was that... was that a pun?"

Crinnan thought about his words and then shrugged again. "I mean... I guess if you want to look at it that way it works..."

With a snort, Thornscale sat up straight in his chair. Crinnan wore a confused expression as he looked at the faces of his team, and then watched curiously as Thornscale shrunk down to their size. The demon, now six feet tall, stepped forward and stared at them.

"I will be... honest with you..." Thornscale said, his voice still booming but taking on a more... realistic tone. "I've been doing this for seventy-five years... I've been sitting in this room... talking into a computer, giving entitled players an opportunity to... move onto the next level." Thornscale breathed out a labored sigh and looked back and forth between the confused expressions of in Crinnan's team.

"W...what?" Milinka asked.

"Look, this is my job." Thornscale said. "It's been my job for nearly a century and... I have never once done anything to actually better anyone's life. Sure, sometimes people get out of the keep and have a breakthrough that lasts a few days, but then they're back to being depressed or... whatever within a week."

"S...so..." Milinka replied. "So... look I'm confused."

"I get it." Thornscale nodded, his tone seeming much more... real... "It's confusing. It's scary, it's weird... Here's what I'm trying to say. Pretty much every day of my entire adult life I've sat in this room for nine fuckin' hours watching players come and go simply to move on to the next level to torture more prisoners. This has not been a fulfilling existence; I have never done anyone any good. But now... here you are. Former prisoners on a grand quest for redemption, REAL redemption, not some simulated storyline."

Crinnan looked over his party and saw that they all were wearing various expressions of shock or disbelief. Was... Thornscale really complaining about his job to them?

"You're actually trying to get out of here, to get back home... This... all this... is *real* to you. I get it... You can't just log out and go eat your lackluster bland dinner and then have boring sex with your wife while your dog watches as you fall asleep covered in the residue of not only your own semen because you're a depressed shit too lazy to clean yourself up like a decent person, but also the thick, thick pain of knowing your life doesn't make a difference to anyone anywhere."

"BTB tell us how you really feel..." Dali smirked.

"I look at you people..." Thornscale said with a sigh. "I look at you people and I see a chance... an opportunity for my life to have meant something. Yes, I know who you are... You are the one that my manager says is trying to break out. You're the one working with the Ancient Life Links remnant. What I'm doing here goes against all the rules in the book, against everything I've been told all my life. What I'm doing right now is highly illegal, but I need this. I need to know that I've actually done something good with my life before I die. Do you guys get that?"

"So..." Milinka shook her head. "Like. You're a real person?"

"Last time I checked; computers don't have existential crises." Dali replied. "You, dude..." She stepped up to Thornscale and patted him on his back. "I get you. Forreal."

"Wait so... what the fuck." Crinnan snapped. "What are we doing here?"

Thornscale turned to Crinnan. "Moving you forward. We're *all* moving forward after this. I'm near the end of my life, so... I have nothing to lose. Now, the situation isn't too complicated. I just have to be defeated in combat for the portal to open. But..."

"Done." Without thinking, Crinnan cut Thornscale off and lunged forward, driving his sword through the demon's chest. The knights and Dali behind him all gasped, and Thornscale's eyes grew wide.

"Idiot!" Thornscale sputtered. He fell backwards, scales ripping from his body and magma looking blood pouring out of his chest. "Whoever kills me... sacrifices themselves... they have to start their journey from the First Level to obtain entrance to the next..." Thornscale fell to his knees and Crinnan threw his head back and looked up at the ceiling.

"You're fucking kidding me." Crinnan sighed. He looked over at Dali, who still held his pistol, and then over to Milinka and the knights.

"What?" Crinnan asked. "What's..." He looked down at his hands and saw that they were slowly... vanishing. "Oh, this isn't good... this is really bad...

this…" Crinnan's voice faded and everything went black. The last thing he heard, was the sound of a gunshot.

You Have Died

Chapter Thirty-Four
Respawn

The First Level

Congratulations, Citizen. You have killed Thornscale and completed the last level of Dread's Keep. Now you must endure Thornscale's final test and prove that you truly are strong enough to earn your place in the Fifth Level of the Hells. Find your way back to Thornscale's throne and show your goddess Dura'ana that you are worthy of being her champion. As it is written the Book of Eveen, Chapter...

"Skip!" Crinnan shouted as he tumbled through the air.

Congratulations, you have conquered Dread's Keep, Level Two.

+500,000,000 Rank

Congratulations, PrettyKitty6969420! You have advanced in ranking!

Previous Rank: 17,306,158,472

New Rank: 16,806,158,472

Previous Percentile: 57%

New Percentile: 56%

Quest Started: Thornscale's Final Trial

You have proven that you are mighty enough to conquer Thornscale, but are you strong enough to return to the portal to the fifth level that now awaits you? Fight through the levels and make your way back to Dread's Keep.

Note: Your portal summoning skills will not be available to you for this challenge.

Crinnan fell...or so he perceived that he was falling. The air blew past his face in the darkness that surrounded him. His hair whipped through the wind; his body burned from the heat that rose from the smoldering ground. Crinnan watched the ground approach, he watched, and he braced himself for the impact.

With sealed eyes and clenched teeth, Crinnan groaned in anticipation of the collision with solid ground. He waited... and waited... soon the air rushing past him slowed, his hair fell back down on his neck, and he realized he was no longer falling. Slowly, he opened one single eye and looked down at the burning ground which he hovered only a few inches over. He reached out, touching it, and then dropped face first.

"Ow." Crinnan groaned as he rolled over onto his back. The flames burned around him but did not harm him. His simple clothes were not consumed by fire, he was... fine. Crinnan realized this must have been the difference between entering the Hells as a prisoner and as a player. Slowly, he rose to a sitting position and then pushed himself up.

"Well shit." Crinnan sighed as he looked around. He was alone, the rest of his party had probably already progressed to the Fifth Level without him. He thought about that and realized that their progression suddenly meant nothing. Without him it didn't matter if they made it to the Seventh Level because they wouldn't be able to escape...

"Well... I should say this looks unfortunate." Sage's voice echoed in Crinnan's mind. *"What... what did you do?"*

"I killed Thornscale." Crinnan replied with a sigh. "The guy had issues... he really hates his life."

"Don't we all." Sage replied flatly. *"So... yes, killing Thornscale is only half the battle. When you kill him, it kills you and you have to respawn in the First Level."*

"Well, that's just so stupid and unrealistic." Crinnan snapped back. "Why would that even be a thing? That doesn't happen in real life."

"...What have you experienced in the Hells so far that would lead you to believe that any of it is grounded in reality?" Sage inquired.

Crinnan shrugged. "Well, the killing is pretty realistic..." He looked around again and thought of Milinka. "I need to get back to... to the keep... I..."

"You want to get back to the girl?" Sage asked, a hint of amusement in his voice.

"Yes..." Crinnan replied, suddenly embarrassed. "I just... need to get to the Seventh Level."

"Sure." Sage laughed slightly and Crinnan's face grew red. *"Look, Crinnan, I should say it is okay to feel the way you do. I would even encourage it. Any fuel to get you to fight harder toward the end goal is good. It's also fine to be in love. Nobody will question the length of your penis simply because you feel things."*

"Why would you explain it that way?" Crinnan asked, perplexed. "Look I..."

"Why are you defending yourself?" Sage asked, cutting Crinnan off. *"It's okay to care for people. End of discussion. Now, you need to focus on getting yourself where you need to be. To the Fifth Level so that you can find your beloved, and then to the Seventh Level so we can end this."*

"How do I do that?" Crinnan asked. "I mean... quickly..."

"You will have to... work... quickly..." Sage replied in a tone that suggested his response was common sense. *"Kill quickly, run fast... and make sure you don't lose that fairess..."*

"The what?" Crinnan asked, confused.

"The fairess... Dali, I believe her name is?" Sage continued. *"Do not lose her."*

"How can I..."

"Hello brother." Dali said as Crinnan felt a hand fall on his shoulder. "It would appear that I was not present when I should have been. For that I apologize, there is currently much going on in Govia and I am very busy."

"Brother..." Sage murmured. "How very interesting... I must go, Crinnan. Get to the Fifth Level, find your love, and then get to the Seventh Level. Hopefully I will talk to you soon."

At that, Sage was gone and Crinnan turned around to face Dali who was standing behind him.

"How are you here?" Crinnan asked.

"Well, I logged in as you killed Thornscale." Dali replied. "I tried to log in sooner to warn you not to kill him but... as I said... my job is very busy right now... no thanks to you."

Crinnan simply grunted as he turned to continue looking around the area. Being alone with his big sister was a strange feeling for him as he hadn't seen her for years. She was supposed to have died when she was fourteen, he recalled his parents speaking frequently throughout the years about her and how they missed her...

"But... how are you here?" Crinnan asked. "As in, how did you get here with me?"

"Oh, well." Dali composed herself and brushed the wrinkles out of her ratty clothing. "When I logged in, I saw that there was a gun in my hand. I saw you killing Thornscale and knew what was about to happen. So, I shot myself in the head."

Crinnan watched her as she spoke and when he was done, he snorted an amused laugh. "They're probably a little bit freaked out now." He said, tickled by the idea of them all watching him disappear and then Dali shoot herself.

"I'm glad you're entertained, Crinnan." Dali said, shaking her head. "But we're back down to the bottom of the barrel. We need to work our way back to the Fourth Level and..."

"Yeah, I remember what I did the first time, Sayraa." Crinnan cut her off. "I need a sword."

"It is not the same as last time, Crinnan." Dali argued. "This time, people know who you are. They have their eye out for you Crinnan, they know it is your fault that they are trapped here. The original players are massing here in the Fields of Misery, they are searching for their own and cutting down any former prisoners ruthlessly."

"Well good, then one of them should have a sword." Crinnan said. "I just need to take it from them."

"Not necessarily." Dali said, holding up a finger. "Hold still."

"What? Why?" Crinnan asked.

"Just do it, I need to scan you." Dali informed him. "It will only take a second."

Crinnan did as he was asked and watched Dali's eyes go out of focus. She reached a hand up and poked her finger in the air, causing Crinnan to cock his head curiously. "What are you doing?"

"I am using my scrying ability." Dali mumbled; her eyes still distant. "Shut up."

Crinnan felt a quick sensation like his arm had fallen asleep, except through his entire body. It only lasted for the blink of an eye and then it was gone. Dali seemed to be mouthing some words as if she were reading and then nodded her head and blinked a few times.

"You have a very significant electric affinity." Dali said. "All your affinities are... substantial but electric is your best one so we will focus on that."

"What are you talking about?" Crinnan asked, confused by her words. "What is an electric affinity?"

Dali rolled her eyes and shook her head at Crinnan's ignorance. "Just toss context out of the window. That is fine." She said sarcastically. "An affinity is a numerical value assigned to your natural talent with a specific type of ability. It is a reflection of your real-world affinities, for you are born with these affinities. They can be augmented and grown so that you become more powerful. In this case, we are focusing on electricity."

"Yeah, I really don't understand what you're talking about." Crinnan replied dumbfounded.

"You can use magic, Crinnan." Dali said impatiently. "Electric magic. Like lightning?"

"Oh." Crinnan nodded his head. He grimaced at the idea. "Yeah, I don't know about that, I've never really done anything like that before."

"Well, you are about to Crinnan." Dali said. "I want you to think…" She paused. "You know what that is right? Hearing words in your head?"

"You don't need to be a bitch." Crinnan replied, unamused. Dali smiled and let out a small chuckle.

"I want you first to turn away from me, then hold your hand in front of you." Dali instructed. "Then, in your mind I want you to think Bolt Level One. Can you do that?"

Curiously, Crinnan turned from Dali, held his hand outward and thought *Bolt Level One*. To his surprise, a flash emitted from his palm and then a bolt of lightning shot outward. Crinnan stumbled backward from the unexpected recoil, and he watched the bolt fly forward, ultimately striking some person in the distance. Crinnan heard a yip of pain, and watched the person fall over. He knew he shouldn't, but he couldn't help but laugh.

Player: BigMoHunter EXECUTED

Player Rank: 15,845,129,587

Congratulations, PrettyKitty6969420! You have advanced in ranking!

Previous Rank: 16,806,158,472

New Rank: 16,325,600,029

Previous Percentile: 56%

New Percentile: 54%

"You did it!" Dali chirped. "I mean, yeah it was amateurish and sloppy but. Yeah, that was a good bolt. The harder you focus on it, the longer you charge it, the more powerful it will be. Remember that when you go to use it."

"I mean..." Crinnan grunted as he got to his feet. He looked down at his fingertips to see that they were smoking. "That was pretty damn cool, I'm not even going to pretend like I didn't like that. What happens if I..." He held out his palm and thought *"Bolt Level Two"* He charged it for a second like Dali told him and her eyes grew wide when she realized what was going on.

"Crinnan that's a bad idea!" She barely got out before a much larger bolt of lightning fired from Crinnan's palm. Crinnan was blasted into the air and he screamed as he flew in an arc nearly fifty yards away, finally crashing to the ground and rolling to a stop. He coughed and a small plume of smoke fluttered up out of his mouth. He looked down at his arm and saw that his veins had turned black as if they were burnt, and his entire hand sizzled like bacon on a skillet.

Dali appeared a moment later, standing in front of Crinnan and shaking her head. "How..." Crinnan asked. More smoke came out of his mouth and the smell of electricity filled his nostrils. "How did you get here so fast?"

"I phased, Crinnan." Dali replied. She reached her hand out and grabbed his forearm, helping him back to his feet. "Because I am strong enough to handle it. If you know the incantation or command you can will any ability into being, just like in the real world... but most high tier ones will just rip your body apart so, do not will anything but what you know you can handle... and for Dura'ana's sake... do NOT attempt to phase."

"Right..." Crinnan replied, but he couldn't help himself. Seeing Dali just teleport across the ground like that was amazing. He had to try it. He nodded at her, turned and thought "Phase". He suddenly disappeared out of existence, and a split second later... a puddle of gore broken bone and body parts appeared out of nothingness and splatted to the ground.

You Have Died

"Dura'ana save us all..." Dali sighed, looking down at the puddle that had been her brother. Crossing her arms, she shook her head and tapped her foot. Nearly twenty minutes later, she heard the sound of screaming as Crinnan plummeted toward the ground. She phased over to his location, grabbed him by the ear, and "helped" him to his feet.

"You are, without a doubt, one of the biggest morons in existence." Dali chided him. "Had you done that in real life you would have died.

"You sound like mom when you put it like that." Crinnan groaned at the pain coming from his ear. "Can you... fucking let go?" Dali flicked her wrist and Crinnan stumbled forward. She stepped back and watched as he found his footing.

"Thanks..." He mumbled as he turned to her. "So... I get what you mean by don't try other abilities..."

"You could have just listened." Dali replied, raising an eyebrow at him. "You do not have to just... ignore people for the sake of it. Sometimes in life people know what they are talking about and you cannot just rely on your own experiences to get you through whatever you are facing. Trust people sometimes, kid. Like I need you to trust me now."

"Why should I?" Crinnan barked in response. "You abandoned the family to run off and join the Govian Empire. You are a fucking traitor. You're just as dead to me today as you were yesterday."

Dali's nostrils flared and she took a breath and closed her eyes. "Crinnan, that is a severe oversimplification of the circumstances that led me to my current position. I understand that you do not know said circumstances, however I do request that you save your judgement for..."

"Fuck off." Crinnan said, waving his hand in Dali's direction. "The fact of the matter is that you ran away. You joined the Empire; you didn't come back. You're a traitor and you're no Jamiso."

"I was kidnapped, Crinnan." Dali called out to him. "I was seduced by an evil man; I carried his child... I watched the child die in front of me. And then I was taken by Govia, I had no choice."

Crinnan stopped and lowered his head. He chewed on the inside of his cheek for a moment and then turned to face Dali. "You should have run."

"You are not truly that cold, Crinnan." Dali said, stepping forward and shaking her head. "I know your parents, your brothers. I know myself... You are not truly like this. You just want to be like this... No. I could not have run, Crinnan. You do not run when you are in a cage..."

"This is how I am, Sayraa." Crinnan corrected her. "This is how I've always been and I'm not changing because you don't believe me. I wouldn't change for you anyway, not when you abandoned us..."

"I *never* abandoned you, brother." Sarasin hissed. "I prayed every night for your safety, for mother and father's safety. I prayed for Rubii and Kiersen... and even little Cris who was just a baby when I was taken. I bled, I cried, I sacrificed everything I had so that I could just keep living... and I grew powerful. I was entrusted with secrets, with missions. I watched over the family from Govia, I made sure that everybody stayed safe and undetected."

"Yeah right." Crinnan rolled his eyes. "You sat in your mansion riding whatever guy you wanted and..." Dali reached out and slapped her palm against Crinnan's cheek. Crinnan's head spun ninety degrees and a frown formed on his face. His lips curled up into a snarl as he slowly turned his head back to look at the body his sister currently inhabited.

"You're going to apologize for that." Crinnan hissed. "You were..." Dali raised her eyebrow and punched Crinnan square in the nose.

"No, you disrespectful little shit." Dali growled as she stepped forward. "You are going to purge that filth from your mouth, your mind and you are never going to speak to another lady like that again, am I understood?" Another slap across Crinnan's face sent him tumbling to the side. "I am Bishop General Sarasin Fyr, and I am your sister. I love you and nothing will change that. Now, if we can..."

Crinnan spun toward Dali and roared as he charged forward. He launched himself through the air and wrapped his arms around her midsection, tackling her. However, by the time he hit the ground, she had phased out of his grasp and now stood behind him.

"That was stupid." Dali said flatly as she extended a palm over Crinnan, who was now face first against the ground. A blast of invisible power slammed against Crinnan, cracking the brittle glowing ground beneath him and he shouted in surprise in pain. He thought it was over and moved to stand, but Dali did it again, pushing him back to the ground. Dali knelt down, grabbed Crinnan's ear and pulled on it until he was on his knees and her lips were only an inch away.

"I *never* abandoned you." Dali growled at him. "I *never* will. Why else do you think I'm here right now?"

"F-fine..." Crinnan groaned. "I get it..."

"And?" Dali asked expectantly.

"And what?" Crinnan replied. Dali twisted his ear and he yelped in pain. "Oh! And I'm sorry Sayraa. I'm fucking sorry!"

"You will never speak to another lady that way in your life, right little brother?" Dali asked.

"Y-yes..." Crinnan replied. "I m-mean no! You know what I mean!"

"Good." Dali let go of Crinnan's ear and then pushed the top of his head forward. "Now. Get on your feet. We have a lot of ground to cover."

Crinnan did as he was told, wiped the tears from his eyes, and followed his sister.

Chapter Thirty-Five
Welcome to the Bloodgames

The First Level

"Attention, citizens: As you are aware, Hellscape is temporarily on lockdown pending the capture of the entity called Crinnan Jamiso. We understand this continues to be a concern to those of you who have no way of logging out. We are also aware of the condition that many of you are experiencing where your "Player" status has been revoked and you are temporarily unable to protect yourselves. We assure you; solutions will be provided quickly. Until that time, we encourage all citizens afflicted with this condition to find the nearest gamemaster so that you can be properly identified and protected.

"Furthermore, we declare that a bounty has been placed upon the head of Crinnan Jamiso. We will issue a one-thousand shard reward to any who deliver Crinnan Jamiso to a gamemaster. New players, we encourage you not to engage Crinnan Jamiso as he is armed and dangerous. For the rest of you, it has been reported that he is currently in the First Level. We are working diligently to provide you all more information on his whereabouts so that we can end this lockdown as quickly as possible. Remember everyone, Dura'ana is with you, and the Emperor Cidro commends you for your bravery."

The message ended and Crinnan snorted. "So, they're sending the entire Hells after me." Crinnan smiled and cracked his knuckles. "Should be easy enough to get to where we need to go then."

"Sajinious has encrypted your character information." Dali said to him. "We... Govia cannot accurately track your exact location, we only know which level you are on as players report you... apparently the person you blasted earlier reported you for PvP. Also, Sajinious deactivated most of the Gamemasters abilities, they are just like regular players now."

"Whatever that means." Crinnan shrugged. "So, I guess it's time for us to go kill some people? Move on to the next level?"

"Yes." Dali nodded. "We need to be smart; we need to..."

Crinnan ran forward and held his palm out. A bolt of lightning shot out from him and struck a player in the distance. Dali tried to protest but Crinnan charged forward, sending another bolt into the person. After a few hits, Crinnan knelt down and picked up a sword from the ground and ran back to Dali.

Player: DukeofDorks EXECUTED

Player Rank: 15,977,159,178

Congratulations, PrettyKitty6969420! You have advanced in ranking!

Previous Rank: 16,325,600,029

New Rank: 16,151,379,603

Previous Percentile: 54%

New Percentile: 53%

"Got a sword." Crinnan reported with a small grin on his face. "Now I don't have to use the magic."

"Crinnan..." Dali sighed and shook her head. "You need to..."

Crinnan's eyes grew wide and he pushed past Dali. After a few moments, Dali heard another scream and watched him walk back wiping the blood on his sword off on his pant leg. She stood with all her weight on one leg and arms crossed. As he approached, she raised an eyebrow.

Player: BloodAdept EXECUTED

Player Rank: 12,884,157,987

Congratulations, PrettyKitty6969420! You have advanced in ranking!

Previous Rank: 16,325,600,029

New Rank: 14,517,768,795

Previous Percentile: 53%

New Percentile: 48%

...

NEW PERCENTILE ACHIEVED! Congratulations, you are showing your true power. Your buffs have been modified.

Cosmetic Items unlocked! See your wardrobe for more details!

...

Congratulations! You have crossed the threshold of the 50th percentile and into the 40s.

...

New Ability Pending.

"That was a good one." Crinnan said after the voice in his head silenced.

"Are you going to listen to me?" Dali asked.

"Probably not." Crinnan shrugged. "I'm ready to get out of here."

"Fine." Dali said. She vanished from his view, Crinnan heard a cacophony of screams in the distance, and then suddenly she was in front of him again. She smiled and tilted her head as a swirling blue portal opened up in front of her. "That's the Second Level." She said with a grin. "As it stands, I believe I am winning."

"Hold the fuck up." Crinnan said. He wrinkled his face and stepped in front of the portal. "You don't get to disappear and teleport or phase or whatever. That's fucking cheating. I'd say we're tied right now."

"Oh, but you get to use every ability available to you?" Dali inquired.

"I only have one!" Crinnan snapped back. "We need to make this fair."

"Crinnan..." Dali stepped forward and thumped him in the forehead with a finger. "Get serious. Are we not getting you back to the girl you love? Are we not trying to break you out of the Hells?"

"I mean..." Crinnan thought of Milinka and freedom. He smiled as he thought about the kiss they had shared back in Dread's keep, and the thought of being a real person breathing real air again really made him miss home. But then he realized Dali was cheating again. "Hey fucking wait a damn minute. You're the one who started this game. Don't just crawl in my head like that."

Dali couldn't hold back the laugh. She looked at Crinnan and shook her head gleefully. "There are some brains in that skull of yours." She said, thumping him in the head again. "Fine. No phasing unless I have to but... we do this quick. We *have* to get you to where you need to be, understood?"

"Right." Crinnan nodded, suddenly wanting to see Milinka again. "But what's the score?"

"Five to three." Dali replied. "You are losing." At that, Dali pushed against Crinnan's chest and he fell backward into the portal. She smiled and followed closely behind.

***

The Second Level

Attention citizens: It has been reported that Crinnan Jamiso has passed through a portal. He is currently located somewhere in the Second Level. The bounty has been raised to two thousand shards. Praise Dura'ana, Praise Cidro.

"Oh boy." Crinnan snorted in response to the voice. "Looks like we're in trouble now."

"Come on." Dali said, ignoring his sarcasm. "We have got to go and find players to kill. It will not be hard; they are abundant as this level is commonly referred to as the Bloodzone and people partake in a variety of different game modes here."

"Bloodzone, huh?" Crinnan repeated. "That's a weird name. I wonder why they went with…"

"Suns out guns out boys and girls. The skies are clear, the suns are out. There isn't a cloud in sight! It's a beautiful day to die!"

"Well, that's not the same voice." Crinnan whispered looking over at Dali. "There's no suns? Where are all these loud voices suddenly coming from?"

"We portaled into a warzone." Dali sighed. "They're randomly generated… and it looks like we won't have time to get out of the radius. Basically, it's a last person standing free for all where up to one hundred people fight to win… weapons and items are scattered around the area and we have… about an hour to be the last person alive."

"Oh, that's easy then." Crinnan nodded. "Like the stories of the Bloodgames that the humaan people tell."

"Yes, Crinnan." Dali said with a regretful tone. "They *are* the Bloodgames."

"As you all know my name is DJ and I am your host for the next hour. You know the rules. Fight, slaughter, bathe in the blood of your enemies! I ask you, are you ready to prove that YOU are the mightiest amongst your peers? Are you strong enough to survive? Let's see if you have what it takes to WIN the Bloodgames!"

"Oh, how tacky." Crinnan sneered in response to the sound of the obnoxious voice. "Is this guy for real? Do we have time for this? Can't we just. Not?"

"We are already locked in." Dali informed him. "We have to fight... listen. Both of us cannot survive. We will team up for the fight and then in the end you will have to kill me. When it is all over you will be able to travel to the Third Level... this is actually a good thing, it will be a quick way for you to get to where you need to go. Do you understand?"

"Not at all." Crinnan shook his head. "I never have any clue what anything you say means."

"I get it." Dali said. "Just. Stick with me, we will see our way to the end and get you out of here okay?"

"Yeah." Crinnan replied. "No prob..."

The ground suddenly crumbled. Crinnan lost his footing and fell. He yelped in surprise, and instead of hitting the dirt like one would expect he was in a freefall.

"What the fuck!" Crinnan yelled. His body tumbled through the air and he was blinded by an unexpected light. It was bright and warm and gave him a nostalgic sense of comfort... it was something he hadn't experienced for what seemed like a lifetime.

When Crinnan's eyes finally acclimated, he found he was surrounded by a white haze. He wondered what it was for a moment, but it was gone as quickly as he noticed it. Looking up, Crinnan saw a cloud... and behind the cloud was a brilliant blue sky. He stared at the color in amazement, and then gasped when he saw the source of the light.

Hanging in the sky above him were the twin suns; The Brothers as they were called. His heart was filled with a longing to return home, to bask in their light, to breathe real air and actually worry about dying. He stared at The Brothers long enough for his mother to have a heart attack, and then a mass suddenly zoomed past him. It broke his concentration and looked down.

The world beneath him was beautiful. He saw a small island with sandy beaches and a green core surrounded by endless blue ocean. The sight was refreshing, a welcome break from the blacks and greys he had grown so accustomed to. Strangely however, the air suddenly started filling with multiple colored circles. He looked on in confusion until he realized what he was looking at.

"Parachutes?" He internally asked. They started appearing all over, and he watched as they glided toward various points on the island. Crinnan reached up, feeling his chest and found that he had straps over his shoulders. He found a ripcord and wrapped his fingers around it. He had only parachuted a few times in his life and was a bit nervous about the whole situation.

The ground drew nearer and Crinnan pulled on the ripcord. His parachute opened behind him, jerking his body and slowing his descent. He watched the other 99 participants of this sudden and unexpected deathmatch navigate to their landing spots, and he found a clearing amid the woods nearby and aimed himself for it.

A few minutes later, Crinnan's feet hit the grass and he crashed into the ground. His parachute collapsed on top of him and he struggled to remove it. He fought with the canvas for a few moments before finally emerging and turning toward the tree line.

"Okay this isn't so bad." Crinnan mumbled to himself. "So, I have this magic shit... and my sword..." He looked down at his hip and groaned when he realized his sword was no longer with him. "What the Hells!"

"Your weapons from the Hells don't carry over to the Bloodgames, kid." Yet another strange voice rattled off in Crinnan's head. This voice was deep and gravely, and he had a Dust accent like Karston. *"You're gonna have to get creative. Figure out solutions to the problems as they're presented."*

"Who are you? Where are you?" Crinnan replied, looking around him.

"Kid don't worry about me. I'm just here to answer any questions you may have." The voice replied. *"Do you have any questions for me?"*

"Yeah, how do I get a weapon?" Crinnan asked.

"Look around. You'll find one eventually. They're all over the map." The person instructed. *"Guns, melee weapons, kitchen utensils... Hells you could go break a limb off a tree and start bludgeoning your opponents with it if you want."*

"Not really..." Crinnan replied. "I'd rather find a gun. Or use my ability."

"Sure kid." The voice said. *"Let me know if you need anything else."* The voice vanished, and Crinnan was left alone.

"Okay, need to find a weapon... again..." Crinnan whispered to himself as he spun in place. There was nothing in his immediate area which led him to frown. He ran into the tree line, not knowing what it was that he needed to find. Surely they wouldn't be glowing or spinning or anything that would allow him to recognize them from a distance. He stopped running for a moment and once again took in his surroundings.

The guttural sound of a battle cry pierced Crinnan's ears and he spun to face the roar. Something hard, circular and metal slammed against Crinnan's face and he gasped as he heard his nose crunch. He stumbled backwards just in time to receive another blow, this time to the side of the head. He saw stars but tried to fight through it. His attacker had pulled his arm back for another blow, and Crinnan was seeing double. He snarled and launched himself forward in a tackle towards the center of the two images he saw.

Crinnan made contact with flesh, and he and the other person both crashed to the ground. He heard the sound of the heavy metal object striking a rock on the ground. Crinnan didn't waste any time. He pounded his fist into the other person's face, roaring with fury as he heard bones crack and teeth break free. The other player quickly fell unconscious and Crinnan reached out and grabbed the heavy metal object that the person had struck him with.

For a split second, Crinnan examined the object in his hand. It was a cast iron skillet. Crinnan snorted at the crudeness of the weapon and then raised it into the air to strike his opponent. He thought about it for a moment, and then turned the skillet ninety degrees so that the edge would hit the player, and not the flat side. He felt that had been the player's mistake, hitting Crinnan with the bottom of the pan and not the edge.

Crinnan slammed the skillet down against the person's forehead and heard a pop. He reeled back, repeated his action, and the skull split in two. Crinnan did this two more times for good measure, stood up, and kicked the person square in the ribs.

Player: Deverash EXECUTED

Player Rank: 13,457,214,988

Congratulations, PrettyKitty6969420! You have advanced in ranking!

Previous Rank: 14,804,297,295

New Rank: 14,130,756,141

Previous Percentile: 49%

New Percentile: 47%

"Idiot!" Crinnan yelled at him. He spit a glob of blood out on the corpse and sighed when he realized his weapon was a fucking pan. Whoever the voice was that had reached out to him hadn't lied. Kitchen utensils *were* viable weapons.

Sighing, Crinnan turned toward the trees and ventured further into the forest to find more people to kill. But not before he heard the announcer's voice again.

"Twenty dead already! This is going to be a quick round! The Hellfire has been ignited and will be closing in. Keep your eyes on your maps so that you don't get immolated. Eighty players remain, go gettem boys and girls!"

Chapter Thirty-Six
Grandpa's Helper

The Bloodgames
The Second Level

"I don't want a damn frying pan." Crinnan groaned as he walked in search of a more substantial weapon. "This is shit. I don't like it; I don't want it... I don't have to have it!"

"You sure do complain a lot." The mysterious voice from earlier called out to Crinnan. *"You know if you channeled some of that bitching into productivity then maybe you could win this damn match."*

"I *can* win this fucking match." Crinnan spat. "I don't need positive butterflies fluttering around in my ass to get me there."

"Well damn there hotshot, sorry for doubting you." The person said with a chuckle. *"Look I'm having a shit ton of trouble monitoring your progress. All your data is corrupt and doesn't make a lick o' sense. You gotta name?"*

"No." Crinnan replied. "I'm not here to make friends. I'm here to kill people and move on."

"Well, aren't you just the little badass then." The voice said sarcastically. *"Look, you're cool, you remind me of some folks I... dealt with... a long ass time ago. Specifically, a little girl that pretty much hated everything that moved. That doesn't matter though. Listen, these matches generally run around twenty to thirty minutes long. You have the pleasure of being paired up against a number of high-ranking players. Highest in here today is rank 42, couple in the 100s and then about a dozen under 500. They're the ones you're gonna need to watch*

out for as they will fuck you sideways long dick style without your permission and then sneak out while you're sleeping and not call you the next morning."

"That's. A weird way to put it." Crinnan said, scratching the back of his head. He wondered what the term "long dick style" meant, but ultimately shrugged. He didn't have time to ponder over things that didn't help him find a better weapon. "So, can you help me find something better than a frying pan to fight with?"

"Negative, buddy." The voice replied. *"I'm just an advisor. My sole purpose here is to ensure that you have a firm understanding of the rules and mechanics as you go out there and kill your peers. I can't tell you how to fight, when or where to fight, or what to do."*

"Well, I already know how to fight." Crinnan said with a snort. "I don't need any help with that."

"Sounds good to me. But look, if you have any questions just give me a holler." The voice went silent again and Crinnan continued his journey deeper into the woods.

Crinnan wandered around, frying pan in hand for a few minutes before he finally chanced upon something. He saw it, a small silver cylinder hovering above the ground glowing and spinning in place. "Guess I was wrong." He mumbled to himself as he approached. He knelt down and grabbed the cylinder, lifting to inspect it.

"What is this?" He turned the cylinder over in his hands, examining it. It was about nine inches in length, black rubber surrounding it for grip and a small red button where his thumb would go. He looked down at it, noticing there was a hole in the top and could see the sunlight catch something shining inside.

"This looks useless." He said. He held the weapon outward, pushed the red button and then jumped back as a steady stream of red light blasted out the hole. Crinnan gasped and stared at the light. It hummed strangely and didn't vanish as long as Crinnan held the button down.

"What is this?" Crinnan asked in a disgusted tone. "A sword? Made of light?" He waved it around a bit and his face wrinkled up in disappointment. "No way, this is garbage." He let go of the button and the light disappeared. "I can't fight with this flashlight; it's not balanced at all." He tossed the light sword hilt over his shoulder and sighed as he marched onward.

After a few more moments Crinnan chanced upon another weapon. A magazine fed pump action shotgun and a box of shotgun shells was just sitting there waiting for him. It wouldn't have been his first choice in the real world, but it went boom and killed people and wasn't made out of light, so he knelt down and picked the weapon. He ejected the double stack mag and noticed that it was already loaded with ten slugs. He appreciated the fact that he was provided with slugs instead of buckshot, or Brothers forbid birdshot. This would give him greater range and versatility. He replaced the mag and racked the weapon.

"Don't have anywhere for that." Crinnan shrugged as he looked down at the box of slugs. "Ten should be enough though..."

"What the hell do you mean you don't have any room for that?" The voice suddenly appeared. He sounded confused and a little annoyed. *"Box barely weighs anything, just put it in your inventory."*

"I don't have a bag!" Crinnan argued. "I'm not just going to carry around a box of slugs."

"Are you..." The voice lowered a bit, the confusion not leaving him. *"Are you stupid?"*

"Hey, fuck you." Crinnan spat back.

"Man, just open your inventory." The advisor snapped. *"Put the shells in and use them when it's time to reload."*

"Okay clearly I'm not understanding something." Crinnan sighed. He looked around him for hostiles before he committed to a conversation with this strange voice. "What the fuck are you talking about?"

"You... are playing this game and... don't know how to use your inventory?" The advisor asked in a dumbfounded tone. *"Is... that the case?"*

"I guess?" Crinnan replied, equally as confused.

"Ah Jesus fuck you're one of them, aren't you?" The advisor groaned. *"One of the prisoners who were turned into players?"*

"Maybe." Crinnan answered.

"You know I'm going to have to report this right?" The advisor asked. *"I can't just have you..."* He paused for a moment and Crinnan heard a slight hum come from the advisor's end. *"Wait. You're not that Crinnan boy I keep hearing about, are you?"*

"Look asshole, I don't..."

"Crinnan... Jamiso right?" The advisor continued. His voice held a certain tone of recognition and mystery. *"Tell me kid... what was your daddy's name?"*

"Is this a joke?" Crinnan asked. "I don't have time for jokes."

"No, it ain't a fucking joke." The advisor continued. He sounded serious. *"Tell me your daddy's name."*

Crinnan sighed and sucked on the side of his cheek for a moment before he shrugged. Govia already knew his father's name. His father had been giving Govia trouble for decades. "Same name." Crinnan relented. "Crinnan Jamiso."

"And his daddy before him?" The advisor continued prodding. *"What is your grandfather's name?"*

"I don't fucking know!" Crinnan snapped. "Look, I don't have time to be going through my entire genealogy with you here..."

"I get it kid." The advisor cut him off. *"Look... long time ago I knew of a baby named Crinnan Jamiso... He was named after a small village on..."* The advisor paused for a moment and then found his words. *"...well. Just a small village... he was the son of a..."* The advisor sighed deeply. Crinnan sensed a bit of regret in his tone. *"...a good friend..."* The advisor fell silent.

"Alright, neat story." Crinnan sighed. "But I have..."

"Holy fuck you are impatient." The advisor groaned. *"Look... I... I can't sit here and help you kid..."* The advisor's tone had softened, as if he were speaking to someone he cared for. *"But listen to me real quick. Do your best, get through this... I've seen a lot since we... landed all those years ago but nothing has ever compared to the time I spent with... well... my friends. I let them down all those years ago. I..."* Crinnan heard the advisor begin to sniffle softly. *"God damnit, just go north. I ain't gonna tell you what's there and I ain't gonna tell you why to go north but be fucking careful... Hell, who knows, maybe ol' Grizzly will finally get a good night's rest tonight."* The advisor laughed and Crinnan couldn't help but wonder what the fuck he was talking about.

"So… north?" Crinnan asked the rambling person.

"North… go north and…" Crinnan heard a sudden loud thud come from the advisor's end of the conversation. "Ah shit. They're banging on the door… fuck it. Here." Crinnan heard what sounded like some furious typing on a keyboard and then felt something small strike his feet.

"Old back door still works." The advisor said with a hint of mirth in his voice. "I haven't used it in years… pick that shit up, hold onto it. It's called a skipping stone. It's single use and can't be lost when you die. It's something only I know about, I programmed it years ago and integrated it, but the higher powers said they didn't want it becoming a mechanic, so it was just forgotten about. Whenever you're ready to use it, break that crystal and you'll be able to open a portal to the next level. I can only spawn one reward at a time… I hope it's helpful…"

The pounding grew more intense and Crinnan heard the advisor sigh. "I hope your granddaddy can forgive me… I owe him at least this. Guess I may see him soon… good luck, Jamiso… lots of folks here at Farseer would sure love to see you succeed… if they only knew. Tell your daddy uncle Grizzly wishes him the best." The sound of a door breaking free of its hinges filled Crinnan's ears and then he heard shouting and fighting. After a moment, the transmission ended and Crinnan knelt down and picked up the small pink crystal from the ground.

"Well… that was weird…" Crinnan mumbled as he thought over the entire exchange. He held the skipping stone up to the sunlight and looked at it. It was just a simple stone, pink in color, translucent and a bit foggy in the center. Crinnan examined it, shrugged his shoulders and slipped into his pants pocket.

"That guy…" Crinnan whispered as he began walking again. He thought over what "Uncle Grizzly" had said. The person talked about his father and grandfather as if he had known them. Crinnan had never met his grandfather, and his father never talked about him when the topic was brought up.

Crinnan was used to people talking to him about his father. It had been that way his entire life. In the real world, Crinnan's father was famous, or infamous depending on who he was talking to. Crinnan Jamiso Sr., or Commander Crinnan as he was more commonly known, was a hero amongst Black Knight and a villain to anyone allied with Govia. Without his quick thinking and decisive action Black Knight would have never liberated the island nation of Exgrane twenty years prior. Crinnan was both greatly annoyed and, much more quietly, deeply proud of who his father was.

"This is taking too long." Crinnan impatiently groaned as he walked for a few more minutes. "Aren't there supposed to be one hundred people running around? Where are they?" He pushed his way through a thicket and emerged onto a paved road. He looked around and raised his eyebrows when he saw an abandoned ATV parked on the side of the road. Curiously, he approached the four-wheeled vehicle and examined it.

"Full tank..." He said, looking at the gas gauge. "Key's here..." Looking around, Crinnan hopped onto the ATV, squeezed the brake, and turned the key. The vehicle's engine kicked on and Crinnan climbed onto the seat. He released the handbrake and gave the vehicle a little gas as he pulled onto the road.

"Okay, here we go." Crinnan said to himself as he drove down the road. "This should make things faster." He gave the ATV some more gas and sped up. After only a few moments of driving, Crinnan grinned as he saw a player a few hundred yards ahead of him. He leaned downward, and rotated the throttle, giving the vehicle more power. He watched the player grow closer and closer, and finally, Crinnan slammed into the person, running them over. As Crinnan climbed a hill he chuckled at the player's bad luck. When he reached the top of the hill, however, he quickly hit the brakes.

Player: Woah77 EXECUTED

Player Rank: 15,625,148,133

NO RANK CHANGE

Current Rank: 14,130,756,141

Current Percentile: 47%

In the valley below, Crinnan saw and heard what he could only perceive as complete chaos. People were emptying full magazines as they shot everything but their target and driving vehicles like they were drunk and blind... he saw someone squat over another person... and then stand... and then squat again... only to get domed while he was distracted by another person wielding a large axe.

"What the fuck..." Crinnan whispered as he watched the scene unfold before him. "It's like... a bunch of drunk twelve-year-olds were given keys to an armory." He grinned at the sight, realizing how easily it would be for a person like him to finish this match very quickly. With a snort, he gave the ATV a little more gas, and drove forward into the valley.

Chapter Thirty-Seven
Auroch

The Bloodgames
The Second Level

Crinnan kept his head low as his ATV roared toward the battle in the valley below. He steered the vehicle with one hand, and in his other he held his shotgun tightly. He was ready to enter the fight.

As he drove, he watched an unsettling wall of fire in the distance draw closer and closer to his position. Based on what the announcer had said before, Crinnan knew that the fire would not stop moving until only one person remained. It moved slowly and swirled like a tornado, burning everything in its path. Crinnan seriously didn't want to deal with that.

He quickly approached the town, "Torpedo Town" he realized it was called when he read a sign on the way in. He thought the name was strange considering it was situated in a valley, but Crinnan wasn't about to ponder on naming conventions. His first targets were in sight, he squeezed the brakes and turned the handlebars of the ATV so that he skidded to a stop, threw it in neutral and then raised his shotgun to his shoulder. Within only a moment he had his target sighted and a smile spread across his face.

"Bye." Crinnan whispered as he squeezed the trigger. The weapon discharged and a slug flew out and through the face of his target. The person's body flew backward from the impact, what was left of his head slamming against a brick wall behind him. Glowing weapons and items flew from the person's body, landing all around him. Crinnan didn't waste any time, he dismounted his ATV and ran forward.

Player: OldNothing EXECUTED

Player Rank: 12,488,415,336

Congratulations, PrettyKitty6969420! You have advanced in ranking!

Previous Rank: 14,130,756,141

New Rank: 13,309,585,738

Previous Percentile: 47%

New Percentile: 44%

"Sword..." Crinnan mumbled to himself as he scanned the dropped items. He didn't see one and cursed. He had discarded his frying pan long ago because he had nowhere to put it, and only had a few shells in one of his pockets. He didn't want to run out of ammo or get caught up in a melee situation and not have any way to fight back. "I'll just take this then." Crinnan said as he knelt down and grabbed a pistol. He shoved it into the waist of his pants and kept running.

BOOM

Crinnan discharged his weapon again, dropping another player. Again, no sword. This really frustrated Crinnan and he moved onto his next target.

Player: Artie1231 EXECUTED

Player Rank: 1,232

Congratulations, PrettyKitty6969420! You have advanced in ranking!

Previous Rank: 14,130,756,141

New Rank: 6,654,793,485

Previous Percentile: 44%

New Percentile: 22%

NEW PERCENTILE ACHIEVED! Congratulations, you are showing your true power. Your buffs have been modified.

Cosmetic Items unlocked! See your wardrobe for more details!

...

Congratulations! You have crossed the threshold of the 40th and 30th percentiles and into the 20s.

...

New Ability Pending.

"Holy shit!" Crinnan shouted as he fired his weapon. Unfortunately, the notification had distracted him, and he only grazed his target's neck. The person returned fire and Crinnan quickly dipped behind a brick wall for cover. After racking his weapon, he waited for his opportunity and popped up when his opponent's rifle clicked empty.

"Next time shoot in bursts." Crinnan advised before firing a slug through the being's chest. He flew backwards, crashing into the ground dead. Crinnan snorted at the sight, but then heard footsteps approaching quickly behind him.

"Not today!" Crinnan shouted as he spun around and slammed the stock of his weapon into his would-be attacker's nose. She screamed and fell to the side, giving Crinnan an opportunity to spin his weapon around, rack it, and blast her in the back of the head.

Player: merry9209 EXECUTED

Player Rank: 14,218,573,699

"Spear?" Crinnan snorted as he saw the weapon she was charging with. "You got that close... with a spear? What were you going to hit me with the shaft?" He rolled his eyes and turned, waiting for his next victim.

"Only thirty players remaining, boys and girls! This is where the shit really starts to stink my friends. The iron is glowing, time to strike it while it's hot! Let's see some BLOOD in these GAMES!"

"Oh, shut up." Crinnan grumbled. He did a quick count in his head. Realizing he only had five slugs left, he found cover and ejected the mag. Quickly he dug his hand into his pocket and grabbed the handful of shells he had taken from the box, feeding them into the magazine. He filled it, having two left over and one in the chamber. With a nod, he hopped up and ran toward the nearest sound of screaming.

Crinnan ducked into an alley, shotgun in hand. The world he was in felt much more like the real world and it was invigorating. The presence of the suns, water, plants... it all fueled him in a way the darkness, screaming and fire hadn't been able to. For the first time in a long time, he felt... alive. He felt like he was an actual person and that what he did mattered. And then he felt a knife in his side.

Crinnan grunted as he was tackled to the ground by an unknown force. Instinctively he reached his shotgun above his head, tossing it as far from his attacker as he could so that it couldn't be easily used against him. Crinnan drove his knee into the person's crotch, pounded his fists against their back and slammed his forehead into their nose. He heard popping, groaning and the thump of knuckles on flesh but the person on top of him didn't move.

Crinnan felt pressure against his arm as the being pushed against it with one of his hands. He pulled his other hand back, revealing the knife that had stabbed Crinnan only moments before. Crinnan didn't have time to think, he had time to make one move and so he pressed his palm against the person's chest, snarled, and thought "Bolt Level One"

The lightning passed through Crinnan's palm and blasted the person backward. Crinnan skidded back on the ground a few feet, but quickly got to his feet and pulled the pistol from his waist. He hurried over to his attacker, lifted the weapon and fired. A chunk tore free from the person's head as the bullet ripped through him and with a scowl, Crinnan finally lowered the gun.

Player: HydratheVillain EXECUTED

Player Rank: 8,766,411,544

NO RANK CHANGE

Current Rank: 6,654,793,485

Current Percentile: 22%

Silently, Crinnan ran back and claimed his shotgun. He looked down at the dead attacker and exhaled a breath he had been holding. "Stab me in the neck next time, idiot."

Crinnan snorted at the sight of the dead person and ran to the entrance of the alley. He pressed himself up against the wall, shouldering his weapon and peeked out. He checked his left and right, noting an explosion further down the road and then took a hard right, heading deeper into town.

As he jogged, Crinnan noticed that the wall of fire was already flirting with the outskirts of town. The heat was palpable and the hot wind that it gave off blew against Crinnan's skin. It wasn't like the wind he had experienced as he fought to cross the corridor back in Dread's Keep, but it most certainly was present.

Crinnan ignored the fire and the heat. He had more pressing matters to take care of, and according to the infernal wall closing in on his position, he was running out of time. He had to finish this game as quickly as possible.

"Come on." Crinnan grumbled as he ran. "Where are you!" He heard explosions and gunfire all around him. Shouting, fighting... the sounds of combat. He chanced upon two people fighting and dashed forward. With his shotgun raised he blasted one, racked the weapon and then shot the other. They both fell to the ground, and then the sound of a vehicle accelerating filled his ears. He turned and quickly threw himself backwards, landing on his ass as he watched the truck plow over the dead bodies.

Player: Icarus5645 EXECUTED **Player Rank: 7,977,158,546**
NO RANK CHANGE **Current Rank: 6,654,793,485** **Current Percentile: 22%**
Player: NotaGaian77 EXECUTED **Player Rank: 7,977,158,547**
NO RANK CHANGE **Current Rank: 6,654,793,485** **Current Percentile: 22%**

"Damnit!" Crinnan yelled as he got to his feet. He fired a slug at the truck, hitting the tailgate. The slug tore through the thin metal body of the vehicle and they flew back toward the forest. The tires of the vehicle screeched as the driver spun it around so the front was facing Crinnan. He frowned at this sight and raised his shotgun.

"Wait." Crinnan whispered. The truck revved its engine and Crinnan set the shotgun down. He faced the vehicle and held his palm out just as wheels squelched against the pavement.

"Bolt Level One" Crinnan thought. A quick flash of lightning snaked from his hand and toward the incoming vehicle, but he missed his target. He stumbled backward with a curse on his lips, but quickly forced his balance and held his palm out again.

"Bolt level one!" Crinnan yelled. His shot once again was wide, and he was out of time. As he found his balance again, he realized that there was a very small likelihood of him being able to avoid the truck. He could dive to the right or left, but the truck would just swerve and hit him.

In the split second that Crinnan realized this, he watched as the driver side of the cab smashed inwards. With a loud crunch of metal and shattering glass, the truck flipped so that its passenger side door was facing the ground and then it began to roll away. Crinnan watched the truck tumble into the roiling firewall that was closing in on them, picked up his shotgun and shouldered it.

"Don't shoot!" A familiar voice shouted. Crinnan turned his head and watched as Dali approached him. He lowered his weapon and started walking toward her.

"You're here." Crinnan called out to her. "And you... just destroyed a truck..."

"That I did." Dali replied. She looked over at the wall of fire and smirked. "Not the first one in my life. Probably not the last one either."

"Oh. Well okay." Crinnan rolled his eyes at his sister. "Come on, we have people to kill."

It was Dali's turn to roll her eyes, but she followed him as he turned. "Hey Crinnan, wait." She called out as he started to walk. "Come with me. I need you to listen to me before this ends."

"By the Brothers, what?" Crinnan asked with an annoyed tone. She grabbed his wrist and pulled him into a warehouse looking building. They quickly swept the area, and then stopped. Dali turned to face Crinnan, and he noticed that she had a slightly bothered expression.

"You are going to have to kill me." She said bleakly. "To win, I am going to have to lose... Which means you will move forward, and I will move back."

Crinnan nodded at this, understanding her words. They had already talked about it, but he hadn't spent *too* much time thinking about it.

"Listen. We are down to thirteen people in the match." Dali continued. "The battle will be over soon, and I will do everything in my power to ensure that you win so that you can get the fuck out of here and continue your life... but... look Crinnan, as your big sister I *need* you to promise me something."

Crinnan raised an eyebrow, trying to keep an indifferent demeanor. He was, however, interested in what she had to say. "What do you want?" He asked.

"I want you to fight your hardest." Dali replied, her tone sincere. "Get back to the world and... go after everything you believe in. Kill whatever gets in your way, tear down whatever holds you back. Do not react to situations, learn how to control them." She paused and bit her lower lip as she looked down at the ground. "I have done a lot of bad things in my life, Crinnan. Things I hate myself for and that I know there is no coming back from. I am... in too deep... I am broken... but you... you have died, and you are about to be reborn. Use this to allow yourself to become someone new and strong. Be better than you ever were and never apologize for it... Bring that Milinka girl with you, hold her and kiss her and be happy with her... there is just... too much pain in the world, please do not add to it..."

"Sayraa I..." Crinnan started but Dali shook her head.

"Crinnan you will probably never see me again after you leave the Hells." Dali said softly. "And... if you do, it will probably be your job to kill me... and it will be my job to kill you... just know if we are ever in that situation, I will lose the fight on purpose. There are... very few people in my life that I love, brother." Dali started to sniffle slightly. "But you are definitely without a doubt one of them. I promise you; I love you brother and I don't... I do not..."

Crinnan felt tears gather in his own eyes but he blinked them away. He stood in the warehouse and stared awkwardly at his sister. He wanted to comfort her, but he didn't feel like he truly loved her the way she loved him. She was supposed to be his enemy... but at the same time, he was supposed to be her brother. He sucked on his two front teeth for a moment as he pondered the situation, and finally with very heavy feet, he took a step forward.

"Hey…" He whispered. She looked up at him and he looked down at her. For a moment they stared at each other and then Crinnan, suddenly unburdened, lunged forward and wrapped his arms around her. Dali gasped, but quickly responded by grabbing hold of him tightly. She grasped the cloth on the back of his shirt and buried her head into Crinnan's chest, suddenly weeping uncontrollably.

"I've… I have been alone for so long, Crinnan." Dali sobbed. "You, Kiersen, Cris, Rubaan… Mom and Dad… they were all I knew when I was taken… the thoughts of you are all I have had…"

Crinnan felt his heart melt at the sudden outpouring of emotion from his sister. He realized in that moment that in all those years it was just easier to believe that she was dead. When she first revealed her identity to him in the Hells, he wanted to hate her, to believe that she was evil and a traitor to his family. That was easy for him, it meant that he had no responsibility in the situation, that he could just… shrug it off and paint her as an enemy…

But Sayraa or Sarasin as she called herself wasn't his enemy. This realization was painful to Crinnan, it didn't make sense, it was paradoxical in a way. The two fought on opposite sides of the war, they had different goals and followed completely different people, yet they were also brother and sister. They had the same parents; the same hopes and dreams and love had been bestowed upon them. They couldn't deny the fact that they, despite their positions in the world *were* linked by love.

"Hey, stop." Crinnan said as he pulled back from his sister. "Listen to me. We're going to be okay. *You're* going to be okay. The world we live in is so fucked to shit, but that doesn't mean we stop trying, right?"

Dali nodded at him. She sniffled and closed her eyes for a moment and Crinnan continued. "Look I… I don't know. I haven't seen you in years and… I don't know you anymore. I shouldn't care, I don't want to care but… I get it. You came to the Hells to help me get out. You're risking… everything. I know that means something, and I won't take it for granted… and when I get out maybe one day… maybe we can talk."

Dali snorted and shook her head. "Crinnan my fate is solitude." She said in somber response. "I am bound by my oaths, I am… I have nowhere to run. No *way* to run. I…"

"Shut up." Crinnan said. He leaned back in and gave her a quick hug. She exhaled heavily, once again resting her head against Crinnan's sternum and closed her eyes. It all ended too quickly for her, but it was enough. One of the few people in the world whom she loved had been able to love her back, and that brought her joy.

Crinnan stepped back and nodded at Dali. "It'll all be okay. I promise…" Dali smiled, and then her head suddenly jerked to the side. Brains and bits of skull blasted out the right sight of her face and she dropped to the ground like a ton of bricks. Crinnan's eyes grew wide and he immediately raised his shotgun, firing blindly in the direction that the sudden attack had come from. He quickly strafed to his right, hoping that his covering fire would allow him time to find safety…

> **"Six players remain! This is where it gets dirty, boys and girls. Get ready for the fight of your lives! The fire is closing in on you, victory is within reach! Do you have what it takes, players? Are you going to the be the victor of the Bloodgames!!"**

Crinnan tossed his empty shotgun to the ground and pulled his pistol from his pants. He dove through an open window and rolled behind a smoldering truck for cover. He looked behind himself for enemies but saw nobody there. The fire wall was within fifty feet of him and closing in by about an inch a second.

"Brothers fuck it all!" Crinnan hissed. He heard shooting from nearby and peeked out the side of the truck. A bullet pinged off the metal. He ducked back behind cover and grit his teeth in fury. "Okay… think… think…" A single idea popped into Crinnan's mind. He had to act on it, he had no time to think it over. Crinnan reached his hand around the right side of the truck and blasted a bolt of lightning where he thought his attacker should have been. He blasted backward a few inches and then bolted to his left, pistol at the ready. It took a few seconds for the attacker to spot Crinnan, and that was all the time he needed. Crinnan charged forward, opening fire and striking the person square in the chest two times. She screamed and fell backward, dropping her rifle in the process. Crinnan approached, shot her in the head and then bent down and picked up her assault rifle.

Player: DanFLARE EXECUTED

Player Rank: 10,897,325,652

NO RANK CHANGE

Current Rank: 6,654,793,485

Current Percentile: 22%

"Cool." Crinnan said as he tucked his pistol back into his pants. She had dropped a few magazines on death, so Crinnan scooped them up and replaced the used one for a fresh one.

"Three enemies remaining! The fire cometh, my friends! Prepare yourselves for its cleansing flames!"

"Weird." Crinnan said in response. He shouldered his rifle and hurried to find cover. The fire was drawing closer and closer and Crinnan had no way to avoid it. He *had* to find the other two players and kill them. Pressing himself up against the brick wall of a building, Crinnan leaned out to check for movement. He quickly spotted someone running across the street. Crinnan zeroed in on him, and fired a burst, sending the person to the ground. They started crawling, and Crinnan fired another burst. Finally, they dropped face first and lay motionless. Crinnan watched the flames crawl over the corpse, reducing them to ash and gulped as he turned around to search for the final enemy.

"And then there were two! The final showdown between...
PrettyKitty6969420... and none other than our very own Rank 42 player
Auroch! As many of you know Auroch is a professional Bloodgames
combatant, wins nearly every game he plays in and streams it all to
viewers at home just like you! Make sure you like share and subscribe to
Auroch's channel"

At that, Crinnan heard a loud crash. He spun around and his face paled when he saw a creature that looked like a half bull half person. It stood at least eight feet tall, its shoulders were broad, its body was covered in coarse brown fur, and it had two massive horns atop its head. In its hands was a massive sledgehammer and it had powerfully smacked aside the truck that Crinnan had used for cover earlier.

Wasting no time, Crinnan opened fire. His bullets hit their mark but Auroch seemed to shrug off the attacks as his body was surrounded by a blue forcefield that Crinnan recognized using when he was in Sincroft. Auroch's nostrils puffed out two plumes of grey smoke, and he lowered his gaze to meet Crinnan's.

"Rank... Six billion?" Auroch bellowed in a deep rough voice as he stared at Crinnan. "Pitiful, absolutely fucking disgraceful!" He kicked his right hoof against the ground and charged forward with a speed Crinnan didn't expect. Quickly, Crinnan darted to the side to evade the attack and Auroch blew past him. Crinnan used the opportunity to fire a few bursts at the creature, but his bullets simply bounced off the blue forcefield.

"Hold still you little shit!" Auroch yelled as he turned and swiped at Crinnan. Crinnan jumped back, firing a few more shots. Auroch belted a laugh at Crinnan's futile attempt and burst forward, crashing his shoulder into his chest. Crinnan went flying backward and skidded against the ground before finally coming to a halt only a few feet in front of the fire wall.

The heat bore down on Crinnan and he began to sweat. He quickly jumped to his feet and emptied the rest of his magazine on Auroch. When it clicked empty, Crinnan didn't bother reloading, he simply dropped the weapon to the ground and pulled out his pistol. He fired relentlessly, stepping forward so that the wall wouldn't consume him. It did him no good.

"You're empty, little buddy." Auroch roared with laughter. "Any last words?"

"Come get me." Crinnan said. At that, Auroch huffed and charged forward. Crinnan waited for the last second and then dove out of the way again. Auroch came to a screeching halt, and spun, baring his teeth.

"I said hold still!" He yelled as he raised his hammer into the air. Crinnan scrambled to his feet and held out his palm.

"How do you like your steak!" Crinnan shouted. Auroch squinted his eyes briefly, but Crinnan didn't give him a chance to respond. "I like mine well-fucking-done!"

At that, Crinnan whispered "Bolt Level Two" and a lightning bolt passed from his palm and into Auroch. His shields took the blow, but the force behind the bolt pushed Auroch backward and into the wall of fire. Crinnan watched as the half-bull-half-person's body was engulfed in flame. He writhed for a moment before turning into ash, and Crinnan couldn't help but smirk at the sight.

Player: BULLetFLOOF EXECUTED

Player Rank: 42

Congratulations, PrettyKitty6969420! You have advanced in ranking!

Previous Rank: 6,654,793,485

New Rank: 3,327,396,763

Previous Percentile: 22%

New Percentile: 11%

NEW PERCENTILE ACHIEVED! Congratulations, you are showing your true power. Your buffs have been modified.

Cosmetic Items unlocked! See your wardrobe for more details!

...

> **Congratulations! You have crossed the threshold of the 20th percentile and into the 10s.**
>
> **...**
>
> **New Ability Pending.**

> *"PrettyKitty6969420 wins! What a display that was, it is always amazing to watch a new player rise in the ranks. After that display of strength, this new player has crossed the 1000 rank threshold and is now rank 653! We will all keep a keen eye on you, my friend. State your name, so that your new fans know who to look for, and so that your new enemies know who to hunt."*

Crinnan watched as the wall of fire stopped moving and seemed to just disappear altogether. He spun in place for a moment and looked around at his surroundings one last time, knowing that he was about to go back to the darkness of the Hells. He looked at the green trees, the blue sky and warm comforting Brothers above... A blue swirling portal opened behind him. He was tempted to walk through the portal without saying anything at all in response to DJ's inquiry, but an even bigger, much more petty side of him simply couldn't help himself.

"I'm Crinnan Jamiso." He declared, looking all around him. "Centurion of Black Knight. The guy who's been fucking your day up. Whoever is listening to this, let me tell you one thing. Go fuck yourselves. I hope you get a chance one day to rot in here just like I have... just like centuries of innocent people have. Fuck you, fuck your goddess, and fuck your small-dicked emperor. Oh. And make sure to like, share and subscribe... whatever that means." At that, Crinnan lifted his middle finger, waved it for all to see, and then turned around and walked toward the portal. As he was about to walk through, he paused though as a thought entered his mind.

"Sayraa..." He mumbled. "Thank you..."

Chapter Thirty-Eight
Dead End

Sincroft
The Third Level

"Ah fuck, not this place." Crinnan cursed as the portal closed behind him. He looked around, saw the tall grey and gloomy buildings, the dark sky, the cobblestone street… the… fucking gravlins nipping at his feet. Crinnan kicked one of the little shits and it rolled out of sight. He looked around, making sure nobody saw, and he could only sigh when he got a better view of his surroundings.

Sincroft was on fire. Everywhere he looked, he saw flames, heard the sound of buildings collapsing, the wood cracking and weapons being discharged. A heavy fog of smoke and dust filled the air, and those who were still sane ran in all directions.

"This is… chaos…" Crinnan said as he looked around. People were trampling each other, running from one danger to the next. They screamed and pushed and shoved, and Crinnan was all of a sudden in the midst of them all.

"What's going on!" Crinnan shouted as he was forced to run alongside them. "Why are we running!"

Nobody responded, they only continued screaming in terror and running to wherever they were going. If Crinnan stopped, he risked being trampled like the others he had seen and at this point he was about to risk respawning if he didn't have to. So, he ran.

"Seriously!" Crinnan shouted as he ran with the group. "What is going on!"

"Shut up and run!" Someone yelled back to him. "The players are here!"

"Well fight them!" Crinnan snapped. "There's got to be more of you than there are of them!"

"They's killin' us!" Crinnan heard another declare. "We's too weak!"

"Brothers fuck it all!" Crinnan growled. He pushed and shoved and fought his way to the front of the group. When he finally emerged from the crowd, he took off in a sprint, trying to put as much distance between them and himself as he could. When he felt like he had achieved that, he turned to the right and took off down a street.

The blood in the streets boiled. Crinnan watched it bubble for a moment as he reached down and felt the sword on his hip. He was glad that the weapon he carried before transporting into the Bloodgames match was still with him. He was *really* growing tired of having to find weapons all the damn time. He pulled the sword free of its scabbard and started jogging.

"Market." He said aloud to remind himself how he had escaped Sincroft the last time. "Just have to get past the market... where is the damn market..."

Crinnan looked around. The street he was on was lined with... buildings. The same looking buildings that filled the rest of the city. He had no idea where he was or where he needed to go... he was lost and that frustrated him.

A loud explosion erupted from his right and debris rained down around him. Crinnan ran to avoid being struck by anything big and wondered exactly what had triggered the explosion. Shortly after he heard screaming, footsteps and the sound of gunfire.

"This doesn't seem right..." Crinnan said to himself as he ran away from the danger zone. "All these guns seem..."

"I should say it is not right, Crinnan." Sage said. *"The Govian Inquisitors have sent in teams to begin executing prisoners-turned players. They want the ranks thinned, they want everyone to respawn at level one so that they can herd them and keep them from becoming a threat."*

"That's bullshit." Crinnan snapped in reply. "They gotta fuck with us in life and then they have to dominate us in death?"

"For some people, simply being in charge is not enough." Sage sighed. "Unfortunately, those people run our world."

"Yeah... get me out of here and they won't much longer." Crinnan growled. "This... isn't right. None of this is right. People have to rest eventually no matter who they are."

"Oh, I agree, young Crinnan." Sage replied. "Evil people always find a way to take the best of intentions and run them into the ground. The people around you, those screaming and running for cover. The mindless ones who are unaware of what is happening around them... they all deserve better. They should be living in paradise right now. They should be enjoying the Afterscape... but those who wanted power, those who line the throne room of the Imperial Palace in Cidroska... they were not content with allowing their enemies and those that disagreed with them to die in peace."

"How does someone fix something like this?" Crinnan asked as he looked around. He saw people running on the sidewalks, ash settling from the fires around him... the blood in the streets beneath him continued to boil and the ground shook with every explosion. "How can we... just let people die in peace?"

"In time the answer to that question will become evident, Crinnan." Sage replied solemnly. "However, I should say that is not what you need to worry about right now. All that you need to focus on is moving forward. You need to find the portal out of this accursed city and reach the throne room of Dread's Keep. The portal you opened there waits for you, when you find it you will be able to catch up with the girl you love..."

Crinnan groaned. Why did Sage have to say things like that? He ignored his thoughts though and nodded his head. "Okay." He said with a deep sigh. "I can do this."

"Of course you can Crinnan." Sage replied. "You have lived your entire life waiting for this moment. You are the key to everything my... my young friend. I believe in you... I will talk to you soon."

Sage left and Crinnan started jogging again. What had Sage meant by that? The... key to everything? Crinnan didn't believe he was anything extraordinary. He was good at fighting, but he was shit at everything else. The whole idea confused him.

Crinnan rounded a corner, hoping he was heading toward the market district only to stumble upon a scene he hadn't expected. He found a group of six Govian Inquisitors dressed in traditional Inquisitor attire: a suit of thick synth-fiber armor, with blue clothing showing underneath and a synth-fiber helmet with a black visor covering their faces. Their upper arms were bare, and their forearms were covered by synth-fiber gauntlets. They each aimed an AT34 Carbine, an automatic combat rifle, and had a short sword strapped to their hips. Their weapons were trained on a group of kneeling Sincroftians, and when Crinnan came to a halt, his eyes grew wide and he turned to run.

"Get him!" Crinnan heard one of the Inquisitors shout. As he ran the sound of six rifles being shot at once filled the air and Crinnan knew that all the prisoners had been executed. After that, the Inquisitors gave chase, a few firing at him as they ran.

Crinnan ducked into an alley, hoping to shake his pursuers. The sound of the footsteps did not cease though and Crinnan soon realized he had made a grave mistake. The alley was a dead end and Crinnan came to halt, realizing he could go no further. Slowly, he turned around, spun his sword in his right hand and prepared his left to fire a bolt.

"You!" One of the Inquisitors shouted. "I know your face! Get on your knees, you're coming with us!"

"Come and get me." Crinnan rebutted, taking an aggressive step forward. The Govians all trained their rifles on Crinnan and took a step of their own in response.

"Bishop General Klaus wants you alive. Submit, Black Knight, drop your weapon and get on your knees!" The Inquisitor ordered. They all took another threatening step forward, and Crinnan reactively took a step back, bumping into the wall behind him.

"I'm not going anywhere with you!" Crinnan hissed. He extended his arm, pointing the tip of his blade toward the Inquisitor who had spoken thus far. "Come on!" Crinnan knew that if he died he would just start over. That would be an inconvenience but was preferable to being captured.

A sudden sound jarred Crinnan out of the moment. It sounded like a metal canister being dropped on the ground nearby. Distracted, Crinnan looked and saw exactly that. A small silver cylinder rolling underneath the feet of the

Govians. Before he could react, heavy white smoke began pouring from the cylinder, quickly filling the area around them. Crinnan heard a gunshot and immediately dropped to the ground. For a moment, all he heard was the sound of bullets being discharged, the howling of Inquisitors, and bodies hitting the ground.

When the smoke began to dissipate, Crinnan hurried to his feet and got in a defensive stance. He was confused about what had just happened, but then he watched as a figure stepped through what remained of the smoke. When he saw the person, he lowered his sword and snorted a laugh.

"Ain't you about had enough of this shit?" Karston asked, his tone dry and a little bit angry. He held a smoking revolver in each hand, had his wide brimmed hat on top of his head and wore his long duster jacket. He stepped forward, licked his chapped lips and looked Crinnan up and down. "Shit boy, looks like you've had better days."

"Karston…" Crinnan said as he stepped forward. "How did you know I was here?"

"I seen you a few blocks back." Karston replied. "Watched you run like a stud bein' sent into a fairess den. Then I seen all them… what'd you call em? Grovlian?"

"Govian." Crinnan corrected.

"Sure whatever. I watched them all chasin' you and… well I figured why the fuck not?" Karston holstered one of his pistols and began loading the other as he walked toward Crinnan. "Look, you son of a bitch." He said as he looked down at his weapon. "I been havin' thoughts ever since you left. Thoughts of… getting' outta here, pavin' a new path… findin' my family like that sluttly little fairess girl said. I shoulda gone with you the first time but… well… I reckon I mighta been a bit too scared."

"It's fine." Crinnan nodded and walked to meet Karston. "Can you get us out of here?"

"Reckon I can." Karston said, sliding the cylinder of his revolver into place. He holstered the weapon and pulled his second one free to reload it. "Can you get me to the Seventh Level to find my family?"

"I can try." Crinnan replied.

"Good enough for me." Karston slid the bullets into his pistol, put the cylinder in place, then spun it in his hand so that the handle was facing Crinnan. "Last time I seen you, you was a pretty damn good shot. Would be handy to have two sets of eyes who can make their bullets land instead of one. You agree?"

"Works for me." Crinnan said as he grabbed the revolver. He tucked it into his pants and Karston turned toward the entrance of the alley.

"Probably can't use those can we?" He asked as he knelt down and grabbed one of the Govian's carbines. The weapon vanished when he touched it and Karston shrugged and got back to his feet. "Oh well."

"Just like in real life." Crinnan snorted. "Fuckers lock their weapons. They call it bricking."

"That information doesn't do shit for me down here." Karston said as he beckoned for Crinnan to follow. "Come on, marketplace is this way. Let's get your dumb ass out of here so that we can move on with our lives."

"You think the portal will be in the marketplace again?" Crinnan asked. "Isn't it random?"

"Hasn't been today." Karston replied. "Ever since the players and the Govians showed up, portal's been open. I guess it's a retreat option or something for them or some shit, I don't know. Can't imagine why they would need to retreat; it's been a bloodbath."

"Is there any kind of resistance?" Crinnan asked.

"Yeah, some folks been showin' up. More and more of 'em. They're all gathered at the belltower, I heard some of 'em callin a couple of 'em Commander, heard the word Centurion thrown around..."

Crinnan grinned at that. "Take me to the belltower then." Crinnan said. "They're... friends. Let's get there, and then we can get to the portal."

"Sounds good, kid." Karston said. Crinnan started to walk but Karston called out to him. "Hey, Crinnan?"

"What?" Crinnan asked, turning to look at him.

"I don't know how to say none of this or anything..." Karston said, his tone clearly uncomfortable. "And I ain't trying to be sappy or corny or no dumb shit like that but… well… I'm glad you're here. For the… for the first time in… who knows how long… I got a little hope in me."

Crinnan fell silent at the old elf's words. He let them soak in while he tried to come up with a response. He wasn't… *trying* to help anyone. He didn't mean to be any kind of hero or anything like that. He simply… was following a voice trying to get back to his life. Hearing Karston's perspective on the matter rattled him a little bit.

"I…" Crinnan stammered, but then decided just to remain silent. He nodded his head and gave Karston a quick uneasy smile. "Okay."

"Alright then." Karston said with a knowing nod. "Let's get to that bell tower."

Chapter Thirty-Nine
Personal Army

Sincroft
The Third Level

Attention Citizens: It has been reported that Crinnan Jamiso is in Sincroft. Anybody in Sincroft capable of fighting, we need you to apprehend this criminal. Do everything you can to capture him. His bounty has been raised to ten thousand shards. May Dura'ana be with you.

Explosions and gunfire erupted in the distance as Crinnan and Ander arrived at the Belltower. The obelisk was made of the same boring gray stone that made up every other building in Sincroft, and Crinnan looked up at the rusted old bell that hung under a canopy at the top. He saw the Black Knights gathered behind it and hurried forward.

"Jamiso!" The voice of Commander Emilio called out as Crinnan approached. "Crinnan Jamiso! I am both saddened and delighted to see you. It pains me that you didn't make it past Dread's Keep, but I am filled with joy that you are well."

"Yeah, cool." Crinnan quickly said, shaking his head at the commander. "Look, we have to go. Now. A portal out of here is open in the marketplace and is guarded by Govian Inquisitors. If we get through there, we can get back to Dread's Keep and then I can progress to the next level."

Emilio looked at Crinnan and smirked. He didn't need further convincing. He raised his hand and turned around to address the small army behind him.

"Time to fight, brothers!" Emilio shouted to them all. "Jamiso has returned to us, it is our job to get him where he needs to be. Come, let's follow him to the battle!" Emilio turned back to Crinnan and nodded. "Wherever you need us to go, we will, my friend. We *must* get you to the final level." Emilio reached his arm out, and Crinnan grasped it.

"Thank you, Commander." Crinnan nodded to the Lycaani who had been his Commander throughout his childhood. In that moment he felt a strange sense of equality with him, one that wasn't addressed or instigated by the Commander, but more so one that Crinnan felt he had... in some way... earned.

"Move out!" Emilio shouted as he let go of Crinnan's arm and turned to the army. "Time to show these Govians how scary dead Black Knights are!"

***

The Black Knight army was small. It was composed of about fifty soldiers with weapons they had scavenged from the players they had ambushed on their way to Sincroft. There were only a few guns between all of them, the rest were equipped with swords, bows, axes, spears... whatever they could get their hands on. They all ran as one with Karston leading them.

"We're almost there." Karston said as he came to a stop and turned to Crinnan. "Just up the road a bit, then we take a right at the next road. That'll take us directly into the marketplace."

"Good." Crinnan said. He turned to Emilio and the other Commanders. "Alright. We're going to have to surprise them and force our way through... we... we will probably take heavy losses here... are you sure you're up to it?"

"What is there for us to lose, Crinnan?" Emilio asked. "We will respawn, we will regroup, and we will fight again. We intend to keep the fight going here in the Hells. We are the Seraphim; we will *always* fight."

Crinnan nodded and looked past Emilio at the rest. He saw his friend Elia's mother smiling warmly at him, he saw Xiwaine and Xibelle Phoenix standing side by side. Xiwaine had his head held high and gave Crinnan the slightest of nods. He saw Vassili Emmal, Milinka's grandfather. The large elf gave Crinnan a supportive wink. Finally, he looked at Jeph Scaven, his former squad mate. He wouldn't be so bold as to call him a friend. But... yeah Crinnan knew him. The rest stood there, weapons in hand and hearts aligned with Crinnan's. Once again, they were about to give everything they had in support of pushing him forward.

For a moment, Crinnan felt a strong sense of... gratitude. He was lucky to have people who would stand there and rally to support him even in death. He thought about what Black Knight had stood for, and what had bound them all together back in life and then he looked upon the generations of soldiers who stood before him.

In spite of the politics, the squabbling and all the internal fighting... Black Knight was family. Crinnan looked upon all of them. He felt a strange compulsion to reach out and thank every single one of them, he wanted to sit with them all and hear their stories and drink with them... he wanted to spar with them and rush into battle alongside them... a hundred thousand words passed his mind, countless ways he could express how he felt, support them and encourage them before they went into battle with and for him... but only two words managed to come out in that moment.

"Thank you." Crinnan said softly. The emotion was bubbling inside him and threatening to come out if he said any more words. He bit the corner of his lip and nodded his head rapidly as he quickly turned his back to them all. He wasn't going to let himself cry. Not there. He nervously tapped on the hilt of his sword before his fingers ran down and wrapped around the handle. He pulled it free from its scabbard, and then the pistol that Karston had gifted him found its way into his hands... and suddenly, words weighed down his tongue and his heart and he had to release them.

"Whatever happens..." Crinnan called back to the soldiers behind him. "I will never forget you all. None of you!" He looked over at Karston and the old elf gave him a solemn nod. "This... this is all just the beginning!" Crinnan's words turned into a shout and he turned around to face his brethren. "None of our lives are over. No, we were just... waiting... for this moment. For every moment that follows... we... we fought for something that mattered back in life. That carries over to our deaths... all we want... all we truly *ever* wanted... was to live our lives in peace. That fight won't end until we can do that, and I promise you I will do everything I can to make sure that happens... So again I say brothers; thank you. Now, let's go kill them all."

***

In spite of Crinnan's impromptu speech, and in spite of the encouragement that the speech swelled their hearts with... the Black Knights were no match for the guns that the Govian soldiers had. Crinnan charged forward, flanked on either side by his brethren and he watched as they all began to fall to the bullets raining down on them.

"Shields up!" Vassili Emmal shouted. "Protect Jamiso!"

"We'll get you there, Crinnan!" Jeph shouted as he sprinted alongside Crinnan. "Don't you fucking worry. You'll get there!"

A bullet passed through Jeph's eye and he dropped to the ground, dead. Crinnan snarled at the sight but couldn't focus on it. He had to keep running.

"Just up ahead!" Karston shouted. "The portal, fifty feet! Push!"

Crinnan heard the sound of shields bashing the Inquisitors as the shield bearers in the front pushed forward. They trampled over a few, and Crinnan made sure to stomp hard on their throats as he passed. Black Knights were getting shot up all around him, their blood was spraying his body, but they stayed true to their word. They protected their brother with their lives, they swung their swords, fired bows and fought with everything they had to get him that fifty feet...

"Stay on your feet!" Crinnan heard Vassili Emmal scream at everyone. "That is fucking order! Do not fall!"

"Keep pushing!" Commander Emilio roared. "We are almost there!"

Crinnan felt something pass through his arm and he yelped in pain and spun straight into the arms of Xiwaine Phoenix. Xiwaine held him up, pushed him forward and screamed for Crinnan to find his footing. Crinnan finally did and ran.

The ranks were thin, there weren't many Black Knights left and Crinnan could hear bullets whizzing all around him. The portal was in sight, it was right there, he was almost there... the gunfire around him, the screaming, the fighting... it drowned out his thoughts. Crinnan could only focus on what he saw, and he saw blue.

"Break off!" Vassili shouted. "Engage enemy! Run Crinnan!"

Crinnan took off in a full sprint with Karston at his side. He heard the screams of the Black Knights and Govians alike as they fell, he listened to bullets whizzing past his head... but he focused on the blue light ahead of him.

"We did it!" Emilio shouted before he fell to a knee. "You're there Crinnan! You're there brother! Go, run, fight and save us all!"

"We believe in you!" Aura Sols shouted as she fell to her back.

"Be fierce!" Xiwaine Phoenix screamed as his throat was cut.

The last thing Crinnan heard before he and Karston dove through the portal was the sound of laughter. The few Black Knights who had not fallen were cheering and laughing as they died to protect Crinnan. Crinnan felt only rage and adrenaline as he passed through the blue light.

All his life... every breath he had taken he had hated the idea of caring for others. He had actively lived to avoid everyone. He expended all this effort only to find in death that so many would all be willing to fight for him. Crinnan's vision went dark as he passed through the portal, his tears fell from his eyes and he realized what it was truly like to care for and to be cared for by others.

Crinnan and Karston emerged from the other side of the portal and Crinnan fell to his knees. He dug his hands into the dirt beneath him, lowered his head, and all he could do was cry. The outpouring of support was too much for him to handle, they had helped him knowing that they may not be able to escape. His Black Knight brothers had all but pushed him through the portal so that *he* could have an opportunity to live again...

This did not make sense to Crinnan. Why would anyone be so willing to endure such pain just so one person could have a chance? Why him? Crinnan threw the dirt in his hands to his sides in a fit and Karston knelt down next to him.

"Look, partner," Karston said softly yet sternly, "we can't sit here and wait for those Govians to come through the portal. All them folk who just died did so, so that you can keep movin' forward. Now ain't the time for restin' or cryin'. Now's the time to find that strength inside of you and keep your feet movin'."

Crinnan nodded at Karston's words. He looked over at the elf and sighed. "I'm ready for this shit to be over." Crinnan whispered.

"You're preachin' to the choir there boy." Karston chuckled. The elf took hold of Crinnan's arm and lifted him off the ground. "I been ready for this shit to end ever since it started... Lost my mind a few times, found it again, then lost it again... if what you're doin' can change all this for the better... if you can... I donno, get us outta here or give us a fightin' chance even then I'd say it was all worth it. Hells, boy. I been here I don't know how many lifetimes, and I ain't never seen nothin' like this. Now come on, get your ass up off the ground, quit your blubberin' and let's put some distance between us and this portal."

Crinnan snorted and pushed himself up off the ground. He looked over at Karston and nodded in confirmation that he had heard the elf's words. He took a deep breath in through his nose, clenched his fists together, and looked at Dread's Keep ahead of them.

"Alright." Crinnan said as he wiped the last tear from his eyes. "Let's fucking go."

"That's what I like to hear." Karston said, and slapped Crinnan on the back. At that, the two stepped forward, and started running toward the castle.

Chapter Forty
I Am...

Dread's Keep
The Fourth Level

"Well, this place is spooky as shit." Karston's voice echoed off the walls of the keep as they walked through the doors. "I don't have fond memories of bein' here. Never stepped foot inside but I've been killed outside the walls plenty of times. Got skinned once, they hung my hide like a banner off the walls. Weird shit."

"That sucks." Crinnan replied, not fully knowing how to respond to something like that.

"I mean. it wasn't fun." Karston said, not familiar with the term 'sucks'. Crinnan nodded in response and the two jogged through the large room that the doors of Dread's Keep had led them to. Crinnan hadn't seen the room the first time he had entered, it had been completely black, and he had endured Thornscale's trial there. In reality, it was covered in black mold and had broken down and rotting furniture discarded all over the place. Crinnan saw tables and suits of armor from the Age of Blood, he saw broken swords and blackened skeletons. It was all very grim and as Karston had put it, spooky as shit.

"Where do we go from here?" Karston asked.

"I don't know." Crinnan replied. "It... could be anywhere... I guess we just have to..." A sudden laugh reverberating off the walls silenced Crinnan and sent a chill down his spine. He looked around anxiously and drew his sword in response.

"The fuck was that?" Karston snapped. He produced his revolver in one hand and pulled a knife from his belt with the other. "We ain't alone in here, Crinnan."

"Well no shit." Crinnan hissed back at him. "Be quiet, don't give up our position."

"They know where we are." Karston replied with a shake of his head. "We've made too much noise in this place already not to be noticed. I reckon we got another fight on our hands."

Crinnan growled as he scanned the area all around him. He heard movement but couldn't find the source of it. Somebody was fucking with him, and Crinnan did not like being fucked with.

"Alright, come out!" He shouted as he pulled his revolver free. "Enough of this!"

Crinnan heard footsteps, and in the dark it was difficult to see the form that was approaching him. Both Crinnan and Karston raised their pistols in anticipation of an attack. Finally, however, the figure stopped. He held his arms out as if to show that he was not armed, and then every torch and brazier around them suddenly lit, illuminating the area and revealing the identity of the person before them.

"I wondered if you were going to come back for me, my dear friend." Ander said jovially. "I watched you... shoot me... watched you leave me behind. And then I thought to myself: No. Not Crinnan, he is one of the good ones..."

"Ander!" Crinnan gasped. "You... you're alive?"

"No, Crinnan I am dead." Ander replied with a thin grin. "Tis why I reside with you in the Hells. But we can change that, no? We can... all go back home together."

Ander's tone was unsettling and sent a shiver down Crinnan's spine. He didn't sound angry or vengeful as he should have, he sounded... warm, but distant; as if he were trying to be comforting, but it was coming off very creepy.

Crinnan stared at Ander for a moment, worried about the situation. He didn't know what to say, he had shot him the last time they saw each other. Ander did not seem to harbor any resentment over that fact, but Crinnan could clearly see the bloodstain and the hole that his bullet had left in Ander's robe.

"Are... are you okay?" Crinnan asked. He felt a shock of fear spread over him as he looked into the vampre's eyes. "What has... happened to you?"

"Rebirth, child." Ander replied quickly and simply. "That which was buried has been exhumed. I am whole once again, and my path has been made clear. At your side, I will be able to walk this path that I may uncover my destiny."

"That's not a fucking answer." Crinnan groaned.

"I do not expect a boy to fathom what perplexes even those who are centuries old." Ander replied. He grinned warmly and reached his hand out, gently placing it on Crinnan's shoulder.

"Hey there, back it up." Karston said, stepping forward. Ander's vision snapped to the elf, and his free hand quickly reached out. Karston was suddenly lifted into the air, his arms stretched out to their full length at his sides and his face turned upward toward the ceiling.

Crinnan watched silently, he had a deeply rooted feeling that Ander's power was beyond anything he could hope to fight. It was immense and scary, and Crinnan watched in fear as Karston groaned in pain.

"He's..." Crinnan squeaked as he looked at Ander. "He's a friend. Let him down."

"And me?" Ander asked with a tilt of his head. "Am I a friend, Crinnan?"

"I..." Crinnan knew he should just say yes, that he should just placate the vampire to avoid being the target of his power. But Crinnan was also a young fool. "I don't know..."

"From the mouth of babes..." Ander said softly as he gently placed Karston back on the ground. He turned his head and looked at him as he regained control over his body. "Forgive me, elder but one cannot be too careful when it comes to strangers in the Hells."

"Fair enough." Karston panted as he straightened out his jacket. "Next time, it'd be fine to just ask me to step back though..." Ander smiled at Karston, and then his vision went distant. He gently pushed Crinnan aside and strode.

"We have company..." Ander announced as he strode toward the door.

"Shit!" Crinnan cursed as he readied his revolver. He ran up to join Ander; Karston quickly followed suit.

Moments later, Govian Inquisitors began flooding through the doors. There were dozens of them, all with their AgraTec 34 Carbines shouldered and ready to fire. Ander stood and watched in silence as they filed in, it looked like he was waiting for every last one of them. He seemed to *want* them there.

Finally, a tall figure in full battle armor and a long blue and gold cloak stepped in. He had an authoritative air about him and walked with his back straight and his eyes focused on the three beings before him. Finally, he stopped, removed his synth-fiber helmet, to reveal his long pointed vampre ears olive skin and short buzzed dark hair, and quickly strode toward Crinnan and the others. A soldier flanked him on each side, and when he stopped before Crinnan, he handed the helmet to the soldier on his right and composed himself.

"Do you recognize me?" The vampre asked with a smooth, deep voice. He looked at Crinnan with piercing eyes and Crinnan noticed the scars that covered the left side of his face.

"I think so." Crinnan replied. "You're Bishop General Klaus, right?"

"I am." Bishop General Klaus replied. "And the fact that I am here should be unnerving to you, Crinnan Jamiso. You see, it is an uncommon occurrence for a Bishop General to be sent after a single person. You have caused a great many problems in the mainland, problems that require worldly judgement. It is... unheard of for prisoners of the Hells to commit crimes that carry over into the world but... well, here we are."

"So, what do you want?" Crinnan asked. "You want to... kill me?"

"Quite the opposite, young one." Klaus replied with a shake of his head. "I wish to take you home. I want to learn more of what it is that is going on here. You see we are in a very precarious situation back in the corporeal world. We cannot allow people to leave the Hells which is why the lockdown is in effect, and why you are experiencing this... occupation of my forces." Klaus paused and glanced over at the faces of Karston and Ander. He smirked at them and then looked back to Crinnan.

"Crinnan Jamiso, innocent people are hurting because of this... virus that has been allowed to run free in this place. We cannot permit people to log into the Hells and risk being trapped here. You see there are two billion citizens in mainland Govia. Do you know how many of them are in the Hells right now?"

"No." Crinnan replied with a stern uninterested tone.

"There are three hundred million Govian citizens currently trapped in the Hells. Three hundred million lives all at risk because of the actions of your benefactor. I wish to fix this, there is no reason for three hundred million civilians to be in harm's way and I am certain you would agree with this sentiment for I do not take you to be a cruel or evil person."

"Three hundred million?" Crinnan asked, surprised at the number. "Where... where the fuck are all of them?"

Klaus gently laughed. "Each level of the Hells is roughly the same size as the continent of Redodra, though much of that space is simply unused. These people are here, and they are there... with all that space, there is more than enough room for everyone on our planet, for all the prisoners..."

"So why do I keep going to the same damn places then?" Crinnan asked. "If the Hells are so big?"

"Because you are following one of the hundreds of introductory storylines. Your path to the seventh level was randomly selected. For most players, upon reaching the Seventh Level the entirety of the Hells becomes unlocked and they are then free to explore... but none of that matters, and I apologize for wandering from my initial focus." Klaus bowed his head gently to Crinnan and then continued speaking.

"Crinnan Jamiso it is at the request of not only Supreme Father Eckaart and his council, but also of our beloved Emperor Govia Cidro himself that you be extended the opportunity to be reborn, forgiven of the crimes of you past life, and allowed to live as a free citizen in the mainland of Govia. All we ask in return is that you surrender any and all information you may have concerning Sajinious Lynx and the Life Links remnant."

"Wait, what?" Crinnan asked. "Are you saying... you'll just... give me my life back?"

"We will provide you with a body, therapy to help ease the transition, a home and riches." Klaus said. "You can have anything you ask as an esteemed ally of the great Emperor Cidro, son of the Goddess Dura'ana. We will give you all the freedom you fought for in life, you will never have to want for anything again."

Crinnan fell silent at the offer that was extended to him by Bishop General Klaus. It sounded too good to be true, he could simply... live in peace for the rest of his life if he gave up what little information he knew about Sage? He mulled it over. He didn't truly know Sage; he wouldn't feel like he was betraying him. Sage had to have been doing all this because he had something to gain out of it too, so... would Crinnan be wrong to act on his own best interests as well?

His mind shifted as his heart began to speak. But what about his family? What about his parents, Black Knight, his friends Alec and Elia? Could he just... pretend like they never existed? What about those who had fought to get him so far in the Hells... what about Milinka? Could Crinnan truly live a good life knowing he had abandoned her to rot and burn in the Hells forever?

"Withdraw your troops from Canrom." Crinnan suddenly demanded. "Forego the occupation of all lands north of Izla'Axi and west of Mrask. Let the people live freely and decide their own fate. Those are my terms if you want me and your three hundred million people back."

"You are bold." Klaus said with a respectful tone. "However, this is not a negotiation. This is an offer for you to retain your pride. We *will* figure out a way around this virus and withdraw you forcefully in only a matter of time, Crinnan Jamiso. Either accept our generosity now or face our wrath soon."

"So... that's a no then?" Crinnan asked. Klaus formed his lips into a smile and nodded his head.

"Forgive me for not being entirely clear." Klaus said. "Lest the people you wish to free fully surrender themselves to Emperor Cidro, then they will never know freedom. You are correct, Crinnan. Govia will not entertain..."

Crinnan fired his pistol, knocking Klaus back a few steps. Before the Inquisitors could react, Crinnan had lifted his weapon and fired again, sending a bullet through Klaus' forehead.

"Fuck you!" Crinnan roared. "Fuck you and your snake tongue you piece of shit Govian!"

A blue wall of light suddenly appeared between Crinnan and the Govians and he watched as they fired their rifles relentlessly on Crinnan and the other two. Karston stepped back, surprised by the ethereal wall and Crinnan looked up to see that it stretched all the way to the ceiling.

"You..." Crinnan whispered, looking over at Ander. "You did this?"

"I am impressed by your audacity, child." Ander said, not taking his eyes off the Govians in front of him. "You hold a great power within you, one that upon returning to the mainland must be unlocked..." Ander turned his head and smiled. "And with that power, we can reshape the world... together..."

Crinnan rolled his eyes and Ander's feet suddenly lifted off the ground. "You have never beheld true power." Ander said as he hovered above the floor. "Watch and realize the friend you have in me."

Ander floated forward, past the blue wall, and extended his arms out from his body. The bullets that were being fired at him simply... dissolved when they came near Ander, leaving ripples of translucent space behind.

Crinnan watched as Ander rose higher into the air, his arms extended as if he were being crucified. The Govians' resolve seemed to falter as they watched him rise, and a few turned to run. The doors to the keep, however, slammed shut and the Govians began to panic.

"Be among the first to speak the name of your true redeemer!" Ander bellowed, his voice seemingly amplified through some technique or ability he had. "Abandoned in life, cast aside by those that formed him. Used and discarded like a tool in the hands of the ones who believed their ambitions to be the only way... wrought in the fires of perdition, formed in the smoke by centuries of clarity that could not be found in the world that birthed him; I am he who deliver unto the masses the true way. I am reborn, I am Eon!"

Ander brought his hands in front of him, and the bodies of the Govians quickly rose into the air. The Inquisitors screamed and writhed in fear, trying to find balance but they were defenseless. Some continued firing their weapons, while others simply dropped them out of fear or surprise. Crinnan watched with wide eyes as their bodies began twisting, their bones breaking under whatever force held them.

"And so ends your story!" Eon declared. The Govians ripped apart like paper, their limbs being tossed in all directions and their screams blotting out any other sound that would pass through the room that they all stood in. Blood fell like rain upon the floor and pooled beneath them. Crinnan watched fearfully as a few bodies burst and painted the walls with gore. He took a step back and could feel his heart pound in his chest. Finally, Eon released his hold on them all, and the crumpled masses of flesh fell and splashed into the blood beneath them.

Eon floated backwards, passing through the blue light wall behind him and landed softly on the ground next to Crinnan and Karston. The two of them looked at Eon with terror and concern in their eyes and Eon simply nodded.

"Those who seek the true way, those who ally themselves with me... any who wish to call me friend will be spared from this fate." Eon gently purred. "Come, my friends. There is no more time to tarry. The end is nigh, I know the path. Let us all venture forth, and lay claim to our fates."

"Ander..." Crinnan whispered as Eon turned and began walking toward one of the sets of stairs. "Ander what..."

"Ander is no more." Eon corrected him. "May he rest peacefully. Thank you, Crinnan, for returning me to my true form, for enabling me to awaken and live once more. Remember my name and call me friend. 'tis a delight to meet you, Crinnan Jamiso, I am Eon."

Chapter Forty-One
A Risky Betrayal

Dread's Keep
The Fourth Level

Two pistols, a sword and an ammo belt laid on the ground in front of the corpse of Thornscale. Crinnan looked down at them, they had been his before he had killed Thornscale and respawned back at the First Level of the Hells. He called Karston over, handed him the pistol that he had been gifted and scooped his old equipment. He holstered the pistols on his ribs, clipped on his ammo belt, and put the sword on his back.

The blue light from the portal that remained open shone on Crinnan. He stared at it for a moment, feeling grateful that he had made it back. He was finally caught up to where he had been, finally able to continue to the end...

Congratulations, Citizen. Your faith in Dura'ana and our great Emperor Cidro have led you to the end of Thornscale's trials. You have proven that you are strong and diligent enough to overcome even the greatest of odds. For that, you are to be commended. When you log out, please visit your local Inquisitor's station and you will be provided new job opportunities. Now, walk through the portal and enter the Fifth Level. You have earned it!

Pending Abilities Available:

Portal (Level 4)
Portal (Level 5)
Portal Abilities Re-Enabled

"Job opportunities..." Crinnan snorted. "Yeah right." He didn't even want to think about what kind of job a citizen would be offered for having done what he did.

Three more levels..." He said softly to the others. "We're... we're almost there."

"Then we must not tarry, child." Eon replied. "Come, arise, let us venture forth into the unknown that we may finish this."

Crinnan grunted as he stood. He was tired, not physically but mentally. He felt like he had spent a lifetime fighting. The end was so close and all Crinnan wanted to do was rest... he looked over at Karston though and sighed. The old blood rancher had spent literal lifetimes in the Hells... he had fought, lost his mind, sought his loved ones and... ultimately given up so that he could have a chance at peace in Sincroft. Crinnan realized as he looked at him that he didn't deserve to rest. He stood to his full height and took a deep breath.

"Then let's go..." He said. He turned toward the portal and immediately thought of those who were waiting for him. He thought of Edmaan and Demyan, the knights who had impacted his life so greatly when he was younger. He wanted to make them proud, to show them that he was strong and that Edmaan's teachings hadn't gone to waste... and then Crinnan thought of Milinka.

"I have to find her." Crinnan whispered to himself. He would not let her down again. He *would* find her like he had promised so long ago. There was simply no question in his mind about what he needed to do. He would not leave the Hells without her.

"Come on." Crinnan said as he approached the portal. "Time to go." He watched as Ander and Eon both passed through the portal and then stepped forward himself. Before he could pass through, however, Sage spoke.

"Crinnan... can you hear me?" Sage all but shouted. *"Can you hear me Crinnan!"*

"Yeah, I'm here. What?" Crinnan asked, a bit annoyed.

"Listen to me very carefully." Sage implored. *"You have to get away from Eon. I wish I had known that Ander was him sooner, had I known..."*

"Yeah, he's fucking crazy." Crinnan agreed. "But... how?"

"That skipping stone in your pocket." Sage said. *"When you get to the Fifth Level, use it immediately."*

"I can't just leave the others behind." Crinnan argued. "I won't abandon Milinka."

"Crinnan I understand that you love her, but you cannot allow Eon to get to the Seventh Level." Sage shouted. *"He must not leave the Hells!"*

"Look I'll do everything I can." Crinnan said. "But none of this is happening without Milinka."

"You do not know what you speak of..." Sage growled. *"If only you realized what kind of power Eon truly has..."*

"Sage... I'm getting Milinka." Crinnan said, cutting him off. "There's no question about it. I haven't truly... loved anyone but myself my entire life, I can't just... run away now. I'm doing this."

"I... I understand." Sage replied with a defeated tone. *"Truly I do... Look, if I cannot convince you to skip the Fifth Level... then please. Find Milinka, and then do whatever you can to get away from him. Remember, once you pass through a portal you create, it closes."*

"Great." Crinnan rolled his eyes. "Is there anything else important I need to know?"

"Dali is your sister?" Sage replied.

"Yeah, figured that out already." Crinnan said.

"Then no..." Sage said. *"Finish your journey, I will be waiting for you on the other side."*

"Okay Sage..." Crinnan said. He looked back up at the portal in front of him and sighed. "Hey Sage?"

"Yes, Crinnan?"

"I guess I haven't said this yet but..." Crinnan fidgeted nervously, hating the taste of the words on his tongue. "Thank you... I guess." Sage fell silent for a moment but eventually replied.

"I... owe it to you." Sage nearly whispered. *"Now, we both have to go. Get moving, Crinnan. I will see you soon."*

At that, Sage fell silent and Crinnan walked through the portal.

***

The Fifth Level

Crinnan stepped out of the portal and into a field of crimson grass. The sky above him was grey, the Fifth Level was a bit... brighter than any of the preceding levels. Crinnan looked around, appreciating the landscape more than he had any of the others.

"This isn't so bad." He said with a shrug of his shoulders. "Kind of nice..."

Atop a nearby hill Crinnan saw the upright forms of Karston and Eon. He jogged toward them, quickly climbing the hill. As he neared, he noticed that they were staring down into a valley. He walked up next to them and glanced down to discover what they were looking at.

"What!" Crinnan shouted. He saw hundreds, perhaps thousands of players gathered in the valley below. They were engaged in combat with another army, a horde of shrieking and screaming touched that scrambled in a large mass toward them. The players were easily outnumbered ten to one, but they were, at least for the moment, holding back the feeble bodies of the insane yet empowered prisoners that were assaulting them.

"What is going on?" Crinnan asked, mesmerized by the battle.

"The touched are hunting." Karston replied. "They've learned that they can kill... they're massing together by instinct I reckon. God look at them, it's like an ocean..."

"There's so many." Crinnan replied. "So many people that have been driven to insanity here... after all the years of torture and pain." Crinnan shook his head at the sight and then surveyed the player encampment below. "These are the players who killed Black Knight back at Dread's Keep..."

"I would venture to guess that that is a correct assessment." Eon said. "They killed... and then they moved on. They had no reason to enter the keep."

"So, they're out hunting prisoners then." Crinnan realized. He snorted. "Guess they found them."

Karston chuckled alongside Crinnan at the situation that the players had found themselves in. Karston reached out and patted Crinnan's shoulder. "Alright then, let's get away from here. We got ground to cover." Crinnan nodded and turned to leave but... something caught his eye. He stopped walking and squinted at a large group of about fifty or sixty people sitting on the ground. Their hands were bound, and their heads were lowered.

"Prisoners..." Crinnan whispered. "They're taking prisoners? Why?"

"You don't want to know." Karston called over to him. "Remember... the Hells is where these players come to sin..."

"Ah fuck no." Crinnan snapped as he started running forward. "No, Milinka could be in there. I'm not leaving them to get raped or tortured by the players. This shit is getting shut down."

"Crinnan, wait!" Karston shouted after him, but Crinnan ignored him. He ran down the hill and when he reached flat ground again, he drew his sword. He sprinted forward in the direction of the cluster of prisoners. It didn't take long for one of the three guards to notice him. When he did, he ran forward to engage Crinnan.

"Dumbass." Crinnan snorted as he readied his weapon. Within a matter of moments, Crinnan and the player had reached each other. The player swiped his two-handed axe at him, and Crinnan stepped to the side, evading the attack. He quickly swiped at the back of the player's neck, severing his spine and ending his life.

Player: Duckie9689 EXECUTED
Player Rank: 9,977,158,546
NO RANK CHANGE
Current Rank: 653
Current Percentile: 11%

The other two guards approached. Crinnan didn't have time to fight. He dropped his sword, drew his pistols, and fired on each of them until they were on the ground. Afterward, he holstered his weapons, retrieved his sword and brained both the players to make sure they stayed down.

Player: PiousVenom0666 EXECUTED
Player Rank: 11,187,589,577
NO RANK CHANGE
Current Rank: 653
Current Percentile: 11%
Player: Outhouse69 EXECUTED
Player Rank: 9,977,158,546

"Idiots." Crinnan snorted as he ran away from their bodies. It wasn't long before he had entered the player's camp and approached the group of prisoners.

"Come on!" Crinnan shouted at the nearest one. "Get on your feet, time to get out of here!" He ran up and cut the rope that bound the prisoner's hand. "Here, take this." He handed over one of his two swords and pointed at everyone else. "Cut them free, hurry we don't have time to waste!"

"Who are you!" The prisoner Crinnan had freed shouted. By then the other prisoners had noticed the commotion and gotten to their feet as well.

"Crinnan." He replied. "I'm... a friend." Crinnan started cutting through more bindings. He looked over and saw Eon and Karston keeping watch. "Karston come help." Crinnan said to him. "Let's get this done!"

"On it!" Karston replied, pulling his knife from the sheath on his belt. He ran over and started freeing prisoners left and right.

"Don't push, fucker!" Crinnan yelled at one of them. "Just wait your turn!" He cut another rope, freeing another prisoner and they hurried and gathered about ten feet away. "Come on, we..." Crinnan was suddenly cut off as he heard the sound of footsteps running toward him. He quickly turned, ready to fight only to find Milinka standing there in front of him.

Crinnan gasped. He dropped his sword and reached his hands up. Placing a palm on each of her cheeks, he pulled her in and pressed his lips against hers.

"Crinnan!" Milinka cried softly as their lips briefly parted. "I... I thought it was over. I thought you were gone for good..."

"Yeah, well. I made a promise to someone a long time ago." He whispered back. "That I would find her one day."

"Nope." Milinka said with a grin. "You already broke that promise." She leaned in and kissed him again. "But here's to second... or, well third chances now, right?" Crinnan couldn't help but smile. He placed his head on the back of her head and held her tight.

"Okay." He whispered into her ear. "Yeah, second chances..."

"Ahem." Karston cleared his throat next to them, and they quickly let go of each other. Milinka cocked her head at the sight of the elf and a wide smile formed on her face.

"I am so happy to see you again, Lord Karston." Milinka said with tears in her eyes. "I guess Crinnan dragged you with him this time?"

"You too, madam." Karston nodded his head and couldn't fight the smile that formed on his own face. "Yeah, he's definitely a little shitstain ain't he."

"Truer words have never been spoken." Milinka held her hands out and Karston cut the ropes that bound them. He gave her a wink and then turned to the next prisoner.

"We have been found." Eon declared from behind Crinnan. "I will keep them at bay." Crinnan glanced over and saw that a detachment from the player army was rushing toward them from the battlefield. Bodies began exploding in the distance, and blood flew into the air like fireworks. Crinnan frowned as he turned to Milinka.

"Where are the others?" He asked. "Edmaan, Demyan?"

"They didn't make it." Milinka sighed. "Players cut through them..."

"Damnit." Crinnan hissed. He looked over at Karston and frowned. Quickly he picked up his sword and helped the elf cut through the rest of the prisoner's bindings. He sent them to the hill and then turned toward Karston and Milinka.

"We're leaving." Crinnan whispered to both of them. "Now."

"Without him?" Karston asked, a hopeful tone in his voice. "How we don't have a portal?"

"I do." Crinnan said. He reached into his pocket and produced the skipping stone that Grizzly had gifted him back in the Bloodgames. "We're going to the Sixth Level. All of us."

"Prisoners too?" Karston asked.

"Sure." Crinnan nodded. He grabbed Milinka's hand and led her over to the prisoners. He dropped the stone on the ground, stomped on it and then started pushing the prisoners inside.

"Go!" He whispered sharply to them. "Get through, everyone. Hurry up!" Crinnan glanced back at Eon and noticed he was busy blowing people up. It didn't take long for the majority of the prisoners to pass through the portal, but when there were a handful left, Eon turned his head.

Crinnan locked eyes with the vampre, and for a moment, they stared at each other. Crinnan wore a look of guilt, though he didn't regret what he was doing. Eon simply shook his head and waved a finger in Crinnan's direction. For a single tense second, Crinnan held the gaze and then he felt Milinka tug on his arm. When he was pulled back to the moment, Crinnan knew Eon could have ended him right then and there. Finally, he nervously looked away from Eon and hurried through the portal.

Chapter Forty-Two
The Calm

The Sixth Level

The Sixth Level of the Hells was unlike all the other levels Crinnan had seen. As he, Karston and Milinka emerged from the portal, they found that the Sixth Level had a dark sky full of twinkling stars. Crinnan looked up at them for a moment filled with wonder, and then turned and stared at the giant orange, green and blue moon that took up nearly half the sky. Everyone's eyes were transfixed on the moon, but it didn't take long for Crinnan to realize something. They weren't looking at a moon; they were looking at Duraan itself.

"It's..." Crinnan stammered, finding it immensely difficult to speak. He couldn't pull his vision from the planet; it was as if there was a magnetism drawing his eyes to it.

"Home." Milinka whispered as she slipped her fingers between Crinnan's. The two stood, surrounded by those who had been damned for centuries and stared in silent admiration at the only home they had ever known. "Do you think it is real?"

"I doubt it." Crinnan whispered. His boots were planted on the green grassy ground and as he looked around himself, he saw lush trees and vegetation. The only place he could have possibly been was Igo, the green moon that had illuminated the sky every single night of his life. "If it is real, then that means..."

"Igo is the Hells?" Milinka finished Crinnan's sentence. "If it's real, it means everything is really happening, all the bodies, the magic, death, and blood...."

"It can't be." Crinnan shook his head. "It is all too crazy, too advanced; our world couldn't make something like this."

"I should say, your world did not create such a thing." Sage's voice rang out. *"Mine did."*

"Yours?" Crinnan repeated.

"The great minds of the Ancients." Sage continued. *"We created all this. We dreamt it, designed it and made it a reality. I should say it truly was a beautiful thing... once."*

"Before the Empire..." Crinnan mumbled. "Before Dura'ana..."

"Indeed." Sage sighed heavily. *"I have seen it all Crinnan, everything. I have been to the stars, seen other worlds... the Humaans showed me everything they knew. I wanted to bring that to my home, to make it as amazing as I could... I fought the Church in the Sin Wars, I commanded much of the AOC, but we just could not win against the ignorance of the people. People want to believe what is not real. They want to think that something that does not exist is more beautiful and desirable than all that does. How do you fight that Crinnan? How do you win and survive against such delusions?"*

"You wipe it out." Crinnan found himself saying. "Like a fucking weed, you burn it, poison it, cut it down... whatever it takes."

"A bit morose, but not wrong. Perhaps you will succeed where I failed." A remorseful sounding Sage said. *"Your path is greatness, Crinnan. Only greatness, I truly want that for you."*

Crinnan remained silent. He squeezed the handle of his sword and looked down at the grass at his feet. He did not care about greatness, he just wanted to be home again. His eyes wandered back upward toward Duraan and he spoke.

"Am I truly on Igo?" He asked.

"No." Sage replied. *"It is all a computer program. Igo is much more beautiful than what you see right now."*

Crinnan sighed and looked over at Milinka. "It's not real. It's all computer shit."

"Well Brothers fuck it all then." Milinka sighed. "It's still pretty I guess."

"So where do we go from here? How do we get back to reality?"

"You are on the cusp of it." Sage's voice sounded hopeful and excited. *"The Sixth Level of the Hells is where the prisoners are sent for good behavior. I can summon the portal to the Seventh and final level of the Hells for you. This is the only level where I can do so, for I should say anyone has the ability to depart from this level at will, but I don't trust you to be able to figure it out on your own. You can leave whenever you are ready... Crinnan this may be the last time we speak before we meet. If that is the case, then... well, I should say that I rather look forward to meeting you."*

"Yeah." Crinnan replied, nodding his head. "I look forward to it too." To his surprise, his words were honest. He really was interested in finding out who Sage was and why he had chosen to guide Crinnan back home.

"The portal is opening. The final level may be difficult, the demons have amassed there and are waiting for you...but I should say that once you arrive, you will not be alone in your fight. Lucaas and I have called out to all the prisoners; told them that they can fight... told them that you will lead them in a battle for vengeance. There are many who await you."

"Okay." Crinnan stood and reached his hand out toward Milinka. She grabbed it and he pulled her up. As she got to her feet, the portal to the final level opened.

"Can we have... just a few minutes?" Crinnan asked Sage.

"Yes." Sage replied. His tone sounded warm and a bit jovial. *"Send the prisoners through... and you two... say what you need to."*

"Don't fucking watch." Crinnan snapped.

"I would not dare." Sage replied. *"Goodbye Crinnan."* At that, he was gone and Crinnan turned to Karston.

"Can you take these prisoners and go through the portal?" Crinnan asked him. "We'll be right behind you I just... I need to..."

"Shut up." Karston said, giving Crinnan a pat on the back. "I'll take care of it partner. You take a little time for yourself and kick boots with that girl."

"No not that!" Crinnan hissed. Karston's entire body shook with laughter and he nodded.

"You behave." Karston said with a tip of his hat. "You're… you're alright partner. I'll see you on the other side."

"You are too, Karston." Crinnan said with a nod. Karston smiled and turned to the prisoners.

"Alright, saddle up!" He shouted at them all. "Time to get through the portal so these two can fuck in peace!"

"Brothers damn it all." Crinnan said as his face flushed red. Milinka burst into laughter and Karston gave her a wink. After a few moments everyone was gone except for Crinnan and Milinka.

"So… here we are." Crinnan said when he was sure the two of them were alone.

"Here we are." Milinka replied. She took a seat on the soft green grass and looked up at Duraan. "So close to home…"

"Yeah." Crinnan whispered as he sat next to her. He looked up at the planet and sighed, allowing himself just a moment of rest before he dove headfirst into the chaos he knew was waiting for him in the Seventh Level.

Milinka laid her head on Crinnan's shoulder and closed her eyes. "You know. It would be nice if we didn't have to leave this place." She said softly. "We could just sit here… together… and stare up at the stars."

"Might get boring after a while." Crinnan replied. Milinka lifted her head from his shoulder and he snorted a laugh when he looked over and saw the stink eye she was giving him. "I'm just kidding. Yeah, I could do this… for a long time…"

"You better." Milinka pouted. She leaned back on her arms, grabbed Crinnan's shoulders and pulled him down so that the back of his head rested on her lap. He was apprehensive at first, but when he was laying down he felt more comfortable than he had in years.

"Thank you Crinnan." Milinka said to him as the two of them lay there. He heard her sniffle a bit and turned his head, looking up at her as a tear dripped down off her chin and onto her chest. Crinnan sat up and locked his eyes on hers.

"What's wrong?" Crinnan asked. He reached up and wiped another rogue tear away. "Are you okay?"

"This has all been... such a... I do not know. It's been terrible but it's also been..."

"I get it." Crinnan said tenderly. "Seeing you again has been one of the best things that's ever happened to me. Sure it all happened in the worst place possible, but... I don't know, maybe if you hadn't been here then I would have given up a long time ago."

"I mean..." Milinka grinned. "It's nice that I'm one of the best things ever, but you apparently have never had double chocolate fudge cake."

Crinnan's face wrinkled up and his nostrils flared. "I like white cake... but I'll take steamed cabbage over cake any day."

"You are fucking gross." Milinka said before bursting into laughter. Crinnan joined her and nodded his head.

"I like what I like..." Crinnan said in defense of himself.

"Yeah?" Milinka asked. A look of longing was in her eyes, and Crinnan cautiously nodded his head.

"Yeah." He leaned forward and pressed his lips to hers. The tension keeping Milinka sitting straight dissipated, and Crinnan reached an arm up and cradled the back of her head. Slowly, he lowered her down to the grass and passionately kissed her. Their kiss lasted as long as they wanted this time, and nobody was there to interrupt them. After a few moments, Crinnan pulled back and pressed his forehead against Milinka's."

"Before anything ruins this..." He whispered, his lips gently trembling against hers. "I just want you to know..."

"Yes?" Milinka whispered. She breathed heavily, and her heart pounded in her chest. Crinnan reached up and stroked her cheek.

"I love you Milinka." He whispered. "I have since we were kids..." Goosebumps spread over his arms, and Milinka felt a cold shiver come over her as well. She wrapped her arms around him and pulled him close to her.

"I love you too, Crinnan." She replied softly. "I really do." Crinnan smiled and laid down next to her. She wrapped her arms around him, hugging him from behind as she rested her forehead against the back of his head. Crinnan grabbed her hands and for a moment the two just laid there in silence.

"We can't lay here forever." Milinka whispered into Crinnan's ear. "We have to go..."

"Just five more minutes?" Crinnan whined.

"Nope." Milinka let go of him and sat up. Crinnan groaned and pushed himself to his feet. He reached his hand out to Milinka, she grabbed it and he pulled her up. Crinnan leaned in and gave her one last kiss on the cheek and they turned and started walking toward the portal. As they approached, however, a second portal appeared and Eon stepped out of it.

"Hello, my friends." Ander growled as he approached the two. "I do hope I am not once again interrupting a tender moment between the two of you. 'Twould be a great shame to impede on young love." He threw his hand out and a powerful force pushed Crinnan onto his back.

"'tis a great shame that you felt compelled to abandon me the way you did." Eon declared as he approached. "Why I have never wished to do any more than help you."

"Milinka get out of here! Sage are you still there!" Crinnan shouted as he found himself immobile on the ground. "Sage?"

"Yes." Sage replied. "What is going on?"

"Eon... Eon is here..."Crinnan croaked. "He has gone crazy."

"Crazy?" Eon repeated, looking up at the stars. "Sage... Why, Sajinious Lynx my old friend. Is that you?"

"How does he know..." Crinnan asked.

"Damn it all!" Sage yelled. "Crinnan he has locked me out, I cannot help you... Let him go Dryak!"

"Oh worry not my friends." Ander said as he knelt and stroked Crinnan's cheek. "I will bring Crinnan and his muse no harm, for you see, he has liberated me from this prison! Without him I may never have been given the opportunity to establish my kingdom on Duraan. For all this, I thank you all."

"Dryak, stop it!" Sage hissed. *"Leave him alone, get out of here! You do not deserve to come back!"*

"Oh, Sajinious." Eon smiled, holding his arms wide toward the planet of Duraan above him. "Not only will I come to the planet, but I will rebuild it all in my image. I will restore order to the world; I will obliterate all that you and all that Govia has created. All will have no choice but to fall to their knees and declare Eon as their King and savior!"

"Dryak... Eon, that is enough!" Sage shouted. *"If you come here, I promise you I will find you and purge you. You know my power exceeds yours! Stand down and leave the children alone."*

"This conversation bores me." Eon waved a hand and Sage could be heard no more. He looked to Crinnan and smiled a warm smile. "I will always consider you a brother for what you have done for me, Crinnan Jamiso. Fear not, for although I may seem wicked, know that I am just." Eon reached out his hand and beckoned Crinnan and Milinka toward the portal to the Seventh Hell.

"Shall we?" Eon asked with a smile. "The end is upon us, let us march forth and claim our destinies."

Crinnan felt whatever force was holding him down recede and he quickly sat up. He wanted to draw his sword and attack Eon but he knew he wouldn't stand a chance. Instead, he looked at Milinka. She wore a look of apprehension and her hands trembled. "I am here." Crinnan whispered as he leaned into her. "It's... it's okay." At that, he slipped his hand into hers and the two of them followed Eon through the portal.

Chapter Forty-Three
Before

The Seventh Level

Attention Citizens: You have failed to apprehend Crinnan Jamiso and he has arrived at the Seventh Level and risen to the 11th Percentile. It has never been more imperative that this demon be captured, for if he is successful in what he aims to achieve, you will all be in great peril. I now implore *all* citizens to pursue Crinnan Jamiso to the Seventh Level regardless of ability. He must be stopped, and whoever is able to apprehend him will receive an award of ten thousand shards. I am opening portals in all the key areas on all levels for...

The transmission suddenly stopped and Crinnan watched as blue portals began to pepper the landscape all around him. The Seventh Level was dark, and the land was composed of black ebony rock. No vegetation grew, and the ground on which Crinnan stood was flat though he saw shadowy mountains looming in the background.

"This doesn't look good." Crinnan growled as he watched players begin to file out of the portals. A seemingly endless stream of them began to crowd into the landscape and Crinnan took a step back, bumping into Karston and the others they had saved who had apparently been waiting for them.

"Yeah, partner." Karston sighed. "I don't know how you reckon you're gonna get out of this one..."

"We will." Milinka replied. "We won't give up no matter how many of them come out of that portal. We have to fight, and we will win."

"Look at them though." Crinnan argued. "They're still coming... there are so many of them..."

"They are nothing." Eon hissed as he stepped forward. "They could not hope to stand against me."

"Against us." Milinka corrected him. "You're not the only one here." Eon turned his head and snorted at Milinka.

"Child, I am all that will ever be." Eon corrected her. "None can stand against me, I will crumble the seat of the Empire with my own hands, I..."

A bright flash of light suddenly filled the sky, cutting off Eon and forcing everyone to shield their eyes with their hands. A loud static sound briefly filled the air, and Crinnan, even through his shielded eyes saw that the light was shifting and changing colors like a video at nighttime. Curiously, Crinnan peeked over his hands and his eyes grew wide at what he saw.

An image floated in the sky... it looked like a movie or a television program, but it was just a close up of a wooden desk in what looked like an office. Everyone in the Seventh Level stared at the image, curious what it was... but then a few moments a figure stepped into view seated himself behind the desk.

The elf was handsome, clean shaven and had a well-groomed head of blue hair that was silvering at his temples. He was initially silent as he slowly lifted his hands and straightened the tie that disappeared into the blue vest that he wore over his collared shirt. He cleared his throat, chewing on his tongue for a moment before a warm smile formed on his face. His teeth were among the brightest Crinnan had ever seen.

Folding his hands together in front of him, he sat up straight and stared directly at all who watched. His nostrils briefly flared, and his eye twitched ever so slightly. Everyone in the Hells was silent. The players who stepped out of their portals looked up in curiosity at the strange image before them. The elf simply sat in silence as if he were waiting for a cue. Finally, with a clear Ancient accented voice that Crinnan recognized, he spoke.

"Hello, my fellow citizens." Sage said with a tone that demanded attention. "I do find myself humbled greatly by this privilege to speak with you today. My name is Sajinious Lynx, founder of the Life Lynx corporation and former president of the great republic of Izla'Axi. I come before you today not as a leader, but as an equal... as a suffering servant whose greatest desire is to see the spark of life shine once again in all of your eyes. Let none of you mishear my words, for I do not speak only to the dead. I speak to all who would hear, even those of you who have perhaps ignorantly delivered an immeasurable amount of pain unto you fellow Duraanians."

Crinnan stared up at Sage completely in awe. The elf's voice was captivating, his appearance and posture was much more than Crinnan expected. He carried himself in a way that pulled Crinnan in and wouldn't allow him to break free. He *had* to listen.

"For the first time in nearly one thousand years I am able to rejoice in the fact that I can sit here with you and discuss something that affects us all in one way or another. You see my friends, no matter which side you fight for in this final battle that has been thrust upon you all, you will not wake up tomorrow the same. I have had the absolute pleasure of equalizing the 'playing field' if you will. I have personally taken it upon myself to make certain that you all are on level ground. You may be asking yourself why I would ever do such a thing. I should say that I do not believe you are evil, oh citizens of Govia. I am not punishing you... and on that note I did this because I want everyone to understand that those of us who have died are not deserving of punishment, and even if we were then those of us who still live are not the ones responsible for dealing out such punishment. Death *is* our punishment... as it is also our reward. A conclusion of life, a ceasing of sensation and experience and learning... but also rest... and perhaps a new adventure for us all.

"Or so that was what the universe had in mind... A millennium ago, I changed that because I was afraid. I did not do it for money, I had plenty. I did not do it for fame... for such a thing grows boring. No, I sought to end the finality of life once and for all because I lost the person who was most dear to me. I altered the natural course of life because my wife Amanda was taken from me and I didn't want anyone else to feel that pain again. Goodbye is... very difficult to say, and in some circumstances even harder to accept. I wanted everyone to have the opportunity to commune with those they loved for all of eternity... and so I created the Afterscape..."

Sage paused for a moment to collect himself and then continued.

"I was a fool." Sage said. "When the Church won the war, everything that I hadn't lost was taken from me. My assets were seized, my life's work was twisted into hideous perversions of their original forms. The Afterscape, once a utopia where any could forge their own eternities, was transformed into the Hells and I have carried the blame with me for centuries. My friends, my desire today was to come before you to apologize for having failed you... you have endured many lifetimes of torment and pain because I could not handle my own. I can never make amends for this, but here I sit doing everything in my limited power to at least make it end for you... I have no expectation of forgiveness, but I do ask that you take to heart what I have said..."

Crinnan looked over at Eon who was snarling at the image of Sage. His hands were aflame, and he trembled with fury. There was clearly more to their relationship than Crinnan was aware of.

"The first step in the end of your torment is for Crinnan Jamiso to escape, for he holds the key to all our salvation. Govia is opening portals all over the Hells as we speak. These portals will lead you to the Seventh Level. I implore you, friends, take your exhumed lives and strength and go to the Seventh Level that you may aid Crinnan in what may be one of the most important events in the history of Duraan. Your lives are at stake as are the futures of your descendants and all who dwell on Duraan. My friends, I beg of you. Do not tarry and do not fear, together as a people we can all create a better tomorrow for those that will come after us."

Crinnan glanced at Milinka who stared up at Sage. She took a deep breath; her shoulders raised and lowered as her lungs filled with air, and then she reached down and took hold of the axes hanging from her hips. With a ferocious look, she pulled the weapons free.

"My time with you all is quickly running out." Sage continued. "Together you are all powerful. You can resist those who have hurt you for so long. You can fight and you can win. Get to the portals. Join Crinnan Jamiso in the Seventh Level and show everyone who has ever lived that you will not bow down. Show them that you are strong, you are able... and in spite of your own deaths and torment... you are still here." Sage closed his eyes and nodded his head gently before unfolding his hands and placing them face down on his desk.

"Thank you... my friends... for hearing me once again. For those of you who escape today, I will see you soon. For those of you who remain in the Hells, I am proud of you." Sage pushed himself up, and without another word he walked away, and the video faded out of view.

"By the Brothers..." Crinnan gasped as he watched what had to have been thousands of people pouring through the open portals all around him. They carried their weapons, loaded their guns... a few of their hands ignited with magical powers. They were all very obviously preparing for combat in their own way.

Crinnan heard shouting and the sounds of combat as the people flooding through the portals tried to find their sides. Guns discharged and swords clanged against the metal of armor. The unfortunate cried out as they fell as the chaos erupted around him.

Crinnan watched the former prisoners roar with a vigor that was renewed by Sage's appearance. Even though they were outnumbered they clashed against the players, fighting viciously to gain the upper hand.

"What do we do?" Crinnan asked. He looked around nervously for a way out or something from Sage. "We're here... how do we... how do we escape now?"

"I am certain we will know when we see it." Eon spat with a frown. He stepped forward toward the fighting, not bothering to look at Crinnan. "These things... they take time. All we have to do is stay on our feet until the way home presents itself."

Crinnan glanced at Eon but didn't let his gaze linger. The sight of Eon scared Crinnan, his power was immense and Crinnan didn't want to be responsible for Eon going back to Duraan. It was becoming increasingly apparent, however, that Crinnan would not be returning without him.

"Put your trust in me, my young friend." Eon said as he continued forward. "I will deliver you, even if I am forced to carry you."

"Great." Crinnan replied with a sigh. Somehow, he found his fingers interlocked with Milinka's and he looked over at her.

"Almost done." She said as the two walked forward. There was a look of what Crinnan thought could have been disappointment on her face. He looked around at the others, stopped to let them pass, and then turned to Milinka.

"Maybe we should just stay here." Crinnan said. Milinka snorted in response and then looked to the battle that was growing ahead of them.

"Crinnan and Milinka? Finding love and living happily ever after in the Hells?" Milinka asked. "It's cute but... I'm ready to go home."

"Yeah, I get that." Crinnan let go of her hand and reached up to stroke her cheek. "Well. Then I guess I have no choice but to go with you then."

"Good." Milinka said. Crinnan smiled thinly and then they turned back toward the battle. "Our forces are massing. The two sides are separating... this is... this is going to be rough."

"Bring it on." Crinnan said as he watched the two armies split. This was going to be his last fight in the Hells, and he was eager for it to be over. His army ran toward him in a large mass while the player army pulled back.

"Time to be your father." Milinka said, patting him on the shoulder. "They are all here for you after all."

"Well fuck." Crinnan replied.

Chapter Forty-Four
The Storm

The Seventh Hell

"It's him!" Crinnan heard someone shout. "He's here! He's over here!" Thousands of sets of eyes were suddenly upon him and Crinnan stopped dead in his tracks. His vision darted back and forth as he nervously looked at everyone. Then his free hand awkwardly raised in greeting.

"Uh... hey." Crinnan called out. At that, the people erupted in cheering. Weapons were raised into the air and a chorus of voices drowned out Crinnan's thoughts. He pursed his lips together and looked over at Milinka.

"What... do I do?" He asked. "I've never..."

"Stand tall." Milinka replied. She squeezed his hand, and he straightened his back. "You're their leader..."

"By the Brothers." Crinnan griped. "I'm no good at shit like that."

"You're a fucking Centurion and they're staring at you!" Milinka hissed back. "You look like an idiot!"

"I *am* a fucking idiot!" Crinnan whispered. His head snapped up and he imitated his father by putting on a fake cheesy smile. He looked around, examining the hopeful faces that surrounded him. He wasn't sure exactly what to do so he let go of Milinka's hand and drew his sword. He raised the weapon in the air and the cheering erupted again.

"Well, they're easy to please." Crinnan snorted.

"They just want to see that you are confident." Milinka replied. "Watch this." She cleared her throat and stepped forward.

"Good people..." She shouted as she motioned for them to quiet down. She waited for a moment and the roar hushed. "I do not know how long you have all been here... whether it has been a century, a decade or even only a year. Truly it does not matter. What matters is that we are a people all bound together through a common experience. In our time here we have endured the sins and the oppression of the people of the Govian Empire. We have been killed, burned, tortured, raped, maimed... we have been treated like insects for the entertainment of the Govian citizenry! We are not people in their eyes. We are merely and simply objects to be played with..."

"This ends today!" Milinka continued. "We are no longer cockroaches scurrying about in an effort not to be squashed or eaten. No, we are people, and we are a people united! We have been extended an opportunity, one that will enable us all to get revenge on those who have treated us like trash for so long... I know we all have so much time separating us, so many years in between the eras in which we existed. We may not necessarily like the person standing next to us for whatever reason, but today we put those differences aside so that we can fight and destroy those who seek to dominate us. This is it, my brothers and sisters. Today we show Govia the power of the people! Our actions will reverberate for years to come, and those who come after us will know never to lay down and give up again. There is *always* a way and we have found ours! People of Duraan, if you hear my words raise your swords to the sky!"

Swords and weapons were lifted all around. Milinka grabbed Crinnan's from him and lifted it. Crinnan shrugged at this and just lifted his pistol into the air.

"To us!" Milinka shouted. "May this movement be the catalyst that ultimately undoes the tyranny and oppression that has held us down for so long!"

The army erupted in cheering once again and Milinka smiled and handed the sword back to Crinnan. He grabbed it and shook his head at her.

"Pretty neat huh?" She asked with a wide smile on her face.

"You're good." Crinnan acknowledged. "Much better than I would be."

"Yeah?" Milinka asked innocently. "Well. Now it's your turn." Milinka placed her hand on Crinnan's back and pushed him hard. He stumbled forward and suddenly all eyes were on him again. He looked out at everyone, feeling a lump growing in his throat. His jaw suddenly went slack, and he felt a drop of sweat drip down his back.

"Right." Crinnan said as everyone quieted down.

Many of the people nodded their heads at him, while some just patiently looked on. Crinnan cleared his throat and blew out a nervous breath.

"Well, I'm Crinnan." He said anxiously. He could hear the sound of Milinka's palm smacking against her forehead behind him. He cleared his throat, again, and took another step forward.

"So, all my life I've been a soldier." He said. "I've fought for what I believe is right. I've killed a lot of Govians, I've seen a lot of my allies die. I've bled, sweat and fought for people who couldn't care less." He nodded his head and took in a breath through his nostrils. "Yeah. For people who would rather just sit and let the Govians tell them what to do... I've seen the Govian normal. They barge into your homes, search through your stuff. They scan your bodies with computers and arrest you without reason... I've seen Govians burn down towns and execute any survivors on the side of the road... all for submission, all for wealth and power. They force their citizens into shard mines to dig up the crystals they use for power and currency, they tell us how long we are allowed to live and force us to believe in their goddess..." He paused, not exactly knowing where he was going with what he was saying. "It's all fucking stupid and I'm sick of it!"

A few murmurs of agreement echoed out of the crowd and Crinnan nodded along with them. "Yeah, why should I live the way they want me to, you know? Why is it that because I'm alive I have to submit to Govia! Why do I have to go to bed at night worrying whether I'll wake up on fire or on a cross or with a noose around my neck? I mean I just want to grow old and have a damn cabbage farm!"

"Crinnan get to the point." Milinka leaned in and whispered.

"Sorry." Crinnan said, probably too loud. "Look, the point is. We're all here because Govia decided we had to be. It's not enough to control us in life, they have to control us in death too and it's time for that to end. I don't know how this fight is going to end, I don't know who will make it out alive or who will respawn in the First Level or what... but I do know that no matter what happens we are about to send Govia a message that even though we're dead we can still fuck them up!" Crinnan finished speaking and nodded confidently at his words. The crowd was silent. Crinnan cleared his throat for a third time, as he looked at all the faces out in front of him. Awkwardly, he turned and looked at Milinka.

"Why aren't they cheering?" He leaned forward and whispered.

"Always end in a question." Milinka replied.

"Oh. Okay." Crinnan nodded and turned back to the crowd. He stepped forward, raised his head, and took in a deep breath. He opened his mouth to speak but... couldn't think of anything. He paused for a second, looked back out at the crowd and then saw Commander Emilio push through to the front.

"So, who is ready to take the power?" Emilio shouted. The crowd stirred at this, and the volume of Emilio's voice rose. "Who is ready to reach out with their hands, take hold of the power that Govia uses against you, and wrap it around their necks?" The crowd cheered and Emilio pumped his fist into the air.

"Who has the real power?" Emilio yelled.

"We do!" The crowd disjointedly answered.

"Say it loud so that the enemy can hear you!" Emilio continued.

"We have the power!" The crowd screamed.

"Then today, let's join the true Demon Crinnan Jamiso, let's fight harder than we ever have before, and let's break this fucking place so that no one will ever suffer here again!"

The crowd went wild, and Emilio turned and walked straight to Crinnan. He reached his hand out, walked past Crinnan and Milinka gave him a high five. Crinnan frowned but nodded his head.

"A little more practice, my young friend." Emilio whispered into Crinnan's ear. He gave his shoulder a pat and then Crinnan turned to him.

"Where did you come from!" Crinnan nearly shouted.

"Why, one of the portals." Emilio replied. "Sajinious Lynx told us all how to get to you."

"Oh, Sage." Crinnan nodded.

"Yes. I know not who this... Sage Lynx is." Emilio shrugged. "But for some reason, he wants you to live."

"We all have our reasons." Another voice said. Crinnan turned and saw Dali walk up to him, and next to her was a slender hooded she-elf with thick red hair emerging from one side of the hood. Crinnan gasped at the sight and he approached the two.

"You're here..." Crinnan said to the red haired one. "Like... in person?"

"Yes, Crinnan." Sarasin replied. "I decided to fight alongside you... in my own body. Don't worry, they won't recognize me, and I'll be right at your side, so do not fear."

Dali smiled and punched Crinnan in the shoulder. "Hey you." She chirped. "You made it. That makes me totes happy." She glanced over at the others and gasped. "You!" She shouted, pointing at Karston. "Come on. I want to take you to someone before the fight starts."

"Me?" Karston asked, scrunching up his brow.

"Yes, you. Come on." She beckoned him to follow and Karston shrugged and took a step. "Someone wants to see you." His eyes grew wide as he realized where Dali was taking him.

"My... my family?" The tone of his voice suddenly went up and he looked over at Crinnan as a large smile formed on his face.

"Who else?" Dali asked with a smile. Karston closed his eyes and choked back his tears as he turned to Crinnan.

"Well, If I don't see you again..." He said with a trembling voice. "You done did me right, partner. I ain't never gonna forget what you done for me here. You're alright in my book, Crinnan Jamiso." Karston extended his hand, and Crinnan grabbed it. Karston quickly pulled Crinnan into a hug and patted his back hard. Finally, with a sniffle, he let go, straightened his hat, and walked away.

"Oh, and don't forget what I said back there." He called back. "Don't you ever guess what she wants. Be a real badass and talk to her." Karston gave Crinnan a wink, and then followed Dali away.

Crinnan watched Karston walk and couldn't keep back the smile that formed on his face. The old rancher deserved whatever happiness was in store for him. Crinnan nodded his head and sighed heavily, it was about time for him to find his own happiness too…

"Let's get this moving." Crinnan said as he turned around. Sarasin, Milinka and Emilio looked at him and nodded, and then Crinnan briefly glanced at Eon who stood off to the side watching with a contemptuous smile on his face. Milinka, Emilio and the Black Knights all followed Crinnan as he made his way to the front of the army to set into motion whatever was about to happen.

***

Sage

"Yes, I know he is in the Seventh Level." Sage snapped at Lucaas as he worked frantically to bypass the extra security measures that Govia and Farseer were actively deploying. They were fighting against him; they knew something was about to happen and they were working hard to ensure that Sage failed.

"I'm just saying, dad!" Lucaas argued. "It's time!"

"Not just yet, son!" Sage said through gritted teeth. Taking down the firewalls and encrypting the codes to gain access to the stream that controlled all the data going out of the Hells was tedious, and Sage didn't have room for error. He furiously typed at his keyboard, and then reached up and wiped the sweat from his brow before it dripped into his eyes.

"They're really putting up a fight…" Lucaas admitted. He too was hammering at his keys, and was nearly panting from all the effort he put in. "It's like they're pulling new code out of their asses… if I could just…" Lucaas' eyes went wide, and he leaned in closer to his computer monitor. He gasped and his fingers started gliding across the keys faster than they were before. "Oh yeah, there we go!" He smashed the enter button and spun in his chair to face his father with a wide grin on his face.

"They're fucking locked out!" Lucaas cheered. "We have full control over the data stream!"

"You amazing boy..." Sage said before he belted a laugh. He stood up from his chair, walked over and wrapped his arms around his son. "You have done it! I should say you have outcoded *me*, son..." With tears in his eyes, Sage lifted Lucaas off the ground and spun in place. He put the boy down and leaned in closer to his computer.

"Fortify it." Sage ordered but reached out and began typing commands on Lucaas' keyboard. "I will call the security team and inform them that we have access so they can bolster our defenses. This will not last forever but..." He looked over at his boy, his eyes nearly glowing with pride. "I should say, you just... undid what has taken the Govians centuries of coding to accomplish..."

"Welp." Lucaas said, his smile nearly as wide as his father's. "I learned from the best." Sage's fingers halted for a moment and he sighed. With a sad nod, he looked over at his son and reached up. He touched the boy's cheek and sighed.

"That you did, my son." Sage said as he finished his code and stepped back from the terminal. He pulled out his phone and motioned for Lucaas to continue. "Okay, time to get back to work... I am... I am proud of you, Lucaas."

***

The Seventh Level

Crinnan stood alongside Emilio and Milinka at the front of the army. Across the battlefield, they could see the horde of players was larger than Crinnan could have imagined. Their armor and weapons glowed, they jumped in place and a few were... dancing? Crinnan watched the strange sight and then turned to Milinka.

"What are they doing?" Crinnan asked with a confused tone. "Why are they... moving like that?"

"Because they are idiots." Sarasin replied, shaking her head at the sight. "Morons dance like that in the real world too. They think it's... funny..." Crinnan snorted and then turned to Milinka.

"Well, this is it." Crinnan said. "Now we just... wait for something to happen."

"Ancient NaNe users on me!" Eon shouted, smiling as he walked past Crinnan. "We will be your vanguard, Crinnan. Let us, the mightiest here charge into battle wielding the power we created that we may lay waste to our enemies in your name and pave the way to your glory."

"Sure..." Crinnan nodded, then turned and looked at Milinka. "Will you stay by my side?"

"Always." Milinka smiled and then Crinnan lifted her hand and kissed it. She took a deep breath, and as she exhaled, she pulled her axes from her hips. "Let's do this."

Crinnan walked forward and raised his sword. The army behind him followed suit and as Crinnan got closer, he spoke again.

"Let's do this for the ones you still love!" He shouted. "For their memory... do it for the hope that all this one day may end, that we all may somehow find peace. Fight for yourselves, for every thought your mind has ever created. Make it matter, make it worth something... it's time to show these fuckers what you can do, it's time to shove our fucking blades down their throats!" Crinnan looked over at Milinka and she gave him a look of expectation.

"The question." She whispered.

"Oh..." Crinnan replied. "Who's ready to turn these shitheads into a stain on the ground?" The army behind him cheered and Crinnan looked over at Milinka and smiled widely.

Eon's feet floated up off the ground and many of his Ancient warriors did as well. "Advance!" He shouted. At that, hundreds of Ancients charged forward, hovering, phasing and running behind Eon. The player army followed suit, their largest and heaviest armored running forward to intercept the first wave. Crinnan looked to Milinka and then Milinka turned toward the enemy.

"Archers!" Emilio shouted, raising his hand into the air. "Nock your bows, wait for my mark!" Nearly a hundred soldiers lined up in rows in front of Emilio. He stood behind them all and held his open hand in the air.

"Twenty more steps!" Emilio shouted. Crinnan turned to his right where Vassili Emmal stood with a wide grin on his face.

"I guess that leaves us." Crinnan shouted toward them "The infantry."

"Five steps!" He heard Emilio shout. "Steady… Aim… loose!" A volley of arrows shot over Eons division and struck the charging demons. Some fell, and the rest continued moving forward with their assault.

"Infantry, prepare your swords for feeding!" Vassili shouted to the soldiers with him. "We determine outcome of battle. Here is best advice I have. Stay on feet, don't drop sword!" Vassili heard laughter from within his ranks and he smiled a bit himself.

"Let's go, fuckers!" He shouted. At that, Crinnan and Milinka ran side by side as they hurried to reinforce the first wave. For a moment it was quiet. All the sounds, the chaos around him, it all died out and Crinnan only heard his breath and felt his pulse. The battle was getting closer… closer… Finally, he spun the sword in his hand and charged past the Ancients and into the fray, immediately driving his sword through the chest of the first player he saw.

Player: Kevolution EXECUTED

Player Rank: 2,478,654,789

Congratulations, PrettyKitty6969420! You have advanced in ranking!

Previous Rank: 3,327,396,763

New Rank: 2,903,025,776

Previous Percentile: 11%

New Percentile: 9%

NEW PERCENTILE ACHIEVED! Congratulations, you are showing your true power. Your buffs have been completely removed.

Cosmetic Items unlocked! See your wardrobe for more details!

...

Congratulations! You have crossed the threshold of the 10th percentile and into the top 10!

Ability Unlocked:

...

Portal (Level 7) - Grants player the ability to summon a portal to the Seventh Level of Hellscape anywhere portals are permitted.

As the sounds around him returned, he heard the war cries of the infantry as they burst into the battle. The sound of steel on steel, the cries of the dying and the steady hum of magic filled his ears and as he pulled his sword from the player, he turned to make sure Milinka was still with him. He watched her cleave through a player's throat, and nodded as he charged forward, engaging another.

The player swung an axe at Crinnan. He jumped backward, bumping into someone as he did and raised his sword to block another attack. "Fuck off me!" He shouted as he spun, slicing through the demon's arm and relieving him of his sword hand. The player reeled back and Crinnan watched as a heavy two-handed axe removed his head. The headless player fell to the ground, and Crinnan saw his former squad mate Jeph Scaven give him a wink and charge back into battle.

A player charged Milinka, but she ducked down and swiped her leg at him, knocking his feet out from under him. He tumbled forward and before he could hit the ground, Milinka had planted both her axes into his chest. Crinnan ran past her and threw a lightning bolt into the demons ahead, knocking a few over and allowing him to decapitate the one who still stood.

Player: Neb EXECUTED

Player Rank: 67,112

Congratulations, PrettyKitty6969420! You have advanced in ranking!

Previous Rank: 2,903,025,776

New Rank: 1,451,546,444

Previous Percentile: 9%

New Percentile: 4%

"You okay?" Crinnan shouted at Milinka.

"Awesome!" She returned as she pulled her axes from a demon's back. "You?"

"Ready for this to be over." Crinnan growled. "Ah shit, incoming!"

Crinnan watched as at least a dozen demons charged his way. He and Milinka stood side by side, prepared to engage them when Crinnan suddenly heard the sound of... hooves. Looking to his left toward the direction of the sound, Crinnan watched as a mob of ethereal horses charged forward, all being ridden by people with wide brimmed hats, revolvers and repeater rifles.

They whooped and laughed as they rode, and Crinnan watched the white smoke lift from their weapons as they mowed down the players. Any who still stood were trampled by the horses. Crinnan saw Karston among them being flanked by who he could only assume were his sons and couldn't help but smile.

"Get back in the fight!" Sarasin shouted as she phased in front of him. "Watching is for losers!" She phased forward and Crinnan watched her employ a strange sort of martial arts paired with her magic attacks. She punched a player square in the chest leaving a hole from the impact and then sent his body flying across the battlefield. She threw waves of invisible power, knocking people to the ground, and Crinnan even watched her kick someone in the head and literally punt the head into the distance.

The darkness above groaned and trembled and Crinnan looked up as the sky seemed to split open. A brilliant blue light emerged from behind the crack that had formed and Crinnan immediately realized that he was looking at his way home.

"That's fucking it!" Crinnan shouted, amazed at the sight. "That's gotta be the way home Milinka!" He looked back at Milinka and saw that she was struggling to fend off four players.

"Get off her!" He shouted as he leapt forward. He cut through one of the player's skulls and then crashed down on top of another. His sword impaled the player in the chest, and Crinnan lost grip of it. He rolled forward, grabbed the player's face, and blasted into it with a lightning bolt. The player's head exploded, and Crinnan blasted onto his back.

Player: DarkontraTrout EXECUTED

Player Rank: 7,776

Congratulations, PrettyKitty6969420! You have advanced in ranking!

Previous Rank: 1,451,546,444

New Rank: 725,777,110

Previous Percentile: 4%

New Percentile: 2%

"That was dumb!" Milinka shouted as she ran over and helped Crinnan up off the ground. Crinnan found his balance, kissed Milinka on the lips and then turned and wiggled his sword free from the player's chest. He brushed his hair out of his face and pointed upward.

"I hit the one percent." Crinnan snorted. "And I don't even fucking care!" He pointed up at the portal that had opened in the sky. "That's where we need to go!" He shouted. He saw that a great number of his army had turned to run toward the blue rift in the sky. He also saw that many of them were being cut down as they ran. He cursed and grabbed Milinka's hand.

"Let's go." He said, nodding forward toward the rift, "Time to end this."

Milinka nodded, but before they could run, they were both blasted violently onto their backs.

"It seems that the way home has presented itself." The voice of Eon declared as he appeared in front of them. "It is then time for me to take what I need and leave this place."

"Fuck off, Eon!" Crinnan yelled as he scrambled to his feet. "Just go! Nobody is stopping you!"

"You see, that could not be further from the truth." Eon said as he floated closer to Crinnan. "You, Crinnan, are stopping me. I need what is locked away within you!"

With a growl, Crinnan darted forward, swinging his sword toward Eon's chest. Eon, in turn, held his hand out and Crinnan suddenly froze in place with his sword hovering only inches from Eon's body. His spine felt ice cold, and he couldn't move anything but his eyes as he watched Eon.

"Your... parents... seems to have put something special within you." Eon said softly as he stepped forward and cupped Crinnan's cheek in his hand. "Something... something you were born with... something that has *always* been there. I feel it is mine to take, Crinnan, for it is of no use to you."

"Get away from him!" Milinka shouted as she dove forward, axes at the ready. Eon caught her midair with his abilities and slammed her to the ground. Milinka screamed, and Eon snarled at her. "I could destroy your bodies right now, you foolish children. I could blast you into nothing... or wait... I could make you cut her throat and drink until you burst Crinnan." Eon snarled and placed his hands against each of Crinnan's temples. "It is time for you to open the repository, my friend. For the knowledge contained within..."

"No!" Eon suddenly shouted as he dropped his hands and stepped backward. He started panting heavily, and Crinnan and Milinka were both freed from their captivity. Crinnan stumbled forward, crashing to the ground, and Milinka ran to his side.

"Run... Crinnan..." Eon struggled to shout. "Go... home!"

"Ander!" Milinka gasped. She moved to run forward, but Crinnan grabbed her arm and pulled her back.

"I... cannot hold him..." Ander growled. "Th... thank you for being... my friend..."

"Ander!" Milinka yelled. "Ander I'm so sorry!"

"No!" Ander insisted. "Go! Go and… go and… live!" At that, Eon's face formed into a furious scowl as he took back over. Ander did not say another word, and Eon stomped forward.

"I have endured enough of this foolishness!" Eon growled. He threw his hand out, knocking Crinnan and Milinka onto their backs again. "Do not resist!"

Crinnan felt his ribs crack as he slammed against the ground and yelped in sudden pain. He stared up at Eon with fury in his eyes. He was so close to getting Milinka out of there, he could see the rift only a few hundred yards away…

"I will have it!" Eon continued. "It is mine!" He reached forward only for a wave of invisible power to slam against the side of his body. He tumbled to the ground, surprised, just as Sarasin ran into view and blasted him again, holding him down with her abilities.

"Fucking go!" Sarasin yelled; her voice strained by the amount of energy she was using. "Now!"

Milinka got to her feet, but Crinnan could barely move. He struggled to push himself up, and then he felt Milinka hook her arms underneath him. "Come on." She encouraged him. "We're almost there. Get up, come on!" Crinnan groaned in pain as she helped lift him to his feet. He put his weight on her and she grunted as she helped him walk forward.

Slowly the two inched toward the portal. Every step sent a shock through Crinnan's broken body, he felt like there was no way he was going to make it. Gravity kept pulling him down, and finally, Milinka could hold on no longer and he tumbled to the ground again.

"I can't…" Crinnan whispered. "I can't breathe, I can't walk… you… you go and save yourself. That's all that really matters to me…"

"No!" Milinka insisted. She tugged on his arm, trying to force him to his feet, but Crinnan didn't have the strength to stand. "No, I won't leave you!"

"You have to…" Crinnan tried to yell back. "Please!"

A shadow fell over the two, and Crinnan turned his head to see a tall white corpulent monster towering over them. He wore a grin on his face and held a large hook out in front of him.

"Well, what an opportunity we have here!" ByggDykk declared as he stared down at the two. "How easy it would be for me to get my revenge."

"Go away!" Milinka shouted. She got to her feet and raised her axes toward the demon who had bitten Crinnan's head off so long ago. ByggDykk rolled his eyes and lumbered past Milinka, gently pushing her aside.

"It's okay." He said as he tossed his hook to the ground. He knelt down and picked Crinnan up, cradling him like a baby. "Sometimes... people have to look death in the eye to realize exactly how big a piece of shit that they are." ByggDykk stood back to his feet and looked toward the rift. "Lead the way, little lady."

Milinka nodded and ran toward the rift. As she got closer, she felt the pull of the blue portal grow in intensity, and saw that people were tossing themselves in by the dozen. As they ran, others formed up behind them protecting them from incoming fire and anyone who would wish them harm.

Dali ran up alongside ByggDykk and grabbed Crinnan's hand, sending as much healing energy as she could into him. Crinnan felt some strength return to him, though his pain did not fade. They finally reached a place where the rift's pull could only barely be resisted and ByggDykk set Crinnan down and gently helped him to his feet.

"Well, that was weird." Crinnan grunted as he babied his ribs. "Thanks... I guess..."

"No, Crinnan Jamiso." ByggDykk said with a shake of his head. "Thank you for showing me the way... Things are... things are going to change in my life... I promise you."

"Good... I guess." Crinnan said. ByggDykk nodded to him, and then stepped forward. Crinnan watched as the lumbering demon was sucked into the rift and then looked around him.

"Go Crinnan!" He heard Commander Emilio shout. "Go home! The Seraphim have no place there, we will remain behind and guide those who follow!" Crinnan nodded to Emilio and turned to see Sir Edmaan on his other side.

"I'm proud of you, Crinnan!" Edmaan shouted. It was hard to hear him over the wind, but Edmaan reached out and slapped Crinnan on the shoulder.

"Take care of my sister!" Sir Demyan added. "Just so you know... I approve of all this..." Crinnan nodded to Demyan Emmal, and then turned to Milinka.

The deep, rolling sound of roaring and crackling fire filled their ears. The wind created by the release of the immense power surging around them blew their hair in all directions. Everything was covered in a blue hue from the rift that pulsed above, yet they somehow found themselves standing calmly in the middle of it all, safe only because they had each other.

Above them in the pure and absolute blackness of the sky, the rift had surged; a swirling blue gash hung in the never-ending nothingness. They felt the unknown force tugging at them, beckoning them to enter.

"I will find you!" Crinnan whispered his promise as he leaned into Milinka's ear. He pulled back and stared at her. "I promise you Milinka, I will come back to you, wherever you are!"

"I will be waiting!" She shouted as the force of the rift lifted her feet off the ground. Crinnan held onto her hand tight and he could not take his eyes off her. The rift pulled at her harder, but his love gave him the strength to pull her down and push his lips against hers one more time.

"I love you." He whispered as he finally let go of her hand. Her fingers caressed his cheek and she smiled as the rift pulled her upward. Their eyes remained locked and Crinnan saw her mouth the words.

"I love you too."

"I *will* find you Milinka, I promise!" A moment later, she was gone, carried into the sky just like Crinnan had been back when they were so young in Kamlot. When he was left alone, Crinnan spun in place as he surveyed the Hells one last time.

The battle raged on as people scrambled to get into the rift. He saw an entire horde of touched get sucked in, watched as players and prisoners alike threw themselves at the swirling blue light... Crinnan looked over to where Sarasin and Eon had been and saw they were both gone. He sighed and spun in place until he too was looking at the light.

"Go Crinnan!" Dali shouted as she approached him. She grabbed his arm and squeezed tight. "Thank you... so much... for saving us all..."

"Dali..." Crinnan replied. He reached out and grabbed her hand, squeezing hard. "Go finish your life."

"I will." Dali sniffled as she stood on her tip toes and kissed him on the cheek. "And you be good to Milinka, be good to yourself... I will never forget you."

At that Dali reached forward and pushed Crinnan. He lost his balance, dropped his sword and the rift plucked his body from the ground. The blue light grew brighter and brighter as he got closer and eventually, he was sucked into it and it became all that he could see.

The world of the Hells quickly faded from his mind and as the blue light that surrounded him turned to white, Crinnan Jamiso opened his eyes and he heard a simple sentence uttered by a very familiar voice...

"I should say, whoever touched the thermostat is going to get it..."

End of Age of Reckoning: Book One

A Word from The Author

It's been 20 years since I first birthed this world. I hope you enjoyed what was essentially the opening cinematic. I know I loved writing it for you. Keep your eye out for Age of Reckoning Book 2, starring Sarasin Fyr (Crinnan's sister who used Dali's body to help him get out of the Hells.)

-CJG

Other Works by Christian J. Gilliland

Bloodgames: Season One